With love from
Stuart

Hope you like
this author!
All the best

BLOOD BROTHERS

Janus Oggsford

Illustration: Wendy Rawding

Published by
The OX PRESS
P.O. Box 378
Kidlington
OX5 2DW
UK
© Janus Oggsford 2013

The author asserts the moral right to be identified as the author of this work

ISBN 978-0-9573932-1-9

This novel is a work of fiction. Any references, explicit or implied, to historical, current or future events, to flesh-and-blood humans (living, or dead) and/or to real locales are offered only to convey a semblance of reality and authenticity.

Other names, characters, institutions, places and incidents are the products of a fevered imagination, and any inferred resemblance to their presumed real-life counterparts is entirely coincidental.

All rights reserved, all wrongs righted. It is forbidden to reproduce this publication in whole or in part, likewise to store it in a retrieval system or to transmit it in any form whatsoever and by any means whatsoever, without the prior written permission of the publisher.

The book is sold subject to the strict condition that it shall not, by trade or otherwise, be lent, re-sold, hired out or otherwise circulated without the publisher's prior written consent in any form or binding or cover other than that in which it is herewith published and without a similar condition being imposed on any subsequent purchaser.

Printed in the UK by TJ International Ltd
Trecerus Industrial Estate Padstow PL28 8RW

Cover Design by Anton Maverick
www.antonmaverick.org

For Adam

Acknowledgements

The Author and Publishers wish to acknowledge the presumed copyright holders of the following songs/lyrics, of which mere snatches appear in the text:

The Donkey's Serenade - 1937
Rudolf Frims/Allan Jones & Nat Shilkret

Nature Boy - 1947
Eden Ahbaz/Kerli

Old Man River - 1927
Jerome Kern/Oscar Hammerstein

---

and thanks, as always, to the ever-helpful
Stewart Roach
of
Cherwell Graphics, Kidlington

Prologue

The quarry seemed deeper than on Samson's previous visit. It looked as though a great deal of stone had been gouged out from the southern face, causing the crumbling church to teeter precariously on the very edge - an effect emphasised by extensive undermining. Almost every building in Old Guinea, from once-imposing edifices such as Foxgloves Hall and St. Peter's Church, to the meanest hovel or pigsty, likewise the miles and miles of tumbledown dry stone walls - all these were constructed from sandstone hacked from the quarry. During building booms the quarry was busy from dawn till dusk, with blasting twice a day. A makeshift railway was used to raise rock from the face, down in the bottom of the quarry, to a platform of old railway sleepers at the summit, where the waggons were unloaded. The waggons were hauled up the long, twisting incline by a noisy stationary engine working through a complex system of cables and pulleys, and unloaded by manual operation of levers which opened their bottoms. After being unloaded the waggons were allowed to freewheel back down to the workface. At first their progress was very slow, because the axles were never oiled and the track poorly maintained. Occasionally waggons would be derailed by stones on the track, and once, a quarry worker had been killed by a waggon which jumped the track and plummeted some thirty or forty feet onto him: it still lay there over patches of rust, upside down and with one set of wheels at a crazy angle. Samson wondered if the patches of rust had originally been pools of blood.

The most dangerous area was, of course, the lower slopes. Once the waggons got moving they came to a steep section of the track, down which they plunged with a shrieking rusty roar; they then raced round a long, curved, almost level section (in effect, a ledge of up to fifteen yards wide, before descending, more steeply again, to the workface.

The level section was where the fun was to be had, and fortunately (being technically out of bounds to St. Peter's children) it was out of sight both from above and below, thanks to substantial overhangs. The game was, to wait behind the dynamite hut, about ten yards from the track, like novice steeplechasers under starter's orders - and there, with bated breath and bumping heart, to listen for the roar of the waggons as they began their descent of the steep upper section. Then, of course, the first one to run across the track in front of the roaring waggons was 'chicken', and the last one 'the kiddy'. Both Samson and Snorky excelled at the game: both were experts at cutting it fine. Speedy, of course, was never invited to play: instead, someone would shout 'Corner!', whereupon he would shuffle off and stand at the back of the hut until collected.

A chain of three loaded waggons was now clanking up the last few feet of the upper section, just prior to unloading. Within a minute or two they would have been emptied and cast loose. It was time to get ready.

'Okay?' Snorky checked, getting to his feet and performing a few jerky limbering-up exercises.

'Right when you are,' Samson replied resolutely.

'Right: the showdown,' Snorky said grimly, his tense voice reduced to a whisper.

'The showdown,' Samson agreed. Then, remembering Speedy, he turned to him and shouted: 'Corner! Corner!'

Normally Speedy would have obeyed the command mechanically, but on this occasion he failed to budge, even when Samson repeated the command twice. There was nothing for it, therefore, but to resort to a bit of quick magic that never failed: Snorky's 'magic circle'. This involved using a clog toecap to inscribe a crude circle in the dust around where Speedy stood: he would stay there all day, if necessary - or if, as on the trip to Blackpool, he was forgotten. (Once, he had been accidentally left inside a circle all night: he was only found the following lunchtime, as cold as a hibernating skunk.) On this occasion he failed to follow precedent: he stepped out of the circle.

From far above came the noise of the waggons being emptied, and a vast cloud of dust rose up, plunging the level section into semi-darkness. Time was running out. Something had to be done, and soon: a bit of inspiration was called for.

'Stay there, you thick twit!' Snorky shouted.

'Yes, stay where you are - please.' Samson's voice was tinged with desperation.

In response, Speedy smiled angelically, and slowly and deliberately withdrew his tongue from his left nostril. Then his lips parted as though he was going to belch: instead, incredibly, words came out:

'Me pay, Sansan. Me pay,' the unfamiliar voice wheedled.

'You haven't got any flipping money, you stupid gormless idiot!' Snorky shouted.

'No ... I think he means "play",' Samson said. 'What do you think? '

Snorky blinked and shrugged, but said nothing.

'Okay ... come on, then!' Samson shouted to Speedy, then all three of them sidled over to the starting line. Urgently, Samson tried to explain the rudiments of the game to Speedy, who - after returning his tongue to the nostril where it belonged - began nodding enthusiastically.

Samson himself, in addition to having lightning reflexes and a wonderful sense of timing, had developed a foolproof system based on careful observation. Reduced to its essentials, the system was, to start counting when the waggons' roar changed quality, and to start running on the count of three-and-a-half. This, unfortunately, was slightly beyond Speedy's counting range, so some other system would have to be adopted - and soon.

'Any moment now!' Snorky called out, setting himself.

'I know: we'll give him a start,' Samson shouted back, and Snorky appeared to nod agreement, though he might just have been counting down. Samson motioned Speedy to a point about three yards from the track: from there, even a tortoise would have ended up 'chicken'.

Samson gouged a line in the dust, making it extra bold by repeated use of his clog toecap: his head was lowered, and his breathing was hard, more from tension than exertion. The overall effect was not dissimilar to that of an angry bull. Speedy watched him, perhaps wondering if the line was a new kind of circle.

'Listen!' Samson commanded, racking his brain for a suitable instruction ... a simple instruction ... an instruction so simple that even an idiot would be able to understand it. Fortunately, inspiration was immediately forthcoming:

'Listen!' he commanded again, and unconsciously switched to the vernacular. 'Reet? When tha 'ears t' truck, run like fuck!' The rhyme was the important thing, of course, not the swearword.

'Tuck ... fuck,' Speedy repeated, intense concentration contorting his features.

'Again!' Samson demanded, using his hands as might an Italian choirmaster, to elicit a *fortissimo.* 'Again! Truck ... fuck!'

'Tuck ... fuck,' Speedy obliged, this time more fluently thanks to having withdrawn his tongue from his left nostril, for the second time in as many minutes - a world record, Samson wondered? 'Tuck ... fuck .... tuck ... fuck ...... tuck ... fuck .. fucktuck ...'

Speedy's incantation echoed back and forth across the quarry and set itself up inside Samson's head. Samson felt faint, perhaps from loss of blood. His heartbeat seemed to double in speed, then to double again.

The noise from above changed character. Samson settled beside Snorky in his special crouch, which favoured a particularly explosive start and hence permitted a very late one. At the same time he began his silent count, half-closing his eyes in an effort to overcome the interference from Speedy's continuing chant. It didn't work, but at least it reduced Speedy to a blur, so he didn't have to think about him.

'One!' Samson shouted, inaudibly. *Damn!* At this moment, the blur shifted: Speedy had turned round and was looking back at him.

'RUN!' Samson shouted - this time publicly, exaggerating his mouth movements to compensate for the fact that the words were probably inaudible above the roar of the approaching waggons. Speedy grinned, as though he was getting the hang of the game and beginning to enjoy himself.

'TWO!!' Samson shouted hoarsely. 'RUN!! RUN!!'

Momentarily, Speedy turned towards the track: then, clearly

confused, he turned back as if awaiting new instructions - though his mouth movements, like those of a drowning fish at the surface of a polluted pond, suggested that he was still continuing the original chant.

'THREE!!!' Samson screamed. 'RU-U-U-U-U-U-N!!!!'

He and Snorky shot forward at virtually the same moment. Speedy, crazy boy, started to run back towards them: finding himself going the wrong way, he turned to follow them across the track.

It was too late. There was no special sound distinguishable from the terrifying roar of the waggons, only inches away: no shout, no scream. But when Samson and Snorky skidded to a halt and turned, as one, to look back, they saw Speedy's body lying face down beside the track, absolutely still except for the erratic swinging of his 'Napoleon' earring. There was a huge bloody gash across his left temple, but blood only seeped from it, rather than gushed or spurted.

White with shock, Samson and Snorky looked at each other, back at the body, then at each other again. Snorky grabbed hold of Samson's lapels and pulled him close.

'Listen!' he wheezed, his burning eyes seemingly on stalks. 'I know nothing ... you know nothing ... we know nothing - okay?'

'Nothing?' Samson quavered.

'No, nothing.'

'What - nothing at all?'

'No: nothing ... nothing at all ... absolutely nothing.'

Slowly, Snorky released his grip. Then the two of them spontaneously did what Speedy should have done: they ran like fuck.

1. A Song in The Air - 1

It had been a dark and stormy night, but the new day was ambivalent. From time to time a break appeared in the clouds and narrow rays of sunshine stabbed out, suggesting that it might turn out to be a beautiful summer's day after all. Young Samson Smalley is to be found in the drawing room of Foxgloves Hall, the family seat deep in the Pennine foothills. He is at the pianoforte, trying to pick out the tune of The Donkey's Serenade *with the index finger of his right hand: at the same time he is mouthing the words, just audibly:*

There's a Song in The Air ...

Samson was a long way from having developed the flowing technique to which he aspired, and which the venerable instrument clearly merited. 'C. Steinbeck & Sons, Gold Medal Oldham 1899' the faded gold lettering inside the lid proclaimed, so that Samson felt it wrong to blame his difficulties on missing notes or chipped ivories: already, at the tender age of nine, he knew the saying 'only a bad workman blames his tools'. No, the problem wasn't technical - though it would have been nice to have a proper Ottoman instead of the creaking, worm-ridden three-legged milking stool which, being so low and rickety, obliged him to kneel precariously instead of to sit. The real problem was, to turn a deaf ear to the four clocks which ticked competitively, and at times even ominously, from the dim recesses behind him.

Viewing the room from above and taking Samson himself to be facing twelve o'clock, the instrument nearest to him was at about twenty-past. This clock, a stylish late Victorian grandmother, was a most pleasing feature of the room: with her soft, quiet and regular tick she made an ideal metronome for a beginner. Slightly further round, interposed protectively between the grandmother clock and the extraordinarily life-like bas relief serpent threatening her from the original 'Garden of Eden' fireplace, stood a stout grandfather clock, an early Victorian piece with a feeble, irregular but endearing tick-tock, like an arthritic cripple stumbling along over uneven cobble stones with the aid of two metal-tipped walking sticks. Behind him hung, slightly askew, a disabled but otherwise perfectly healthy cuckoo clock, ticking away jauntily but without benefit of an hour hand and with only one half of its call functioning, so that it sounded more like a hoarse pigeon than a sonorous cuckoo. Finally, at exactly half-past, a fourth opinion as to the time was offered by a cheap-and-nasty World War 2 tin clock, urgent and metallic.

Samson hated the tin clock - not from any precocious snobbery, but because of the dirty trick it had played on him a few days earlier. During a well-earned break from practice he had turned to consult the two old clocks, whereupon the tin clock. perhaps feeling left out, began ticking more and more loudly. Samson, intending to stare at the tin clock in an intimidating way, had turned quickly through the necessary extra thirty degrees or so. In the event the clock had the better of the confrontation: Samson felt a sudden painful click in his neck, and for a few awful moments he experienced the terrifying prospect of having to spend the rest of life with his head the wrong way round. Subsequently he had tried to assess, coolly and calmly, the pros and cons of that condition. It was almost all cons, he decided. For a start it would ruin his chances of ever becoming a world-famous pianist of the calibre of, say, Ravitz or Landauer (whom Samson, perhaps viewing their duets as competitive rather than co-operative, had misheard from the wireless as 'Rabbits' and 'Landowner', without his appreciation having been compromised). It would make eating and drinking much more awkward ... blowing the nose, too. It would also increase the risk of tripping over - though, as against that, at least he wouldn't fall flat on his face.

Samson now reminded himself of the need to take revenge on the tin clock at the earliest opportunity. For the moment, though, the most pressing need was to get on with the practising, at least until the whole of *The Donkey's Serenade* had been slogged through once, from beginning to end. With commendable self-discipline he launched into the piece again, *Da Capo*:

      There's a Song In the Air
      But the Sweet Senior Eater ...

Mrs. Smalley backed into the room, half-carrying, half-dragging a huge cauldron of nutty slack with which to damp down the fire - somewhat prematurely on this particular morning since the fire, although kindled as always at half-past six, was still blowing back and threatening to go out. She put the cauldron down with a thud and a clank, gave vent to a loud, lingering sigh, then went over to the window. Conveniently, her cardigan sleeves were still pulled over her hands, so it was the work of moments to clear a circular patch of condensation. She peered out, her impassive features belied by the urgent way she sucked on a hollow tooth. Samson, equally good at hiding his feelings, watched her from the corner of his eye, his index finger poised above the keyboard and twitching like the tip of an angry cat's tail. New condensation formed almost as soon as the old had been smeared away, so Mrs. Smalley was obliged to change sleeves. After several more increasingly half-hearted attempts to keep a small area clear she shook her head in resignation, then gave Samson what she herself would have described as an 'old-fashioned' look as she left the room. Samson affected not to notice her exit.

About to resume his practising, Samson suddenly realised that he had no idea how much time had slipped away. It was no good getting careless, because from around nine o'clock it would be necessary to put himself on red alert, whatever that was. So: the time .... Samson turned round slowly, gingerly: the recent near-disaster had left his neck very stiff and fragile, so that by the time he had the grandmother clock in his sights he felt he had reached the limit and must give up. Fortunately at this point he had a brilliant idea: he would calculate the time. The grandmother, if he remembered correctly, was seventeen-and-a-half minutes slow with respect to the grandfather - who, for his part, was twenty-eight minutes faster than the tin clock (which had been put right by the six o'clock news only days before, and rarely gained more than two or three minutes a day). So: there were still twenty-seven minutes of practising time left, give or take the odd half-hour. The ease with which he had managed the tricky calculation bolstered Samson's self-confidence no end. Even so, he was careful not to waste too much time basking in self-satisfaction. Without further ado he turned back to the piano, relocated what passed for middle 'C', and began again.

Mrs. Smalley quietly re-entered the room and went to the window by the most direct route, which involved squeezing between Samson and the Chesterfield. Suspecting that she had deliberately brushed against him so as to put him off, Samson turned to protest. However, he thought better of it when he saw how, with a single imperious sweep of the entire forearm, she cleared an area the same size and shape as would have resulted from the action of a windscreen wiper. He also noticed that her lower jaw was quivering. Accordingly he contented himself by testing middle 'C', his eyes unfocussed in unwitting imitation of a blind piano tuner.

Mrs. Smalley suddenly executed a reverse wipe, as though to put the condensation back: then she turned away abruptly and went straight to the fire. Getting down on one knee, she seized the poker and, after giving the fire a wary prod, suddenly mounted a frenzied attack on it, inflicting several deep stab wounds, and exposing little red patches suggestive of fresh blood. Samson observed her thoughtfully, wondering if by any chance she might still be smarting from his well-meant criticism of the day before: something of an expert on fires, he had drawn her attention to the error of poking the heap of coals at the top. Well, whatever the problem, the brief flurry of activity seemed to calm her down. She now withdrew the poker from the coals with the smooth, unhurried action of a victorious duellist and held it up like an extended forefinger to make an important point to Samson, who had been watching the whole performance through the tilted mirror above the sideboard.

'I though I told you to keep an eye out,' she said, jabbing the poker towards him for added emphasis.

'I am ... I was,' Samson replied, coolly returning her accusing stare.

'I don't know for the life of me know why you have to keep fiddling with that blessed piano,' she continued. 'If -'

'I wasn't fiddling,' Samson protested.

'You were!' she insisted. 'You still are!'

'I wasn't fiddling,' Samson insisted back. 'That's violins.'

'You silly ass!' she snorted. 'Hmph! We'll see how clever

you are when he comes - or should I say, if. Now come on! You've got weeks and weeks to ... to mess about with that.'

She paused, took a deep breath, then continued more resignedly:

'*Eeeh*, all this upset ... I wonder what that beggar's up to.'

'If he's coming, he'll come,' Samson shrugged. 'I don't see -'

'There's a lot of things you don't see,' Mrs. Smalley retorted. 'The point is, knowing him, he'll not even bother to give the gates a proper try. Oh, you can laugh ... they found a whole bunch of letters in the ditch just beyond Ramsbottoms', the Christmas before last.'

'The snow *was* twenty feet deep,' Samson pointed out. 'Perhaps -'

'Twenty!' she scoffed.

'More, probably,' Samson insisted. 'Almost buried the gateposts.'

'Well anyway,' she said, 'I can't imagine why they employ such people ... where they find them, even. Now: get over to that blooming window and keep your eyes skinned, or I'll skin them for you, if it's the last thing I ever do. Now, come on: look sharp! I don't want to have to tell you again -'

'Oh, alright,' Samson sighed.

He eased himself off the stool and, taking the long route around the Chesterfield, shuffled to the window. He took up station between the far curtain and the grandmother clock. From there, by crouching like a stick insect, he could keep the approaches to Foxgloves Hall under constant surveillance without running much risk of being spotted in the process.

Samson fixed his gaze on the great wrought-iron gates, undeterred by the glare of the early-morning sun, which was attempting to sneak through a gap in the clouds. It would be some time before it rose above the twenty-five-foot-high gates and released Samson from the need to squint. There had been times when the gates made Samson feel as if he were in a prison, for although they were unlocked and the key long since lost, they had dropped on their hinges and sunk into the clinker driveway so as to be immovable. There were also times, like the present, when the gates had a reassuring fortress-like quality, promising security against intruders, and at such times Samson swelled with justifiable pride, recalling Mr. Smalley's proud boast that the gates were, 'without a shadow of a doubt, the finest in Lancashire, bar none'. By almost shutting his eyes when looking at them, Samson was able to visualise the gates as they must have looked when first erected, an integral part of the awe-inspiring approach to Foxgloves Hall.

Samson now recalled the sense of insult he had felt one morning when Meredith, the Methodist preacher man, came by on his ridiculous Shetland pony, his toecaps dragging through the cinders. Meredith had stopped to inspect the gateway. and had burst into uncontrollable sneering laughter as he poked with his riding crop at the stone pillars, now sadly eaten away and listing, as if their present state in some way detracted from their original magnificence. Obviously he was unaware that the gateway's deterioration was largely the fault of a runaway carthorse which, perhaps tormented by the spirits of the night (Old Guinea being, of course, boggart country) had in pitch darkness careered into the gates at a speed reckoned to be in excess of thirty miles an hour. The colossal impact, beyond dislodging a few decades of rust, had left the gates themselves virtually unscathed, though the pillars had been rocked to their foundations. One had lost its stone ball: this, miraculously surviving the drop intact, had then rolled down the steep slope beside the drive, cut a swathe through the massed rhododendron bushes and - after coming to rest, of course - acquired a thick coating of moss. The horse had come off worst: its head was so tightly wedged between the bars that it had to be removed. Fortunately, rather than being hacked off willy-nilly by any Tom, Dick or Harry, the head had been expertly sawn off by the then butler, one Thomas Sharples. Known to posterity as 'Stuffer' Sharples on account of his passion for taxidermy, he had immortalised both himself and the demented horse by expertly stuffing the sawn-off head with horse hair, mounting it on a beautifully-beeswaxed oak board carved into the shape of a heraldic shield, and adding on a discreet brass plaque below, at his own expense, the simple, dignified inscription 'MAJOR'. Ever since, the head had peered out over the grandmother clock's shoulder, as it were, its flared nostrils and generally-distorted features serving as a constant reminder of the dangers of thoughtless action - or, from Samson's point of view, of the delirious pleasures of taxidermy. How wonderful to be able to make dead animals even more lifelike than the real thing! Samson had spent countless hours scouring the surrounding countryside for specimens on which to learn the taxidermist's art. On a couple of occasions he had been fired with excitement at the prospect of producing a jaunty pied wagtail (or was it a young magpie?), a majestically-soaring seagull or, best of all, a murderously-squinting barn owl, but all three finds had been rotten almost to the point of being unrecognisable, heaving with maggots and stinking to high heaven. At such times Samson would have given his right arm for luck like that of Sharples.

Mrs. Smalley announced her return by tapping Samson on the shoulder, making him jump.

'When I said to keep an eye out,' she said, prodding him for added emphasis, 'I didn't mean for you to give yourself a stiff neck. I don't for the life of me know why you have to crouch like that, all twisted up, when there's a perfectly good little stool to sit on.'

'Stop poking me!'

'Well, straighten up, then, .. come ON!' The last two prods were particularly severe, being successfully aimed at a sensitive spot just inside his right shoulder blade.

'*Ouch!*' Samson squawked. 'If you do that again ...'

Mrs. Smalley backed off. Going over to the hearth, she picked up the poker very resolutely (so that Samson flinched, even though she was nowhere near him), but then suddenly seemed unsure what to do.

'Eeeh, dear,' she said quietly after a long pause. 'Still no sign, I suppose?'

'No.'

'Mmm? What? What did you say?'

'I said "No".'

'What, nothing?'

'No, nothing. Nothing at all.'

'Nothing at all?' Mrs. Smalley was beaten now, drained

of all resolve. She stared abjectly at Samson, the poker dangling lifelessly from her limp wrist, reminding Samson of a cocker spaniel with a thorn in its paw, that he had once seen.

'No,' Samson said, clearly and decisively, tightening the last notch of the screw even as a lump came into his throat. 'Nothing ... nothing at all ... absolutely nothing.'

2. A Song in The Air - 2

There ensued a long silence, during which Mrs. Smalley stared vacantly into the fire and Samson observed her clinically. The silence was finally broken by Mrs. Smalley: she shook herself and laid down the poker.

'Well, this won't win the war,' she said to herself, 'just waiting and waiting ... and waiting. I'd better get on and do, I had that. *Hee!* And I was going to make a start on *Love's Labours Lost* today, but what can you do?' Then, turning to Samson: 'Now you, stay where you are. There's still time, if I'm not mistaken.'

She rose tiredly to one knee, then stayed in that position for several seconds, like a boxer taking advantage of a compulsory count. Sighing deeply, she somehow managed to leave the room without however recovering an erect posture. Samson permitted himself the luxury of a quick smirk. *Hmph*, 'waiting'! What a waste of time! Waiting ... waiting to see whether he had won a scholarship to the Grammar School. *Hmph!* As if it really mattered ... whatever happened now, he would be separated from the love of his life, the beautiful ... *no*, the *beautiful-beyond-compare* Rita Wrigglesworth. In any case it was ridiculous - yes, *ridiculous* - as if anyone from St. Peter's could ever win a scholarship to a Grammar School! It was probably a million-to-one chance, near impossible. Yet this year, both he and his best friend Snorky Horrocks had made history by sitting the Grammar School's entrance examinations, so the chance of the two of them getting scholarships was ... at least two million to one - in other words, absolutely impossible. It was as unlikely as Snorky's transformation from a simple swineherd to Prince Charming in the last-but-one school pantomime.

Snorky ... ha! Dear old Snorks! He had made history by starring three times in consecutive years' New Year's Eve pantomimes, progressing from the lead in *Aladdin* to the Wicked Stepmother in *Snow White and the Seven Dwarfs*. He was the only one who had ever been word-perfect. Actually it was not too difficult to see how Snorky could have won a scholarship to the Grammar School. In almost every respect he was a cut above the other children. There was his appearance, for example: he was always immaculately turned out - hair slicked down with lashings of Brylcreem, a clean white shirt twice a week, and those boots: Snorky's trademark Cherry-Blossom-black boots, boots with such a brilliant shine that you could see your face in them, in marked contrast to the dull clogs or muddy wellingtons worn by almost everyone else. Nor was there any doubting his abilities. Though not always a match for Samson at - for example - mental arithmetic, he was a noted speller, and his handwriting was 'copperplate' (whatever that meant), constantly held up as a model to encourage others who could read and write, and to humiliate those who couldn't. Then there was his prowess as magician and illusionist. Here he was in a class of his own, putting on show after show in which you were so enthralled that you could be forgiven for thinking that he had cast a spell over you: such was his dexterity that he could skin a full-grown frog in two minutes dead. It was a privilege, an honour just to have known Snorky. But for the two of them to have been best friends ... blood brothers, more or less ... was more than anyone could reasonably ask of life. *Hmph!* What on earth had happened to Snorky? Had something terrible happened to him? Could he have brought a curse down on himself? Well, whatever ... he certainly seemed to have disappeared off the face of the earth. Gone. Vanished. But why? Why? WHY?

Samson jerked his head around in frustration and suffered a severe blow to it as he collided with Major's.

'WHY?' he repeated involuntarily.

Samson forced back urgent tears and lifted his heavy gaze clear of the towering gates. The sun had abandoned its aspirations, retreating behind massive black clouds which looked so heavy that they might have been turning to stone, ready to crash down on Foxgloves Hall and raze it to the ground. Everything so black, so bleak ... and yet it seemed only yesterday that the inseparable trio comprising Samson, Snorky and their dim-witted hanger-on Speedy Ramsbottom, famous or infamous according to the deeds of the day, had been the hub round which everything at St. Peter's revolved -

and into which the new Vicar, the Reverend Pilkington (soon dubbed 'Polecat' by the children, in reference to his sharp face and bushy white eyebrows) had put his spoke at every possible opportunity. The 'Three Esses', he had dubbed them - though come to think of it, given his 'Oxford' accent, it might have been the 'Three Asses'. It was strange that he should have an Oxford accent, Samson had always thought, given that he was Bolton-born-and-bred and had married a woman from Harrogate. Anyway, the man had a nose for trouble, an uncanny knack of putting two and two together correctly, and of making great leaps of intuition where lesser minds might merely have stumbled to wrong conclusions. For months the dratted man had dogged their elusive footsteps, though he had never been able to pin anything on them until a dinner-time episode when Snorky, believing the coast to be clear, indulged his passion for swealing in the patch of gorse beside the caretaker's little orchard. The wind had changed direction unexpectedly, blowing smoke in their faces, and Polecat had caught them red-eyed, swooping down on them from behind and hoisting Samson and Snorky onto their toes with bony hands that gripped like talons.

'Haha! Where there's smoke, there's fire,' he shouted exultantly, then proceeded to shake them mercilessly, as if they were rag dolls. Then, just when Samson's brains felt as if they were the consistency of rice pudding, Polecat tossed him aside and spun Snorky round, grabbing him by the lapels so viciously that the poor boy started choking. Having thus secured Snorky's full attention, Polecat proceeded to lecture him about the dangers of fire, reminding him that the ultimate horror was Hell Fire. Then he slackened his grip and searched Snorky's sphinx-like features for signs of repentance. Finding none, he pulled Snorky's face level with his own and resorted to a figure of speech which would have had special significance for the latter:

'If I ever catch you again with so much as a spent match, I'll skin you alive.'

He then released his grip, whereupon Snorky slumped to the ground in a crumpled heap.

'I doubt he'll come by aeroplane,' Mrs. Smalley said, catching Samson by surprise, then before he could work out whether she was referring to Polecat or to the postman she added: 'Did you really remember to put your name at the top of every single page?'

'I told you,' Samson groaned. 'I must have told you a hundred times.'

'I know ... but you did forget, once,' she pressed, referring to a test at St. Peter's three years earlier. 'Lost twenty marks just through that one silly oversight.'

'I still came second,' Samson countered.

'Well that's no good ... no-one wants to be second,' she insisted. 'Hee! It'll be a different kettle of fish at the Grammar School, I can tell you. No use being second there. It'll be "dog eat dog" ... I mean, well ... I know you say you remembered, but can you actually remember doing it - on every sheet of paper?'

This was too much. Samson turned round and fixed her with a murderous glare.

'Well, all right ... if you're absolutely sure,' Mrs. Smalley relented. 'Eeeeh, I say! I don't like those clouds, do I heck This weather ... I've never known anything like it, I haven't really ... it was exactly the same this time last year. Well anyway .. .. let's hope there's a silver lining, eh? But do keep an eye out, for goodness sake. It's not much to ask ... I can't do everything. He could still come, I suppose.' With a deep sigh and a hopeless shrug, she left the room.

Samson dutifully examined the clouds for signs of a silver lining, and his optimism was rewarded by the appearance of a tepid ray of sunshine which squeezed through a tiny gap in the clouds and shone straight into the drawing room. It was undoubtedly an omen, a reminder to Samson of the only ray of sunshine in his troubled life: Rita, youngest of five daughters of the landlord at 'The Dog', an old coaching inn on the old toll road to T' Back o' Beyond. Rita had transferred to St. Peter's half way through Samson's penultimate year there, and though that was over eighteen months earlier he remembered that electric moment of first contact. He had been standing behind her in the milk queue, his nose poking into her gorgeous waist-length black tresses, breathing in slowly and deeply so as to capture the intimate, intoxicating smell, a heady cocktail of beer, tobacco smoke and *eau-de-cologne*. She had turned slowly to investigate the intrusion, and that first incredible glance of hers had transfixed him like Cupid's arrow whanging into a table jelly, setting it permanently aquiver. For more than a year after the first meeting, their love had smouldered rather than burst into flames, latterly because of Samson's deep involvement with his friends Snorky and Speedy. All that had changed on a school trip to the seaside, and any residual doubt as to his and Rita's mutual feelings had been put to rest at the Whit Monday fête, thanks to the close contact of the three-legged race.

Unfortunately Rita had not sat for a scholarship to anywhere, and so would be transferred to the nearest Secondary Modern school. For that reason Samson was resigned to not seeing her again until the following Whit Monday - now, thankfully, less than three hundred days hence. In a rare snatched moment of intimacy they had more or less pledged their undying love for each other and promised faithfully to see each other at the next fête. Already Samson had started saving his pennies for this wonderful occasion, imagining buying her ice cream after delicious ice cream until she could not face another lick ... once, in a wonderful dream that he had never succeeded in re-running, they had sloped off to the churchyard together, and there in the intimate shadows of timeless gravestones he had systematically licked all traces of ice cream from her - first, her hands and arms; then her face, lingering awhile to clean her lips and inside her luscious mouth, then on to her swan-like neck and finally the front of her gingham dress where, to tease him, she regurgitated a constant stream of vanilla ice cream.

Suddenly Samson had a terrible vision: the fête was in full swing, throngs of present and former pupils throwing themselves enthusiastically into the rich programme of activities - sack races, egg-and-spoon races, tugs-of-war, relays, rounders - while the adults disported themselves on the grass, gorging on food and drink and tapping their feet out of time to the brilliant silver band in which Rita's older brother was a trombonist. Meanwhile Samson himself hovered around the perimeter, desperate to catch a first sight of the beautiful creature who belonged, and always would belong, to him and him alone. But she didn't turn up.

Involuntarily jerking back into full consciousness, Samson banged his head severely against Major's rock-hard lower jaw. He saw stars and heard a muffled clash of cymbals. Then, remembering his own musical aspirations, he abandoned his fruitless vigil and stumbled back to the piano.

3. Nature Boy

Thank God for the piano! Without it, life just recently would have been unbearable. Celebrating his return, Samson indulged in a few fancy flourishes, like an ageing conductor loosening up before a performance, then nonchalantly flicked his way through the first few notes of the serenade, at the same time wishing that he had mastered the rest of this wonderful piece of music. Running through the whole piece would have been an excellent preparation for grappling with a much more challenging musical composition - *Nature Boy*, his favourite. As it was, the best he could do was to ensure the optimum playing position by conscientiously performing the elaborate kneeling-down routine that he had perfected over a period of many weeks.

Nature Boy! Himself, of course! Himself to a 't'! Samson had a deep respect, a fundamental respect for Mother Nature: not the snivelling, cringing respect which is born of fear and a sense of inferiority, nor the patronising kind which stems from arrogance and a conviction of superiority - but rather, the respect which one has for a good and true friend: a healthy respect. He felt as much a part of Nature as any other living creature. He felt no mawkish sentimentality when watching an earthworm being tugged from its underground home by a starving thrush, yet at the same time he himself had not the slightest wish to harm any other living creature, great or small. 'Live and Let Live' was his motto: a Buddhist by inclination, though not yet by conviction, Samson would not knowingly have hurt a fly.

Nowhere did Samson experience this feeling of oneness with Nature more intensely than on the wooded slopes of Dead Man's Clough, barely a stone's throw from Foxgloves Hall. Though he had often, at St. Peter's, been accused of having two left feet when subjected to the mechanical routines of P.T. (in fairness to himself, it was always because he had something else on his mind), in the woods he was as surefooted as any deer; he could move swiftly yet noiselessly, seeming to float from one bit of cover to the next; and he could crouch in such a compact heap, or stretch himself out into such a long thin streak, that he was almost invisible almost anywhere. He knew every inch of the woods, as if they were an extension of his own body. He could detect the slightest movement of bird or beast, unerringly interpret the faintest crackle of a twig or almost inaudible rustling from the dense undergrowth, and so be supremely alive to everything going on around him. Thanks to his wonderful hearing his radius of awareness was far greater than vision alone permitted, given that during the usual drizzle visibility was often down to a few feet. Only in respect of sense of smell did Samson acknowledge himself to be inferior to the average animal. With scarcely any success so far he had tried to overcome his innate disadvantage by developing a special kind of breathing, based on hours of painstaking observation of Major: it involved breathing in slowly and deeply, through flared nostrils, then exhaling forcefully and with a slight snort, through the open mouth.

Nature Boy! Oh yes, that was him alright: an amalgam of Robinson Crusoe, Alan Breck and the real Lord Greystokes. The first was Samson's resourceful self, improvising rude shelters, crude spears and dugout canoes; the second was his dour, determined self, sustaining himself on tepid porage whilst fighting a one-man battle to put the world to rights; the third was himself as raw power, monarch of all he surveyed. Of the three heroes, Samson had always identified most comfortably with the last, going to extraordinary lengths to emulate the apegod's remarkable abilities, even to the extent of stripping down to his vest and trousers when practising swinging from bough to bough. However, deep down he knew that he would never be more than a pale imitation of that particular idol.

Samson's subconscious yearning for a more suitable model came to a happy conclusion when he was awarded *The Last of the Mohicans* as a school prize. Here at last, in Uncas the noble savage, Samson discovered himself, and little imagination was needed to see Snorky as the cool, calculating Hawkeye, the Vicar as the evil Magua, and Rita as the dusky maiden Cora. The part of Old Man Chingachgook was more difficult to fill, with only Speedy left on the casting couch: after so many years as back end of the obligatory pantomime horse, would he have the versatility to assume a new, more human persona? Probably not.

The Last of ... - ha! The full significance of the title had impressed itself on Samson ever since he had broken up for the summer holidays and temporarily lost all contact with his dear friends: the drama had to be played out just by himself and Polecat. The latter was a familiar figure among the anarchic maze of lanes and tracks which criss-crossed the less inaccessible parts of Old Guinea like a dirty old string vest. He marched indefatigably hither and thither, up and down, a poor man's Grand Old Duke of York. From time to time he would stop abruptly to scribble urgent notes in a little red notebook with a spiral wire binding - at such times it was not difficult to think of him as a venomous black spider anxiously inspecting a damaged web. Wherever he went he was instantly recognisable. When in full swing he suggested a living version of the strange 'jummitry set' which Snorky had once proudly shown off: he was all straight lines and sharp angles and perfect arcs, and the regular irregularity of his slightly limping stride was emphasised by the almost metronomic ticking of the pedometer strapped to his left gaiter.

Polecat's incessant patrolling stimulated much speculation, of varying degrees of wildness. One short-lived rumour was that he was a spy (a variant on this being that he had a screw loose and was pretending to be a spy). The most popular theory was that his activity was essential research for writing murder stories. Mr. and Mrs. Hodgson of Windy End Farm, founder members of the Old Guinea Crime Circle, which had met every Thursday evening, come rain or shine, for two-and-half years until they themselves were murdered by a tramp for no reason whatsoever, had been heard to suggest off the record that all three of the published murder mysteries of one 'Agatha Sotheby' were set in a place which, allowing for changed names, could only have been Old Guinea. Samson certainly subscribed to the last theory, and had a desperately uneasy feeling that the next of Sotheby's mysteries would involve the discovery of a nine-year-old boy's mutilated corpse in mysterious circumstances.

Ever since the summer holidays had started, Polecat had taken to patrolling the high ground on the far side of Dead Man Clough, from where he could keep Foxgloves Hall under constant surveillance. Immobile for rnost of the time, when he did move to a new observation post he disguised his gait as though in an effort to tread as softly as possible, so that his hunched figure, seen in silhouette, strongly reminded Samson of an injured magpie he had once almost caught.

There was no way in which Samson could leave Foxgloves Hall without being spotted. He had tried wading through the duck pond and then sneaking past the No. 2 chicken house; he had tried crawling backwards through the dense hawthorn bushes forming the eastern perimeter fence; on his most recent attempt, he had gone down on his belly and, after squirming along the exposed part of the cinder drive, somehow managed to wriggle under the gates, thereby skinning his knees and working bits of cinder into the abrasions so that his knees threatened to stay blue-black, like a coal miner's, for the rest of his life. Unfortunately every such effort had been a waste of time: Polecat had always spotted him without difficulty, so that by the time Samson reached the clough the Vicar would already have scrambled down the far slope, crossed Stranglers Brook and begun ascending the near slopes in order to cut him off as a preliminary to cutting him up.

The first couple of times, more by good luck than good management, Samson had been able to avoid Polecat's clutches, and felt smugly confident in his own superior woodcraft. The third and fourth times, however, were near-disasters. The memory of the swealing episode, of being shaken like a rat, and the threatened live skinning of Snorky, were enough to convince Samson not to risk a third encounter of the close kind: it would be third time unlucky.

Samson cursed. Here he was, with a perfectly good piano in front of him - well, it wasn't too bad ... better than nothing, anyway - and wasting his time worrying about something that could be avoided simply by staying indoors. By now, according to recent calculations, he ought to have mastered *Nature Boy* and moved on to an up-tempo rendering of *Oh*

I Do Like to Be Beside the Seaside. So: practice, practice ... practice practice practice practice practice ... crowd out the stupid thoughts and get on with something useful. Thank God again for the piano. It was high time to have another stab. Samson readjusted his position, cleared his throat, and began:

There Was a Boy ...

'Hee! Almost nine o'clock! ' Mrs. Smalley announced, virtually injecting the words into Samson's left ear. 'I can't make head nor tail of it, I can't really. In fact, I do sometimes wonder ...'

Samson sounded middle 'C' percussively until she left the room. Apart from being extremely irritated by the pointlessness of her concern - what did it matter which school he went to, if he was to be separated from Rita? - he was worried by the fact that he had not heard her re-enter the room. This was the danger of single-minded practice, this loss of vigilance. It was at just such a moment that Polecat might squeeze through a gap in the hedge, creep round to the front of the house and rap on the window. There would be no escape: he, Samson, would be caught like a rat in a trap. He wondered whether it might be possible to rig up some kind of alarm system in the grounds, something with a trip wire and a bell ... but what with?

Samson shook himself like a wet dog and prepared to resume his musical self-development. For a little while he agonised over the question as to whether, in the event of making a mistake, it might be a good idea to play the piece backwards to the beginning - not only as a kind of punishment, but to improve flexibility. No ... he would keep that trick up his sleeve. Shuffling an octave towards the treble end of the piano, where he would be better concealed from anyone lurking outside the window, he began again:

There Was a *BZZZZZZZZZZZZZZZZ* .....

His instant reaction was that the imaginary alarm system had been triggered, hut half-way through his dive to the floor he realised that the noise was being made by a giant bluebottle which - severely overloaded, by the looks of it - had crashed into the leaded window with a sickening thud and was now trying to screw itself through the glass. Christ! How could anyone seriously be expected to practise with that kind of thing going on? The temptation to swat the offending fly had to be strongly resisted: clearly, leaded windows, though obviously less expensive than stained glass ones, would nevertheless be well beyond his limited finances - even if he won a scholarship to the Grammar School and, equally unlikely, his father kept his promise and rewarded him with the princely sum of ten shillings. Samson attempted to dislodge the fly by blowing at it, but succeeded only in stopping it buzzing. It seemed to know it was safe. Sleek and shining, bursting with rude good health as though fed on all the best cuts, it busied itself in an elaborate and quite unnecessary grooming session.

Samson turned back to the piano. Immediately, the bluebottle taunted him anew, buzzing very very loudly by flying on the spot. Samson, unwilling to lose the near-perfect kneeling position which he had had the good fortune to adopt, blew again - much harder this time, at risk of internal injury. The bluebottle eyed him coolly, insultingly, obviously full of itself. Samson, determined to get across his seriousness, smashed an angry discord. At this the bluebottle crouched down and prudently adopted a low profile, though only after performing a provocative figure-of-eight dance. *Aaaaarrrrggh!* The best thing to do was, to ignore it, forget it. It would soon tire of the game. Samson turned back to the piano and plunged into the keyboard:

>There Was ....

Almost certainly of course the bluebottle was biding its time, waiting for the most opportune moment to make its next interruption - its last, for sure. Samson whirled round like a dervish, giving his tormentor the fright of its life, and for good measure stabbed a warning finger at it. Ha! That seemed to work! Satisfied that at last he had got his message across, Samson now resumed in earnest:

>There Was a Boy
>A Very Strange and Gentle Boy ...

Gentle ... gentle ... Samson smiled wryly to himself as he murmured the word, suffused with pleasure as he relived the tender feelings that had welled up inside him during those rare moments of intimate contact with Rita. He had blushed then as he blushed now. On one occasion he had felt so strange that he had rushed out into the playground and struck Jimmy Ashworth on the nose, then stood over him with clenched fists, trembling almost uncontrollably, as the latter sank to his knees and looked at him uncomprehendingly before cupping his hands over his bloody face. It was not long after that that chalked hearts had begun to appear in the playground and on nearby trees, with the arrow running from 'SS' to 'RR'. At first he had been barely conscious of them, being above such frivolous nonsense, and in any case had idly assumed that ' SS' stood for Sammy Sharrocks, his own initials being properly 'SSS' because of his rarely-used middle name, 'Singleton'. However, on reflection that was impossible, as Sharrocks had died of chicken pox some weeks earlier. So 'SS' must be himself. But 'RR'? That was a puzzle, a mystery. Rolls Royce? Hardly ... he had seen one, and seen it several times, but not been impressed. It was only when he saw Rita at bay one dinner time, mobbed by a flock of chanting girls, that he made the connection.

Actually, Samson now realised, 'RR' also stood for 'Ronnie Ramsbottom' - his dear friend Speedy. Alone of the St. Peter's children Samson had befriended the poor wretch, and though Speedy stank even in the depths of winter, Samson had often felt protective towards him and, albeit briefly, put a reassuring arm round his shoulder. He had liked Speedy very much, in spite of the revulsion. Speedy had many redeeming qualities. Regardless of what he was or was not or might have been or might not have been, he was a good listener, and unique in never having the slightest malice towards any of his many persecutors. You could pinch him. poke him, kick him, tweak his nose, give him a Chinese burn, even smack him until his face was purple and abuse him until you yourself were blue in the face, and he would think no worse of you. He was the nearest thing to a saint that Samson could imagine, so it was not fair of Snorky to spread the rumour that he had cloven feet, or webbed feet or whatever, and that he had been sired by Th' Owd Lad himself. Poor Speedy!

Poor boy! Years later, faced with inexplicable troubles of his own, Samson would remember Speedy and reflect that life could be cruel, incomprehensibly so, a malicious joke gone out of control.

Mrs. Smalley re-entered the room.

'I was wondering if it could have been your spelling that let you down,' she said.

'Oh ... " i" before "e",' Samson sighed theatrically.

'Well, except after "c",' she was quick to point out. '*Eeeh*, I don't know ... I think it's your memory that lets you down most. You didn't used to be so bad though. Of course, we know where you get it from, don't we.'

Samson crouched hunched and still, staring at the keyboard with his eyes crossed, trying to focus on middle 'C' with his right eye and top 'C' with his left. He was conscious of his mother's breath on the back of his neck but he managed to maintain his attitude until she gave up the unequal struggle and left the room. By this time he had a splitting headache. To cure it, he brought his head crashing down on the keyboard, cobra style - at great risk to his upper front teeth, which in the last few months had begun to work loose.

The reverberations were like organ music. It was Sunday morning. The church bell sounded distantly. The buttercups were in flower, another haymaking season was coming, as Samson searched Ramsbottoms' farm for Speedy. The farm was strangely quiet, deserted. Peering through the cobweb-infested kitchen window Samson saw only the cauldron, boiling dry on the range, and a festering side of bacon swinging eerily in the gloom, like a recently-hanged criminal. In the shippon the cows stood motionless, heads down, subdued. As Samson picked his way across the farmyard, the assorted fowl stared at him strangely, almost accusingly. Only the gander seemed to have any life about it. It was pacing excitedly up and down the long low wall which helped to retain the midden, and when it saw him it started honking loudly and urgently. He quickened his pace and approached the gander as closely as he dared. It was trying to tell him something, and for this once had no interest in attacking him - instead, it stretched out its neck, pointing to a spot in the middle of the midden. Samson's heart jumped as he caught sight of the two wellingtons, upside down and with only the soles and heels above the surface. Speedy!? Another game of 'blind man's buff' gone badly wrong? A .... ? Plunging into the stinking, stinging manure, Samson battled against the powerful drag in a desperate attempt to reach his friend. Successful after an eternity, he tapped on Speedy's boots to alert him to the danger he was in. There was no response: worse, Speedy was slowly sinking. Samson flung his arms round Speedy's legs and tugged manically, but to no avail: Speedy was a dead weight. Samson surfaced, took a deep, deep breath so that he swelled up like a balloon, then dived down again. In spite of being blinded by the ammoniacal sludge he was able to make a positive identification thanks to Speedy's strange hair which, calf-like, grew in tight whorls. Samson ruffled the wiry growth, shouting 'Come on, come on, you'll be all right. One .... two ...' But then his probing fingers discovered the deep cleft in Speedy's temple and he knew that he was dead.

Low overhead, an enormous formation of blood-red bluebottles darkened the sky: even as Samson flinched away they released their bombs, which fell with unerring accuracy into Speedy's ears, the left one and the right one alternately as the head was rocked from side to side. Splits opened up like deepening wrinkles, as if he were ageing a year a second, and they released armies of writhing maggots. A huge slimy red worm pulsated out of Speedy's mouth, then dashed for safety up his left nostril when it caught sight of Samson. It was so long that it stretched all the way to the church door, and so thick that he couldn't get his arms round it to restrain it.

Others in the endless queue jostled Samson, hemming him in at the same time. The church bell clanged loudly, discordantly. In time with the bell, organ music swelled and decayed and the queue surged back and forth. Now the queue narrowed to single file, revealing the Gothic doorway. The music stopped abruptly in mid-phrase, resulting in a deafening silence. Samson hung back, then braced himself as the crowd's momentum bore him onward. Too late he realised that he was about to be pushed into an enormous hemispherical chamber laid out as a three-dimensional snakes-and-ladders set. Equally wary of snakes and heights, he tried to shout out, but no sound emerged, not even a whisper or a whimper. A nurse in an immaculate starched white uniform approached, bearing an ivory die on a silver tray with funny handles. Clearly she understood the meaning of Samson's shouting: beguiling him with an amazing smile, at least a hundred pearly-white teeth set in a perfectly straight line, though black in the gaps from her nervous habit of chewing her pencil, she teased him by offering him the tray; then, as he trustingly leaned forward to take the die she suddenly withdrew the tray and batted him round the ear with it so that he was launched into the void. He was falling, spinning, somersaulting ...

Samson came to with a snort. Holding onto the piano until the dizziness cleared, he surveyed the room for bluebottles. There were none. That was odd: there had been some - one, anyway. It had been over by the window. though it clearly wasn't there any more. Oh well ... Samson yawned, took a deep breath and prepared to resume his piano practice.

The bluebottle had other ideas. It gave Samson a quick double buzz, restrained and yet quite impossible to ignore, from somewhere behind him. Samson resolved to concentrate on the fifth and subsequent notes of *Nature Boy*, determined to make the best possible use of the half-hour or so of safe practising time remaining. He began again:

'A Very Strange anDAMN!'

A wrong note! It was no good: the bluebottle would have to be dealt with - and severely, something a bit more effective than a good talking-to. Samson eased himself off the stool, picked up and rolled up the morning newspaper and crept along the back of the Chesterfield where obviously the bluebottle was hiding. The loose cover, with its irregular clusters of purplish-blue forget-me-nots, was the perfect place for concealment. Samson soon tired of scrutinising each individual floret and took to swatting the cover indiscriminately. Clouds of choking dust flew into the air - but no bluebottle. The explanation was soon clear: the beast was actually somewhere near the table. Though unable to locate it precisely Samson could hear it buzzing intermittently, as if revving up in preparation for take-off. But it prudently fell silent when Samson abandoned the Chesterfield and crept towards it.

It was very odd ... the table was covered as always with its off-white linen tablecloth, and although there were quite a few stains none was dark enough or of the right size to be Samson's quarry. Samson, really meaning business now, dropped to his hands and knees to search the dark underside and legs of the table, giving the crevices an occasional flick with the newspaper. Nothing. Another short, teasing buzz underlined the futility of searching below the table: the bluebottle was above it, after all. Aha ... of course! The cruets! The dark blue salt and pepper containers, in their ornate tarnished silver stand, were an ideal hiding place. Yes, there it was, the blighter! It was on the pepper cruet, frozen in an awkward posture, like an escaping prisoner caught in a searchlight beam and in two minds whether to stay put or to make a run for it. Perhaps, Samson surmised, it was desperately resisting an urge to sneeze; or then again, it might have been risking splitting its seams in a desperate attempt to empty its overstuffed bowels, in the hope of then being able to effect take-off from such a short runway.

Samson paused for a little while, the better to decide his final step: should he persist with the little-by-little approach that had worked so well so far, then launch the beast into space with a vigorous flick which would make it dizzy and force it to make a crash landing, whereupon it would be a sitting duck? Or might it be better to strike out with the newspaper when within six inches or so? The bluebottle, perhaps operating on a more instinctual level, took off - apparently, without difficulty. Samson cursed: not only had his intended victim outwitted him yet again, but also it had denied him the chance to observe its upside-down landing technique: did it get into position for touchdown by executing a forward roll, a backwards roll, a sideways roll ... ? Or was it so completely at home in its chosen element that it could land any way it wanted, anywhere, anytime?

Samson's adversary seemed to know that it was safe up there on the ceiling, out of reach of the flailing newspaper. It gave Samson a volley of short, aggressive buzzes: *BZZZ ... BZZZ ... BZZZ ... BZZZ* which could be interpreted only as mocking laughter because of the way it simultaneously began rhythmically bringing its front legs together, a bluebottle's version of the slow handclap. Samson tossed the newspaper away in frustration, deciding to resort to an old Red Indian trick: to go back to behaving as though everything was perfectly normal. However, he had not struck a single new note when the foolhardy creature divebombed him. Even as Samson waved an angry fist at it, it celebrated its success by executing that most difficult of aerobatic feats, an outside loop. Samson leaped to his feet, retrieved the newspaper, rolled it up specially tight, and climbed up so as to stand precariously with one foot on the Chesterfield, the other on the piano keyboard. The bluebottle accepted the challenge - for a little while. Then either it was winged by one of Samson's flailing blows, or it was upset by the increasingly turbulent flying conditions, for it suddenly wheeled away from the combat zone and made a forced landing on a small amber section of leaded window, there to lick its wounds, carry out running repairs, re-calculate the odds and contemplate its next move.

Samson jumped down just in time to avoid doing the splits. He reminded himself of the wisdom of the old saying 'mind over matter' and went back to his practising. To help maintain concentration in such distracting circumstances he stared straight ahead at the three-duck wall plaque above the piano and struck each new note from an ever-increasing height, his index finger like a stooping peregrine. Good! Excellent! So far, he had managed to hit all the right notes. But could he continue to do so? And ... yes ... then one ... yes ... day ... *YYYNNOOOOO! AAAAAH!* Samson leaped off the stool, staring in disbelief at the spurting index finger, which must have been slashed by the sharp edge of a damaged key.

Retribution was swift and unerring. With a mighty bound worthy of his new hero Uncas, Samson reached the window and destroyed his tormentor with a single decisive thrust. The amber glass against which the victim had been cowering, turned to orange. But, thank God, the window held.

4. A Backwards Step

'*Eeeeh*, I say!' Mrs. Smalley exclaimed, chancing on the scene of the crime and catching Samson red-fingered. '*Hmph!* "As flies to wanton boys!" You want to be careful with those windows, I'll say you do! They cost money, they do that!'

'I only poked it,' Samson protested. 'It's not as if I punched it or thr ... threw a cushion at it. Perhaps it wasn't looking where it was going.'

'I know ... but as I said, you can't be too careful,' she insisted. '*Hee!* You'd know about it, I'll say you would!' Then, noticing Samson's index finger, she added, 'Goodness gracious me! I should wrap that in your handkerchief, if I were you.'

'Well, you're not,' Samson grunted.

Mrs. Smalley ignored him, having weightier things on her mind:

'Where on earth can that blooming postman have got to?' she sighed. '*Eeeh*, this so-called welfare state .. . you could be on your death bed, for all they care these days.'

'Perhaps they forgot to put the name on the envelope,' Samson joked. 'Or spelled the address wrong.'

Mrs. Smalley ignored him again, preferring to turn her attention to the fire. Seizing the bent old poker, she aimed it unerringly at one of the coals. Her skill in this respect always earned Samson's grudging admiration, since he had never had the slightest luck when trying to spear minnows in Stranglers Brook with a similarly bent stick. To fill in the time until his mother left the room Samson poked middle 'C' with the index finger of his left hand, the right one of course being quite unserviceable. Samson recognised that the injury, notwithstanding its annoyance value, could be a godsend, forcing him to reach the same proficiency with his left index finger as with his right. On the few occasions when he had tried to involve the left hand it had proved remarkably independent, as though it had a mind of its own. If in fact mastery of the left index finger proved possible it was not unreasonable to look forward to some future day when the supremely difficult art of playing with both index fingers at the same time could be mastered.

'I suppose I'd better see to your egg,' Mrs. Smalley announced. She gave Samson a very meaningful look as she left the room, though he had no idea what the meaning might be.

The morning egg, during these excruciatingly tedious last few days, had become the high spot of the day, the one thing guaranteed to be a complete surprise. The results, in spite of Mrs. Smalley's best intentions, were utterly inconsistent: one day the egg would be runny-raw - the next, rock hard; and just occasionally, to keep him confused, it would be perfectly done. Samson, try as he might, had found no way of predicting the outcome successfully: there was no pattern whatsoever. Well, the moment of truth was fast approaching. Would the egg be soft for the third morning running, would it be as hard as one of the pot eggs his father used to trick the hens into laying, or - the possibility favoured by Samson - would the mysterious 'law of averages' that his father believed in, ensure that this one was medium-rare?

Mrs. Smalley served the egg and retired to a safe distance. Samson slid over to the table, turned slowly to face the egg, bowed formally, picked up the blackened silver teaspoon with a ceremonial flourish, performed an elegant backlift, then prepared to take a real swipe at the egg.

'Oh. eat it properly!' Mrs. Smalley scolded. The spectacle was too much for her ragged nerves: she left the room.

Samson put the spoon down and began again, following exactly the same routine as before - except that this time he followed through:

WHACK!

Incredibly, the glancing blow failed to make the slightest impression. Samson paused briefly. doubly pleased: first, his second-best guess had proved correct - second, a hard egg was a good omen for the day ahead, promising firmness and decisiveness. Anyway ... the time had come to show the egg who was boss. To this end Samson resorted to his favourite Red Indian trick: turning oh-so-slowly away from the table, feigning complete lack of interest in the egg, he started to rise as though intending to leave the table - then, hands and spoon the merest blur, he swung a murderous two-handed blow without taking his eyes off the target for a single moment. *BANG!* The egg, dislodged from the tarnished silver-plated napkin ring which served as the eggcup, rolled off the edge of the table and dropped to the stone hearth. Samson pounced on it triumphantly before it had stopped rolling, took swift advantage of the hairline crack it had sustained, and prised out the rock-hard contents with the aid of the stone-from-horse's-hoof attachment of the ten-in-one pocket knife which Rita had shoplifted for him as a token of her undying love. The shell fragments, consigned to the fire, gave out little dancing flames with pretty colours.

Samson detected a rustling sound from behind him, and hurriedly concealed the knife.

'How is it?' Mrs. Smalley asked solicitously, peering over his shoulder.

'Oh, just right,' Samson replied, eager to avoid the customary post-mortem.

'Oh well, that's one then, isn't it,' she said proudly. 'Perhaps I'd better take Dad's out, then. He does seem to prefer them on the runny side, for some reason.'

So: a good time to pack up the piano practising and get on with other pressing business in the relative privacy of his bedroom ... Samson mumbled a farewell and bounded up the stairs. Pausing briefly outside the bedroom door to utter the customary hushed 'Meeiaow!' he entered, quietly closed the door behind him, slipped the catch, and prepared to swing into action. First he went to the dressing table. From there he searched the still-drawn curtains for the image of Rita which light passing through a particular pattern of moth holes sometimes managed to create. This time he drew a blank: worse, if there was indeed a face to be made out, it was that of a stern old man with deep-set eyes pierced by pinpricks of cold grey light.

Fortunately there were other ways of bringing Rita to mind. Samson moved his chair to the centre of the room so that it was under the lightshade, then fished inside the cobwebbed bowl for the toy squirrel which, being a present from Rita, he had christened 'Rati'. The name was also appropriate in that the squirrel's tail was uncharacteristically threadbare. Rati was the nearest thing to a teddy bear that Samson had ever owned, and in spite of its poor condition it was very precious to him. The choice of the lampshade as hiding place was also a cause for satisfaction: there was no chance of the squirrel being revealed when anyone turned on the light, because Mrs. Smalley had long ago removed the bulb so as to save electricity, also to prevent Samson from reading in bed.

Preliminaries completed, it was time to get on with some serious work. After replacing Rati and the chair Samson crawled under the bed and lifted up a corner of the tiny square of lino so as to get at the precious sheaf of papers which constituted his life's work to date: a simply wonderful (though not wonderfully simple) classification scheme whereby any British resident or common migrant could be identified from any of several kinds of evidence: appearance, mannersims, song, eggs and - subject to further research - its droppings.

There were still problems in all categories. These problems were in no way Samson's fault: rather, they originated from shortcomings of the published works on which his research was largely based. First and foremost, his three reference books - favourite of which was E.A. Ennion's The British Bird - were in bad condition, with many pages torn and many more missing, including almost the entire section on seabirds. This was most unfortunate, of course, but then beggars couldn't be choosers. The books had been sold to him at a nominal price by his fellow ornithologist and best friend Snorky. The second problem was that they were not very helpful in enabling birds to be identified from their song. Each book offered its own transcriptions, with serious discrepancies between them - as, for example, between '*weeli-weeli-woo*', '*oui-oui-oui*' and '*Whee-o-Whee-o-Whee*'. The use of capital initial letters for the third version was particularly confusing: just how were you supposed to hear the difference? In fact, out of over a hundred different species whose calls were given, there was only one about which the authorities were in agreement: the cuckoo.

Appearance and behaviour, likewise, were far less helpful indicators than Samson would have wished. Too much seemed to depend on whether the bird was young or old, cock or hen, wearing winter or summer plumage, and so on, so that after many hours of intensive study it was difficult to distinguish with certainty between a mature cock pied wagtail and a fledgling magpie. But of course all difficulties are relative, and none proved as daunting as that of identifying birds from their droppings. Here the problem was not so much one of conflicting information, as of dearth of information. So far, fieldwork had done little to rectify the position: evidence was quickly washed away by rain, and there seemed to be a frustrating similarity between specimens from different species. Samson had therefore cheated just a little by writing 'greyish-white' in every column. Now, deeply uneasy, he acted decisively, changing every single entry to 'whitish-grey', pending further enlightenment.

Fortunately, given the numerous and severe difficulties confronting him in this top-priority project, Samson could always turn for solace to his magnificent collection of birds' eggs. Housed in a superior quality Church's shoe box kept out of harm's way on top of the wardrobe, laid out lovingly in fluffed-up cotton wool to give them further protection and to display them to maximum advantage, the eggs never failed to elicit a thrill of satisfaction when he took them down for inspection. They brought back happy memories too: one of the great bonds between himself and Snorky was their passionate interest in collecting eggs. It was Snorky who, borrowing from his long experience of collecting coins and tokens, had introduced the grading system which Samson still applied most rigorously. never afraid to classify a particular specimen as merely 'Fine' where a less scrupulous collector might have succumbed to the temptation of discounting the odd blemish and opting for 'Very Fine', 'Extremely Fine' or even 'Mint'. Samson's scrupulosity meant that his collection had no eggs in 'Mint' condition. and only one with an 'EF' ('Extremely Fine') designation: a perfectly-shaped and highly-polished brown hen's egg, with blowholes so tiny as to be almost invisible - a perfect example of the serious egg collector's art. Strangely hens, unlike all other bird species in Samson's experience, laid eggs in which baby birds never seemed to develop, even if you kept them for months until they became rotten; young chicks had to be bought from somewhere in Yorkshire. This fact compounded the difficulty that Samson had always had in giving a confident answer to one of Snorky's famous brain-teasers, 'Which came first: the chicken, or the egg?'

In terms of condition the 'EF' egg was of course the star of the collection, in a class of its own, for none of the others had earned even a 'VF' label. The 'F' category, however, was well represented. This was largely thanks to Snorky who, putting a higher value on friendship than on competitive collecting, had sold Samson a priceless collection of rare seabirds' eggs for the token sum of half a crown, a mere two-and-a-half months' pocket money - so very little for a collection that might have taken a lifetime to put together - or longer for someone who had only ever been to the coast once, on a day trip to Blackpool.

This collection-within-a-collection was given pride of place in the centre of the box, whereas the hen's egg was consigned to obscurity in the bottom left-hand corner, certainly well out of the limelight; also, the seabirds' eggs were individually identified by little strips of card scissored from old Senior Service cigarette packets, and bore legends executed in the nearest Samson could manage to illuminated script. This central display had much in common with the Crown jewels. Five of the eggs, well matched both in rarity value and size (they were all about the same size as the hen's egg), were set in a perfect circle, sharp ends towards the centre.

There was 'Puffin F'; next, anticlockwise viewed from above, came 'Guillemot F' (a strange spelling which Samson took great pride in having got right); next 'Herring Gull F'; finally 'Skewer F' and 'Petrol F'. At the precise centre of the circle, like a diamond set among emeralds, was 'Great Hawk F' - a magnificent piece, a jewel indeed, as large, as beautiful and as precious as a golden goose's egg. The prudence of providing the seabirds' eggs with identification cards had been underlined quite recently when Samson, distracted by the sound of the gates being rattled, had inadvertently stepped back onto the collection. The hen's egg, as luck would have it, survived unscathed; likewise the seventh and final exhibit, a 'Fair' (only just) cracked and dented song thrush's egg which, as if in answer to a prayer, had dropped out of the sky onto the back lawn, presumably as a result of being laid in mid-air. The seabirds' eggs, by a cruel twist of fate, were all flattened. Their fragility was surprising, and raised questions about the wisdom of nesting high up on the cliffs. Another chance discovery threw some light on this puzzling point: on commencing restoration work, painstakingly picking up each little shell fragment with a forefinger moistened with fresh spittle, Samson found that the mottling smudged badly; obviously, therefore, eggs needed to be laid well out of the way of waves and spray, since their virtually identical sizes and shapes would have made it difficult for the parents to recognise their own eggs. This brilliant insight went some way towards compensating for the damage. The only remaining problem was, whether to reclassify the casualties as 'Poor', or to retain their original 'F' classification on the grounds that their present state was an Act of God. In the end, common sense prevailed.

It was time to kiss the collection goodbye. Samson blew the worst of the dust from the lid of the shoebox, brushed his lips against the lid, spat out, then returned the box and its precious contents to the top of the wardrobe. So ... what next? Get on with the classification scheme? Tackle the job manfully in spite of the contradictions, missing pages and interrupted field work? Or get a pencil and paper and work out how long it would take to acquire replacements for the damaged eggs?

Samson raised the blind. Aha! The weather now seemed to be getting better, i.e. worse. There was now a much more general clouding-over and Samson could see clearly that visibility had dropped considerably in the short interval since breakfast. But it was still too good: it was still possible, looking out across the fields, to make out the ragged line of scrub which marked the far lip of Dead Man Clough, where Polecat usually waited, posing as a stricken oak while keeping

Foxgloves Hall under observation ... yes, there he was, tree/shrub No. 17 on Samson's diagram ... biding his time .... wasting his time, actually, since there was nothing he could do as long as Samson remained indoors. Well, if it was a game of patience he wanted he could have one: time was on his, Samson's, side, since he had clocked up only nine years as against Polecat's fifty-nine.

Relieved thanks to the conclusions from this re-assessment, Samson relaxed and allowed his attention to stray away to the right, to the section of Stranglers Brook downstream from Dead Man Clough: Dobson's Gorge. The far wall of the gorge was a sheer cliff face, rising a few feet higher than the near wall. Perched on top of this wall of rock, like an eyrie, was Belle Vue, a small crescent of rich people's houses with large gardens extending to the edge of the gorge. All the houses were white, so when not obscured by mist they often resembled an upper set of false teeth grinning contemptuously over the peasants across the gorge. At this particular moment small black clouds massed menacingly over the Belle Vue houses and a narrow beam of sunlight picked out the largest and finest one - recently repainted, it reflected the light with dazzling brilliance. This gem belonged to Sid Clegg, the millionaire.

Samson had another reason, an even more compelling one, to look across at the Belle Vue cliffs. For weeks the unmistakable call of a cuckoo (or pair of cuckoos, it was to be hoped) had been audible from the region of Dobson's Gorge. Thanks to painstaking observation and more than a little intuition Samson had established beyond all reasonable doubt that the birds were nesting on a concealed ledge more or less directly below Belle Vue House, the Clegg mansion. On several occasions (but only on Sundays, because of the Vicar threat) he had worked his way downstream to the foot of the Belle Vue cliffs with a view to locating the nesting site, but each time he had been forced to cut short the mission on catching sight of a rival birdsnester whom he had come to think of as 'Boy Sunday'. From the few occasions when Samson had managed to get a proper look at the boy he judged him to be about his own age, similar in height and build too - nevertheless he was absolutely distinctive, being completely and utterly black, like a golliwog. Most of the time he was well concealed, merging with shadows and only visible - if at all - as a set of flashing white teeth, so that at first Samson had thought he was imagining the boy. One day, determined at all costs to get to the bottom of the mystery, Samson wandered around the clough with feigned carelessness until he was sure he was being observed, then suddenly disappeared into a small fissure and lay doggo for the best part of an hour. His patience was amply rewarded: for several seconds Boy Sunday came into full view, moving noiselessly upstream. The boy's impressive woodcraft, his stealth, and the brilliant way he used any available cover all suggested that he was a genuine savage rather than, for example, an apprentice chimney sweep living rough. It gave Samson a tremendous feeling of satisfaction to beat the blackamoor at his own game: savage or no, he obviously lacked Samson's deep ornithological knowledge and was hoping to be led to the nest.

GULP! Sidney baulked as an extremely unpalatable thought bubbled up from the depths: what if Boy Sunday got tired of waiting to have the hard work done for him, and decided to go it alone? The little snake! God ... there was no time to lose - each passing minute made it more and more likely that the cuckoo's nest would turn out to be yet another Old Mother Hubbard's cupboard. It was imperative to beat Boy Sunday to the prize.

'Come on, come on, come on!' Samson exhorted himself through gritted teeth, emphasising each new resolve by banging his fist down on the makeshift little desk where so many of his important projects had first seen the light of day. The split finger throbbed painfully, underlining the element of urgency, and blood started seeping from the wound. In spite of the urgent and worrying nature of his problem Samson was not the kind of person to lose sight of other projects that demanded his time on a regular basis. Getting back to his feet, he went to the wardrobe, rocked it to and fro whilst muttering 'Sorry, sorry' to its occupant;

when at last he heard a gentle thud he dropped to his knees, groped under the wardrobe and retrieved what, until the acquisition of the seabirds' eggs, had been his most treasured possession: his diary. This was no ordinary diary - the beautifully-tooled leather-bound cover made that very clear. Samson brushed his finger tips over the cover several times before opening the ornate brass clasp. 'Racegoers Diary 1936', the exquisite marbled fly leaf announced; above that, in the top right-hand corner, was the beautifully-penned message 'To Eric With Love, Christmas 1935, Better luck with the gee-gees in '36; the signature, for some reason had been scratched off.

There followed pages and pages of useful information about race meetings, tables of winners of classic races going back to the 1832 Derby, and a page about tides and lighting-up times (of little use to residents of Old Guinea, Samson felt, but none the less interesting for that). Apart from the inscription on the fly leaf the diary was almost as new. There were just two lightly-pencilled entries in the whole diary, both for January. The first said simply 'Two pounds each way My Golly'; the second, scrawled rather than written, said 'Leave the bloody gee-gees alone' - presumably a late New Year's resolution. For a long time after acquiring the diary Samson had felt overawed by the quality of the paper and had made a resolution himself: not to use the diary unless something really really important happened. Hence all the blank pages, one for each day, all the way through to 31st March. After this the diary suddenly came to life. 'GA', the first entry announced: the Great Adventure, that wonderful, never-to-be-forgotten day out with Snorky, all expenses paid apart from the bus fare, and culminating in a visit to the cinema to see the greatest film ever made. Also on 1st April: 'BECFS': 'Bought Egg Collection From Snorky'. That momentous purchase had been one reason for the abrupt change from car-spotting to bird-spotting, recorded succinctly on 2nd April: ' FCS-BBS'. The other reason was the cruel disappointment (a triple one, at that) suffered on the afternoon of the second, when for the last time, as it turned out, he made the long cross~country trek to the main road. A little tired, he had settled down stoically, mindful that on the two previous occasions there had not been a single car all day: the only vehicles had been a horse and cart and (from a serious spotter's point of view) an equally useless motor cycle, without number plates; this, as if to tease him, had been driven past at least a dozen times. It had looked as though he was going to draw another blank and he was just on the point of leaving when a bedraggled White Leghorn emerged from the massed horsetails lining the far side of the road and began to creep across. Samson's heart burst into activity, an idling engine suddenly given full throttle: here, purely by luck, was a once-in-a-lifetime chance to discover the answer to Snorky's most perplexing brain teaser: 'Why did the chicken cross the road?'

The chicken, about half-way across, suddenly stopped. It lifted its head and cocked it on one side, the better to examine either the road or the sky. Had it? ... would it? .... Samson, crouched down among a dense stand of horsetails, and holding his breath, willed the chicken to continue its journey. Damn! At this point a huge motor car purred into view: Captain Clegg's Rolls Royce shooting-brake. Some boys might have felt that such a car was worth a dozen ordinary ones, but not Samson. The great machine glid past like a ghost, the huge bulk of Captain Clegg immobile and impassive at the wheel. In truth it looked more like a Dinky toy propelled by an unseen hand.

Clegg's famous 'cauliflower' ear was equally disappointing, being no larger or more impressive than a brussels sprout. Worst of all, the disturbed chicken retraced its steps and disappeared back into the horsetails, taking its precious secret with it.

Nevertheless, from April 3rd things had really got moving, judging from the flood of entries. 'SAT', the first one recorded: 'Saw A Thrush'. April 5th: again, 'SAT', and 'SATA': Saw A Thrush Again': judging from the attempts at correction this entry had originally read ' HSTT', in other words ' Half Saw Two Thrushes'; April 6th: 'SYAT', probably 'Saw Yet Another Thrush'; April 7th: 'STT', 'Saw Two Thrushes' (or just possibly 'Saw Three Thrushes' ... or just 'Saw The Thrush'?) Almost certainly, judging from the angrily-scrawled 'STFTA', the last deciphering was the correct one. Samson still felt slightly uncomfortable about all of the 'thrush' entries. One of his books had talked about 'the common or garden thrush', yet neglected to explain how to distinguish between them. It seemed almost certain that they were all of the 'garden' variety, since they certainly weren't common.

Right: time to begin again, time to bring the records up to date, to put on record the piano-playing progress and the historic victory over the bluebottle. Samson yawned, stretched, and reached out for his trusty pencil ... damn! It had been left in the living room.

Samson got up, stepped to the window and threw out his arms in an appeal to the heavens for help. His prayer was answered instantly, probably it had even been anticipated: great waves of mist had rolled down from the higher ground beyond the clough, reducing visibility to a few yards. Feverishly replacing his secret materials, he flew down the stairs three at a time, threw on his raincoat and wellingtons and was gone.

5. The Cuckoos' Nest

Wonderful ... perfect! Within seconds of being swallowed up in the swirling vapours Samson felt cool and collected, and completely safe in his invisibility - as well-protected as a newborn prophet swaddled in silk or a new-blown egg coddled in cotton wool. Soon, however, the chilly fingers of mist prodded him into the realisation that his sense of security was ill-founded: Polecat would expect him to take full advantage of this hell-sent opportunity to make a break.

On the past three occasions when Samson had risked venturing abroad there had been no mist - he had hared across the fields by the most direct route, banking on reaching the relative safety of the deep woods before the Vicar could intercept him. This time, given the dense mist, this might not possible, since speed across the fields could only be achieved at risk of blundering into some of the thousands of cowpats which made the pasture as tricky to negotiate as a minefield. It was tempting to hope that Polecat, similarly impeded by the mist in his mad scramble across the clough, might trip and break his stupid neck, but it was obviously unwise to depend on such a stroke of luck.

There was a choice of three routes from Foxgloves Hall to Dead Man's Clough. First, there was the aforementioned direct route, a distance of about three hundred yards through the cow pastures on the lower slopes of Ramsbottoms' farm. The other two routes were then like the outer prongs of a very wide and very bent toasting fork. The right-hand prong could be likened to a cocked dog's leg: following it involved squelching along a twisting sequence of waterlogged ditches which, if negotiated successfully, gave access to the clough via Dobson's Gorge. The point of entry was easily recognised from afar by a minor landmark which resembled a Buddha, consisting as it did of an almost spherical stone two or three feet in diameter, representing the head, this perched precariously on a much larger but similarly rounded body. Samson thought of this structure as 'The Whacker Doll' because of its resemblance to the real thing of the same name: Rita's trusty doll, which she had wielded to great effect during her first turbulent months at St. Peter's, and which had survived unscathed until she brought it down too hard on a skull even more impact-resistant than the doll's. Samson rarely chose this route, because after squeezing round The Whacker it was necessary to traverse a narrow path, at best a foot wide and at worst non-existent because of erosion, with a two-hundred-foot drop to the right and only a rickety barbed wire fence to hold on to - plus, for good measure, the ever-present threat from Hamish, a treacherous red bull allowed to roam freely on the other side of the fence.

The third route, the left-hand prong of the toasting fork, involved a long detour across rising ground by way of a succession of hedges and dry stone walls, and it meant skirting Ramsbottoms' farm at risk of being eaten. Here lurked a guard dog of monster proportions, as big as two or three Alsatians put together. It bore no relation to any dog that Samson had ever seen, or even read about. Fortunately Snorky, one of whose aunts regularly exhibited cocker spaniels at the Royal Lancashire Show, had been able to identify its pedigree as half Alsatian, half Baskerville and half mongrel - truly, a dog-and-a-half. The beast lurked behind a disused pigsty and never barked a warning. The first thing you became aware of was the clanking of a heavy chain, then as you peered over the low wall to see what was going on, you saw the beast sailing towards you three or four feet off the ground, all mad yellow eyes and slavering fangs, until at the last moment, just when it expected to sink its teeth into you, it was brought up short by the chain and half-throttled in the middle of an expectant howl: a split second later there would be a sickening thud as the rest of the flying beast fetched up against the wall. There then followed a few moments of safety in which to scurry past, after which there was a quarter of a mile of peaceful, relaxed scrambling until you reached Dead Man Clough immediately downstream of Entwistle's Bottom, where the gaunt bulk of a ruined mill blocked the valley. This area, and particularly the section of valley upstream of the mill, was very much a no-go area, since it was regularly patrolled by one 'Connemara Peggy', alias

'The Crone'. Hundreds of years old, The Crone had originally been an Irish noblewoman caught up in the Jacobean uprisings - information which meant absolutely nothing to Samson. More to the point, she was instantly recognisable from quite a distance by her long black shawl and headscarf, and the clay pipe permanently clamped between toothless jaws. Approaching her was not recommended: though not always ill-disposed to the curious, she had been known to tear out a tormentor's throat with bony fingers that gripped and penetrated like an eagle's talons.

So: which route to the clough to choose? It wasn't necessary to be a genius to realise that the first route was both the quickest and the least dangerous. Of course Polecat too would realise that and, since Samson had given him the slip twice already, would assume that he would choose between Routes 2 and 3 ... in which case, the safest route .... would be Route 1. Slightly confused, but nevertheless pleased with the sophistication of his thinking, Samson boldly put his best foot forward, eyes probing through the thick mist like converging spotlight beams in a smoky theatre, in the hope of avoiding as many cowpats as possible. It proved easier than expected, and in no time at all he was well into the pasture and proceeding, in best Mohican style, at a steady jog.

Christ! What the -?! Samson suddenly went sprawling across a cudding cow. The animal, perhaps more shocked than he was, bellowed loudly as it struggled to its feet and lumbered across the field, setting off a minor stampede of ghostly shapes with asynchronous udders. Samson, shaken but nonc the worse for wear, set off again - this time, with head held high. In this manner he must have got to within forty or fifty yards of the clough, still essentially unscathed, when he tripped over a wire buried in the long grass. He stumbled, but avoided falling. He realised he had been lucky not to go sprawling into a huge cluster of fresh cowpats, and he cursed the thoughtless idiot - a poacher, probably - who had left the wire there. Well, anyway ... this was no time to get agitated. Samson took a deep, deep breath and began counting oh-so-slowly to ten: however, he had scarcely reached two when he heard a strange whirring noise in the mist close by, as of something flying past at quite a speed. Two others followed in quick succession: *whirr, whirr!* What on -? *Partridges*? Yes, of course ... must have been. Perhaps a whole covey of them had been flushed out by a careless cow or a weasel or something ... Samson felt a warm glow of satisfaction at the ease with which he had identified the birds; it was wonderful that, at long last, those countless hours of study had paid off. He stood stock still, scarcely breathing, straining to hear the characteristic '*Fvu! Fvu!*' or '*chirrick chirrick*' as described in 'The British Bird'. Suddenly a fourth partridge, flying even faster than the others (perhaps one with a mental problem, in a vain attempt to catch up) just about nicked Samson's left ear. He flinched and covered his face with his hands, then immediately felt ashamed of his reaction. To recover his self-esteem he set himself in a classic boxing stance modelled on a picture of Gentleman Jim Corbett he had once studied, then boxed the ears off a few shadows. Immediately feeling better, he lowered his guard - prematurely as it turned out, because a fifth partridge, either in too much of a hurry for its own good, or afflicted by navigation problems, ploughed into a large fresh cowpat just in front of him. Wildly excited in spite of having been lightly splattered from head to toe, Samson bent down to examine the crater. It was deep, but - surprisingly - little more than an inch in diameter. Could a partridge - even a partridge chick - be that small? Or ... fantastic! ... could they have been snipe?

Feverishly Samson cast around for a stick or something similar with which to probe the crater, hoping to rescue the crashed bird, resuscitate it, then either keep it as a pet or stuff it. The search for a stick, unfortunately, was fruitless; worse, it proved impossible to relocate the cowpat, there were so many of the damn things. A little disconsolate, Samson shrugged stoically and force-marched himself with the alacrity of a lead soldier across the last few yards of meadow.

First base was a venerable beech tree growing on the very lip of the clough. The tree's thick, smooth trunk rose near-vertically all of fifteen feet before giving off the first branches, the thinnest of which drooped over the clough at a steep angle, bare except for a profuse growth of leaves at its turned-under remote end, so that it resembled the trunk of a feeding elephant. It was on this distinctive branch that Samson concentrated his considerable willpower. Counting slowly and deliberately down from five, barely breaking the rhythm to spit nervously into his palms on the count of two, Samson coiled himself up like a Jack-in-a-box and with a mighty effort sailed out across the abyss. His wildly-clawing fingertips just managed to gain a purchase on the slimy, algae-encrusted branch. For a few seconds he hung there precariously, legs flailing ineffectually; then, when at last he managed to improve his hold, he threw his legs up and around the branch and worked his way, sloth-like, along the underside of the branch until he reached the trunk. It was then child's play to climb ten or twelve feet to reach the secret platform from which he planned to make his reputation as an ornithologist.

The platform was constructed on the principle of a spider's web but lacked the model's delicacy and sophistication and so perhaps could have been mistaken for the dray of an unusually casual squirrel. Radiating out from the central hub, but deliberately randomised for better concealment, were thirty or forty leafy branches culled from other parts of the tree and regularly renewed as their foliage deteriorated.

Samson, hunched up with his knees tucked under his chin, all wellingtons and elbows, inspected the structure as conscientiously as any spider. It was easy to verify that the platform had not been disturbed since his last visit, thanks to the marks he had scratched at the branches' intersections; it would have been impossible for anyone or anything, man or beast, to disturb the platform without leaving a trace. Happy with his handiwork, Samson carried out his final check, satisfying himself that his trusty but rusty tin opener was still pointing due north. It was only then that he felt able to relax and to settle down to a period of intensive listening, straining his ears for tell-tale sounds from the mist-enshrouded slopes below.

Most people, even after a lifetime in the countryside, would be hard-pressed to recognise more than a couple of dozen sounds: Samson, in spite of his tender years, was as forest-wise as any animal. No matter how mysterious, muffled or faint were the animal noises percolating through the trees and bushes and mingling with the sighings and groanings of the plants, Samson could decipher them as expertly as any scholar deciphering hieroglyphic scratchings. Surely there was no animal on earth that could pass, undetected or unrecognised, within half a mile of where Samson now crouched. His confidence was in no way misplaced: not only had he benefitted from countless hours of practice, but also he had made a very important discovery. Noting that, when listening acutely for any given sound, other sounds might be unattended to, he had developed the technique of listening in a completely new way, for everything in general and for nothing in particular, like a sensitive radio aerial disconnected from its tuning circuit. It was a technique he could switch on and off at will, and it was this technique he now chose to employ. Closing his eyes, he opened his ears to the full sound spectrum of Nature's 1001-piece orchestra.

'*Drrrrrrr... Dr ..... Drrrrr .... Dr.......rrrr ...*'

Samson awoke, shivering and anxious. Normally he would have been over the moon on hearing, with amazing clarity, the unmistakable drilling of a woodpecker, so so similar to the noise made by a boxwood ruler being vibrated on a desk top. On this occasion he cursed: twenty feet up in the air or not, he might have given his position away by snoring, or by talking in his sleep. He pinched himself, half as punishment and half as a way of recovering his senses. Actually though, he now realised, he might have been too safety-conscious; he might have been better off getting to the site of the cuckoos' nest as quickly as possible. Well, he would do that straight away - at least, after performing an important ritual: carving 'ITA' ten more times on the side of the trunk facing the clough. Next time he would be up to ninety, and the time after that he would be due for a triple underline: the missing letter 'R' could then be added at leisure. Unfortunately, in the excitement of the moment he let slip his only carving tool, the tin-opener. To search for it now could be profitless, Samson realised, on account of the thick mist: without further ado he edged himself out along a suitable branch (one which, for reasons which will be clear in a moment, stretched in the opposite direction to the abyss), lowered himself gingerly until he was hanging by his arms, then - without being able to see the ground, so thick was the mist, dropped down. The drop was successful: an experienced parachutist could not have rolled over better on landing. With only a cursory nod in self-congratulation Samson picked himself up, dusted himself down and carried on where he had left off.

On the clough side the beech's irregular, twisted roots had been exposed by erosion, while just above ground level were two large round protuberances set close together like a criminal's eyes, so that the whole had the appearance of a sick squid with a tree growing out of its head. Samson now used these exposed roots to work his way round the trunk and to let himself safely down the first and steepest part of the clough. Then, squatting on his haunches and using his wellington treads as brakes he slipped and slithered his way down to the brook. This descent, unlike some previous ones, was a complete success: on fetching up feet first in the shallow water at the edge of the brook Samson treated himself to a brief but nonetheless sincere handshake. At the same time he remained conscious of the need for caution, so instead of clambering onto the bank - which would have made for faster progress, but at risk of leaving obvious tracks - he picked his way downstream through the shallows. All that was then needed was to be careful to avoid stepping into deep holes in the stream bed, slipping on smooth, slimy stones, and dislodging loose ones. In the event he managed extremely well, limiting his scores to 1, 2 and 1 respectively before a sudden amplification of the stream's sounds announced that he had reached the point where two further streams augmented the flow, and the narrow, steep-sided ravine concentrated it: the short section known as T' Cut. Second base, the point at the foot of the cliffs directly below the cuckoos' nesting site, was then easily identified, even in mist as thick as the proverbial pea soup, by a pile of polished boulders each the size and shape of an ostrich's egg.

Samson was beginning to enjoy himself. He had, he

now admitted to himself, overestimated the dangers. The Vicar was out of the picture, likewise Boy Sunday - further, whereas, viewed from across the ravine, the cuckoo cliffs had looked impossible to scale, from close up it was obvious that climbing them would be child's play, the kind of thing you could, with a bit of luck, do blindfolded and with one hand tied behind your back. There were dozens ... hundreds, maybe even thousands of handholds and footholds and little ledges. There was an important lesson to be learned here: never imagine difficulties - always take the trouble to find out what things are really like. Samson crouched motionless for a while and only began the ascent when this lesson had been well and truly internalised.

Samson began the long climb. At first he ascended as a flea might, jumping from position to position. It was a technique pioneered by Snorky's great-great-grandfather in his days as a mule skinner in the Rocky Mountains during the Gold Rush, and handed down from generation to generation like a precious heirloom; it was supposed to be kept as a family secret, but Snorky had said that because they were 'sort of like brothers', he could let him in on the secret. The point was, by jumping from point to point it was possible to avoid the danger inherent in putting all your weight on one foot, which was obviously as stupid as putting all your eggs in one basket. Actually the Horrocks Technique was not necessary here, and Samson soon abandoned it: the climb was like going for a stroll, only vertically instead of horizontally, and he felt that if he did slip, the thick mist would buoy him up and let him drift back down as gently as if he were a sycamore seed. In no time Samson found his head and shoulders emerging from the top of the mist, so for a few moments he was able to imagine something very silly and stupid: that he was a sugar plum fairy embedded in light icing. It was a perfect moment to stop and take stock, because just above was the slight overhang below the cuckoos' presumed nesting site. Getting onto or around this overhang looked like being the first really difficult bit of climbing. This would have been an ideal moment to put the kettle on and have a nice cup of tea with extra sugar, but of course that was not possible. Sensibly, Samson nevertheless stopped for a breather and a chance to take stock.

Stepping sideways onto a convenient ledge, Samson gradually turned round so as to face outwards, and was immediately enthralled by the spectacular, almost magical scene before him. The sun was peeping out, giving the top surface of the mist a smooth, silvery appearance in some places, the delicate texture of freshly-fallen snow in others. The unreality was like that of a pantomime set - in particular, that of the never-to-be-forgotten St. Peter's production of 'Snow White and the Seven Dwarfs', in which the use of some magic stuff called 'dry ice' had resulted in clouds of white vapour covering the stage - the seven dwarfs too, leaving only the heads of the Wicked Stepmother and pantomime horse poking out. The sun was gathering strength by the minute, and the mist melting away faster than butter on hot toast, exposing a panoramic vista which explained why the name 'Belle Vue' had been chosen for the houses up top. The view must once have been, quite simply, awe-inspiring. Unfortunately it had been spoiled at some time: it was as though an anti-social giant had tipped his rubbish down an embankment. One or two items, such as Foxgloves Hall and the ramshackle spread of Ramsbottoms' Farm, had lodged part way down the slope and not suffered too much damage; the bulk of the rubbish had collected at the bottom of the slope and had ever since been a smouldering tip: the great smoking mass known to generations of locals as 'Monkey Town'. According to Snorky, one of whose maiden aunts was a midwife, babies there were sometimes born with a tail - more a stump, of course, than something long and bushy. Until recently such babies, as they grew up, had been obliged to wear special trousers or skirts to conceal 'Th' Owd Lad's Curse', as the affliction was called. Samson had always maintained a healthy scepticism about the special clothes, being aware anyway that some people believed that a tail was not a curse, but a blessing from Almighty God himself - something to be proud of. Monkey Town was a one-industry town set in a hemispherical valley, very similar to the Hell of Samson's dreams. Dozens of huge cotton mills belched thick black greasy smoke into this basin seven days a week, three hundred and sixty-four days a year, several thousand closely-packed houses likewise: thus trapped. the smoke swirled round and round. mixing with the perpetual mist to form a smog so dense that often you couldn't see the end of your own nose - hence the curious local practice of frequent nose-tapping, misinterpreted by strangers as a 'Don't be Nosey' gesture. Having regard to the often zero visibility, some Methodists had started to argue that God had given people tails so that they might find their way to and from work in procession - each holding on to the tail of the person in front in the manner of circus elephants.

It was all coming back now ... Snorky had always insisted that Speedy Ramsbottom had been born with a tail. The poor boy stank - not of the strong but essentially healthy odours of the farmyard, but as though he himself were slowly putrefying. He was the scapegoat for every bad smell in the classroom.

'Who's making it unpleasant for others?' Miss Pollock would ask in her horrible cracked contralto voice. Before the question was fully out a forest of fingers would be pointing at Speedy. His way of sitting there, immobile and with his unnaturally long tongue thrust deep into his left nostril, made him seem guilty whether he was or not.

'Go and stand in the corner immediately, you disgusting shameless lout!' Miss Pollock always screamed - quite unnecessarily since Speedy, slow as he was, would by that time be half way to the corner which he had made his own: it was in fact always referred to as 'Speedy's corner'.

Samson had often felt that Speedy was unfairly treated. After all, since he stank all the time you got sort of used to it, to the extent that you only really noticed it when he moved (which was not often) or when Polecat went and stood beside him: then, the most terrible stench would rise up, so foul that you felt like shouting out or vomiting. Probably this specially nauseating stench was caused by fear, Samson surmised. Polecat, probably wanting to pretend to be a forgiving Christian, never punished Speedy in that situation - instead, he limited himself to giving Speedy a withering look, and muttering an inaudible rebuke. Samson had often tried to lipread this, hoping to make use of it himself when Speedy misbehaved in his company, and as near as he could make out the Vicar's words were suitably restrained and moral: 'So there, you see', or something very similar. Presumably he was trying to get Speedy to see the error of his ways.

A sudden noise from somewhere just above awakened Samson from his reverie. The cuckoos!? They must have moved. Perhaps they had got stiff, sitting in one position for too long hatching their eggs. Anyway, a little fall of rubble gave them away. Samson, himself a bit stiff, turned round to face the cliff and strained his neck in an effort to catch a glimpse of the careless birds. Unfortunately they were being more careful now: perhaps they had heard him move. Well .... the thing to do was, to keep absolutely silent, and tune in to noises from the nest, blocking out all others. Samson now regretted never seriously practising the ear-swivelling exercises which Snorky had often demonstrated - actually he had never had the slightest success, couldn't even make them twitch ... obviously some people were born with the gift ... others, unfortunately not .. so no amount of practising would work. The silence rang oppressively in his ears and he gradually became a bit despondent: there were times, like this time, when it seemed that he only ever had real success with birds when he was with Snorky.

'*CUC-KOO! CUC-KOO!*'

The distinctive repeated call, ringing out loud and clear as a church bell and reverberating back and forth across the ravine, took Samson somewhat by surprise, so that for several seconds he stood there open-mouthed. The cuckoos! So he had been right all along! Had his luck changed, or was he simply being rewarded for patience and persistence? God, what would he have given to see Snorky's face at this moment!

'*CRACK!*' Samson winced and yelped as something nasty nicked his left earlobe and ricocheted off the rock face, threatening to blind him in the process. Another inch ... *Christ!* His first reaction was that he had been divebombed by an anxious cuckoo, but common sense suggested a missile of some sort, such as a stray shot from a poacher's gun. But there had been no bang.

'*CRACK!*'

Another missile virtually exploded not two feet from where

Samson clung. A stone! There was no doubt about it: Samson watched it plummet down into the depths of the ravine. Guessing that there would be more to follow, and terrified of being blinded, Samson nevertheless courageously turned round to face his unseen assailant. He squinted into the sun, unable to use his hands to shield his eyes, and painstakingly scrutinised every square inch of the opposite wall of the ravine. Nothing ... nothing at all .... absolutely nothing. Then, just when he was beginning to wonder if this was really an awful nightmare, or if he was going mad, a squat bush on the opposite wall was bent to one side, a hideously grinning black face appeared, and a very definite V-sign at his expense was made with a huge catapult.

6. Cliffhanging

Flipping heck! The blooming blackamoor! Damn the filthy reptile, damn him ... damn damn damn damn damn him ... and the rest of his stinking tribe! Would that the grinning idiot be struck dead where he now crouched .... be despatched to the uttermost depths of Hell Fire, to end up as a lump of charred meat, or as greasy black cinders! With these and like sentiments Samson sustained himself during those crucial first few seconds of panic.

Oh God! If only he had done what he ought to have done: co-opted Snorky for the final assault on the nest ... there were bound to be at least two eggs, so they would both have come away happy. If Snorky had come along the savage wouldn't have dared show his stupid face - and if he had, he wouldn't have stood a chance, because the two of them would have hunted him down relentlessly, communicating with one another by means of well-rehearsed Red Indian war whoops and, to strike terror into the victim, raucous noises made by blowing through split grass stems held between the thumbs. They would have closed on him in a brilliant final pincer movement, then pounced together and finished the blighter off in their own distinctive ways - Samson by mercilessly beating him to a pulp, while Snorky made bootlaces out of his thick black hide.

Snorky ... *mmm* ... It occurred to Samson that he too might well be in the area ... probably hoping to be led to the nest. When Samson had first confided his supicions about the cuckoos' likely nesting arrangements, Snorky had come up with some cock-and-bull story about cuckoos not building nests - instead, they laid their eggs in other birds' nests, and could even mimic the eggs of birds very different from themselves! Absolutely ridiculous, of course - and if any further proof were needed, there was the fact that the bird books which (to be fair) Snorky had more or less given him, had missing pages not only in the section devoted to seagulls' eggs, but also the page detailing the cuckoos' nesting arrangements.

Come to think of it, it had in fact been Snorky who first

suspected the cuckoos' existence and who finally narrowed down the nest's whereabouts to the general area of Dead Man Clough. Without doubt that had been one of the finest feats of ornithological detective work that Samson had ever witnessed. Snorky had three glass balls, which at first sight seemed to be identical shiny spheres about an inch-and-a-half across. On closer inspection subtle differences could be discerned, differences which stemmed from distinctive arrangements of opaque inclusions in the otherwise clear glass. In one the bits made up a misty pastoral scene with a pale blue stream, pale green trees and pale pink animals somewhere between pigs and cows. Another revealed snow-capped mountains partly obscured by low clouds, with anaemic pink Christmas trees on their lower slopes. The third ball came as something as a shock, especially if viewed last: a scantily-clad mermaid disported herself suggestively on a rock rising out of foaming waves, a marine equivalent of 'What the Butler Saw'. For weeks and weeks after Snorky first unveiled them they were the hottest thing around, and he exploited them to the full in game after game of 'Find the Lady', mollifying frustrated losers by letting them have a quick peek at the mermaid.

Eventually of course the novelty wore off. Samson then went through a long phase of being preoccupied, withdrawn even, and was often to be seen gazing glassily at one or other of the balls in a quiet spot where he felt safe from disturbance. Beside himself with curiosity, he was finally let in on the secret: in certain lights, and with the hands cupped around but not touching a ball, you could see all manner of strange things - in fact, you could see almost anything you wanted to see, also things you would rather not have seen. Sometimes, if you started to lose concentration a little, you could find that instead of you looking at them, they were looking at you, seeing into the innermost recesses of your soul. Snorky, whose willpower was legendary, finally achieved dominion over the three balls and with concentrated gaze forced them to disclose their innermost secrets. In this way were revealed the locations of the nests of two pairs of plovers, three pairs of skylarks and a widowed magpie, all accurate to within ten or twenty yards. The first sightings of the cuckoos, unfortunately, were indistinct, probably because of the greater distance involved. In fact they were so indistinct that poor Samson, peering hard enough to rupture his eyeballs, was unable to make out anything at all.

Not surprisingly it was weeks before Snorky made a positive identification, having hit on the brilliant idea of consulting all three balls simultaneously and waiting until two of them were in agreement. Samson, driven to distraction during the long dragging days of uncertainty, had done a spot of crystal gazing himself, pressing into service his three hard-won dobbers. His initiative was rewarded: on at least two occasions, misty blurs had shown up inside the frosted glass of the No. 1 dobber - blurs which could only have been a pair of cuckoos flying in close formation over the treetops. With that advantage Samson had decided to go it alone, and he had been rewarded immediately by actually hearing the birds in the clough. Now, he must pay the price for going it alone. At that moment, perched on the narrow ledge as precariously as a kittiwake's egg, Samson would gladly have given everything he possessed for even the briefest squint into any bit of old glass. How else could he find out what Fate had in store for him - and cheat her?

'*THWACK!!!*' Another missile cracked into the rock face just beside Samson. Fragments flew in all directions, one catching him on the temple and another on the cheek: either of them, if his sixth sense had not made him flinch just in time, could have blinded him. Panic ran riot within him, loosening his bowels at the same time as tying a knot in his throat. He screwed up his eyes and prepared for the next missile to be a direct hit. Myriad tiny coloured lights flashed in the dark void around him, but it was better than being blinded. The other advantage of screwing up the eyes, tighter than tight, was that by blocking out the external world it was possible to think, to imagine the situation as if you were an outside observer. Only by staying absolutely calm, Samson knew, would it be possible to survive the attack. There followed a spell of virtual self-hypnosis as Samson forced himself to run through uplifting examples from history. There was Jesus Christ on the cross, calmly chatting to his crucifiers and refusing medical attention (though prudently, he did allow salt to be be rubbed into the open wounds); King Harold lying on the beach at Hastings, calmly trying to pull a Norman arrow out of his eye; and, perhaps the example to top them all, Lord Horatio Nelson at the Battle of Trafalgar. St. Peter's headmaster, Mr. Thoroughgood, never tired of recounting Nelson's historic triumph blow by blow, and to hear him warming to his theme on a winter's afternoon as the light started to fail, with torrential rain lashing the rattling windows, you could easily imagine that he himself had been there, even that you yourself were there while the action went on around you. Long-pent-up tensions were released when the Victory's huge cannons boomed into life, spreading death and destruction on a grand scale. The air between the decks was filled with acrid smoke, and ear-shattering noises reverberated from timber to timber. Then an answering broadside of grapeshot from the sneaky, cowardly French raked the deck and men fell over like ninepins, whole arms and legs shot off. And yet amidst this terrible carnage the great Lord Nelson stood impassively, up to his ankles in blood, directing operations - as cool and upright as a lone cucumber in a bed of squashed strawberries.

What a man! Now, fortified by Nelson's heroic example, Samson decided that it was time to take stock of his own situation as a preliminary to decisive action. Either in imitation of the great commander, or to halve his own potential losses, he forced open one eye.

Oh God! Samson had immediate cause to regret his action. A cool breeze had sprung up: the ravine was clear of mist and the last few clouds were bowling along the sky as lightly as if they were made of the finest cotton wool. And so like a condemned man at the scaffold, suddenly having his hood removed, Samson for the first time fully appreciated that he was face to face with death. Below him was a two-hundred-foot drop onto bone-shattering boulders - across the gorge, an armed maniac. Samson clung desperately to the rock face to avoid being sucked off the ledge into the void. And then the very cliffs started to sway, almost to spin. He prayed that he would be dead before hitting the bottom. God ... what would his heroes have done in this situation? What could anyone have done? What could Uncas or Alan Brick or Tarzan have done? Answer: nothing ... nothing at all ... absolutely nothing. Samson suddenly felt a sense of resentment towards his heroes: in his hour of need they had deserted him. It was obvious that their various exploits owed an awful lot to luck, to being in the right place at the right time. But, put any of them in the wrong place at the wrong time ... or was it the wrong place at the right time? or the right place at the wrong time? ... anyway, not the right place at the right time ... and they would quite possibly look very ordinary. Samson closed his eyes again, the better to concentrate, and mentally put each hero up on the ledge in his shoes, like a tin duck at a funfair. Uncas, son of Chingachgook, emitted a bloodcurdling whoop, then flung his tomahawk away in a tantrum. Alan Brick, sitting there sipping his gruel, elected to scowl and bear it - but did nothing. Tarzan ... aha! He had something up his sleeve. He started to fashion a rope, obviously intending to swing across the chasm to attack his tormentor. Good idea! Good old Tarzan!

Samson urgently set his mind to making his own rope ... he could knot his socks together (if he could take them off in the first place, the problem being that if he bent over he would almost certainly overbalance); he could tear his shirt into strips, like prisoners did - perhaps even tear his hair out ... mmm, nothing really convincing there. What about Robinson Crusoe? Surely he could have come up with some good ideas: improvising a rope ladder, or a parachute ... using his braces to fashion a crude catapult ... BINGO! Ripping off his braces, Samson cast around for suitable ammunition. Perhaps, after all, the tables could be turned ... yes: David and Goliath! Samson stretched the braces to test their elasticity. They were a good pair in spite of having been in the family for generations. Great! One thing at least was now clear: whether he won or lost the coming shooting match (or drew, for that matter) he would fight on to the bitter end, neither asking nor giving quarter (whatever that was). Also, very importantly, he would show no trace of fear: if he had to suffer he would do so - but in silence, like a man. He renewed his search for suitable ammunition.

'*AAAAH! UUGGH!*' Samson yelped. A potato-sized stone had just thudded into his solar plexus, knocking the wind clean out of him and creasing him up, so that it was a miracle that he didn't topple over there and then. Inadvertently he let go of the braces. Through the tiny window of consciousness not misted over by pain he followed the braces on their erratic journey. The strange way they fell, the loose ends seeming to chase each other, made Samson think that he would have been better to weight the ends with stones, and use the contraption as a bolas which might have ended up wrapped round the savage's greasy neck, strangling him.

'*CRACK!*' Another stone just about exploded in the exact spot where, if he had not been doubled up in pain, his head would have been.

Enough was enough - in this case, too much. Samson turned to face the wall of rock behind him, threw himself at it, scrabbled at it like a demented mole and - miracle of miracles - somehow managed to hoist himself the ten or twelve feet needed to reach the top of the cliffs. His trousers, without visible means of support, ended up round his ankles, exposing a magnificent target which, thank God, came through the ordeal unscathed. Then, with a final desperate effort, Samson heaved himself onto the springy, rabbit-cropped cliff top turf and, danger seemingly at an end, permitted himself the luxury of a good quiver.

7. Cat and Mouse - 1

Licking his cuts and grazes as he lay collapsed on the orthopaedic Belle Vue turf, Samson now experienced an emotion which, for him, was rare: shame - more precisely, shame with a capital 's': Shame. Not only had he failed to stand his ground and fight like the man he thought he was - though, to be fair, what could he do? - but also he had taken flight in the most degrading fashion imaginable: he had shown his bare behind, and to a savage to boot. And as if this were not enough, the incident also triggered memories of another incident - the one which would surely, throughout his (hopefully) long and eventful life, remain his most embarrassing one.

It was the occasion of his dear friend Speedy's ninth birthday. Unbeknown to Speedy, a spectacular celebration had been planned by his classmates at St. Peter's. Snorky, as self-appointed Master of Ceremonies, also assumed the roles of both choreographer and musical director, and got together a choir and a small wind ensemble. The latter began to rehearse every Monday afternoon, since on that day of the week the school dinner consisted mainly of processed peas, of such an unpalatable variety that second and even third helpings were freely available.

Snorky's preparations were thorough - professional, even: nothing was left to chance. The ceremony was planned for half-past three, to allow time for the peas to be digested - as much as they ever would be. Speedy was waylaid in the cloakroom and held prisoner there until the choir and wind ensemble had taken up stations. When eventually he emerged he was surrounded by the well wishers. Clearly he was bemused, especially when Snorky stepped forward to present him with a home-made birthday card. It had a picture of a sow on the front, and underneath was the crude inscription 'This is Your Wife'. Samson thought the card too offensive, beyond a joke, but he relaxed when Speedy smiled and pointed to the picture with an expression that betokened recognition. Of course, he couldn't read the words.

The well-wishers, straining at the leash, struck up without

waiting for the conductor's baton. They were a trifle ragged, but what they lacked in polish they more than made up for in enthusiasm. Samson, as one of the least unmusical members of the ensemble, had been entrusted with the responsibility of producing a *fortissimo glissando* to underline the honoured person's name:

>Happy Birthday To You
>Happy Birthday To You
>Happy Birthday, Dear *Speeeee-dy* ...

Over-excited, Samson was unable to contain himself. Leaping onto the low playground wall with the agility of a young billy goat, he lowered his trousers to half-mast. Then, sticking out his behind for added theatrical effect, he badly overstepped the mark: there was a disgusting bubbling sound, and moments later the fruits of his efforts were running down the backs of his legs for all to see and smell. Without a doubt this shameful episode set back his conquest of Rita by several months.

Well, there was one good thing about the present situation, Samson realised. This was that his discomfiture had been witnessed not by a mocking crowd, but by a single human being - if the savage could be called a 'human' being, which was doubtful. Actually. his being a savage might be a stroke of luck in that he might not speak English, or write it either, in which case he would probably have to carry Samson's secret to the grave with him .. aha! Now ... there was a thought: by killing Boy Sunday, he would nip the story in the bud. So: the thing was, to fake an accident ... maybe, break his miserable neck .. *crunch!* Lovely ... and then throw him down the ravine. Nobody would ever be the wiser. Unfortunately it was a long trek to where Boy Sunday was stationed, at least a mile of rough going, since it meant travelling upstream for at least half a mile before finding a crossing point ... so so frustrating, since the direct distance between the two of them could not have been more than twenty or thirty feet. Samson wondered what the world long jump record stood at, and whether he could break it, given that Boy Sunday's side was several feet lower than the Belle Vue side. Recognising that his waterlogged wellingtons would be a severe encumbrance (quite apart from the inconvenience of having to hold his trousers up while building up speed - or risking becoming hobbled at the moment of take-off ... or even, landing on Boy Sunday's side trouserless), he decided against any such heroics and resolved to do everything the hard way.

It was time for action, not thought: time, for example, to pull his socks up, because when the hunt was on he would need his hands to hold his trousers up. Careful to keep down out of Boy Sunday's sight, Samson crawled upstream along the top of the cliffs. After a couple of hundred yards there was enough cover to enable him to proceed, bent double and at the double: within half a mile he reached a part of the valley where he could scramble down a not-too-steep and well-wooded bank so as to rejoin Strangler's Brook at the point where he had slid into it after leaving the old beech.

Samson paused, standing still in the stream and resisting the insistent pull of the water on his wellingtons. He had to admit to himself that, though he certainly did intend killing Boy Sunday by faking some kind of accident, he had no clear plan of campaign. That was no good at all, because the reptile might well have several lives, like a cat. Death would therefore have to be a multiple one. He now vaguely remembered something Snorky had once told him, something to do with kilts ... a so-called 'triple death': you stabbed the victim, then strangled him and finally hanged him - or was it, drowned him? The problem now more or less defined, the details of a solution quickly fell into place: first, get his fingers round Boy Sunday's greasy black throat, and slowly squeeze the life out of him ... watch his eyeballs pop out as the pressure built up ... then, when the body had been limp for at least sixty seconds, push it over the cliffs ... then scramble down and hold his curly black head under the ice-cold water for at least five minutes, to drown him ... after that, crash a big stone down onto his thick skull time after time until the brains (if he had any) oozed out, like when Snorky had put Shag out of his misery ... then drag the body back upstream and up onto the bank, then make a fire and burn the body to a cinder - or at least, to a heap of cinders. *Mmm*, that should just about do the trick ... one improvement might be, when strangling Boy Sunday, as soon as he went limp and let go of the catapult, grab it from him and ram it up his black behind, butt first - then finish strangling him, of course.

The cool, clear waters helped Samson compose himself; the power of positive thinking, reinforced by the effervescent quality of the bubbling stream, transposed him to a higher key. He set off, resolutely wading downstream as fast as his game little legs allowed. The course of the stream was fairly straight for about three hundred yards, after which it turned fairly sharply to the right. Just in time Samson realised that, if he continued to walk in the stream, he might be visible from where Boy Sunday crouched, and so lose the vital element of surpnse.

Samson paused to consider how best to amend his plan. The simplest possibility was, to retrace his steps, climb back to the old beech, and approach Boy Sunday along the lip of the ravine; unfortunately, from time to time he would be exposed on the skyline. The only sensible alternative was, to cross the anonymous swamp to his right. Shaped like a segment of an orange, the swamp was about a quarter of a mile long, and about a hundred and fifty yards across at its widest point - with which he, Samson, was now level.

Samson barely knew the swamp. He had ventured into it only once, about a year earlier, and vowed at that time never to set foot in it again. The entire area was dark and dank, overgrown with willows which were so split and intertwined that to a savage like Boy Sunday it could have felt like a mangrove swamp - whatever that was ... On that first, never-to-be-forgotten visit, he had been panicked by a huge black bird with serrated wingtips. It took off from right under his nose, and as it flapped away, disturbing the foul air, it uttered a succession of doleful cries, which sounded to Samson like the cries of someone who had been buried alive. In his hurry to get back to the stream he had lost his sense of direction, blundered deeper and deeper into the interior of the swamp, and come upon something quite extraordinary: an abandoned railway carriage. (What made it particularly extraordinary was that there was no railway track in the valley.) It had been there for years and years, judging from the moss-covered roof and the saplings growing out of the windows, quite apart from the extent to which it had sunk into the swamp. Curiosity had finally overcome fear and Samson inspected it, half-expecting to see some first-class skeletons - or at the very least, a few assorted skulls and thighbones. However, the only sign of human presence apart from the burned-out upholstery and smashed windows was a 'still life with flies' arrangement in one corner, comprising a woman's high-heeled shoe covered in mildew, a pair of torn and heavily-stained pink bloomers and a neatly-coiled pile of excrement, the near end twisted as artistically as a dollop of ice cream in an as-yet-unlicked cornet. Somehow, he managed to keep his imagination in check and remove himself from the scene with scarcely a backwards glance.

Contemplating the vile swamp anew, Samson struggled to contain his loathing and apprehension: at the same time, he came to realise that, since it was the kind of place in which no person in their right mind would ever set foot, it would provide the safest possible route. For a while the negative feelings continued to dominate, but slowly the logic of the argument won out and he implemented his decision before he realised he had made it: taking a deep, deep breath - hopefully, enough to sustain him till he reached the other side, he put his best foot forward.

At this point Samson discovered that he had a passenger - a stowaway. It was a black, slug-like creature about an inch long, sticking to his exposed right calf just above the top of the wellington. Taking hold of an overhead branch in order to steady himself, he shook his leg to dislodge the creature, but succeeded in losing only his boot. Frustrated, he gave the thing a powerful flick with his middle finger, but it clung on like a leech, its muscular body writhing powerfully as it strove to improve its grip. Finally Samson was obliged to tear it off and fling it away: it left an ugly mark, from which blood flowed profusely. The loud 'plonk' as the creature landed in a pool helped remind him of the need to be quiet. Replacing his wellington, he wiped away the surplus blood, took a new deep breath and began to tiptoe through the swamp.

It was soon clear that this was not to be Samson's lucky day. He found himself sinking, and the more he tried not to, the more he got sucked in. Soon he was waist-deep in slime. Disgusting bubbles of gas, disturbed by his exertions, broke the oily surface of the rust-stained water. His imagination began to run riot, turning a simple quagmire into a bottomless pit inhabited by a giant octopus which, accustomed to a rich diet of railway passengers, would look on him as no more than a tasty snack. Perhaps the railway carriage had been dragged there from somewhere by the octopus, after being derailed ...? He waved his arms about wildly, in unwitting imitation of an octopus, and cried out, anything to blank out the unspeakable horror of feeling rubbery suckers attaching themselves to his legs and private parts. Fortunately, his hands encountered a low branch, and with a superhuman effort he heaved himself from the mud and swung onto a fallen willow trunk. Well, at least the mud had rendered him invisible.

Samson resumed his journey. Making a wide detour around the area in which the railway carriage was, he made good progress and soon reached the far side of the swamp, which ended abruptly where the wall of the clough rose from it at a steep angle. After several failed attempts to scramble up the slope he managed to get a hand-hold on an exposed root, then rose shakily to his feet. The whole of this section of the clough was thinly populated by dwarfed and stricken oaks, standing like markers in an abandoned graveyard. Samson experienced a deep sense of foreboding: the hairs on the back of his neck attempted to stand up, but were prevented by the thickly-caked mud. After taking a succession of deep breaths he set off on the last stage of his mission, wriggling up the steep slope on his belly. Every few seconds he stopped, pausing for a few moments to help alleviate a painful crick in the neck. It got worse and worse, but suddenly his wince turned into a broad grin, thanks to an important discovery. He had, he realised, stumbled on the answer to one of Snorky's brain-teasers: Why do we (humans) walk upright, on two legs? The answer was, obviously, so as to be able to see where you were going, without getting a crick in the neck.

A narrow path, about a foot wide, provided Samson with

the opportunity to switch to a Neanderthal crouch. Progress was now more rapid, in spite of the need to place one foot directly in front of the other, as if running along a tightrope. He wondered what would happen on such a narrow path if a careless rabbit or something were to meet him, this amazing mud-covered apparition, head-on. The odds were, that it would either drop dead of shock, or leap sideways and land in the swamp. Could rabbits swim? What would happen if ...? These were good questions, but their timing was poor. As Samson rounded a blind right-hand bend, a huge black figure leaped out at him from behind a tree trunk, uttering a great bellow:

'ST-O-O-O-O-O-O-P!!!'

The instruction boomed into Samson's right ear, so loud and clear that its literal meaning was lost on him and only the loudness and tone of voice registered. Polecat! In a brilliant reflex action Samson leaped sideways to evade the attacker's clutches: landing heavily on the steep slope below the path, he rolled over and over, his head narrowly missing tree after tree, until he landed back in the swamp not ten yards from the point where he had emerged from it. Shaken, confused, disorientated, he was yet conscious of his assailant charging down the slope towards him, two huge boot soles on the end of a body which tapered to a pinhead.

Samson scrambled to his feet and took off. He used all the tricks he had ever learned, to shake his pursuer off: he tried hopping on one leg - he changed his wellingtons over to the wrong feet; he took his wellingtons off and continued in his stockinged feet; finally, probably his best idea, he ran into a patch of mud and then walked out backwards, repeating this sequence several times, until it appeared that a whole army had marched into the mud and vanished without trace. The trick had some success: Samson, though now starting to hyperventilate, watched with a superior smirk as Polecat, having examined each and every set of footprints, ended up throwing his arms up in a gesture of defeat. Now that he had given up, it was Samson's turn to play the hunter. He was soon able to appreciate at first hand some of the difficulties of this role: incredibly, in spite of having size 13 boots, Polecat made scarcely any impression even in the softest ground.

It soon occurred to Samson that, if he stuck on Polecat's tail, he must inevitably be safe. So simple, so beautifully simple! Wildly excited, he decided to forget about Boy Sunday for the time being: he would take his sweet revenge as and when he chose, and in the meantime Boy Sunday could jolly well sweat it out.

Samson was beginning to enjoy himself. As master of the situation he could afford to indulge in showy techniques - for example, haring across open spaces and then landing silently behind a new tree trunk after yet another carefree leap. But there was one flaw in his otherwise impeccable logic: if he tracked Polecat too successfully, he might catch him up and thereby run the risk of being nabbed. This point, which had thus far escaped Samson, was brought to his attention when, more careless than carefree, he blundered into a small clearing. In front of him, not more than three or four yards away, Polecat was sitting on a tree stump - fortunately, he was preoccupied with some running repairs. Removing one of his gaiters, followed by the boot and sock, he exposed his right foot and started to wiggle it experimentally. It was a huge horrible thing, with tufts of hair sprouting from the toe joints. But it was the big toe which captured Samson's attention: it went on and on and on ... and on .. . no wonder the man could move so fast, Samson mused, his big toe was so long that it had already crossed the finish line before its owner had left the start.

A small stream, a tributary of Stranglers Brook, ran past the log. Polecat winced, braced himself for the shock of the cold water, then gingerly lowered his foot and washed between the enormous toes. He appeared to be about to rinse his sock, but then he suddenly glanced up in alarm, sensing movement among the trees in front of him, over to Samson's left.

'*Thwaaaah!*' The noise of a catapult's discharge merged with a yelp of pain from Polecat. He stood up on one leg, clutching the recently-washed foot, then lost his balance and fell back with a jolt. Then he suddenly leaned forward, picked something out of the grass in front of him, and examined it. Samson could just make out that it was a large pebble. Polecat angrily tossed it into the stream and scrutinised the trees again through narrowed eyes.

'*Thwack!*' Another stone sped unerringly to its target, faster than the eye could see - not difficult, since the range was almost point blank. The missile appeared to catch Polecat in the chest: he gasped, and put his hand over his heart; then, seemingly in slow motion, he collapsed to the ground behind the log, ending up on his back with his horrible big toe sticking out above the log. Samson stared at the fallen figure, resolving to get the hell out of the clough as soon as it seemed safe to do so. For the moment, prudently, he stayed put and awaited developments.

Samson's patience was soon rewarded: there was a slight movement in the trees, a group of shrubs was parted and the evil Boy Sunday appeared, casually dangling his catapult by the elastic. As Samson continued to watch, fascinated by the savage's appearance close to - and especially by the gleaming white teeth and the enormous whites of his mad staring eyes - Boy Sunday drew a wicked hunting knife from his belt and started to creep on all fours towards Polecat's defenceless form. *God Almighty!* He was probably going to scalp him!

Just then a most curious thing happened - so quickly that Samson could catch little more than the result. In a lightning movement, a veritable blur, Polecat produced a huge pistol from inside his coat, aimed it very deliberately at the shocked savage, and squeezed the trigger.

'*Phutt!*

8. Cat and Mouse - 2

It was now the savage's turn to utter a cry. The pellet seemed to have struck him on the temple, for he put his hand to his head and looked in terror at the blood which appeared. Then as Polecat made to reload his pistol, Boy Sunday cried out again, turned tail, and went crashing back into the bushes. Marvellous! Wonderful! Boy Sunday's come-uppance at last - and how! Forgetting in the excitement of the moment where he was, Samson spread his arms as a first step toward bursting into spontaneous applause. Fortunately his trousers promptly slipped down and the unwise action had to be aborted.

Feeling foolish for having been about to applaud a mortal enemy, after a long interior monologue Samson managed to convince himself that the best thing would be to let Polecat and Boy Sunday destroy each other. The fact that Polecat had an air pistol certainly needed thinking about. The best idea still seemed to be, to follow him - but with greater care - until it was absolutely clear that he had called it a day and was on his way home to the vicarage. Better to be safe than sorry. Samson therefore waited patiently while Polecat, all fingers and thumbs and big toe, struggled to replace his boot.

Tailing Polecat proved easier than before. Obviously he had assumed that both Samson and Boy Sunday had been scared out of their wits, and would by now be miles away, because he was very careless, never once looking back to see if he was being followed. Nevertheless Samson proceeded circumspectly, always a good twenty to thirty yards behind Polecat, and with his footsteps synchronised. Things were going well, but gradually Samson became puzzled as to where Polecat was heading. Could his destination ... it might be ... yes, it had to be: Bear Island. That was strange, very strange indeed. Whatever could he be up to? Secret target practice? Buried treasure? Somewhere private to do his Number Twos? Well, whatever his game, he wasn't going to keep the secret to himself.

Samson, recognising that he was getting over-excited again, had a quick word with himself before calculating how long to wait before continuing. The only way onto Bear Island was via a rickety old wooden footbridge. That in itself was no problem - but reaching it was: it involved crossing about twenty yards of bare ground; the rim of the island, just beyond the bridge, was similarly bare. It would therefore be necessary to give Polecat sufficient time to get out of sight - enough time for him to reach the bridge, cross it, then walk round the island far enough to be out of sight. It made no difference whether Polecat chose to go left or right on reaching the island, because the distances involved were more or less the same.

Samson allowed twenty seconds (counted as twenty-five pulses) so as to give himself the necessary safety margin. Then, screwing up the front section of his trousers' waistband so as to be able to hold the trousers up with just one hand, he broke cover and made directly for the bridge. Reaching it, he was able to relax: Polecat was gone, out of sight - though not, of course, out of mind. Samson skipped lightly across the bridge, ready in case it collapsed: it really was on its last legs, which were in fact the original ones. Thanks to one leg being completely missing, and another being broken off at the knee, as it were, the original proud and functional structure was twisted and sloping, with several planks missing, two sections of handrail likewise. It bore his weight with little protest, though how it could have supported Polecat was difficult to understand.

Once across the bridge Samson searched the rocky ground for signs of his quarry. He was starting to get a little frustrated, creeping this way and that without any luck whatsoever, but then he remembered that Polecat's left leg was fractionally shorter than the right one, and that therefore he would probably have chosen to go left, in other words, clockwise as viewed from above. Samson therefore went that way too, closely examining the ground for footprints and any lingering scent. He had only gone ten or twelve yards when his acute senses detected a splashing behind him, and his brilliant intuition came up with the explanation in less time than it took him to spin round: there, wading across Strangler's Brook under cover of the bridge, was Polecat - gun in hand. The cunning devil must have been hidden there like a troll. Taking to his toes, Samson shot off like a frightened rabbit, haring along the path and then suddenly veering off up the hill towards the central summit.

To all outward appearances there was madness in Samson's method: apart from presenting a clear (though distant) target, for the greater part of the ascent he had to run through dense bracken, leaving a trail a blind man could have followed. The bracken ringed Bear Island like the hair on a friar's head, and the bald crown was strewn with boulders, among which a few stalwart trees grew at peculiar angles, as if each at some stage in its development had been caught in a hurricane and been left permanently bent. Samson's reason for choosing to make for the summit was that the largest tree had a hollow trunk, accessible only by claiming a neighbouring mountain ash and then wriggling across via interlocking branches; also, the hollow tree had two conveniently-placed knot holes, sufficiently close together to enable him to squint out stereoscopically - or at least, wall-eyed - without being in any danger of being spotted himself. He would stay there, snug as a bug in a rug, until Polecat tired of the game.

Samson got settled just in time. Polecat must have raced up the hill: Samson heard him slump down at the base of his tree like a sack of potatoes: he was gasping for breath. Unable to see down at the necessary steep angle, Samson subdued his own breathing and listened intently. He became aware of irregular yawns and sighs, of shuffling feet and of finger joints being cracked, a noise which he had always hated. He prayed that the thumping of his own heart could not be heard outside the trunk, or vibrating through it. But before he could get really worried, a most curious thing happened: Polecat spoke, quietly but distinctly:

'Where'er thou be ...'

Samson's first reaction was that this was a threat directed at himself, but then an unspeakable, utterly nauseating, smell assailed him. A long-standing mystery was solved at a stroke. The cunning devil! The blooming swine! The twister! All this while, Samson had heard the words as 'Where'er Thou be', words murmured in the classroom every time Speedy was disgraced ... 'Thou' with a capital 'T', a silent prayer ... NO!

It had to be, had to be ... had to be 'Where'er thou be', with a small 't' - the words, Samson now remembered, which were inscribed on an old gravestone in St. Peter's churchyard:

> Where'er thou be
> Let the wind go free
> For it was the wind
> That kill-èd me.

Fortunately, thanks to the excellent ventilation up on the summit, the foul smell soon cleared. Then almost immediately, in its wake, came a new, much fainter smell, as when someone fiddles about with a cigarette lighter. That was odd ... Polecat was a non-smoker. It seemed that Polecat had caught a whiff too, for he stirred and walked forward far enough to edge into Samson's field of view. Samson watched him scanning the slopes below, and heard him murmur:

'What the devil ...?!'

As if in reply. a huge flame flashed up the slope through the bracken, to create an arc of fire which thickened at an alarming rate as it swept towards the summit. Polecat screamed:

'Mercy, mercy, oh Lord!'

He tore down the slope towards the flames, like a martyr of old. Samson watched, amazed, as he charged through the crackling bracken and billowing blue-black smoke, hungry yellow flames licking at his gaiters. Finally, just about through the bracken, he rolled over and over to extinguish his smouldering clothes, before plunging into the brook.

Samson, for once, was lucky. Unable to extricate himself from the hollow trunk, he watched in terror as the flames came closer, then boggled in disbelief as they subsided as suddenly as they had begun. But though he was coughing uncontrollably and almost blinded, he was left in no doubt as to the identity of the perpetrator of this foul deed - the elusive, evil genius behind this latest near-fatal stunt: the blinking blackamoor.

9. The Penny Drops

'*Eeeh*, I say!' Mrs. Smalley exclaimed, catching sight of Samson drifting across the landing. 'I don't know ... you're white as a sheet ... like you've seen a ghost or something ... or had the fright of your life. You're black too, by the looks. And what are you doing in your pyjamas at this time of day?'

'A bad dream,' Samson mumbled.

'I should jolly well think it was,' Mrs. Smalley said. 'Must have a bad conscience about something ... done something you shouldn't have ...'

'Or not done something I should have,' Samson retorted feebly, trying to put her off the scent.

'Such as? Oh, my God ...' Mrs. Smalley recoiled, and even in the dim light visibly paled. 'I knew all along.'

'Knew what?' Samson grunted.

'You!' Mrs. Smalley breathed accusingly. 'Telling me you were sure you'd put your name at the top. And I almost believed you.' Her mouth sagged open, her eyes lost their focus, and she clutched the banister with both hands. Samson seized his opportunity, slipping past her back into his bedroom and bolting the door.

'The fright of his life', indeed. Hmph! Stupid woman! How could you not be pale if you'd been cooped up for weeks on end? If anyone had had a fright, it was the Vicar ... and the blackamoor. No chance of the blackamoor looking pale, no. To give him his due he was cool, very cool. Out of all the people Samson had ever known only Snorky (apart from himself, of course) was so cool in a crisis. That was one reason why having someone like Snorky as a friend was so wonderful. What a friend! Actually all was not yet lost for the future, if he was still alive and kicking. It was just possible that they would go on to the Grammar School together ... in which case life after St. Peter's would not be too bad.

During the early days of Snorky's career as magician and illusionist, when he performed the frog-skinning demonstration as an *hors d'oevre* and followed it up with the three-card trick called 'Find the Lady', Samson had tended to steer clear of him, perhaps intuitively recognising that it was dangerous to get mixed up with someone who dabbled in magic. However, after the incident in which Snorky came to Samson's assistance by setting fire to bully boy Slattery's shirt tails, the two of them formed a mutual admiration society. There followed a period during which Snorky developed his art little by painstaking little: Samson was privileged to witness the incredible patience and persistence involved in the perfection of 'simple' little tricks - some of which seemed absolutely pointless until Samson managed to attune himself to Snorky's twisted mental processes. This was particularly true of Snorky's coin-on-the-glass trick.

On the rare occasions when there was a sunny dinner time, customers at the Nine Bells sometimes took their pints outside and sat on the low perimeter wall. One such day Snorky took Samson in tow and singled out a lone drinker, a slow-witted farmer who had just finished a pint of frothy mild and was staring at the empty glass uncomprehendingly, as if it had a leak or a secret compartment.

''Owdo, Mister!' Snorky greeted the man breezily, 'Hey, does t' wanna see a trick?'

'See a what?'

'A trick.'

'Oh, a trick - what sort o' trick?'

'A brain-teaser,' Snorky replied, at the same time relieving the man of his beer glass and then twirling it round and round by the handle as though he were a gunfighter.

'Eh? What?' the man asked, furrowing his brows. He was probably mesmerised by the revolving glass. (Samson certainly was.)

'Gorra shillin'?' Snorky demanded pushily. 'Just for t' trick. Tha' ll gerri' back when t' trick's done wi'.'

''Ere, lad,' the man said after a long fumble. 'Better be a good 'un. An' 'urry up, Ah'm bloody thirsty.'

'Ta very much,' Snorky said, seizing the coin. 'Ready?'

The man nodded hesitantly.

'Now, sithee -'.

Slowly, very deliberately, Snorky upturned the empty glass on the wall, and with a showman's flourish placed the shilling on the upturned bottom of the glass. Then he fixed the man with the hypnotic stare for which he would become famous.

'Are t' ready, Mister?'

'Aye, come on, lad,' the farmer said impatiently.

'Reet!' Snorky said excitedly, smiling briefly before assuming a serious professional air. 'Reet! Think careful now (*snork!*): is yon shillin' on t' top o' t' glass, or on t' borrom, eh? On t' top - or on t' borrom? Tek thi time, no call to rush.'

The man removed his greasy cap, replaced it, pushed it to the back of his even greasier head, scratched an ear, then tilted his head this way and that so as to view the shilling from several different angles. Samson, noting that Snorky was standing in the man's light, wondered whether this was deliberate: he moved round and crouched beside the man. He glanced from Snorky to the glass and back to Snorky, fascinated by the discovery that Snorky's ears, viewed against the light, glowed luminously like an angel's wings. Perhaps the sticking plaster had come adrift?

'Come on, come on!' Snorky pressed, in his excitement forgetting patience and respect. 'Come on, gerra move on! Is it on t' top, or on t' borrom? Eh?'

Samson had worked out the answer in no time: the shilling was obviously on the bottom of the glass, you only needed half a brain to work that out. He beamed a condescending smile at the slow-witted yokel.

'Come on, buck up!' Snorky shouted. 'We 'aven't gor all day, we're due back at school in a minute.'

'Aye,' the man volunteered at last, '*err* ... aye, it's ... *err* ... it's on t' top.' He looked up at Snorky apprehensively, then at Samson.

'Silly beggar!' Samson said to himself - under his breath, of course. How could anyone, especially a grown man, be so stupid? He was therefore greatly surprised to see Snorky suddenly get very upset and peevishly thrust the shilling back into the man's hand, at the same time shouting accusingly:

'Th ... th ... tha's s .. s .. sin it be ... b .. b .. be ... befoor!'

Samson stared at Snorky in amazement, having never realised or even suspected that Snorky had such a terrible stutter - or even, a stutter at all. He suddenly felt full of admiration for his having triumphed over his disability -

almost, anyway. He was obviously very very upset. The man, for his part, continued to stare at the glass.

'Come on!' Snorky said to Samson, tugging his sleeve. 'We'll be in trouble for bein' late again. We mun run.'

They started legging it back to St. Peter's, but when they were out of sight of the pub Snorky pulled up and consulted his wonderful Newmark wristwatch, the envy of all and sundry.

'We're okay,' he decided.

Samson, a few yards ahead, turned to confront Snorky.

'You were wrong about the shilling, you were wrong,' he insisted. 'Look -'

'Depends which way you look at it,' Snorky replied without hesitation, reverting to his 'better' accent. 'Anyway, it's not important. Come on, let's go to Jericho.'

'Not important?' Samson echoed incredulously, then Snorky's proposal registered. 'Why, what for?'

'I'll treat you,' Snorky said, smiling mysteriously. 'Come on!'

The two friends struck out along the overgrown track which had once led to the hamlet of Sodham, now spooky and abandoned. Samson stayed close to Snorky, not knowing him very well as yet. He felt he needed to be on his guard in case Snorky pulled some kind of stunt, such as running off and leaving him to the mercy of ... whatever. His nagging doubts were soon dispelled, however, when Snorky turned off the track, vaulted over a stile, then led Samson along a well-used muddy path in the shadow of an overgrown hawthorn hedge. Soon they heaved over the brow of a gentle hill and came upon a little semicircle of tumbledown cottages around an ancient well: Jericho. Two emaciated cats huddled together by the well. They shot off as the two boys approached, and to Samson's amazement entered the nearest cottage by leaping straight through the downstairs window; thereupon, as in a magician's trick, two speckled hens, equally agitated, fluttered out. Closer inspection revealed that the window had no glass, also that the front door was heavily padlocked and bore a weather-worn notice announcing that the house was condemned as being unfit for human habitation. Nevertheless it was obviously inhabited, for smoke puffed from the base of the chimney. It suddenly occurred to Samson that this might be the home of the orphaned twins Jean and Joan, surnames unknown, and hence referred to as Jean and Joan Jericho. They had only one pair of clogs between them, and so took it in turns to come to school.

Samson stood near the well, deep in thought. Snorky, meanwhile, marched across to the end cottage, Number 13. It was better kept than the others and sported several enamelled advertising plaques with illegible messages. Instead of going to the front door, Snorky rapped on the window. Samson held back, partly from a sneaking suspicion that the number '13' was unlucky, partly because he suspected that Snorky was up to no good.

Snorky rapped again, and this time got a response: the window was flung open and a beshawled granny figure leaned out, her chin thrust forward aggressively.

''Owdo, luv,' Snorky greeted her cheerily. ''Ow are t' gerrin' on, then?'

'Don't "luv" me, you little beggar! ' she snapped back. 'An' summat else: where did t' pinch that theer beer glass, eh?'

'We found it,' Snorky replied, brazenly returning her stare. The word 'we' registered with Samson and he made a mental note to complain about it when they were alone again. 'What's getten' for a penny?' Snorky then asked, producing money for inspection.

'What does t' want? ' she asked vexedly, pointing to the selection of sweets, several shelves of them.

'What's up theer?' Snorky asked, pointing to the highest shelf.

The old lady heaved a great sigh and disappeared to the back of the shop; she reappeared, puffing and panting, dragging a step ladder. Samson came closer and was shocked to see Snorky pull out a catapult as the old lady stretched to the limit and her skirt hem rose sufficiently to reveal the backs of her knees. Samson pushed the catapult away and the old lady came down, unaware of the threat to her varicose veins.

'These 'ere 'll be just t' ticket,' she informed Snorky, wiping thick dust from the jar with her sleeve before attacking the sticky contents with a metal scoop. 'They were very popular in t' war: penny drops. There's nowt else these days for a penny.'

'Ah'll 'ave some o' them, then,' Snorky said. He and Samson watched, slavering, as the gooey brown balls were prised apart and weighed out. They had to wait for ages until the old lady returned the jar to the top shelf.

'Will there be owt else?' she asked.

'Aye ... *err* ... aye, another penn'orth for mi friend 'ere.'

'You little ... are t' tryin' to make a monkey out o' me?' she rasped.

'No,' Snorky replied, wide-eyed and innocent. 'But if it's too much trouble ...'

He waited to be served again, then handed over a shilling in payment and asked for the change to be in halfpennies.

'Feel richer with a pocket full of money,' he explained to Samson, jangling the halfpennies in his pocket.

Samson felt a bit confused. On the one hand he was bowled over by Snorky's generosity, but as against that he felt Snorky had been very inconsiderate, given the old lady's obvious infirmity. There was also the problem of the wrong answer to the brain teaser, and Snorky's dishonesty in stealing the beer glass. All too confusing, especially since Samson needed all his concentration to suck and munch his penny drops before starting afternoon schooL

During the next few weeks, whenever the weather was fine, Snorky dragged Samson to one or other of the pubs dotted around Old Guinea, accosting lone drinkers and trying out the coin~on-the-glass brain teaser on them. More and more the need to put Snorky straight obsessed Samson; however, it was difficult to come up with an absolutely conclusive argument, especially when you were as stuffed as a Christmas goose on penny drops. Samson's main interest came to lie in seeing what would happen when somebody guessed right - in other words, wrong from Snorky's point of view - and of course eventually this did happen. A stranger, a well-dressed man two or three cuts above the locals - he even wore shoes - summed up the problem in less time than it took Snorky to put it to him.

'On the botttom, of course,' the man replied with a condescending smile. 'You'll have to do better than that, I'm afraid.'

'THA'S S ... S ... S ... SIN IT B .. B .. BEFOOR!' Snorky cried out, obviously heartbroken. 'IT'S NOT F ... F ... F ... FUR!' He thrust the coin back into the man's hand.

Samson found Snorky's behaviour a bit ill-mannered, and turned to walk away. Snorky caught up with him after about fifty yards, and for a while the two of them walked on in silence. Then Samson just had to get it off his chest:

'I thought you said -' he began accusingly.

'Changed mi mind,' Snorky replied, uncharacteristically subdued. He shrugged apologetically, and stared steadfastly down at his precious boots. The reflection was bright enough for Samson to see that Snorky was genuinely ashamed. Samson now fell silent, unsure as to whether he ought to respect Snorky less (since changing your mind was a sign of weakness) or more (because there are very few people who will admit they have made a mistake and yet continue to buy you more sweets than you could eat). The latter argument won the day.

In spite of this setback Snorky seemed to develop new enthusiasm for the brainteaser, as though seeking to make amends to the world after having misled people for so long. From now on everybody got the answer right (really right), and Samson wondered if the word had got round. He was beginning to lose interest in the trick, although still intrigued as to what Snorky's reaction would be when somebody guessed wrong (really wrong). Then when it happened, Snorky instantly changed his own mind, then a couple of days later he changed it back again. Samson could stand it no longer.

'Look!' he said accusingly, obviously very hot under the collar. 'I just don't see what you get out of it. *Hmph!* Beats me.' He shook his head vigorously, almost violently.

'No?' Snorky challenged, his tongue quick as a toad's and his eyes fixing Samson with a penetrating stare.

'Well no ... not really,' Samson replied, suddenly on the defensive.

'Three and tenpence so far today!' Snorky shouted exultantly, jangling the change in his pocket to make his point. 'Come on, let's have some licorice too, I'll treat you!'

'You ... YOU BLOOMING TWISTER!' Samson blurted out as the truth finally penetrated. And sure enough, careful observation of subsequent performances confirmed his hunch: with great sleight of hand Snorky always thrust a useless halfpenny back into the victim's hand, and pocketed the shilling.

10. A Dog's Life - 1

Now that the blinkers were off, Samson was able to relax, and to enjoy Snorky's performances to the full. He learned to suspend judgement as to the merits and demerits of Snorky's actions - he learned that Snorky's most casual gesture, his most innocent remark, as like as not betokened something completely different from what you had at first supposed. Only a slight nervous snork, eyes closed, at the moment Snorky set the trap - as if, Samson thought, he were a blind angler sniffing to check that the bait was securely on the hook - announced the impending trickery. Even then you weren't much better off, because there was no way of guessing what the trick was going to be.

So, the relationship between Samson and Snorky deepened. Samson progressed from accessory-after-the-fact to accessory-before-the-fact and then to full accomplice as Snorky taught him a variety of ways of distracting the victim at the crucial moment. Then, another victim chalked up (Snorky did in fact keep a tally on a fragment of slate), they would race off to Jericho to blow their ill-gotten gains. They were often to be seen together as they roamed far and wide, arms round each other's shoulders. Since they now thought alike, conversation became less important, so that they might spend ten or even fifteen minutes without exchanging a single word. There was, in any case, a good practical reason for speaking as seldom as possible: the penny drops were soon relegated to the status of a dessert, with delicious new black-market pear-drop-flavoured giant bullseye gobstoppers as the new main course - not easy to manage at the same time as trying to chew sticks of liquorice root. Anyway, so much in tune were they that they even marched in step, though there was no mistaking which was which, thanks to the marked contrast between Snorky's brilliantly-shiny Cherry Blossom black boots and Samson's dull clogs, the leather uppers of which were regularly waterproofed by his father with copious dressings of neatsfoot oil.

These were some of the happiest days of Samson's life. He discovered pleasure - pure pleasure, uncontaminated by thought. Quite possibly he enjoyed his endless gobstoppers more than anyone else in the world ever has, does, or will - and yet, his newfound happiness, far from blinding him to the plight of others, helped open his eyes still wider, so that on his wandering along the myriad byways of Old Guinea (there were no highways) he was increasingly struck by the contrast between his own carefree existence and the squalor, the joylessness and the downright misery all around him. For the great majority of Old Guinea's inhabitants, it was a dog's life.

For dogs, correspondingly, it was no life at all. Whereas in most parts of Britain - even Lancashire - at that time the word 'dog' would have called to mind a noble, ever-loyal four-legged gentlefolks' companion, and even best friend, any native of Old Guinea inevitably associated the word with some wretched, ill-treated cur: nobody in their right mind would have kept a dog for any other purpose than to savage trespassers. There were hardly any sheepdogs, even. since Old Guinea was goat country. When, therefore, Samson and Snorky were one day sitting comfortably back to back on a nice grassy hummock, sucking their gobstoppers and generally minding their own business, and a strange animal mooched towards them, nose to the ground as it followed a meandering scent, the boys did not at first identify it as a dog. To Samson it looked more like an overgrown weasel - a yellowish-brown, arched-back creature, Belsen-thin and with its tail well and truly glued between its legs. It shivered as it got within stoning range - unnecessarily, Samson felt, since a large cow prevented Snorky from getting a clear aim. As the creature rounded the cow Samson noticed that it (the creature) was covered from head to toe in cowdung, and his brain became a one-man think-tank dedicated to understanding how and why this was the case. The creature, as if to tease Samson now that it had got his interest, turned back on the cow and nipped its ankles before continuing on its way. Had some other cow, more quick-witted than the present victim, taken revenge on its tormentor. Or -?

'I wonder what it is, and who it belongs to,' Samson said, nudging Snorky with a well-aimed elbow.

'*Ouch!* Eh? Oh .. that ... it's a dog ... got to be someone's.'

'I know it's a blooming dog, you chump!' Samson protested. 'But what make is it? Any idea?'

'Well, it's pedigree, isn't it. Anyone can see that.'

'Pedigree? Alright, but pedigree what? There's lots of different pedigree dogs ... I'm not that stupid.'

'Well, pedigree lurcher, obviously,' Snorky obliged.

'That's what I thought,' Samson said, nodding sagely. There could be little doubt that Snorky was right: at that moment, the creature lurched forward and poached the entire bag of penny drops from beside Snorky. It retired to a safe distance and munched them noisily. Then it squatted, a wild, strained expression in its eyes.

'What the flipping heck ...' Samson exclaimed.

'Ah (*snork!*) spaghetti!' Snorky said. 'Must belong to those Ities up beyond Windy End. He was obviously referring to the Italian prisoners of war who had worked at Higher Moors pig farm.

'Looks more like worms, to me,' Samson mumbled. 'Eh? The war's over - isn't it?'

'One of them stayed on, didn't he.'

'Oh, right ... do you think the other one really was eaten by the pigs?'

'Course he was. Everyone knows that.'

'Blinking heck! I know people eat pigs, but I didn't know pigs ate people.'

'Eat anything, don't they.'

'I suppose.'

To outward appearances the two friends had adopted a stray dog. More realistically, the dog had adopted them. It obviously had a sweet tooth: it had a liking, a craving, an utterly insatiable appetite for penny drops and anything else it could get hold of, including sticks of liquorice root. The dog's constant attentions - in particular, the ill-mannered way it nuzzled Snorky's pockets, created a problem: nasty pawprints on his boots. To minimise this nuisance Snorky started grabbing whole handfuls of penny drops and flinging them as far away from himself as possible, ideally into a clump of gorse or bracken - or, best of all - a good bog. However, it proved impossible to then leg it fast enough to lose the animal, which seemed to find every single sweet in no time. It would then scuttle back for seconds ... and thirds ... and fourths .... Snorky was getting more and more fed up.

'Blooming thing!' he said crossly one day, polishing his toe-caps for the umpteenth time. Although, thanks to the gob-stoppers, there was no shortage of saliva, spit and polish failed to repair the damage caused by the dog's claws, so that Snorky was obliged to bring a larger-than-usual quantity of cotton waste to school each day.

'Why don't we train it, or something,' Samson suggested. In a strange way he had come to like the dog, and was worried that Snorky would insist on getting rid of it.

'Okay,' Snorky unexpectedly agreed. 'Yeah, good idea. Right: the first thing is, to get it to walk behind us instead of chasing round us in circles all the time. Agree?'

'Eh? Oh ... yes, right ...'

'Go on, then.'

'Go on, what?'

'Teach it to walk behind you, bird brain.'

'Eh? How?'

'It was your idea.'

'I know. Flipping heck ...'

After a little head-scratching Samson adopted a teacher's pose, modelled on Miss Pollock. He spoke firmly to the dog, emphasising each point with his index finger, but because the dog snapped at the finger he had to raise his arm higher and higher, until he was pointing skyward. Meanwhile, Snorky watched with undisguised amusement.

'Do something!' Samson begged.

Snorky rose slowly to his feet and produced a short length of rope from one of his many pockets. Then, forming a noose, he lassooed the dog in mid-leap, and with a vicious tug brought it down to earth. Its struggles were heroic but short-lived: soon it was all in, reduced to uttering strange gurgling noises. Snorky handed the free end of the rope to Samson.

'It's all yours,' he said,

Samson loosened the noose by degrees. When the dog had recovered sufficiently to be able to stagger back to its feet

Samson attempted to hold it on a tight rein behind him. The dog was having none of it: it lay on its belly and tried to chew through the rope, in spite of being dragged along the ground at a fair speed. Once again, Samson looked at Snorky for guidance.

'You need to say "Heel!",' Snorky advised. 'Then yank it back. Keep doing that until it understands.'

Samson removed his gobstopper and wrapped it securely in his handkerchief, then cleared his throat and waited till he had the dog's full attention.

'Heel!'

The dog barked, defiantly.

'Heel!' Samson insisted.

The dog howled derisively, and Snorky collapsed, laughing. 'You're supposed to be the boss, not him!' he chortled.

'I know!' Samson shouted back.

'So, shout at him. Show him who's boss.'

'Give me a chance!' Samson said irritably. 'Right: here goes .... HEEEEEL!'

The command reverberated halfway round the parish. The dog performed an involuntary backward somersault as Samson yanked the rope, then struggled to its feet behind him. Samson, confident that he was now in charge, slackened the rope. The dog had other ideas: it went for Samson's heel, administering a vicious nip. Samson fell over very theatrically, clutching his Achilles tendon with one hand while protecting his private parts with the other.

As far as Samson was concerned, that was that. The dog was obviously too stupid to learn anything. Snorky, however, refused to let Samson forget his failure. He took to shouting 'Heel!' again and again as they were walking along, then laughing himself stupid at Samson's over-reaction. Samson could take no more.

'If you're so blooming clever, why don't you train it,' he said crossly, after yet another scare.

'You see, what you did wrong was, to start with something too difficult,' Snorky said in a very grown-up, know-all way which irritated Samson still further, 'When you're training an animal - tame or wild, any kind of animal ... could be a dog or

a lion ... a snake, even - you've got to start at the bottom. '
 'Eh?'
 'I said "at the bottom" - you know, "first things first".'
 '*Hmph!*' Samson snorted. 'I suppose you got all these ideas from your grandfather ... the one in the Rocky Mountains - the mule skinner.'
 'Oh, right ... him,' Snorky murmured, apparently unaware of Samson's biting sarcasm. 'That's right ... mostly from when he used to break horses.'
 'With one hand tied behind his back, I suppose!' Samson growled. He had been prepared to take the mule-skinning yarn on trust - in any case, Snorky's grandfather could not possibly be in the same class as Stuffer Sharples - but the idea that a single man, however, strong, could break a horse, was much too far-fetched.
 'He only had one arm,' Snorky said quietly, eyes downcast. 'The other was bitten off by a cugger. '
 'Oh ...' - Samson was confused and repentant, in equal measure. 'Well, anyway ... so, let's see what you can do.'
 'Maybe tomorrow,' Snorky said.
 'Oh ... fine,' Samson murmured. In the circumstances, he felt he couldn't press him.

The next day, it was difficult to imagine that there had been any bad feelings between them. Snorky made no attempt to tease Samson, who for his part was happy to take Snorky seriously again, especially when he realised that Snorky had not forgotten the challenge.
 'The real secret of training animals,' Snorky began, 'is -'
 'Trial and error?' Samson suggested.
 'No,' Snorky nodded emphatically. 'Reward and punishment.'
 'Oh, yes ... mmm, that's what I meant. Just like school.'
 'Yes, Sir! Reward and punishment,' Snorky repeated. 'That, and starting at the bottom. Right ... the first thing is, I'm going to teach it to sit.'
 'Oh, I see what you mean! ' Samson laughed. 'Yes, that really is "starting at the bottom"!'
 Snorky reached inside his jacket and pulled out a short, thick stick, the size and shape of a small truncheon. Something else

was concealed in his other hand.

'Shag! Shag!' Snorky shouted. 'Here, boy! Here!'

Samson found the name a bit repugnant, and felt a little resentful that he hadn't been consulted: after all, it wasn't Snorky's dog - it was he, Samson, who had seen it first. The dog approached and tried to snatch whatever it was that Snorky was offering. Snorky delivered a short, sharp blow to the animal's skull. The dog recoiled, then tried again, The whole cycle was repeated several times, until finally the dog approached Snorky in a suitably-subdued manner. Then, receiving its reward, it ran off to consume it in peace.

'What was that?' Samson asked. 'What did you just give him?'

'A dog biscuit.'

'Ah, well! ' Samson exclaimed. 'If I'd had some ... '

'Here you are, then,' Snorky said, passing two biscuits to him.

'God, they're very hard!' Samson observed. 'You could break your teeth on them. Not too bad, though ... so, what about teaching it to sit?'

'No problem ... watch me.'

'I'm watching ... funny taste ... a bit fishy ...'

Snorky launched into the next lesson. Samson winced as his friend beat the poor dog into submission, though whether the animal really did obey the command to sit, or was simply unable to stand after being repeatedly floored, was unclear. Anyway, Snorky seemed satisfied. He released the dog and lay back on the grass, and after wiping his brow on a polka-dot handkerchief, he stretched out his arms and closed his eyes.

'*Phew!* Hot work! ' was all he said.

Samson was intrigued to know whether the dog would obey him too.

'Here, boy! Here!' he called, his voice a passable imitation of Snorky's - though of course he could not bring himself to address the animal as 'Shag'.

To Samson's surprise, the dog immediately struggled to its feet and approached him, nose thrust forward and tail quivering in anticipation.

'Good dog, good dog!' Samson said lovingly, giving it a gentle pat on the head at the same time as proffering a penny drop. (The remaining biscuit-and-a-half were too precious to sacrifice, of course.) Now the time was ripe for the test.

'SIT!' Samson commanded firmly. 'S ...'

Repetition of the command proved unnecessary. The dog's response was instant: it virtually threw itself down - unfortunately, so as to sit on Snorky's face.

'SH- I-I-I-I-T !' Snorky screamed, staggering to his feet and pawing at his eyes.

Samson watched in amazement as Snorky went berserk. He really had taken leave of his senses: there he was, still blinded by cowdung transferred from the dog's behind, groping about inside his jacket and bringing out the last of the dog biscuits; he held these out at arm's length, and at the same time called out to the dog in a cracked, croaking voice:

'Here, boy .... here!'

'No no no!' Samson warned Snorky. 'Don't reward him, that's crazy!' To get Snorky's attention, he tugged at his sleeve, but Snorky shrugged him off.

The dog approached Snorky - warily, but obviously intent on seizing the biscuit. Samson was minded to intervene: he sensed that Snorky, in his distress, had forgotten his own teaching, even to the extent of confusing reward and punishment ... if that were the case, all the progress thus far made could be undone at a stroke.

The dog gingerly took the biscuit. Samson was on the verge of saying something again, but was too slow: quick as a flash, the still-blinded Snorky unleashed a tremendous kick, catching the poor unsuspecting animal full in the mouth, knocking it for six. For several seconds it lay where it had fallen, seemingly stunned, a trickle of blood oozing from its mouth. Then it struggled to its feet, shook itself, and carried on as though nothing had happened.

Something was bothering Samson:

'But ... I don't understand,' he said.

Snorky divined Samson's problem immediately:

'Had to find its mouth first,' he explained, his eyes still

screwed shut. 'Water! Water! I need water!'

  Samson heaved a sigh of relief. He had, he realised, misjudged Snorky: far from confusing reward and punishment, the clever devil had simply been trying to find out where the dog's mouth was, in order to kick its teeth in. What other surprises could Snorky possibly have up his sleeve? What, indeed! Perhaps time would tell ...

11. A Dog's Life - 2

So: the dog training proved to be a dangerous activity for all concerned. Samson fared least badly: the only visible injury was a slight limp which, in any case, was at least fifty per cent affectation. Shag, with his tender bleeding mouth and perhaps a dozen invisible bruises, was worse off. But the worst affected was undoubtedly Snorky: the face and hair were eventually put to rights by a visit to the well at Jericho, and indeed his hair took on a new lustre, while a much more serious and intractable problem was posed by the brilliant-white heavily starched gutta-percha high wing collar, so badly spattered with cowdung. Worst of all, Snorky's pride had been hurt; it showed on his face, which went and stayed deathly pale, like a stone with every last drop of blood drained from it. Even Snorky's famous ears, normally reddish-pink or pinkish-red depending on the season, had blanched like red cabbage leaves plunged into boiling water. Samson also noticed that Snorky's magician's hands, normally rock-steady, had started to shake severely.

The two friends trudged round the parish, hither and thither, unable to articulate their grievances and certainly in no mood to go back to school. Samson, deeply uncomfortable, scratched his brains (via his head, of course) for a means of effecting a reconciliation; however, Snorky's moroseness intensified rather than abated, and it was a long time before Samson could bring himself to breach the uneasy silence.

'Snorky!' There was no answer. 'SNORKY ... HEY!' This second call was reinforced by a stiff poke in the ribs, always guaranteed to get a reaction of some kind.

'What?' Snorky murmured, without breaking his stride or turning to look at Samson.

'Why ... why don't you ... you know, when you feel like it ... why don't you teach him to shake hands.' This was a clever suggestion, Samson felt. It was like when you fell off a horse or bicycle, the best thing was always to get back on immediately and rebuild lost confidence, show the thing who was boss. Equally important, shaking hands was the perfect, gentlemanly way to patch up differences. 'Well:

what do you say?'

'Fuck off!' Snorky replied, spitting out the words with enough venom to kill a horse. Samson, surprised and shocked by this uncalled-for outburst, was rendered speechless. However, Snorky almost immediately smiled broadly.

'Only joking!' he said. 'Mmm, good idea! '

Samson was unutterably relieved and, as so often, bowled over by Snorky's acting ability. If he had not known him so well he would have been certain that the earlier words had been spoken in extreme anger.

Snorky sprang into action immediately.

'Shag! Shag! Here, boy! Here!' he called in a friendly, sing-song pulpit-type voice. At the same time he rummaged inside his jacket.

'Drop the stick,' Samson suggested. 'I think he's still a bit scared of you, for some reason.'

Snorky returned the stick to his jacket, and sure enough the dog approached immediately.

'Here, boy! Here!' Snorky repeated. 'Shake hands ... come on, shake hands!'

Even someone as inexperienced as Samson could see that this approach to the training was far too casual: the importance of reward and punishment, likewise such helpful notions as 'starting at the bottom' and 'first things first', had definitely been forgotten on this occasion.

'Try getting him to lift his paw first,' he suggested.

'I know!' Snorky replied - irritably, like earlier. 'And I know how.'

The words were hardly out of his mouth when his heavy boot shot forward and stamped down on the poor dog's right-hand paw. The animal howled, and recoiled on three legs, is injured front paw held aloft. Snorky smiled a cruel, private smile. Samson realised that honours were now even and that the curtain had been let down on the final act of dog training.

Abortion of the dog training programme left a vacuum. Surprisingly, perhaps, Samson and the dog, in spite of any grievances they may have felt, still looked to Snorky for leadership.

'So, what shall we do?' Samson asked when the three met up again the next lunchtime. He turned to face Snorky, who seemed very pre-occupied. Shag, lying down at a safe distance with his head flat to the ground, stared cross-eyed at his two masters. Snorky's head rocked slowly from side to side for several seconds; then the hypnotic motion stopped and a light came into his eyes. He parted his lips slowly in preparation for saying something important, and his attentive audience eased themselves closer.

'I know!' he suddenly announced, standing up so suddenly that he almost overbalanced. Recovering, he thrust his hand unusually deep into his 'magician's' jacket (which Samson firmly believed to be a poacher's), fumbled around, then withdrew a beautiful lacquered black box with brass fastenings. Samson and Shag scrambled to their feet to get a better view. Samson, already in mid-gasp, gasped anew when he caught sight of the lid's intricate mother-of-pearl inlays.

'Crikey!' he gasped. 'What have you got there? 'Can I see?' He reached out to touch the box, but Snorky moved it out of his reach.

'It's magic (*snork!*),' Snorky said, very quietly.

'MAGIC!?' Samson shouted, thereby frightening Shag and making him jump as far as his three-legged condition allowed.

Snorky ignored Samson's excitement. He half-closed his eyes, held the box out in front of him at arm's length, and muttered something that Samson couldn't catch - probably magic words, he supposed. Next, after passing his finger tips over the lid several times, as though caressing it, Snorky suddenly squeezed the box somewhere near the bottom. The lid sprang open, but stayed almost closed, so that Samson was no wiser as to what the contents might be. Snorky, his face a mask of seriousness, stared at Samson without expression before continuing.

At last Snorky raised the lid. Samson gasped again: the box was padded inside and lined with midnight-blue silk on which lay, in perfectly-sculpted depressions, three brilliantly-polished glass balls each about double the size of a dobber.

'Blooming heck!' Samson exclaimed. 'What are they? What are they for? Where did you get them?'

'*Sssh* ...' Snorky whispered, putting a finger to his lips. Then, just as Samson was about to snatch the box from Snorky's lap, Snorky looked up suddenly. Throwing his head back and swallowing forcibly, so that if he had not had such large and translucent ears he would have resembled a drinking chicken, he prepared to speak.

'Well?' Samson pressed again. 'Come on! What is it?'

Snorky held up his hand, palm forward, to silence Samson anew. After another long silence he began speaking again, slowly and ultra-deliberately.

'I spy .... with my little eye .... something ... beginning with -'

'Eh?' Samson queried.

'No: "b",' Snorky corrected, quick as a flash.

'Biscuits?' Samson guessed. 'Barley sugar? Binoculars?'

'I spy ... with my little eye ...' Snorky went on, ignoring Samson's suggestions, 'a .... a .... b-b-b-b-bicycle!'

'A bicycle?' Samson checked, utterly incredulous. 'How on earth ... ?'

Snorky snapped the box shut, thrust it back inside his jacket, then stood up and waved his arms about as if he were a bit unhinged. Samson was reminded of a newspaper photograph of Hitler, that he had once studied. A liquorice stain in the middle of Snorky's upper lip heightened the similarity.

'Come on!' Snorky shouted, slightly hoarse. 'Come on! This way!' He set off at a fast dogtrot: Samson and Shag fell in behind him. After about a quarter of a mile they came to higher, drier ground. Scrambling up to the highest point, they met up with Stony Brew, a steep track irregularly strewn with small boulders and rivulets of sand washed down during torrential rains. Another fifty yards and they ran past a landmark familiar to generations of St. Peter's children as 'The Rock of Gibraltar'- more familiarly, 'T' Rock'. This was a huge, roughly cubic lump of blackened sandstone set into the steep hillside overlooking the lodge of Entwistle's bleachworks. Though superficially similar to the famous Black Stone at Mecca (which the children had even less reason to know about than the real Rock of Gibraltar), the Rock had no religious significance - just as well, for it looked more like it had been thrust up from Hell rather than having fallen from Heaven. Its surface was rough, and at the end remote from Stony Brew was flawed by a transverse crack, up to eighteen inches wide and several feet deep. For these and other reasons it was out of bounds to St. Peter's children, hence a much-frequented spot.

Snorky brought the party to a halt on top of the Rock and the three of them gazed out across the gently-rippling lodge waters while they got their breath back and allowed themselves to be cooled by the gentle breeze.

'What now?' Samson asked. One thing was certain: if the promised bicycle turned out to be at the bottom of the lodge, he would not be the one to recover it.

'What's up?' Snorky asked.

'Nothing,' Samson replied hurriedly. 'No ... I was just thinking about what you told me last time we were here.'

'What about?'

'Well, that pike ... I'm sure you can't have a six-foot pike. Two foot, maybe - no, don't say: I know fish don't have feet - even three foot' - he held out his hands, about three feet apart, then jerked them wider apart - '... but six foot!'

'Definitely there's a six-footer in there,' Snorky said. 'Could even be a seven-footer by now.'

'Oh, come off it,' Samson said. 'Got any idea how long six-foot is?' He stretched out his arms again with a gesture that said, this is nowhere near enough. 'And anyway, not even pike 'd grow at that rate.'

Snorky nodded his head in disbelief.

'No, not that, you clot!' he said. 'Come on, work it out for yourself: Old Grandad Dobson, Jimmy Ashworth's Uncle Whatsit, that stinking old tramp that used to help with the haymaking at Ramsbottoms ... well, okay, it was just his big toe ....'

'You mean ... ' Samson blurted out in astonishment. 'Crikey! I thought you meant -'

'We'd best get going,' Snorky said after giving Samson time to let the real meaning of 'six-foot' sink in. 'Come on! I can almost feel it!'

'What? Feel what?'

'The bicycle, stupid.'

'Oh, that ... yeah, okay.'

The troupe left the Rock to rejoin Stony Brew. They had travelled barely a hundred yards when Snorky stopped dead, held up a hand as if he were a Red Indian tracker, and very theatrically sniffed the air in various directions.

'This way!' he said excitedly, heading straight for a hole in the dry stone wall, about twenty yards further along. Reaching the hole, Snorky paused to examine it minutely, like a detective or an insurance assessor might. Samson, guessing that the hole was the result of an accident, examined the slope on the far side of it, and was immediately rewarded: down in the ditch below, a dead bicycle lay upside down and partly buried in mud. The back wheel, caught by a little gust of wind, ticked enticingly two or three times.

Samson scrambled down the steep bank while Snorky and Shag barked encouragement from the track above. The bike was well and truly stuck in the mire, but Samson, tugging at it manically, finally worked it free. Any modern child would have been cruelly disappointed with the machine, which generally was in poor condition and - more specifically - lacked either a saddle or handlebars. But to Samson it was like finding gold. Covered in mud spots, he dragged the heavy machine up the steep bank as determinedly as a leopard struggling with a recently-slaughtered (and hornless) antelope. Finally successful, he wiped off the worst of the mud with tufts of wet grass. Meanwhile Snorky disappeared briefly, then returned with an armful of sticks. By a process of selective assembly he quickly improvised some wooden handlebars, then succeeded in forcing an L-shaped stick down the seat tube, so that the protruding horizontal part could serve as a very slim saddle of the kind favoured by racing cyclists.

Bicycles, though common in nearby towns, had never caught on in Old Guinea, where the tried and tested clogged foot provided a much more versatile and reliable means of locomotion. Samson had therefore only ever seen one bicycle, the one belonging to Miss Pollock: she, prudently, limited herself to freewheeling, sidesaddle. From patient observation augmented by intense speculation, Samson had learned to appreciate some of the difficulties. He had not, however, realised that the most difficult parts were, getting on and getting started. For a little while, therefore, the two friends took turns at falling off. They had just reached the point of giving up when Snorky suddenly acted as if he had had a brilliant idea.

'Half a mo',' he said, frantically rooting around inside his jacket, then triumphantly taking out a crumpled old photograph. He waved it in the air, and when Samson tried to reach for it he frustrated him.

'Let me see,' Samson pleaded, so pathetically that Snorky relented.

'My old grandad,' Snorky said proudly. 'See the bike? It's the one he used in his act.'

'Bike? Act?' Samson mumbled incredulously, for the photo appeared to show a middle-aged dwarf trying unsuccessfully to balance on a single bicycle wheel, with the handlebars wedged between his nose and upper lip.

'He was a trick cyclist,' Snorky explained. 'Circuses. His special trick was, riding across a tightrope, backwards ... with his hands in his pockets.'

'Sounds brilliant,' Samson murmured. 'God, I wish ...'

'It's just practice,' Snorky said in an off-hand, know-it-all way. 'Here: get on the wall ... now on the bike while I hold it. Okay? Here goes ...'

For a while the two friends took it in turns to push each other. Samson was perhaps the first to overcome the fear of falling off, and certainly the first to be able to freewheel unaided down the gentle initial section of Stony Brew, a feeling so exhilarating that the final painful fall was well worth it. Nevertheless Snorky, though by nature more cautious than Samson, ended up the faster freewheeler through being reluctant to put his boots down to act as brakes. Samson found Snorky's wobbling extremely amusing.

Snorky did not.

'What's up with you?' he challenged, prickly as a hedgehog.

'Well, you' ll never be able to do it properly if you don't learn how to brake,' Samson laughed. 'You'd be better off -'

'What are you talking about?' Snorky shouted. 'And who do you think you are, anyway?'

After this outburst he went into a deep sulk. When Samson tried to humour him, he stalked off up the hill, then sat down with his back to his companions and gazed morosely across the lodge, as though hoping that the gently-lapping waters might soothe him. Samson let him be for a while before going up to him.

'Oh, come on!' he said at last, tapping Snorky on the shoulder in a conciliatory manner.

'I'll tell you what,' Snorky shouted, turning round and giving Samson a cold stare, 'if you think you're so blinking clever, we'll have a race down Stony Brew. Top to bottom.'

'Oh, not starting at the bottom!' Samson joked. 'Come off it! You've got no chance! And anyway, there's only one bike.'

'I know, you twerp,' Snorky retorted. 'What I meant was, to time each other. Come on, a race. Let's have a race (*snork!*). Okay?'

'What for?' Samson asked. It seemed pointless: Snorky would lose, then get even angrier. It could ruin their friendship - and nothing was worth that.

'For the last dog biscuit?' Snorky said.

'You're on!' Samson agreed. 'Shake hands! *Err* ... bags I go first.'

'No, we toss,' Snorky insisted, producing a shilling. He spun it expertly on the back of his left hand. 'Call !'

'Heads!'

'*Err* ... tails! Right: yes, you go first.'

'Eh?' Samson queried, bemused. He had assumed that Snorky would fix the toss, go first himself, then somehow doctor the bike before his, Samson's, own run.

'Then I'll know what target to beat,' Snorky explained. 'Piece o' cake!'

'Not a biscuit?' Samson joked, but Snorky was not amused. 'Yeah yeah yeah ... me first ... suits me,' Samson said. There was only one worry now: that he would not get a proper push from Snorky.

He need not have worried: Snorky, very chivalrously, put his last ounce of effort into getting him started.

'Okay! ' Samson shouted.

Snorky, unmindful of being the architect of his own defeat, continued to give of his best, even at the risk of scuffing his boots on the stones. In next to no time Samson was rattling along famously.

'Okay!' Samson shouted again. 'Enough! Enough! Leggo!!!'

Snorky finally let go. The sensations which Samson then experienced were utterly intoxicating: the machine was much easier to steer at high speed, and the rush of air up his nostrils gave him an intense feeling of freedom. Unfortunately the feeling was short-lived. Shag, now that Snorky had dropped behind, strove to get in on the act in spite of being limited to three legs. Samson was distracted by Shag's attentions. The bicycle went into a high-frequency wobble of the kind known to automobile engineers and devotees of olde-tyme dancing as a 'shimmy'.

'Help!' Samson shouted. 'HELP! HELLLLLLLLLLL ....'

The accident happened far too suddenly for the contributory steps to be recalled in the right sequence with any certainty. However, it seemed in retrospect that the dog leaped through the frame; the improvised handlebars worked loose, then snapped; the bicycle veered off the track and straight out across the Rock of Gibraltar; finally, Samson sailed out over the end of the Rock on his own, a useless length of wood in each hand, thumped down on the grassy hillside below the Rock, rolled dizzily over and over, and came to rest with onc foot in Entwistle's lodge. The faithful bicycle joined him moments later. The world spun round many times before Samson recovered his senses and realised the terrible danger he was in. For a few awful moments his leg refused to obey instructions.

The pike - heck! With admirable presence of mind, Samson wrestled the bicycle free, then grabbed hold of the leg and pulled it clear of the water. After that it seemed to work normally.

Samson scrambled back up the hillside, shaken but not injured. His heart thumped madly - partly from exertion, partly from a premonition that his own disaster had been overshadowed by another: all above was quiet. Reaching the top of the Rock, his fears seemed confirmed: there was no sign of Snorky or Shag, no sound either. Then he caught sight of Snorky's boots, the same colour as the rock - but shinier: they were laid out in front of the transverse fissure, side by side and with the laces neatly tucked in. He raced forward, dropped to all fours, and peered down into the semi-darkness. He was just in time to see Snorky, wedged between the two walls, smash a huge stone down on Shag's head. The dull thud was sickening. As was made clear later, when the two chastened friends made their way disconsolately back to school, Snorky's act had been one of mercy: the dog, he explained, had broken its back in the fall, and would have died a horrible lingering death but for his thoughtful act.

12. The Great Adventure - 1

Samson's spectacular cycling debut/debacle, coupled with the sad loss of dear old Shag, shook him up more than he would have cared to admit. Of course any public show of mourning, such as excessive wailing or the wearing of a black arm band, was out of the question. Samson did however go off his food for a few days, and this at a time when supplies of penny drops and gobstoppers rose to new heights now that there were only two mouths to feed: he was even unable to enjoy the last dog biscuit, which Snorky very generously gave him in spite of the competition not having been properly settled. Samson opted to keep it as a memento, and never ever to bite it, nibble it, suck it or even furtively lick it.

Perhaps what hurt Samson most was not so much the loss of what had been, as the loss of what might have been. With patience and practice, starting of course at the bottom, Shag would almost certainly have regained full use of the injured leg and gone from strength to strength, building up an impressive repertoire of clever tricks - jumping through hoops of fire, for example. Even if he had remained crippled he could at least have been taught to walk on his hind legs. The bicycle had promised even more possibilities. If Snorky was to be believed, you could learn to ride with your feet on the handlebars (if the bicycle had some, of course); sitting on the handlebars, facing backwards; and ducking through the frame. It was not difficult, therefore, to imagine the possibilities opened up by having both a dog and a bicycle.

Possibly, if Samson had had to cope alone with the double loss, he would never have fully recovered his *joie-de-vivre*. Fortunately he had his friend Snorky to fall back on. Friend? *Friend?* No: Snorky was more than just a friend, or even a good friend: he was a real friend, a true one. Although, like anybody else, he had his moods and could be a bit difficult to get along with, you could always rely on him to help you out in times of difficulty. He would help you to feel better by plying you with endless penny drops or liquorice or sherbert or even black market bullseye gobstoppers; he would risk danger, for example by daring to set fire to an assailant's shirt tail; he would even - and this surely went completely beyond the bounds of any ordinary kind of friendship - do something as distasteful as bashing your head in, if in that way he could save you from unnecessary suffering. It was therefore not so surprising when Snorky, obviously acutely aware of Samson's deep sadness in the days following the double accident, insisted on taking him out one Saturday morning for 'a bit o' fun' down in Monkey Town. Though not really in the mood, Samson gladly acquiesced. Thus came about the experience which, for the rest of his life, Samson would remember as 'The Great Adventure'.

The choice of a Saturday for the trip to Monkey Town was ideal from Samson's point of view, since his father would be totally immersed in picking losers in the afternoon's horseracing, and Mrs. Smalley would be up to her knees in mud, feeding the assorted livestock: for those reasons neither of them would be likely to notice any deviation from his usual routine.

Very few preparations were possible in the days prior to the trip: everything had to be left to the Saturday morning. What for some people might have been the vexing question of what to wear on such a rare visit to civilisation was not a serious problem for someone with only one set of clothes: the only real choice was, between clogs and wellingtons. Sensing the greater sophistication of townspeople (Miss Pollock was one, enough to give some idea of what townspeople were like) Samson opted for the clogs. Making an early decision was good, for it meant that he could scrape the worst of the mud off the clogs, and sponge them cleanish, in time for the leather uppers to dry and to accept a quick lick of Zebo grate polish. (It would be too risky to use shoe polish, of course: carelessness like that could give the whole game away.) Mundane matters dealt with, Samson was free to indulge in flights of fancy and outright fantasy: whole streets paved with cobble stones on which his clogs would beat a triumphant metallic tattoo, with sparks flying left, right and centre - Snorky's exciting descriptions - plus visions of shops with huge lit-up windows, stacked from floor to ceiling with toys and toffee, and in which - if you had money or quick fingers - you could pick up anything from goloshes to ear muffs.

The great day arrived, albeit painfully slowly. Samson's excitement was barely controllable, so to fool his mother he pretended to doze off during the egg and made low moaning noises from time to time, as might a sick animal. Not all the moans were put on: a few were genuine, brought on when urgent waves of mental arithmetic regarding his life savings threw up ever-changing totals ranging all the way from 1s 10d to 1s 2d - a discrepancy of well over sixpence, enough to make all the difference between a whale of a time and a wet weekend.

Fortunately Samson was able to cheer himself up whenever necessary by switching attention from the money itself to the priceless repository in which the funds slowly but oh-so-surely accumulated: his wonderful, marvellous, brilliant Black Sambo money box. A bit of self-congratulation was in order too. In the acquisition of Sambo Samson had displayed a high level of business acumen: by arranging to pay Snorky in dobbers, as and when he could, Samson had managed to avoid that cruellest of dilemmas - having money, but no box to put it in; or having a box, but no money to put in it.

Samson knew Sambo intimately. Not only had he spent countless hours in silent contemplation of his every marvellous detail, but also he knew every contour by touch from having taken him to bed every night for weeks and weeks on end, until the weather had turned so cold that even to touch him was torture.

Sambo had been cast as a legless butler - that is to say, not as a drunk, but as as a head and trunk (with arms) standing about eight inches high. He sported a polka-dot bow tie and a natty red waistcoat (sadly, most of the paint had worn off by the time Samson acquired him, but enough remained to suggest how immaculate his original turnout must have been). A well-built negro in his late twenties or early thirties, Sambo had well-modelled features that put Samson in mind of a Zulu chief that he had once seen on a Pathé newsreel. Sambo's ever-open mouth and inane grin were necessary in the interests of efficient operation, as we will presently see. Other features were unambiguously caricaturised to appeal to

European prejudices, though this point was of course lost on Samson, who accepted uncritically the exaggerated 'whites' of Sambo's eyes (they were in fact picked out in luminous green paint, giving a brilliant afterglow whenever Sambo was dragged beneath the sheets for a quick fondle), while the ears, enormous and protruding, would have looked equally at home on a chimpanzee, though apart from being black they were not that much different from Snorky's - when his sticking plaster came adrift, that was.

Sambo's right hand was held palm uppermost in front of his belly, too close to his belly for this to be construed as begging: it was more as if he were carrying an invisible tray, or were giving himself a playful karate chop to the solar plexus. The space between finger and thumb was, of course, for receiving the money. Then, all that was required of the lucky saver was to reach round behind Sambo's left elbow and to depress the short lever which was to be found there. If this action were performed slowly and hesitantly the result was disappointing: the coin slid out from under Sambo's thumb and fell to the floor. A sharp decisive action, by contrast, brought into play a sophisticated system of internal levers: the hand, gripping the coin securely thanks to centrifugal forces, propelled it towards the welcoming mouth; at the same time the tongue retracted, the eyes rolled downwards to show the 'whites' to maximum advantage, and the ears swivelled forwards and downwards. The net result of this wonderfully co-ordinated suite of movements was that the money was swallowed in the most gratifying way imaginable, and without dulling Sambo's appetite in the slightest - being large and completely hollow, his appetite was, for all practical purposes, insatiable.

The foregoing brief account will perhaps give some idea of the tremendous incentive to save offered by the ingenious Sambo as compared, for example, with a battered tin box or a ceramic pig with a slit in its back. Another (and, for Samson, greater) advantage of Sambo was that though the ever-accumulating funds could not be removed casually, at times of real need the entire contents could be repossessed in a trice without any damage being done. This was possible because Sambo had been cast in two halves - a front and a back - held together with a long bolt, the slotted head of which was disguised as the lowest-but-one waistcoat button (the bottom button, of course, being deliberately left undone, for purely sartorial reasons.) When the bolt had been loosened a couple of turns the metal grille corresponding to Sambo's diaphragm could be levered out to allow the entire contents to spill out.

Mrs. Smalley was well and truly fooled by Samson's breakfast table antics. As soon as she had left the room he crawled upstairs, quietly barricaded the door, then sprang into action. Little by little he shouldered the heavy wardrobe a few inches to one side, thereby gaining access to a loose floorboard. By now chuckling as if insane, he groped under the dusty board until - joy of joys! - his probing fingers made contact with their cold metallic target - then instantly, unerringly, after the most perfunctory of caresses the same fingers closed like talons around Sambo's well-muscled neck. In normal circumstances Samson would then have withdrawn Sambo slowly and deliberately from his dark resting place, then stared at him triumphantly, mockingly, as the latter flinched from the cold light of day, eyes flashing impotently, and attempted to wriggle free. However, this was not the time to be indulging in time-consuming rituals. Samson therefore attacked the bolt with an overgrown thumbnail. Almost instantly his life savings tumbled out, closely followed by Sambo's internal organs. Most of the assorted metal fell into the hole in the floor, necessitating further laborious delving before the savings could be extricated and laid out in neat piles: five halfpennies (ill-gotten proceeds of the coin-on-the-glass swindle); a silver threepenny bit - retrieved with some difficulty after having been swallowed with the Christmas cake - and finally, an article much prized by St. Peter's children and known as a 'penny farthing' - a real farthing, squashed to the diameter of a penny through having been run over by a tram in Bury. Neglecting the last two items - which, being of sentimental value, were unspendable - total funds seemed to amount to the grand sum of fivepence-halfpenny, a far cry even from the most pessimistic estimate. Feeling cheated, Samson clanged Sambo's two halves together, just in case any other coins were still lodged there (there weren't), then scrabbled under the floor like a demented mole, eyes closed against the clouds of noxious dust being raised. Nothing ... nothing at all ... absolutely nothing - except for one of Sambo's innards; flinging this down in disgust, Samson then swept the entire heap of parts back under the floor. Then, after a few suitably-deep sighs, it was time to set the room to rights and to make a start on the necessary toilet preparations.

Samson slipped out to the bathroom, holding his nose with his left hand (the lavatory had been unflushable for some time because of a problem with the water supply) while with his right hand he vigorously brushed his teeth with the powerful mixture of salt, soot and baking powder which the Smalleys preferred to slimy commercial toothpaste. Completion of this operation was signalled by superficially black teeth and a taste of blood, after which a quick gargle with cold water revealed sparkling white teeth set in healthy red gums. Next, the hair: taking a chance, Samson sneaked a smear of Vaseline from his father's economy-size tin: this was a dangerous business, given that the top surface of the Vaseline was still largely untouched - Vaseline being reserved for special occasions, while goose grease was the preferred alternative in normal circumstances. Finally, the face: a quick sluice with cold water, followed by a violent rub over with the curtain, brought off the worst of the grime and exposed glowing pink cheeks - in the dim light the residual dark rings around the eyes were scarcely noticeable. Thus slicked up in imitation of a jaded playboy Samson crept downstairs for the final touch: shining his clogs with Zebo grate polish.

Since Snorky and Samson lived at opposite ends of Old Guinea it had been agreed that Snorky would catch the Monkey Town bus at its terminus in the hamlet of Granite Crags - this lay just across the valley from T' Back o' Beyond, on the border with the neighbouring parish of Oakworth - while Samson, for his part, would board the bus at the stop nearest to Foxgloves Hall, the place known to locals as T' Top o' T'

Brew, or more simply as 'T' Top o' T'. This was a small plateau perched on the very rim of the basin that was Monkey Town. From Foxgloves Hall, about half a mile away by crow, it was occasionally just possible to make out a few buildings - the rest of the plateau was given over to long-forgotten Remembrance Gardens dating back to the Great War. For many years the bus crews plying the Granite Crags - Monkey Town route had pulled off the road at this point for a well-earned break, Snorky told Samson, adding that it was an ideal place to take a deep breath or to have a good cough, depending on whether you were just about to plunge down into Monkey Town, or had recently emerged from it.

For as long as he could remember, in moments of enforced idleness Samson had peered uneasily across the fields towards T' Top o' T', knowing that Monkey Town's leading undertakers, J. and J. Wolf, carried on business there. It didn't take much imagination for the brothers to be transmogrified into a pair of greedy vultures, ever scanning the murky depths below for signs of impending death, then swooping down as the victim wheezed his or her last breath. Recently, whilst idly rummaging through the sideboard, Samson had come across the left-hand half of a pair of binoculars, and whenever the coast was clear he had trained the instrument on T' Top o' T' and struggled to make sense of the mosaic image created by the crazed and discoloured lens. He had watched, nervously, the comings and goings of the Wolfs (or was it 'Wolves', he wondered?) though of course it was impossible to see what went on inside the gloomy neo-Gothic house and associated outbuildings. From time to time his attention wandered to the other building at T' Top o' T', a single-storey edifice conceived in Graeco-Roman style and aborted by the use of local clinker brick. It was to this building, the only public lavatory for miles, that the bus crews repaired as regularly as clockwork; and it was thanks to painstaking observation of this routine that Samson felt quietly confident of recognising the bus when he saw it close up, and of catching it.

Samson slipped out of the house undetected, squeezed through the narrow gap between the gates, sauntered across the fields as if heading for Dead Man Clough, then under cover of an overgrown hedge doubled back towards his true goal. Progress was rapid, and the main worry - fouling up his pristine clogs by carelessly stepping into cowpats or muddy ditches - proved groundless. He arrived at T' Top o' T' with time to spare and concealed himself in a clump of rhododendrons until such time as he could get his bearings. This was not easy, because the mist had still not fully risen: neither Foxgloves Hall nor Monkey Town was visible.

Suddenly Samson noticed the signpost. It had been partly uprooted and the arms were twisted and bent to such an extent that it would have been impossible for a stranger to guess where they had originally been pointing. One pointed directly downwards in the general direction of Australia, and announced 'Monkey Twon [sic] 1 mile'. Another, bent roughly skywards like a dislocated thumb, read 'Manchester 14 miles'. Samson nodded knowingly: the damage was almost certainly one of a number of measures used in the war, to confuse German parachutists and spies. The idea of some poor parachutist landing at T' Top o' T' and then finding that, to get to his target, he needed to go back up again for 14 miles, struck Samson as very amusing, and gave him a brilliant idea: he would play a trick on Snorky. 'The biter bit' - or should that be 'bitten', Samson wondered. Well anyway ... yes, he would beat the blighter at his own game, by pretending not to have turned up: only at the very last moment, when Snorky had given up all hope and was resigning himself to a miserable morning spent alone, would he sneak up and board the bus. Wonderful! Marvellous!! Brilliant!!! Fantastic!!!!

Enough ... something was coming, grinding and whining its way uphill. Samson hurriedly picked a couple of rhododendron leaves and put them on his head as camouflage, then crouched even lower. Thus concealed, he only caught sight of the bus (which the thing undoubtedly was, even though it was twice as big as he had imagined it) when it was already half way round the gardens and beginning to pull up. Even so, it was easy to see that Snorky was not aboard. There couldn't possibly be any mistake, because Snorky had promised faithfully to sit in the 'upstairs driver's seat'; and even if he had forgotten his promise, it made no difference because there were no passengers at all on the bus. So, obviously that was the 'up' bus ... unless Snorky had overslept or something, in which case it night have been the 'down' one ... oh, God! Unfortunately Samson had not been able to see which direction the bus originally came from. Scrutiny of the roller blind was not very helpful either, because it was stuck between 'Oldham' and 'Ormskirk' - somewhere around Wigan, Samson surmised, though his knowledge of regional geography was still rudimentary at best.

Another bus arrived, a bit healthier-sounding than the first one. It raced into the gardens, screeched round the gravel and skidded to a halt beside the first bus. Samson stayed out of sight, having deduced that Snorky must be on this one, and that it would be best not to risk being noticed by sticking his head out of the bushes for a sly peep. All ears, he took in the various sounds: greetings being exchanged, footsteps crunching on the gravel, and then uninhibited urination against the outside wall of the public lavatory ... after a slight pause, receding footsteps and increasingly-muted conversation.

A door banged. Samson, crouching like a sprinter on starting blocks, tensed in anticipation. A huge engine shuddered into life. Samson peeped out - just in time. It was the second bus - obviously, the one with Snorky aboard. Samson shot out of the bushes, at the double and doubled up, and leaped aboard as quietly as a cat in spite of being shod with clog irons. The conductor accosted him. Cool as a cucumber, though red as a beetroot, Samson whispered his destination and paid his fare, then crept upstairs as the bus, picking up speed, lurched out of the gardens. Then two things struck him simultaneously, like bolts of forked lightning: Snorky was not aboard ... it was the wrong bus. Samson more or less fell back down the stairs, threw himself off the platform and broke his heavy fall by rolling over and over on the grass verge like an overtrained parachutist or an overpaid stunt man. Then, for the second time in less than a minute, his winged clogs did their stuff, excelling even by their own superlative standards, depositing their gasping owner on the second (i.e. first) bus.

Samson paid again. He was getting good at this, he realised, though any further development of this socially-important skill would have to wait a few months, since funds were now hopelessly depleted. He crept upstairs, placing his feet at the sides of the stairs to minimise the risk of creaking. One ... two ... three .... four ... six .... eight ... ten ... twelve ... emerging noiselessly onto the upper deck, he peered anxiously over the seat backs - and there, like a rabbit that had magically produced itself from its own hat, was Snorky! He was just where he had said he would be, though it was fortunate he was not an upstairs driver because he was indulging in his brilliant 'owl' trick - turning his head through a hundred and eighty degrees and staring madly, his eyes like sorcerers'. Then the lugubrious features cracked open to produce a huge smile.

'Hey! Where were you?' he shouted to the advancing Samson.

'Where was *I*?' Samson shouted back. 'No: where were *you*? You said -'

'Eh? Oh ... ahem ...' Snorky nodded thoughtfully, 'm ... m ... (*snork!*) ... must have being doing mi bootlaces up. Blooming things keep coming undone.'

13. The Great Adventure - 2

It was odd, an incredible coincidence - a million-to-one chance, Samson wondered? - that Snorky should have been bending down to tie his perishing bootlaces just when he, Samson, was engaged in springing a surprise on him. Samson felt a bit cheated and confused, and paused to collect his thoughts. However, any anger he may have felt was short-lived in the extreme because the spectacle of Snorky nodding acknowledgement was so fascinating. Snorky was the only person that Samson had ever met (or ever would meet, for that matter) who nodded his body rather than his head, so that the latter maintained fixed co-ordinates in space, thanks to the rubbery consistency of an exceptionally long neck. Samson was reminded of the expression 'the tail wagging the dog', more than once used by Tomcat Tompkinson, Polecat's predecesor ... maybe it was possible, after all ... maybe it wasn't 'the drink talking', as Miss Pollock had commented ... so could drink talk? Unfortunately there was no time to pursue these and other intriguing questions: discomfited by Snorky's unblinking stare and hypnotic movements, Samson adopted a hare lip and buck teeth as he stepped forward along the gangway; Snorky, for his part, rotated his head with perfect control, enabling his eyes to track his approaching friend whilst preserving the impression that they were as immobile and unblinking as those of a well-stuffed owl - though he flinched when Samson threw himself down in an attempt to squash him.

'Hutch up!' Samson shouted in his ear, at the same time giving his friend a none-too-playful rabbit bite to the side of the neck. Snorky shuffled across to make room, and the spell was broken.

The bus had by now turned out of the Memorial Gardens onto the main road. From where the boys were sitting, up front, it seemed to be on the verge of plunging over a precipice - an impression that was not far from the fact.

'Is this ... ?' Samson began.

'Yeah, Brewer's Drop,' Snorky confirmed. 'One in four.'

'One in four what?'

'Just one in four - no time to explain. Hold tight!'

Following Snorky's example Samson reached out to grasp the horizontal guard rail designed to prevent front seat passengers from being thrown out of the window if the bus were abruptly halted. The boys were thrown around cruelly as the bus bucked and twisted like a bronco with a spiked saddle, and though Samson was having difficulty swallowing his heart, he was reminded of the exhilarating danger of his ill-fated descent of Stony Brew.

Brewer's Drop had been hacked from the side of a huge mound, and being so steep, it spiralled round the mound in a left-hand corkscrew. To the bus's left, subsidence was checked by a brick retaining wall almost as high as the gates of Foxgloves Hall. Here and there an elder had taken root between the coping stones, so that branches drummed an urgent tattoo on the bus's near-side windows and roof: in other places the wall bulged ominously, or was cracked, or leaked water which streamed across the cobbles and drained away at the right-hand edge of the road. This right-hand edge was marked by iron pipes threaded through drunken concrete posts, drawing attention to a twenty-foot drop onto an endless terrace of one-up-one-down houses; beyond these the embankment steepened again, leading down to a slow, foam-flecked black river. The embankment obviously served as a rubbish dump for the houses' occupants, for it was littered with tin cans and holey buckets and pram bodies. It almost had a tractor and trailer too, but perhaps thanks to the restraining influence of the iron pipes, these had failed to clear the terrace, so that the now wheel-less tractor lay on its side in somebody's back yard, while the trailer rested vertically on its shafts, the back end sticking out of a shattered roof.

'Flipping heck!' Samson exclaimed, then: 'Crikey!'

The cause of Samson's second exclamation was that the bus had been plunged into semi-darkness by a huge brick structure which reared up in place of the houses, its monotonous design accentuated by row upon row of windows covered with wire mesh: behind, a colossal chimney rose up, still camouflaged from the war.

'Ebediah Crompton's,' Snorky explained, then seeing that Samson obviously hadn't the faintest idea what he was talking about, he added: 'Fustians.'

'I see,' Samson mumbled, and as if to indicate the level of his understanding the bus lights flickered momentarily. The bus now slowed to a crawl, for the gloom was increasingly exacerbated by patches of the famous Monkey Town smog, a concoction of *cordon bleu* character - that is to say, it was blended from a long list of ingredients, like the culinary pea soup to which it was sometimes compared,

'The gas ... works,' Snorky announced, slowly and deliberately, like a conscientious mother persisting with a mentally-retarded child. For added emphasis each word was punctuated by a stiff poke in the ribs, with a finger so sharp you could easily imagine it had inadvertently been whittled down during a manic bout of pencil sharpening, and was now intent on taking its revenge on the world.

'*Ouch!* .... Does it?' Samson responded. He stared in wonder at the enormous piles of coal and coke, the three colossal gas holders, and - most fantastic of all - the coke ovens, clad in rusting corrugated iron and festooned with leaking pipes. No observer, least of all a nine-year-old country boy viewing such a complex for the first time, could fail to have been overwhelmed by the suggestion of raw power: with its rumblings and hissings and frightful stench it was the industrial equivalent of a volcano. To Samson, watching in awe as great jets of steam curled out from between two pipes, like smoke from an angry dragon's nostrils, the works looked like a group of monsters locked in mortal combat.

The smog continued to thicken: the dim gas lighting providing an eerie glow but no useful illumination. Reality and fantasy became increasingly difficult to distinguish. A thousand questions flooded into Samson's already-soggy brain, gushing to the surface from nowhere, as though this noble organ were an artesian well: did the people down in Monkey Town really have tails (*real* tails)? Was it true that the pub bar stools had special holes cut in the seats? What exactly did the special trousers look like? What would happen if ... ? What might not have happened ... ? Though still able to formulate grammatically-correct questions, Samson increasingly struggled to find the words needed to complete them. Nevertheless he continued in his attempts to put another question together, and so as to save time he opened his mouth. He was too slow: he had barely licked his lips when Snorky's exquisitely-aimed and extremely bony elbow crunched into his already-sensitised ribs.

'*Aaaaarrrggh!*' he gasped.

'*Ssssh!*' Snorky whispered. 'Don't look now, but that girl's that's just got on ...'

Samson looked across and saw that the opposite seat was now occupied by a girl of about thirteen or fourteen, for some reason dressed in her Sunday best even though this was only Saturday. She sat there motionless - like a porcelain doll (or a corpse, even), bloody lipstick and heavily rouged cheekbones contrasting grotesquely with her deathly-white complexion. She shuffled uncomfortably in her seat as she felt the boys' eyes boring into her.

'Yes, yes?' Samson whispered hack from the side of his mouth. 'Yes? What?'

'Reckon she's got the curse,' Snorky said from the complementary side of his outh. Then, very properly, he made a show of staring out of the window beside him, in spite of the fact that visibility was now down to two feet and the conductor was walking in front of the bus, with a red bicycle lamp clipped to his waistband at the rear: he led the bus with a short length of rope, as if it were an elephant even shorter-sighted than usual.

Inside the bus it was still just possible to make out shapes and - as Samson was able to verify by intense squinting - to see the end of your own nose. Fascinated by Snorky's 'curse' remark, which he took to mean that the girl had (or had had) a tail, and revelling in his newfound eye control, he now stared intently at the girl with his right eye whilst peering directly ahead with the left one. Not surprisingly he noticed nothing of interest. However, just when his eyestrain was becoming unbearable, the girl got up to go back down the gangway, her rear end almost impaled on his quivering nose ... and yes, there it was, staring him in the face: a dark red stain about an inch in diameter on the back of her oatmeal-coloured skirt! She must have been one of the lucky few who had survived the operation ... perhaps she had sat on the stump a bit too hard because of the way the bus kept lurching around. But he would never know: she was almost immediately swallowed up in the mist, and the second elbow of the morning informed Samson that it was time to be getting off. The boys raced down the gangway, tumbled down the stairs and hit the town.

Visibility was still appalling, the smog so thick that Samson was hard-pressed to recognise his best friend at arm's length. Fortunately other senses were enhanced by way of compensation, and with each new breath Samson noticed some intriguing new aroma mixed in with the all-pervading stench of bad eggs and refuse: a whiff of bleach, the warm, balmy mell of freshly-baked bread; the pungent odour of fish and chips swamped in vinegar; the acrid fumes of motor vehicles; and even, Samson fancied, the occasional sharp tangy smell of mustard. The ever-changing smells added to the sense of disorientation.

'Where are we?' he asked.

'We're here,' Snorky replied distantly, his quietly-spoken words seeming to disperse into the smog.

'Yes, I know that, you chump!' Samson said. 'But where the blooming heck's "here"?'

'What's up?' Snorky said, a bit irritably. 'Do you think I don't know where we are? *Hmph!* I know this place like the back of mi 'and. Right: time to make a move.'

He set off, groping his way forward, arms outstretched like somebody wading through a waist-deep bog. Samson, not convinced that Snorky knew the area as well as he claimed, prudently counted the steps they took and noted each new left or right turn as they worked their way through a veritable maze of deserted streets.

After a little while the smog began to clear a little, at least in patches. Snorky broke into a brisk march and then into a slow trot. Samson, suddenly worried that Snorky, as a joke, might run off and leave him, grabbed hold of his coat tails as being the next best thing to a real tail - he had long since lost count of the steps and twists and turns. Fortunately they then came to a kind of lamp post on which was a vertical arrangement of coloured lights.

'Traffic lights,' Snorky volunteered in response to Samson's questioning tug. 'They're everywhere in cities.'

Samson immediately committed the words 'traffic lights' to memory before asking, 'What are they for?'

'Well, to prevent accidents, of course,' Snorky replied, staring at Samson as if unable to believe that anyone didn't know the answer. 'The ... err (*snork!*) red light means "go" and the green one's for "stop".

'So, what about the orange one?'

'Err .. . that's for anyone who's not sure,' Snorky replied, but he sounded as if he was unsure himself, so Samson concentrated on memorising the other two colours.

Samson watched, fascinated, as the colours magically changed from green to orange to red. He had a sudden flush of satisfaction when he noticed that these particular traffic lights had a fault: when it was time for the red to change back to orange, the red stayed on until both it and the orange gave way to green. Aha! Even if there were a hundred traffic lights in Monkey Town it would still be possible to recognise this particular set!

At this point Samson almost died with his secret intact. A horse and cart hurtled through the junction while the light was suitably red and was forced to swerve violently to avoid some idiot who was trying to sneak across the junction on green. The combination mounted the kerb, came halfway across the pavement and forced the boys to dive for safety into a shop doorway.

'Phew! ' Samson exclaimed, struggling to his feet and dusting himself down. 'I wouldn't fancy being run over by a horse and cart, would I heck!'

'We can't always choose what happens to us,' Snorky replied in the stuck-up, know-all kind of voice which, if he had not been such a good friend, would have been really irritating.

'What do you mean?' Samson checked. It was annoying, having someone speaking in riddles in an emergency.

'What about my great-aunt Hetty, then?'

'Search me,' Samson shrugged. 'Why - what about her?'

Actually he wasn't sure which aunt Snorky was referring to ... perhaps the one who had been a 'lady in waiting', in other words some kind of highwaywoman. Or .... ah! Was it a different one?

'Do you mean the missionary?' he checked.

'Yes, her,' Snorky said. 'Do you think she had any choice?'

'About what?'

'About how she died, of course. What do you -?'

'I don't know ... why - what happened?'

'I thought I told you once before,' Snorky said. 'She was the one who was eaten alive in Tonga - cannibals.'

'Eaten?' Samson exclaimed. '*Eaten*? By *people*? God! how did they cook her?'

'They didn't,' Snorky replied quietly, then he turned away to hide the deep sadness he must have been feeling.

That particular conversation was obviously over, but the theme of human flesh was kept alive by the window display at which Samson now found himself staring: mis-shapen plaster dummies sporting corsets and ladies' underwear. The trussed dummies, which would have looked grotesque in any light, looked particularly grotesque in this particular shop window thanks to the changing colours issuing from the traffic lights: they looked particularly ghastly in green light. Samson, in spite of his feeling of revulsion, examined the display with interest. Snorky meanwhile bent down to retie his bootlaces: when he straightened up, Samson felt the silence between them needed to be broken.

'So ... what shall we do?' he said, turning back towards the pavement.

'Err ... let's see what turns up, shall we,' Snorky replied. Then: 'Christ! (*snork!*) Do you see what I see?' He nodded to the pavement in front of them. What appeared to be a ten-shilling note fluttered there enticingly.

'God!' Samson exclaimed, making to push past Snorky to go and pick up the precious note ... five shillings each, if Snorky agreed to share it!

'Leave it,' Snorky said nonchalantly, at the same time restraining Samson quite firmly with a rigid arm. 'We don't need it,' he explained. 'Let's leave it for someone who does.'

Samson hesitated, feeling uncomfortable at disclosing just how hard up he was, but before he could make up his mind he was pre-empted by Snorky, who took out a great wad of notes and flicked an expert thumb across them.

'Crikey!' Samson burst out. 'How much have you got there?'

'*Sssh* ... enough for a good time,' Snorky whispered, and he winked merrily.

Samson grinned, happy that Snorky was back to his usual cheerful, happy-go-lucky self. However, Snorky's expression was short-lived, changing quickly into one of deep sadness, with a suggestion of tears in his eyes.

'Poor old girl,' he muttered almost inaudibly, nodding discreetly in the direction of a little old lady who was steaming towards them arthritically at about half a knot.

Samson, glancing longingly at the note every few seconds, watched the old lady approach. The thought of Snorky's generosity, more than the restraining arm, deterred Samson from rushing forward to seize the money.

'It's rude to stare,' Snorky whispered. 'Let's pretend to be looking in the window.'

They turned round and took advantage of the reflections. The old lady finally reached the vicinity of the ten-shilling note. She stopped, badly out of breath and wheezing terribly. After looking round to check that she was not being observed she stabbed at the note with her walking stick. Her aim, confounded both by slight palsy and by little movements of the note, was not good enough. Once again Samson pulled against Snorky's restraining arm, this time with the altruistic motive of picking up the note and handing it to the old lady.

'Easy come, easy go,' Snorky whispered, continuing to restrain Samson. The latter smiled, because although Snorky was obviously suggesting that the old lady would enjoy the money more if she had to struggle for it, he might just have easily have been talking about himself. He was, after all, extravagant to a fault - embarrassingly so at times.

The old lady, adopting a different tack, put down her voluminous shopping bag, propped her walking stick against the shop front, and with an almost audible creaking of ancient bones got down on her knees and reached out with both arms, pilgrim-style. The crumpled brown note, caught by the gentlest of breezes, danced merrily like an autumn leaf, coming to rest a few inches to her right. Obviously in considerable pain, she turned, and tried again: the note, as if Fate had decreed it should stay at liberty, danced away again. This was too much: letting out a great gasp, she tried to fling herself on top of the note: when that failed, she started to crawl after it.

'RUN!' Snorky suddenly shouted. At the same time he reeled in the note, which had been secured at the end of a long thread of brown cotton running under his instep. Then he and Samson jumped over the old lady and hot-footed it round the corner until they were safely out of sight.

They were still laughing breathlessly when they arrived at what was obviously the main street in Monkey Town. The smog was beginning to clear, so that across the road from where they stood panting they could see a cinema, outside which a poster advertised the main feature, a western entitled *They Died with Their Boots On*.

'Is it about -?' Samson said, aborting his question. He had been about to make a joke to the effect that the film could be about Snorky, who almost certainly slept in his boots, but the time didn't seem quite right.

'It's about Cowardy Custard, isn't it.'

'Eh?'

'Cowardy Custard - him and the Sixth Cavalry at Little Bighorn. My uncle Ephraim ...'

But Samson wasn't listening. Instead, his attention had been claimed by the second feature, a film called *Beautiful Dreamer,* apparently about a beautiful girl and an even more beautiful chimpanzee. The picture enthralled Samson and it took several well-aimed stiff elbows from Snorky to bring him out of his trance, and to redirect his attention to another wonderful sight, just along the street: a mobile hot-food stall, from which a mouth-watering smell teased them: steam from the cart rose enticingly, mixing with the chill smog and their own excited breath. An artistic hand-painted sign announced a choice of black puddings and roast potatoes.

'Come on, let's have ourselves a feast!' Snorky shouted. 'Money's no object!'

He ordered a black pudding each, and laced them with thick creamy yellow fresh mustard. The first desperate mouthful told Samson that this was the greatest treat he had ever enjoyed, and though it would have been nice to make the black pudding last (it was scalding hot, anyway), he found himself gulping it down with the voracity of a starving wolf.

'Another (*snork!*)?' Snorky said chirpily.

'God ...' Samson began, but just then warning bells sounded in his subconscious. The horse, he noticed, had recently deposited some steaming droppings, almost the same size and shape as the black puddings. It was just possible that while he had been losing himself in the first black pudding his fun-loving friend had picked up a lump of horse dung with a view to doing a quick switch; such was his sleight of hand that it would he difficult to spot the changeover ... laced with fresh mustard, it might fool even a connoisseur of black puddings until the first fatal mouthful had been wolfed.

'No thanks,' he ended weakly.

'Suit yourself,' Snorky shrugged, apparently not too offended by the refusal. 'I'm still hungry though ... God, I could eat a horse! Not this one, but -'

'Me too! ' Samson admitted. 'Can I change my mind?'

Snorky sidled round to the counter, jangling the money in his pocket, and Samson took up station at the horse's rear end. It was possibly too late, of course, but if the switch had not been made yet it ought to be preventable: with luck, years of diligent observation practice would pay off.

Snorky came back, chuckling. As he handed Samson another black pudding he burst out laughing, almost uncontrollably. The cause of his merriment was not difficult to ascertain: he himself was holding not another black pudding, but the largest potato Samson had ever seen, and it was shaped like an enormous bum - like the horse's! It didn't look very good value (it was terribly charred - so much so that one end of it was pure charcoal, still glowing a dull red), but the sheer size of it!

'It's marvellous ... magnificent ...' Samson breathed, between gulps of black pudding. He searched desperately for words to describe it. 'It's ... it's majestic!' he finally gasped.

'Actually it's a King Alfred,' Snorky said. He leaned forward and attempted to cool the potato by blowing on it.

'You chump!' Samson laughed. 'That's not the way!'

Anyone with experience of rekindling fires should have realised that. It was the worst thing Snorky could have done: the charred region glowed bright red, then the entire potato burst into flames.

'Eh?' Snorky queried - still, incredibly, blowing his heart out.

'No, seriously,' Samson insisted. 'You can't do that!'

But Snorky's mind was elsewhere:

'Christ Almighty (*snork!*)' he suddenly exclaimed - his attention on the horse, not the potato.

Haha! A typical Snorky trick! You could always expect some kind of diversion when you were trying to put him right about something: he hated being corrected.

'What?' Samson asked, remembering to keep one eye on Snorky's potato, one on his own black pudding, and both on the horse droppings.

'Well,' Snorky said, 'what I want to know is, what's a street trader doing with a blooming racehorse (*snork!*)?'

'A *race*horse?!' Samson laughed, deciding to play along with him, then turn the tables when the time was ripe. There was nothing to fear here: he was on home territory, being something of an expert on animals. Actually it wasn't necessary to be an expert in this particular case: any fool could have seen that the beast was no racehorse - it was incredibly old, scraggy and moth-eaten, long overdue for the knacker's yard.

'What's so blooming funny?' Snorky challenged. *Aha!* He was obviously getting rattled!

'Well, it's no racehorse,' Samson said, still chuckling. 'It's either half asleep or half dead - or both!' He walked round to the front of the horse, to play his trump card. 'Come here ... if you don't believe me, come and look at its teeth. It's a great-grandmother at least!'

'Sod the teeth! ' Snorky shouted, refusing to budge from the horse's rear end. 'Just look at these fantastic muscles. I've never seen muscles like these on a horse! *Phew!*'

'Yeah, yeah, yeah,' Samson countered. 'And you - you look at these teeth.'

Samson, from his nodding familiarity with the game of chess, recognised this as a stalemate situation, only resolvable when one of them tired and backed down. He steeled himself for the coming trial of strength, but need not have bothered, for the argument was immediately resolved in an unexpected way. The horse raised its tail to produce another batch of imitation black puddings: the next moment, Samson was flat on his back across the pavement, bowled over when the horse bolted. In the split second that it all happened he was just able to catch sight of Snorky ramming the smouldering potato under the horse's tail: the shocked animal, irrationally, gripped the potato tightly under its tail instead of letting it drop to the ground.

Snorky, barely able to stand through laughing, helped the shaken Samson to his feet. Then, gathering up an armful of hot potatoes from the pavement where they lay scattered, he escorted his dear friend across the street. Moments later they were safe from all possible retribution, swallowed up in the bowels of the cinema - and with enough ammunition to last until the interval, enough money to gorge themselves sick on delicious ice creams - and, in Samson's case, enough bruises to make this his most memorable adventure ever. The films were unforgettable, too.

14. Happy Returns - 1

The morning after the desperate business down in Dead Man Clough, Samson had woken up wonderfully rested and relaxed - reborn, almost: the nearest thing to a holiday he had ever had: his recent adventure had already faded into insignificance. It was all thanks to the wonderful memories stored up over the last couple of years: memories of events and feelings which could never be repeated. Without such memories, he believed, he might have felt drained, like an empty bladder. How much better to be bursting with memories! He felt he knew what it must have been like to be Midas - but whereas the boring old king had only his cold old gold to play with, he had a treasure house of precious memories, stacked so high and packed so tight that sometimes it was a problem to retrieve one. He felt he could lose everything - his money, his bicycle (if he had one), his teeth, his hair ... anything at all, except perhaps his collection of birds' eggs ... provided that he still had his memories. He could be frozen solid in an igloo in Timbuktu, or trussed up tight in a wigwam in Siam, and his wonderful memories would sustain him.

'Thank you, God!' Samson said, quietly and respectfully. Though he didn't really believe in God (not exactly, anyway), he nevertheless felt that he was incredibly lucky to have been given such a fine memory - his mother's jibes notwithstanding. The only worry was, that this precious gift might be lost or destroyed through a tendency to carelessness. Now: memory had something to do with the brain ... the brain, therefore, was the most important part of the body ... at all costs the brain must be protected. He resolved to make a list of the possible causes of brain damage when he got up. Some, of course, were common sense: heading wet footballs or walking under ladders, for example. Others were less obvious, therefore all the more important to identify by energetic thinking ... like - thinking too much?

The Foxgloves Hall thrush, perhaps to contrast the dangers of excessive thinking with the joys of mere existence, suddenly burst into joyous song only feet from where Samson sat ruminating. God! How could it possibly sing like that after stuffing itself full of fat juicy worms every daylight hour of every single day for the past three months or more? Perhaps it, too, had memories: something to sing about.

Samson prised himself out of bed, perhaps realising that the quality of his ruminations was not getting any better. He was a bit stiff, but otherwise felt great. It was already a most beautiful day. The sky was almost cloudless, and wonderfully clearish and cleanish and bluish: the golden sun, so often watery and apologetic, was confidently shining its heart out, so that little imagination was needed to feel the warmth. Samson got dressed and headed downstairs. From the landing another beautiful sight met his eyes: down in Monkey Town, lazy spirals of pure black smoke rose heavenwards from fifty or more towering mill chimneys, going up and up and up before subtly disappearing. Perhaps the Wolf brothers would be able to take the day off.

Samson entered the drawing room and looked around. Though the room was still essentially familiar a few changes had obviously been made - little changes: slight rearrangements and tidyings, nothing fundamental though. But certainly, mysterious.

'Oh, you're down at last,' Mrs. Smalley exclaimed from behind him, breaking the spell. 'I was beginning to wonder if you'd woken up dead, perhaps. I had expected you earlier - by dinner time, at least.'

'Woken up *dead*?' Samson checked, almost inaudibly. Was such a thing possible, he wondered?

'*Eeh*, I say! You did come in in a state yesterday ... I can't think what on earth you must have been up to ... anyway, many happy returns! '

'Hey?'

'Hay is for horses,' Mrs. Smalley corrected.

'No: that's 'aitch',' Samson countered. '"A" is for "asses" -'

'You'd know all about that, wouldn't you!' she retorted. 'Anyway ... the word you need is "Pardon?" *Eeeh*, don't say you'd forgotten ... I mean, fancy forgetting your own birthday! It's like Christmas, only comes once a year. We thought we'd treat you to a new pencil this time ... it's -'

'*Mmm*? Birthday, today?!' Was it possible, he wondered? A

quick check told him it was: certainly, the first of April was long gone, so it was not her customary 'April Fool' trick.

'HB, they're the best,' Mrs. Smalley continued. 'I mean, pencils always come in handy. Well, what do you say?'

'Oh ... thanks a thousand.'

'A million, I think you mean. Well, I shouldn't waste it. I should keep it for the Grammar School if I were you - if you get in. Your birthday comes at an awkward time, I'm afraid. But a pencil always comes in handy. Use it if you have to, of course, but ... well, don't go wasting it, scribbling away in your bedroom.'

'I DON'T SCRIBBLE!' Samson protested. Then, concerned that the vehemence of his denial might be taken as an admission of his top-secret projects, he added feebly: 'Well, perhaps I do, just occasionally.'

'If you're stuck for something to do,' Mrs. Smalley said, gathering steam now that she had gained some advantage, 'you could practise your spelling - or your sums, even .... or go and have yourself a game of chess.

Samson shook his head emphatically.

'Why not?' she queried.

Samson shrugged, but offered no answer.

'Whyever not?' she persisted. 'You must have some reason.'

'I'm tired of winning,' he replied, then permitted himself the luxury of a secret smirk.

'Oh, and Dad says you might as well have these old pen knibs too,' Mrs. Smalley continued. 'There's nothing really wrong with them. Anyway, one thing's certain: you can't beat education. Believe me, I should know: I had to leave school at thirteen. No, if you've got education, the world's your oyster.'

Samson's egg, perhaps as confused as he was by the unfamiliar metaphor, spilled out over the edge of the plate.

'*Eeeh*, they get funnier, I swear they do,' Mrs. Smalley remarked apropos the calamity. 'Must be this funny weather ... upsets everything, if you ask me. Well, I was going to do you another one anyway, being as it's your birthday. No, you can't beat eggs ... full of goodness.'

'What about education?'

'Don't be silly.'

'Alright then: what about scrambled eggs - or omelettes? They're beaten.'

'An egg's an egg when all's said and done,' Mrs. Smalley said. 'But we can have scrambled for tea, that's a good idea. Perhaps with French toast. Yes, that ... and your favourite.'

'Rhubarb?'

'Mmm ... warm.'

'Custard, then?'

'Getting warmer.'

'Rhubarb and custard? Hot?'

'Yes, rhubarb and custard,' she conceded. 'Hot or cold, it's all the same. *Hee!* Ten today! Ten out of ten! It takes some getting used to, it does that! It seems only yesterday ...'

Ten ... ten out of ten ... however you put it, it didn't seem that fantastic, certainly not worth making a song and dance about. Now, a hundred: that would really be something to shout about - if you still had the lung power. But ... ten? No ... everybody lived to be ten - well, almost everybody. Poor Speedy, of course, had fallen short - a point so ably brought out by Polecat at the funeral: 'tragically run out before reaching double figures' was how he had put it, and though Samson had only heard the words at second hand he had savoured them ever since. He still vividly remembered the small knot of mourners standing there in the persistent drizzle with their heads bowed, like so many solemn umpires concurring in a verdict of dismissal.

'Eeeh, it's a game, isn't it,' Mrs. Smalley sighed, derailing Samson's train of thought as effectively as if she had been a cow on the line. 'I can't see this weather lasting, can I heck. I wouldn't be surprised if we had a storm later on.' She slurped her tea with a suitable degree of apprehension.

'How on earth can you foresee a storm in a teacup?' Samson joked.

'Well, just see for yourself how they've settled,' his mother said, thrusting her empty cup under his nose. 'All higgledy-piggledy, on top of each other. I don't like the looks of them at all, do I heck. Anyway, I should stay in today: I think you've done enough messing about recently to last you a lifetime. I know: tidy your bedroom, or something. Clear the decks for action. You never know .... I mean, don't go mauling about the countryside any more, or people might begin to think you've a screw loose. You know how people talk.'

Mrs. Smalley left the room. Samson permitted himself the luxury of another quick smirk, this one in response to the stupidity of her last remark. Yes, perhaps he did have a screw loose - but in that case, everyone else had a whole head of loose screws. Now, a chance remark by his mother enabled his own loose screw to slip neatly back into place. 'It's a game', she had said, apropos of nothing. That was it, precisely: life was a game. Seen in this way, many of the confusing experiences of the last year suddenly began to make sense. However, Samson felt that, before going into details, it was a good idea to record this wonderful insight. What better use for a new pencil?

'Life's a game life's a game life's a game,' Samson chanted under his breath, determined not to allow this gem to slip from his grasp. God, yes! There were players and spectators .... winners and losers ... rule-keepers and cheats ... in a fever of excitement, worried that some of the weaker thoughts might get killed in the rush, Samson sharpened his new pencil into the half-empty eggshell, then started scribbling furiously on the back of an old cigarette packet which he had purloined a few days previously and kept inside his shirt for just such an emergency. Speed was of the essence: suddenly worried that his mother might sneak in and catch him in the act, he downed tools, restoring the packet to the inside of his shirt and sticking the pencil up his sleeve, sharpened end first. Then after munching the remains of his egg as best he could (the combination of egg and pencil sharpenings was not something he could develop a taste for, he felt, though the sharpenings did add a certain crunchiness), he repaired to his bedroom.

Safely installed in his sanctuary, the door locked, Samson took out a piece of virgin white writing paper culled from an old diary of his father's and preserved for some extraspecial task such as the one he was now minded to engage in: an exhaustive set of categories for 'life as a game'. The new pencil, unfortunately, repeatedly shied away from the task: when Samson tried to show it who was boss, it broke. Intensely frustrated, Samson was very near to putting the pencil across his knee and snapping it. Fortunately his thoughts kept straying from the intellectual task to contemplation of the birthday cake which, he knew, would be biding its time in the pantry. The year before, he had got into terrible trouble for taking currants from the top of the cake.

'It must have been a mouse,' he had suggested, when confronted with the crime.

'Yes, a two-legged one,' his mother said knowingly.

'Or a one-eyed one, perhaps,' Samson said obtusely. 'Anyway, how can you be so sure?'

'Because there were nine fresh currants on it when I put it in the oven, and nine burned ones when I took it out,' she said. 'But when I went to put it on the table there were only four. Do you think I can't count, or something?'

Later, enjoying the cake legitimately, Samson realised why the currants were restricted to the top of the cake: Mrs. Smalley had planted them on top during the baking, to give the impression of richness - a trick learned, without doubt, from her wartime 'Make Do and Mend' classes. This practice, of taking the cake out of the oven half-way through the baking, would also explain why her offerings were not only burnt, but sunken in the middle too.

It was not until Samson was in the pantry admiring this year's cake (yes, sure enough, there were ten burned currants on it) that a solution to the problem came to him. Upending the cake, he gouged away at the soft underbelly, reasoning not unreasonably that the clean cut of a knife would be too incriminating. It was not until the fourth or fifth such visit that the extent of the excavations began to get a bit worrying. Once again he would be forced to swear that the culprit was a mouse: the added problem this time would he to explain how the creature had first gnawed its way through an inch-think slab of solid Welsh slate - and without leaving a hole in it. Perhaps suffering from inter-species guilt Samson picked up a few stray crumbs and took them upstairs to give to Hercules. In a way it was his birthday too.

Time passed like lightning. It seemed only a matter of

minutes between finishing brinner and feeling the pangs of teatime.

'You can come down now,' Mrs. Smalley shouted from the landing. 'It's all laid out. Come on, before everything gets cold.' She scuttled back down again.

Samson, suitably excited, hurriedly hid his papers behind the wardrobe. Then, after popping Hercules up his left sleeve, he raced down the stairs three at a time. It was incredible: a veritable banquet awaited him. The drop-leaf dining table had been extended, graced with a fine white embroidered Irish linen tablecloth and set for three; the solid-looking birthday cake, taking pride of place on a Dresden-style cake stand in the centre of the table, now sported a jaunty full-size white blackout candle, which leaned a little drunkenly as though in anticipation of the revelries to corne. Virtually every square inch of the table top was taken up with steaming hot pans containing variously scrambled eggs, rhubarb and custard. Closer inspection revealed a dainty spherical teapot which Samson had never seen before, and an unexploded pre-war Christmas cracker. But for the absence of people, Samson felt, the scene was highly reminiscent of that depicted in the 'Last Super' [*sic*] painting hung in St. Peter's. Mrs. Smalley now went some way towards making up for the deficiency by going to stand beside the table, hands clasped in front of a cleanish white apron, striking a pose appropriate to that of a faithful old family retainer.

'Well, sit down,' she prompted. 'You might as well start straight away, don't let it get too cold. I did French toast for the scrambled, by the way. If you want more you've only to ask.' She plopped a great dollop of egg on the glistening toast, then held up the pepper pot, like an auctioneer might have done, to show Samson where it was.

'I thought I was supposed to be ten,' Samson complained, nodding towards the solitary candle.

'Yes, but that's a *real* candle,' she explained. 'Well, I thought we could count it as ten. Only, birthday candles are dear for what they are, they are that. We can light it later - no sense in burning it just for the sake of it. Is your scrambled alright?' Interpreting the absence of a reply as favourable, she now joined Samson at the table.

For a while they ate in silence, apart from the sounds of mastication. Then suddenly Mrs. Smalley spoke:

'*Hee!* It seems funny, doesn't it - just the two of us.'

'Three,' Samson corrected, with a clever smile hastily fashioned from a wince. Hercules had just nipped the sensitive skin high up on his forearm.

'No: two,' his mother corrected. 'I'm afraid Dad won't be able to join us. More rhubarb and custard?'

'No ... no thanks.'

'Well, you usually -'

'The rhubarb's a bit lumpy,' Samson joked.

'It shouldn't be,' his mother replied, brows furrowed. 'I picked it fresh only this morning. And mine looks alright. Well, you know very well ... Dad always insists -'

'Where is he, then?'

'Oh, he's ... *err*, he's gone out - gone to see a man about a dog.'

'A DOG!! !???' Samson blurted out, jumping to his feet. 'Oh, I've always wanted a dog!' Even before his mother could answer, the dog of his dreams was taking shape: basically white, brindled perhaps, highly trainable - and it definitely wouldn't be called 'Shag'.

'It's an expression,' Mrs. Smalley laughed.

'Oh, I know: like an alsatian, only -'

'No, an expression. It's just an expression. It means ... well, private business, that sort of thing.'

'Oh.' More than at any other time in Samson's bittersweet life the inadequacy of mere words was felt poignantly. He stared downcast into the remains of his rhubarb and custard, idly playing checkers with the last few lumps.

'Hee, I'll give you "a dog"!' Mrs. Smalley scolded good-naturedly. 'What would you want with a dog, eh? As if we haven't enough livestock ... they can eat you out of house and home, can dogs.' She got up and closed the curtains, as though to emphasise that the 'dog' discussion was over.

'We could always feed it on scraps,' Samson persisted doggedly, still chasing the lumps round the bowl. Then more defiantly he added, 'I could always buy my own.'

'Pull the other one,' his mother said. 'Now: close your eyes!'

'What's the point?' Samson asked sulkily. 'I can't see anything anyway, with the curtains drawn.'

'Just do as you're told,' she insisted. 'The trouble with you is, you always think you know best. Just close your eyes, do as I say.'

'But why?'

'Because I say ... because I've got a little surprise for you, if you must know. Now: close them! And no peeping, or else!'

Samson rested his head on cupped hands and, to make up for being unable to see anything, strained his ears. He recognised the sound of tearing paper, and of his mother moving stealthily about - first to the range, then back to the table, finally to somewhere behind him. What on earth was going on? Was she really going to give him a proper birthday present - something a bit more exciting than the usual socks? Was there in fact a dog, after all? Was she waiting for Mr. Smalley to bring it in? Had she let the cat out of the bag, and was now trying to cover up? A cat ... was the dog a red herring? Could it be a fish? Or a kitten, maybe ... a fluffy black kitten ... a playmate for Hercules?

'You can open them now,' his mother's disembodied voice called out.

As Samson should have guessed from the smell of wax, the solitary ten-in-one candle was burning merrily and casting a warm yellow light around the room, its flame dancing in response to the ever-shifting draughts from the window. Mrs. Smalley was seated at the piano, her nicotine-stained fingers and thumbs laid out over the keys like so many half-cooked pork sausages. Suddenly they jerked into life, as though the heat had been turned right up: she began to knock out a crude accompaniment to the words of 'Happy Birthday'.

Unfortunately the work was too demanding and had to be abandoned after the first few bars.

'I didn't know you could play the piano,' Samson said, genuinely impressed.

'There's a lot of things you don't know, just remember that,' Mrs. Smalley said. 'Eeeh, I'm afraid I'm all fingers and thumbs, for some reason. I know: I'll just loosen up with a bit of Ivor Novello first.'

For a couple of minutes Samson watched entranced as the assembled fingers proclaimed their intention of gathering lilacs the following spring. Unfortunately Mrs. Smalley was too out of practice even for this piece, and obliged to begin over and over again, the lilacs in more danger of being squashed than plucked.

Samson began to get bored: Hercules likewise perhaps, for he administered a series of vicious nips. Samson, unwilling to chastise Hercules on their joint birthday, took him out from the sleeve, lifted up the birthday cake on one side, and allowed Hercules to have a good nibble at the bottom of the cake. The opportunity was seized gratefully: probably by coincidence, mouse droppings began emerging from Hercules' rear end, creating an impression of a busy mouse-droppings factory in operation. Samson expertly removed the incriminating evidence from the table cloth by flicking the droppings at the flowers on the curtains. His performance was very satisfying: two direct hits and four or five very near misses in as many seconds.

Suddenly, without warning, Mrs. Smalley banged down the piano lid.

'*Eeeh*, it makes me so mad!' she said disgustedly, ' I used to be so good, I did that. Well, never mind, I suppose ... I know: we can have some cake now.'

There was no time to catch hold of the busy mouse. Instead, Samson dropped the cake back onto the stand so that Hercules was safely imprisoned inside the hollowed-out bottom, his tail curled round his feet. Phew! A close squeak!

Fortunately it seemed that Mrs. Smalley had not noticed anything wrong: instead of coming over to inspect the cake, she went across to the sideboard and opened the drawer. Samson's sixth sense, reliable as ever, alerted him to imminent danger. He turned round quickly, just in time to see his mother bearing down on the cake with a huge carving knife.

'*Meeiaow!*' he cried out. '*Meeiaow! Meeiaow!*'

'*Eeeh*, you're a funny lad, sometimes,' she sighed. 'As if

cats eat cake! Come on, then - blow it out.'

Samson, who could easily have blown the candle out - through his nose, even, if he had wanted to - was deliberately unsuccessful. Mrs. Smalley therefore came to his assistance. The stubborn candle flickered a few times, then went out; at the same time it toppled over in slow motion and finally fell onto the tablecloth.

'Do you want a big piece?' Mrs. Smalley asked. 'Or will a little piece ...? I think perhaps I'll .... *AAAARGGHHHH!*' She dropped the knife and collapsed against the wall. The cause of her consternation was not difficult to guess: Hercules, having eaten his fill, had taken advantage of the candle's detachment to pop his head out of the cake and have a good look round.

15. Happy Returns - 2

Ten! Ten years old!! Ten out of ten!!!!!!!!!! Put like that, it sounded really something, like reaching double figures at cricket, or spelling 'diarrhoea' correctly. However, back in the bedroom, away from the hurly-burly of the party, the achievement didn't seem much to write home about. After all, anyone who reached the age of nine had a pretty good chance of hanging on for another year. This was borne out by the fact that, out of St. Peter's top class of thirty or so children, only three had died in the last year. One of those didn't really count, anyway: to be struck by lightning while sheltering under an umbrella, as Ginger Thomas had been, was a million-to-one chance, since nobody in their right mind in Old Guinea used an umbrella: if you needed protection from the howling gales and driving rain you got yourself a sou'wester.

Actually it had always seemed to Samson that, apart from obvious exceptions such as Ginger, those who were going to die young had been earmarked from birth. Many cases quickly sprang to mind: Deirdre Unsworth, the hole-in-the-heart girl who had sometimes looked like she was wearing purple lipstick ... Derek 'Gobber' Gutteridge, with galloping consumption and a hump like a bactrian camel's (he had bad breath too, not surprisingly) ... or of course poor Speedy who, apart from being little brighter than a freshly-sliced turnip, was said to have been born with ingrowing feet (information which was almost certainly correct, coming as it did from one of Snorky's aunts, who was a midwife). The first two of these had been weeded out before reaching nine.

Reaching nine had special significance for Samson: his own life had taken a dramatic turn on his ninth birthday, even though he had felt like crying when he learned that his present was, yet again, a handkerchief - what was the point of having three handkerchiefs? That apart, it had been more a case of 'one over the eight' than 'nine out of nine'. It was as though he had drunk a whole wellington full of champagne and been transported from one fantastic happening to another, his feet scarcely touching the ground. There was the Great

Adventure, the Blood Brothers business, the crucifixion spectacular .... then the bubbles had burst all of a sudden and all together. Since then time had seemed to stand still, with Samson himself slipping slowly backwards. It was as though a hurricane had appeared from nowhere and cut a swathe through Old Guinea, whipping everything into a thoroughly topsy-turvy state, leaving devastation and a total vacuum in its wake. For weeks now he had been wandering round with a head full of spelling and arithmetic, an expert on birds and horses and nature in general, even to the extent of knowing the difference between a butterfly and a moth, yet unable to remember even simple things such as whether or not he had put his name on an exam paper ... or his own birthday. Years later he was to invent a new word to denote this peculiar combination of omniscience and faulty memory: omnesia.

Even now, weeks after the momentous happenings and with much of the dust settled, many things were still as puzzling as they had been at the time - and none more so than the question as to what had happened to Snorky. Was he still alive and kicking? It was impossible to imagine someone like Snorky ever dying ... but if he was still alive, why had he dropped out of contact? Only days before they had last seen each other, Snorky had asked for a detailed sketch map of the anarchic maze of lanes and tracks leading to Foxgloves Hall, so that they could meet up 'every single day' (Snorky's exact words) of the summer holidays. They had planned to scour every single square inch of Old Guinea in order to put together the finest duplicate collection of birds' eggs the world had ever seen. Day after day, week after week Samson had stayed in, twiddling his thumbs and wearing out the clock faces, but Snorky hadn't put in a single appearance. After all the fun and games, the adventures, the comradeship and the promises: nothing ... nothing at all ... absolutely nothing. It was quite incredible. The thought had crossed Samson's mind that the whole thing had been a set-up, one of Snorky's little jokes, but of course that would have been ridiculous because Snorky would have been just as much a victim. No: there must be some other explanation. The only thing to do was, to go back to the area of St. Peter's

- to revisit the scene of the crime, as it were: to refresh memories that were fading fast, perhaps even to call unexpectedly on Snorky and see what the beggar had to say for himself. Though Samson had never ventured as far afield as Granite Crags it should not be too difficult to find.

Enough! It was time for action, not thought. Samson thumped Hercules down on the dressing table, crept up behind him on the blind side and administered a none-too-playful flick on the ear as a birthday souvenir before snatching him up again and popping him back in his box in the wardrobe. Then he threw on protective clothing and set out on his mission. Prudently, he filled his ears with soggy cotton wool borrowed from the egg collection and moistened with spittle, worried that Snorky might rise to the occasion and come up with some perfectly plausible excuse just as his rubbery neck began to feel the steely grip of his best friend's fingers.

'Don't go too far,' Mrs. Smalley warned. 'Don't go getting yourself wet through and catching your death of.'

'I suppose so,' Samson shouted back, walking off purposefully and quickly settling into the slightly lurching gait typical of seasoned country dwellers. Today nothing would deter him. After trampling across the vegetable garden, he squelched round the duck pond and marched straight through the orchard to his favourite secret hedge gap. Soon he was nearing Ramsbottoms' Farm, and he now found himself mechanically vaulting a five-barred gate so as to make a wide detour around the cluster of dilapidated buildings. God! The detour had become second nature. Samson suddenly realised with a shock that he had behaved guiltily ever since the accident. It would have been far better to carry on as though nothing had happened, or to offer condolences and maybe help with the haymaking again. Because until the accident he had been a constant visitor to the farm: a part of the furniture at times. In the haymaking season there was no greater fun than lending a hand. Turning the hay was the only uncomfortable part - sheer hard work, palms quickly blistering through struggling with the heavy man-sized wooden-pronged rake. Everything else was fun, great fun, even the equally hard work of stooking, because you could break the monotony by diving into the hay and rolling about, or by running about covered in hay like some kind of monster. The best thing? Riding high on the swaying cart, on top of the huge and precarious load, the nearest thing to heaven-on-earth. After sundown, in the huge but low-ceilinged farm kitchen, itching fit to scratch yourself to death, came the greatest treat imaginable: meat-and-potato pie, a whole enamel washing-up bowl full of it, and ... mmm! ... lashings of home-made cider or lemonade to wash it down. You had to be quick to get your fair share: Owd Ned, the tramp who turned up every haymaking, was quite capable of eating and drinking the whole lot by himself; it was rumoured that, like a python, he could eat enough at one sitting to last a month. Afterwards he would repair to the barn and sleep like a log till daybreak, his ferocious snores affording him magical protection from the myriad rats which infested the farm, and which regularly killed and ate the cats brought in to deal with them.

Happy days ... though in some ways winter was just as good, especially around milking time in the late afternoon. The tiny shippon, dimly lit by a single swaying storm lamp, was another world, a womb without a view. Always warm and cosy thanks to the body heat of thirty cows, it bewitched the visitor with a thousand reassuring sounds: the gentle chewing of cud, the swishing of tails, the low-pitched mooing and moaning. The cows seemed to know the routine perfectly: you could see by the way they twitched their ears when Ramsbottom put down the three-legged milking stool and gripped the rusty old bucket between his cheesy knees. At first you heard rhythmic metallic squirts as the jets of milk hit the empty bucket, with an occasional one missing as one of the surviving cats was given a treat. Frequently there was the impressive sound of splattering manure as one of the huge beasts arched its tail. Then Samson or Speedy, taking it in turns, would struggle manfully with the enormous stiff brush in an attempt to propel the manure along the drainage channel and thence out through the gap under the door: it would then well back, serving as a natural draught excluder. Finally, job done, the two of them would sidle into the adjacent dairy and scoop up palmfuls of warm risen cream from the kits. Once there had been the terrible shock of bringing up a drowning rat, then seeing how Ramsbottom, rushing in to see what all the fuss was about, expertly seized the struggling animal by the tail and killed it by cracking it like a whip in the same action he used to lift it out.

Happy days ... alas, gone forever. With a deep sigh Samson slid off the gate and made the necessary detour, picking up the lane again two hundred yards further along. Progress was slow, because from time to time it was necessary to mount the wall in order to keep clear of treacherous ruts and puddles, some of them three or four feet deep - no joke for a non-swimmer. Then, no sooner had this difficult section been negotiated than a second detour was called for, this one around Sharrocks' Farm. There were two reasons for this precaution, both of them compelling. First, Sharrocks was a pig farmer. His pigs roamed the fields at will, and they were maneaters: an Italian prisoner-of-war allocated to the farm had been found dead after dinner by his returning fellow workers; the pigs had eaten half of him and all of his ham sandwiches. The second reason was the farmer's son: he was a 'bad lot' according to Mrs. Smalley, and 'certifiable', according to Mr. Smalley. Just to mention his name was a crime in the Smalley household. When Samson had once asked, in all innocence, 'Why is everyone so afraid of Shagger Sharrocks?' Mrs. Smalley had buffeted him around the ears unmercifully, the only sustained physical assault in ten years of conscientious mothering.

'Don't you ever mention that name again, not in this house at any rate,' she had warned, 'or else you'll get another crack - and I'll tell your father!'

Poor Shagger! It was so unfair ... he was blamed for everything: whenever anyone's hens stopped laying, a cow had a still-born calf or a hay rick caught fire, it was put down to him. Samson had always had a vague plan to get to know him, though there was no real hurry - certainly it would be silly to risk the success of the present mission by having his head kicked in, quite apart from the pigs problem.

On this occasion, as so often, the dangers proved to be

imaginary. Samson completed his detour without incident, without even hearing a grunt, and though slightly out of breath from holding his nose for so long, he soon started to make good progress - so good, in fact, that before he knew it he had reached Skeining Row, a terrace of tiny cottages belonging to Entwistles' dyeworks. For some reason (or possibly for no reason, it occurred to Samson) the cottages had been constructed with triangular front bays, so that the inhabitants, now all widows bar one, could only look out at forty-five degrees, up or down the lane. The widow occupying the first cottage had refused to submit to the alternatives offered, it seemed: she was very markedly wall-eyed and seemed to spend her entire day looking up and down the lane at the same time; meanwhile, she oscillated gently in a strategically placed rocking chair. The second widow was stranger still: summer or winter, rain or snow, she sat hunched on the front step, an unlit clay pipe upside-down in her mouth, and all the while she knitted away at a uniform pace, in spite of not having any yarn. Last, but certainly not least, as you drew near, the third widow watched malevolently - or should that be 'femalevolently', Samson wondered? - then as you passed the cottage she switched to the other window, her eyes burning holes in the back of your neck: in the unwise event that you stopped to return her stare she would rush out, waving a rusty toasting fork and screaming threats. During his last year at St. Peter's Samson had resolved to stand his ground if she tried to frighten him again, and either kick her shins or punch her on the nose. Day after day he had psyched himself up on approaching Skeining Row: day after day the widow had thwarted him by hiding away. It was something of an anti-climax to find out, one day in May, that she had died the previous November.

The most scary thing was, passing the last cottage. Five times the size of any of the others, it sported a T-shaped extension originally built for use as a breakaway Methodist chapel. After the war the building was taken over as a part-time outpost of the Monkey Town public library and as such would have generated no anxiety whatsoever. However, the librarian, a grim-faced and heavily bearded Yorkshireman with the extremely unlikely name of O'Evans, had a most sinister demeanour. It was rumoured that he was a struck-off doctor: certainly a good proportion of the books were on medical subjects. It was believed that he was trying to keep his hand in until allowed to work as a doctor again: why else would so many cats and dogs have disappeared from Old Guinea since the setting-up of the library, and why else would he wander round the reading room, long after closing time, wearing a white laboratory coat? On several occasions Samson had risked being nabbed and possibly dissected, just to find out whether the rumour had any substance. Each time, he had been disappointed: O'Evans would simply pace up and down, reading aloud from an open book which could very well have been a bible.

Christ Almighty! Samson suddenly had a most arresting thought: was anybody in Old Guinea sane? The thought was indeed so arresting that he stopped in mid-stride and began to topple over. Only by applying the mysterious 'law of averages' that Mr. Smalley invoked when totting up his losses on the afternoon's horse-racing could the question be answered reassuringly: someone, somewhere, must be sane - surely? Thus comforted, Samson picked himself out of the ditch, baled out his clogs and squelched on. There had been no threat at all from anyone in Skeining Row, and it was beginning to look as though this was a lucky day.

Though temporarily afflicted by a slight limp Samson broke into a happy trot. Progress was now rapid. Soon, the proximity of Entwistles' was announced by the presence of lint on the hedgerows, and by the distinctive sickly smells of bleaching and dyeing when Samson reached a Heath Robinson culvert carrying frothing, swirling effluent which mysteriously disappeared underground. The works was in two parts separated by the old toll road to T' Back o' Beyond, yet functionally connected by two catwalks and dozens of iron pipes about ten feet above the road. Jets of hissing steam leaking from the pipes were quickly subdued by a stiff breeze sucked along by the boiler furnaces fifty yards further along the road. Because of this breeze Samson had often, on rounding the corner from the lane, been blown onto a swaying weighbridge set into the road, creating a tremendous clattering tattoo of unco-ordinated clogs. Just occasionally - just to keep him on his toes, as it were - a sudden powerful gust of hot, acrid black smoke would shoot the other way, and it was largely thanks to this threat that his breath-holding ability was so well developed.

Usually, therefore, to go through the works was a challenging experience, but as against that there had been many a bitter winter's day on which the works provided a brief respite from the searching cold. Outside the boiler house huge heaps of coke were tipped, sometimes so large that they obstructed the road for hours on end, obliging Samson to clamber over them. The voracious boilers were fed by a team of four stokers who would briefly yank open the cast iron doors by means of long iron hooks, then frantically shovel coke into the white-hot interiors - not so much from love of hard work or money as from the realisation that, if they took their time, they would be roasted alive. Even out in the middle of the road, atop the coke heaps, Samson felt the heat to be unbearable, so that whenever he lingered there to thaw out his vitals before tackling the snowdrifts on the second half of the journey to school, he would revolve slowly but steadily, like an unplucked chicken on an invisible vertical spit, so as to get cooked as evenly as possible. His last action was always to open his coat front, facing the furnaces until he could take no more, then hurriedly do up the steaming cloth so as to trap as much heat as possible. Once, this habit had almost been his undoing: a heavy lump of white-hot coke shot out, following a loud explosion: hitting him in the stomach hard enough to wind him, it then burned through pullover and shirt, and badly scorched his thick woollen vest. Ever wary of a recurrence, Samson had taken to revolving with his eyes closed, a practice which, unfortunately, quickly led to dizziness.

Immediately beyond the works the cobbled surface of the toll road gave way to a new, ultramodern tarmacadam surface which attacked the steepening hills leading to T' Back o' Beyond in a perfectly straight line. Even at the age of nine, Samson had wondered if tarmacadam might be the greatest invention ever to come out of Scotland, and regardless of the answer he was impressed by the brilliant thinking that had brought together the happy combination of stones and tar. It even crossed his mind that perhaps the Scots had a special talent for bringing together pairs of apparently-incompatible materials - oatmeal and blood, for example, or mincemeat and egg. Perhaps his own favourite dish, rhubarb and custard, was also a Scottish invention?

Actually the road was every bit as inviting as a dish of rhubarb and custard, and you felt that, if you stepped on it, you would be transported effortlessly up the hill. Samson had never fancied this route, however, because just beyond the point where it steepened, it disappeared under an arch of blackened elms where a large colony of rooks set up a constant clamour. Beyond this was boggart country, and although Samson, deep down, did not believe in them he was prudent enough to avoid finding out if he was wrong. Accordingly, as always he scraped through a rickety barbed-wire fence, ignoring a prominent 'No Trespassers' sign to which a crudely-drawn skull and crossbones had been added in red and black paint, also an incorrectly-designed swastika in red, and headed resolutely across the rough ground rising above Entwistles' lodge. Soon he was within striking distance of St. Peter's.

By following a broken line of hedgerows and dry stone walls Samson described a rough semicircle around St. Peter's and eventually reached a large sloping field called Preacher's Meadow, home to an irascible donkey which many St. Peter's children had tried to ride, with varying degrees of failure - with one notable exception. *Ha!* The donkey was still there, searching as always for the odd blade of grass which had escaped being trodden into the mud. It looked up once and stared at Samson briefly, but there was not the slightest flicker of recognition on its part, much less any kind of greeting. Offended, Samson cocked a snook at the ill-mannered beast, and when that got no response he resorted to making long bacon at it. The donkey thereupon shook its outsize head ambiguously, as if trying to dislodge a troublesome fly, then pointedly turned its back on Samson and ambled off down the slope. Samson kicked a divot after it and resumed his journey. He was now so near to his objective that, if he had been approaching the coast, he would have been able to smell the sea.

The upper end of Preacher's Meadow was marked off by a low sandstone bluff, three or four feet high, worn away here and there by children's improvised slides. By scrambling up one of these slides Samson set foot on the higher field, the landmark known to locals as 'Tit Hill'. Samson, proud of his ornithological knowledge, had always found the name a bit odd; however, there had obviously been a huge tree at the summit, he realised (now, only a great fat stump remained) and he guessed that the tit or tits in question had nested there for generations. He would dearly have loved to know what kind of tits they were - blue, coal or great. Actually a knowledge of human anatomy would have been more useful to him: viewed from a distance the sawn-off stump resembled a turgid nipple on a firm and well-shaped young breast. Oval in cross-section when viewed from up close, the stump was hollowed out at the tapered end and solid at the wider end. It was easy to imagine it as a simple boat, possibly an ark, stranded at the top of the hill when flood waters receded. Anyway, ark or not, the hollow stump provided a perfect vantage point. Clambering aboard, Samson settled down to drink his fill of the intoxicating scene before him.

16. Snow White

Tit Hill overlooked a complementary identical hill set at a slightly higher level such that an early art critic, sampling the best of Old Guinea's landscapes from a magic carpet prior to the establishment of civilisation there, might have been put in mind of a reclining Reubens nude. Samson, as yet a stranger to the world of fine art, nevertheless experienced a similarly uplifting feeling as he settled down to contemplate this second hill. For there, nestling cosily together, were the three buildings around which so much of his life had thus far revolved.

The three buildings - church, pub and school - were restricted to the near side of this second hill because the far side had been quarried away to provide sandstone for the buildings, and for dry stone walls throughout the parish. Occupying the nipple position right on the edge of the quarry was St. Peter's Church, a curiously tall and narrow structure which, having been blackened by decades of pollution, protruded from the hill like a dirty thumb with an even dirtier extended nail, a monument as much to man's defiance of the elements as to God's glory. Slightly lower down, and to the church's right from Samson's vantage point, the Nine Bells clung awkwardly. It appeared to have been literally thrown together from cheap bricks, haphazardly whitewashed: now grimy and flaking, the whitewash drew attention to (rather than hid) the building's sinful purpose, like cheap make-up on a low-class prostitute. Finally, down in the cleavage, St. Peter's School nestled cosily, secure as a limpet, its cunning roof offering scant leverage to the often gale force winds, and yet efficiently draining the torrential rains into the bog at its rear. For this latter reason it was familiarly known not as 'St. Peter's', but as 'T' Swamps'.

Samson smiled fondly and his eyes moistened as he drank in the scene before him - so tranquil, with just a single solitary figure approaching the Nine Bells ... probably, from the looks of him, a lost hiker: one of those strange townspeople who wore shoes and who couldn't tell the difference between a longhorn and a leghorn - though admittedly, more likely to know about shoehorns. God! How different it would be when winter came and the shouts and screams of a hundred happy children brought the place to life again. September was always a lovely time after the boredom of the summer holidays once haymaking was over. There were new friends to be made and old routines to be re-established - settling the 'puncing order', for example. This was to the boys what the pecking order is to chickens, the parallel symbolised by the title 'T' Cock o' T' Swamps'. Like the better-known 'pecking order' described by Schjelderup-Ebbeover some 20 years earlier, it was established and maintained by threatening behaviour backed up by the willingness to fight. The only real difference stemmed from the fact that whereas chickens have beaks and spurs, the boys had knees and clogs. To keep lower-down boys in their place you would sneak up behind them as they were walking, and kick their raised ankle sideways, causing them to stumble.

If the victim retaliated in any way whatsoever he and his assailant were obliged by tradition to settle the matter in a gentlemanly way in accordance with simple well-established rules. Just beyond the Nine Bells, tucked away on a south-facing hillside, was a little cock-fighting amphitheatre with grass terraces rising over a circular patch of grass about eight feet in diameter, the whole screened from prying eyes by a ring of thick gorse bushes interwoven with brambles. The rivals had to take up position in the middle of the circle, and with arms outstretched, to hold each other's shoulders. Three stewards checked that everything was in order, then the chief of them shouted 'Three ... two ... one ... PUNCE!' At this each combatant, without removing his hands from the other's shoulders, kicked out at his shins. The boy who fell to the ground first, screaming - often helped on his way by a well-aimed knee to the groin as he started to crumple - was of course the loser. Contests were almost always fair, though occasionally a boy would kick on or just after the count of three, or remove his hands from the other's shoulders to gain some advantage. Such tactics were risky in the extreme, because the stewards' responsibility - and reward - was to jump on the cheat and kick him black and blue.

Establishing the new puncing order never took more than a week or so, and once that was out of the way and the new T' Cock o' T' Swamps enthroned, life's other little pleasures could be indulged in. Favourite amongst these were blackberrying on the undulating slopes beyond Windy End, and scrumping crab apples from the caretaker's orchard: then, belly distended, during the brief period before stomach cramps doubled you up, you could have a lovely game of marbles or conkers while the girls played hopscotch or skipping in the opposite corner of the playground. The season for such pleasures was, however, very short: before you knew where you were, the days had shortened, the clock had been put back, and fingers of freezing fog were clawing at the exposed slopes. This fog was far worse than the alternatives of drizzle, rain or sleet and at times really made you wonder if life was worth living. The fog was numbing and corrosive - it made your eyes red and streaming; it got up your nose and clogged your nostrils with something resembling lampblack; and if you were careless enough to breathe deeply it sent cruel stabbing pains through your vitals, leaving influenza, bronchitis and pneumonia in its wake. As the long, long Michaelmas term wore on, only one thing really kept you going - not Guy Fawkes night (because every scrap of wood was snapped up for domestic fires) or even Christmas (Santa had been very hard up since the war) - but anticipation of what was unarguably the greatest event in the Old Guinea social calendar, eclipsing even the Whit Monday fête: the New Year's pantomime.

T' Panto ... ha! It was much more than a pantomime: it was really a grand party, a general good time for one and all, a chance for people from the length and breadth of the parish to let themselves go and to experience, however fleetingly, a sense of community. Parents and grandparents; uncles and aunts; nephews, nieces and cousins once, twice or thrice removed; godfathers, stepfathers, foster-mothers and even mothers-in-law - these, every kind of in-law and out-law, raided their larders and struggled through freezing fog or blinding blizzards, often pressing into service sledges or farm carts or even the occasional pack horse. They came loaded down with home-cured ham and bacon; pork sausages, pickled trotters and tripe and cow heels; cakes, scones and oatmeal biscuits - and, everyone's favourites, parkin, flapjacks and mouthwatering treacle toffee. All of these, and more, were piled high on rickety trestle tables, ending up like barricades erected to delay an invasion by starving hordes.

The period of organised chaos was brief, half an hour at most. It lasted until the Headmaster had completed his speech of welcome and the Vicar had started to intone 'For what we are about to receive ...' At some point during this sentence the children (swollen in numbers by addition of past pupils and relatives, and waiting like unbroken horses constrained by a starting gate) erupted in a mass stampede. Scattering the unwary and the infirm, the children fell on the food like an army of foraging ants, devouring all in their path. Trestle tables were overturned, some broken; quantities of food and drink were thrown to the floor and trampled into a filthy mess whilst smaller children, on hands and knees, grovelled blindly amongst flailing limbs and fallen tables, scooping up food by the handful or even eating, like starving dogs, directly from the pitch-pine floorboards.

Within fifteen minutes at most, the orgy was over, the children back under control. The surviving trestle tables were moved to one end of the schoolhouse and pushed together to form a makeshift stage, then three lines of desks, turned back to front, were set up for use as seats by the grown-ups: the children stood around the walls or sat on the window cills. When everyone was more or less settled the stage was illuminated by two hurricane lamps, and any other lighting doused. Then the show began.

First came the recitations. Two or three local farmers, tongues loosened by copious draughts of Thwaites' Best Bitter, gave brief renderings of such perennial favourites as *T' Lancashire Rose* and *T' Blacksmith's Tale/Tail* against a barrage of prompts and catcalls. Though entirely lacking in artistic merit these performances provided a period of time in which the audience could settle down; then, it was time for a recitation with a difference, by one of Old Guinea's favourite sons, nonagenarian Ted Bradshaw, grandfather of the ill-fated Snotty. 'Grandad Brad', as he was affectionately known, was one of the few natives of the parish to have ventured outside of his own free will, having run away to sea at the age of eight. In the famous Battle of Jutland he had had his right ear and half his hair burned off. Small wonder then that his performance of the classic *The Boy Stood on the Burning Deck* had the stamp of authenticity: long before he had reached the end the sweat was standing out on your brow and you felt yourself sickened by the stench of burning flesh. After this dramatic *tour de force* someone else would give a rendering of the Norman Evans sketch *Over the Garden Wall*. Finally, topping the bill, a virtuoso vaudeville performance by the school caretaker, Dick Diggle. Diggle - ha! For three hundred and sixty-four days of the year the most miserable, sour-faced killjoy you could ever hope to avoid was for this one occasion transmogrified into a performer of such polish that, if you had had a seat, you would have felt as though you were sitting on the end of it.

Diggle's act always began with a rendering of Stanley Holloway's *Three Ha'pence a Foot*, which catalogued the epic battle of wills at the time of the biblical Flood between obstinate Bury shopkeeper Sam Oglethwaite and the penny-pinching Noah: the former clinging to the top of Blackpool Tower as the flood waters rose inexorably around him, and persisting in demanding the full asking price of three-halfpence a foot for his bird's eye maple (which Samson misunderstood as 'Bird's Eye Mabel' without this in any way diminishing his enjoyment): the latter, circling round and round the tower in increasing frustration, refusing to improve his offer. Next, a spell of nifty juggling with some empty beer bottles, just to warm the audience up. Finally Diggle cast his props into the audience and snatched up a three-string ukelele, and without pausing to tune up the instrument went straight into an up-tempo rendering of George Formby's immortal *When I'm Cleaning Windows*. You soon forgot that he didn't know half the words and strummed the same chord throughout, because of the fascinating way that his ferrets started writhing about in his sewn-up trouser leg, as if dancing in time to the music; the climax of this performance, a feat to rival even the supreme Buddhist challenge of clapping with one hand, a whole chorus whistled with one tooth. After this, the adults took a back seat. The lights were dimmed, shadowy scenery began to be scraped across the stage, and for one all-too-brief hour in an otherwise hostile calendar the whole world belonged to the children.

Samson always enjoyed the New Year's Eve buffet. Though well fed by local standards, with virtually unlimited eggs, porage, rhubarb and custard, he found the buffet fare refreshingly different. As far as the pantomime itself was concerned, however, he was normally apathetic. This was not because he lacked a sense of wonder (he did not) or because he felt superior (he did), but because for the past three years he had been cast in the same restrictive role, as the front end of the obligatory pantomime horse - purely because nobody else would share with Speedy. However, Samson did have a special reason to look forward to the last pantomime of his years at St. Peter's: it was *Snow White and the Seven Dwarfs*, and it starred the beautiful Rita. In spite of its theme being the understandably attractive one of a socially disadvantaged girl ending up marrying a handsome prince, *Snow White* had never before been attempted. This was entirely because of casting problems: there was of course no shortage of 'dwarfs': rather, the problem had been the lack of a suitable female lead. So, when the variety acts finished, Samson felt the tension mounting. He had not been present at dress rehearsals, since all that was required of him and Speedy, as in previous pantomimes, was to trot on stage when Miss Pollock launched into *Campdown Races*.

The hurricane lights were dimmed. Miss Pollock struck up *There's No Business Like Show Business,* and the first scene was under way. Samson, watching from the wings (Miss Pollock's classroom), strained his eyes to make out the single seated figure occupying centre stage - Rita? Well, it was ... then again, it wasn't: it was *a* Rita, but not *the* Rita ... more like a sack of potatoes ... yes, it was 'Big Tatty', the generously-proportioned Rita Tattersall. Samson felt a little cheated, but there was nothing he could do but wait. Miss Pollock broke off the opening refrain with an abrupt *glissando* and then launched straight away into *White Christmas*, thumping the keys as if trying to frighten a ghost away. Samson guessed that this was some kind of signal, and his interest revived. The music faded, the lights were dimmed further ... could this be the moment? *Could* it?? No, it wasn't: all that happened was that Big Tatty took out some knitting and began mumbling into it. At the same time, for no apparent reason (as far as Samson was concerned), white downy feathers started falling from the ceiling, like giant snowflakes. Samson, noticing that the onset of the 'snowstorm' coincided with fowl noises and sounds of shuffliing from up in the open rafters, peered up into the darkness and was just able to make out the silhouette of his one-time rival Jimmy Ashworth. It seemed an odd thing to be doing, now that Christmas was over, and it also struck Samson that Jimmy would have done far better to kill the chicken before plucking it.

Ah well .... not his business. He had work of his own to do: sorting out the sewn-up blankets into which he and Speedy would need to climb. The previous year, they had got themselves into a terrible tangle through failing to notice that the near-side leg was inside- out. The easiest thing was to pick the whole lot up and give them a good shake. God! How dusty they were!

Big Tat sneezed, twice: a quiet suppressed one, followed by a veritable explosion. '*Atchoo ... ATCHOOOOO!!!*' The second sneeze was fantastic - powerful enough to launch a thousand ships in a dead calm, and it reverberated throughout the building. Almost immediately, as if in reply, a third sneeze came from up in the rafters, followed by a loud shout; a body then crashed to the stage, closely followed by a half-naked chicken. The former lay immobile where it had landed; the latter careered offstage into the audience - half running, half flying. The panto was interrupted for a short while to allow Ashworth to be dragged off stage, and the chicken to be recaptured. Samson went back to the blankets and found that Speedy had already climbed inside. Further shaking was therefore out of the question, and a slight change of plan was called for: far better to have a little sport than to endure the tedium of further waiting. Samson accordingly set to work poking Speedy through the blankets - slowly and methodically at first, quite happy to take his time and save the best digs till later, then finally reduce him to a gibbering wreck. Unfortunately, just when Samson was getting into the swing of things, to put together some really good one-twos and one-two-threes in place of the opening routine of individual digs and pokes, he was distracted by a loud burst of cheering and applause. Rita? At last? At last! Yes ... a vision, an apparition ... perfection itself ... a perfect miniature lady dressed in incredible finery so perfect that she might have been plucked from a millionaire's Christmas tree. Every detail was special. The long, snug-fitting high-heeled boots were of exquisite black calfskin, with elaborate cross-lacing all the way from the arch of the foot to where they disappeared under her multi-tiered black satin dress, with its wasp-waist emphasised by an ornate gold belt and its bodice trimmed with white lace and spattered with dancing sequins. A fantastic stole (probably porcupine skin, Samson surmised) graced the lady's proud neck and helped set off the huge flashing earrings. Yet all of these touches were well and truly eclipsed by the ultimate finishing touch, the elaborate icing on a rich fruit cake: the hat. For the hat was a veritable work of art - so much so, Samson felt, that if the lady had been wearing nothing else, she would still have created a sensation. Actually it was more aviary than hat. Essentially it consisted of a gnarled forked branch in which was wedged a huge birds' nest: on this cavorted a pair of richly-plumed birds the size of large tits - the original inhabitants of Tit Hill, Samson wondered? One of the birds hung precariously upside-down, its head cocked coyly to one side, while its mate attacked a delicious-looking bunch of large juicy berries which Samson, recalling an illustrated copy of Aesop's fables, recognised as grapes. God! The boots ... the dress .. . the stole ... the earrings ... the hat ... . each, in its own right, was worthy of prolonged applause - but it was the way the parts complemented each other to create a rnore-than-perfect whole that threatened to bring the house down. It was magnificent ... it was wonderful ... it was unbelievable ... it was spellbinding .... and, Samson realised with a start when the lady turned towards him and lifted her short veil to reveal an exquisitely-made-up face - it was Snorky Horrocks!

Snorky Blooming Horrocks ... hmph! Stone the flipping crows! Samson, unable to tear himself away from this fantastic creation, involuntarily raised his right arm and pointed at her/him, and at the same time inched forward until, unwittingly, he was on stage and in full view of the audience. The lady, sensing his approach, turned round, lifted her veil again, tilted her head back slowly, then gave Samson a wink. It was not a wink of the conspiratorial variety, with a silent message such as 'Don't let on', but the ultimate in brazen flirtatious advances - and if there were any doubt on that score, the accompanying blown kiss dispelled it immediately. Samson coloured up and retired in total confusion, tripping over his own feet as he scuttled backwards. The audience laughed merrily, adding to his discomfiture. He shuffled back into the dressing room, the laughter still ringing in his ears. He felt utterly confused, as though he were seeing things, and he had a desperate need to get back on stage and take a second look. If only .... of course! With scarcely a moment's hesitation Samson clambered into the blankets, goaded Speedy into action, and in this guise returned to the stage. A ripple of applause greeted the horse's appearance: it (the applause) died quickly, because the lady was now looking into a mirror and speaking:

'Mirror, mirror on the wall, who is the fairest of us all?'

The audience's reaction was mixed: half, vehement boos and hisses; half, enthusiastic approval.

'You are, you are, you are,' her supporters chanted rapturously, and the lady preened herself so proudly that she might have been a queen. Next she turned royally, more or less floated across the stage in the process of making her exit, then at the last moment she raised her cane and gave the horse a tremendous whack across the hind quarters.

'Giddy up there!' she shouted. 'Giddy up!'

Samson was almost knocked off balance by Speedy's sudden lurch, and needed every ounce of his phenomenal self-control to stand motionless while the stricken hindquarters threshed around like a harpooned whale. Muffled laughter penetrated the blankets. Samson, to his credit, realised how funny it must have looked to the audience, but any amusement on his part was short-lived in the extreme - stillborn, in fact. The cause of this abortion was chemical: foul, noxious fumes which quickly filled up the inside of the horse, forcing their way into every nook, cranny and extremity. Samson, digging down to a new tranche of self-control when a desperate urge to baulk threatened to overwhelm him, steadfastly held his breath, ground his teeth, then jerked round with explosive force, smashing his elbow into Speedy's midriff so violently that, even though bone met bone, the elbow seemed to go right through its target. The action was theatrical: the effect, dramatic. The back end of the horse collapsed - not in the dignified, defiant style that a well-bred cavalry charger might have affected, but ignominiously, folding up like an overloaded clothes horse.

Strangely. this contemptible behaviour was greeted not by renewed laughter but by an explosion of applause. The whole building reverberated as the audience rose to its feet and jumped up and down. Samson, utterly confused, strained to peer with watery eyes through the limp strands of thick wool which had survived from the original mane. He was staggered by what he saw. It was another member of the fair sex: a *real* girl, this time. She was beautiful, incredibly beautiful ... so beautiful, in fact, that Samson stared at her so hard that he began to sway, and might easily have toppled over. She stood stock still, reginal, statuesque, a living doll with lovely pink cheeks and with crimson lipstick which made the most of her Cupid's-bow lips. Framing the picture, gorgeous tresses, black and silken, cascaded over her shoulders and tickled her bottom, shimmering as she moved. Lightning struck for the second time in the same place: Samson's brain. It was Rita! And she was Snow White!

From this point on the pantomime was real, and Samson watched entranced as the wonderful story unfolded. The audience too was enthralled, spellbound, frequently applauding or shouting advice and warnings: 'Don't open t' door! .... 'Be'ind thee, be'ind -! ... 'it 'er wi' thi 'andbag!' And so on.

Only in the final scene did their mood deteriorate. This was when Snorky came on and performed a most unladylike clog dance in boots. The audience hissed and booed themselves breathless.

Samson struggled back to the changing room, dragging Speedy's dead weight behind him. Once out of the blankets he grabbed hold of one corner and gave a tremendous tug, with the result that Speedy rolled out, coming to rest lying face downwards. Samson dug his toe under Speedy's ribs and rolled him over. The poor boy looked half dead: his breathing was rapid and shallow; his complexion deathly pale except for some nasty purplish blotches and bluish lips; his tongue swollen, protruding, lifeless; his eyes, when at last they re-opened, crossed and unfocussed. Otherwise he seemed fine. In fact, after a few good slaps he recovered sufficiently to start moaning like a sick animal. Samson picked him up, gave him a fireman's lift until they were out of the school and across the playground, then set him down and frogmarched him to the church and thence into the graveyard. The two of them sat there for a while, cooling down and taking great grateful gulps of lovely frosty air. Meanwhile, down below, a stream of tiny lights flowed from the schoolhouse, splitting into three subsidiary streams. The individual lights gradually dimmed and coalesced before merging with the general gloom. Samson, watching them contemplatively but without any specific thoughts on his mind, eventually realised that he and Speedy were completely alone together.

Alone? Alone??? Samson laughed. Normally, he realised, being alone in the churchyard late at night would have given him goose pimples, and even an imagined rat would have sent shivers through him. But on this occasion he felt different. They were alone, but they weren't alone: somewhere up there was the great bear that Tomcat had once told him about, and the man in the moon (invisible at the moment, because the moon was still fairly new), and God himself, invisible by nature. Also of course the graves around were populated with dead souls, as much at peace with the world as he was. Idly, Samson read inscriptions on nearby gravestones. At first he was deeply impressed by the quality of the spelling (there was scarcely a mistake on any of them), but then suddenly felt that it was a bit ridiculous to go to such lengths, given that the messages were all to the deceased. How much better, he mused, if the messages could have been passing the other way, from the dead to the living, but of course ...

God! At that moment Speedy shifted slightly, revealing the inscription on the huge tombstone behind him: the tomb of one Alderman John Farrow, who had died at the ripe old age of sixty-six. The message was short, sweet and very much to the point, and Samson memorised it word for word, in a single pass:

> Where'er Thou Be
> Let the Wind Go Free
> For it Was the Wind
> That Kill-èd Me

Thus encouraged, Samson broke wind in no uncertain manner. The explosive noise, ripping through the still night air and reverberating magically amongst the gravestones, brought Speedy to his senses: he grunted, looked quizzically at Samson, then made to get up and go. Samson waited a few seconds for the dangerous gases to clear, then took out his jam jar and, with great care, lit the enclosed candle stub which his mother had kindly allocated for the return journey.

The long trek home passed off as in a dream, with the two friends communicating on a mystical plane by breaking wind. It occurred to Samson that it might be possible to communicate with any animal, or plant, or even lakes and mountains, if only you could learn the other's language - come down to its level, so to speak. Perhaps God's secret was that He alone could speak every language in creation, human or otherwise - that, like a celestial wireless receiver, He could tune in to any wavelength. A sudden rumble of distant fireworks, which Samson mistook for thunder, suggested to him that God, seated on his magnificent throne in the limitless heavens, had heard their thoughts and sent his acknowledgement. Perhaps ....

Samson's brief dabble in mysticism was brought to an abrupt end when his candle went out. For the remainder of the journey the two friends stumbled blindly onwards, guessing the way, colliding with stone walls, getting tangled in barbed wire and falling helplessly into ditches. It was not until Speedy had been safely delivered to the reassuring smells of Ramsbottoms' Farm, leaving Samson to continue alone in the general direction of Foxgloves Hall, that Samson recognised what a strange state he was in. And it was not until he went sprawling for the umpteenth time, and fell headlong into a stinking ditch which he had known was there and could so easily have avoided, that he finally accepted what he should have realised weeks earlier: he had fallen head over heels in love.

17. White Snow

Like winter wheat, Samson's love for Rita germinated precociously but was slow to develop thereafter. It was, it turned out, a very bad time to fall in love. Within hours of his return home from the pantomime the notorious winter of '47 was to seize Old Guinea in its paralysing grip. When Samson collapsed into his little bed, dog-tired but happy as a Cheshire cat, he felt the world was a different place. His whole body aglow, he snuggled down under the heaped bedding, closed his eyes tighter than tight, and set about conjuring up images of intimate interludes with his beloved. Unfortunately the magic failed to work: time and time again it proved impossible to get Rita on her own, away from spying eyes and wagging tongues. When his persistence did finally pay off the results were still frustrating: they walked together down an interminable leafy lane, their hands brushed together and a thousand things needed to be said, but cissy feelings welled up and not a single sentence could be put together.

When Samson awoke, the world really was a different place, chill and hostile. He felt as though he had been reduced to a mere skeleton, held together by tightly-stretched skin in imminent danger of splitting as he shivered uncontrollably. His bones and his skin tingled maddeningly, except for the end of his nose, which felt numb: carelessly checking this last condition with a probing forefinger, he broke one icicle just below his left nostril, and loosened the shorter one which had formed in the other nostril; fortunately, a vigorous snort was all it took to clear both nostrils, upon which the icicles tinkled on falling into the chamber pot strategically placed on the floor, on the blind side of the bed.

So far, so good ... gingerly showing an arm and a leg, Samson hoisted the blind, and shuddered. The usual morning mist was absent: all that could be seen was, a grim slab of black cloud low overhead, blocking the morning light as effectively as if it had been the roof of a tomb. Even as Samson peered out, and continued to shudder, snow began to fall - snow so heavy, that within seconds the sky had become invisible, replaced by a flickering white wall.

For seven days and seven nights the snowstorm continued unabated, so that it seemed as though God had decided to create the world anew - to start again with a clean sheet, as it were. When the snowstorm finally ceased, as suddenly as it had begun, it could be seen to have formed a blanket at least six feet thick: the rhubarb and gooseberries were completely obliterated, while only gentle mounds showed where the rhododendrons were. More than anything else the world now resembled a Christmas card conceived on a gigantic scale - and as such, it was near perfect: quiet, peaceful, beautiful, magical. Only one detail was missing: the obligatory cock robin - in its place, round by where only the tallest brussels sprouts protruded, was a very dead thrush. It appeared to have fallen out of the sky, or at least, to have been thrown out of an upstairs window - it lay on its back, tilted slightly to its left, partially embedded in snow: its right foot was extended skywards, creating a strong impression that its owner had died in a valiant attempt to block the falling snow and so to avoid being buried alive. Samson stared at the poor bird for ages, in deep contemplation. Although the thrush (and almost certainly it was *the* thrush) had, during its lifetime, struck a rich variety of statuesque poses, none of them matched death for dramatic effect.

The scene, likewise, was short-lived. Within minutes of the sky's clearing, a breeze sprang up: it stiffened by the minute, and soon a gale was blowing, whipping up huge clouds of powdered snow. At the same time the temperature plummeted anew. Even as Samson stared in amazement at this second transformation, his hurried breath froze rock-hard on the window pane, and before he could scrape it off, the view was progressively obscured by snow building up on the outside. It was as though the artist, annoyed by a single wrong detail of the original picture, had petulantly splashed white paint over the entire canvas - or perhaps, more decorator than artist, he simply wanted nobody to witness the work in progress until it was complete, and sloshed whitewash everywhere.

The temperature was soon sub-sub-zero, on any scale: Old Guinea became a province of Siberia. Samson, notwithstanding a tough constitution, well case-hardened by previous winters, and being generously anointed with goose grease, felt the cold strike through to the marrow. His priority, on diving into bed each evening, was to keep his body ticking over - to keep the motor running, as it were, lest it should seize up. Within minutes of tucking himself in he would be shivering himself stupid, teeth chattering like maladjusted tappets, and knees knocking like worn-out big ends. Each morning he woke up tepid, the hot water bottle frozen if it had strayed too far from his body, and with icicles sticking out of his nostrils as if, he thought, he were a two-legged (and very skinny) walrus. He found that it was fatal to shift his position, even by the merest fraction of an inch: he learned, instead, to alternately tense and relax his entire body, rhythmically and with increasing intensity, until the itching of childblanes announced that the thick, slow blood had penetrated again to his extremities. Then it was time to count 'One .. . two ... three!', repeating this perhaps a dozen times before tricking his other self into leaping out of bed, tumbling downstairs, throwing on trousers and pullovers over his pyjamas, then filling up to the brim with steaming, wholesome, life-sustaining porage. Then, by huddling in front of the fire for the next twelve hours (with a refill of porage every two hours or so) it was just about possible to build up enough body heat to face another night with a reasonable expectation of not 'waking up dead' - a turn of phrase which had been given a new resonance of late..

Of course, Old Guinea winters were always hard, and attendance at St.Peter's did nothing to make life easier. If you could afford underwear, and if your mother took her duties seriously, then as early as October you would be smothered in goose grease and sewn into your underwear until the following spring, with just a small flap, secured with press studs, for essential one-way communication with the outside world. It was a season of balaclava helmets and wellingtons, and - for the better-off - two or more pairs of thick woollen socks. You frequently had to struggle through snowdrifts eight or ten feet deep, and as a matter of necessity you memorised where the walls were so that you could walk along the tops of them wherever possible. At last - late, exhausted and deep-frozen - you would sit down heavily on the bare plank schoolroom floor, and help each other to remove wellingtons from chafed legs and childblaned feet. It was then a tremendous relief to peel off your sodden socks (no matter how careful you were, snow always managed to find a way down your wellies) and leave them on the pipes. The next problem was, splinters in your behind - something to take your mind off the excruciating pain as the blood fought its way back to your various extremities, and to pass the time while waiting for the milk to thaw.

Heating at St. Peters was rudimentary: just a single, ancient coke-burning stove in the middle of the schoolhouse, so that throughout the winter the sliding partitions between the classrooms had to be left open for the warmed air to circulate. The heating took some time to take effect, so morning assembly was designed to get the circulation going. Gentle songs such as *All Things Bright and Beautiful* were put under wraps until spring, to make way for more rousing numbers such as *Onward Christian Soldiers*, so that everyone could stamp their feet in time to the martial beat. It was only after guzzling two or three bottles of iced milk at break time, finding your socks (if they hadn't been stolen by Catholics) and rushing out into the playground to pummel someone, or to pelt some poor unsuspecting idiot with snowballs formed around lumps of clinker, that you began at last to feel warm. From mid-morning the stove really began to make its presence felt. The fumes were powerfully soporific, so that by going-home time you were as drowsy and cold-immune as if you had been chewing coca leaves.

Even in '47, the worst winter for two hundred and thirty-five years (Mrs. Smalley said - but how could she know, Samson wondered?) it was unthinkable to miss a single day's education. So, the first day of the new term, Samson stepped out of the landing window to begin his journey, all downstairs doors and windows being blocked by snowdrifts. He was wrapped up like a mummy, in layer upon layer of woollen clothes, communication with the outside world being limited to narrow slits in his balaclava, roughly corresponding to his eyes, nose and mouth. For extra protection the exposed areas had been smeared with Vaseline. In spite of these precautions Samson was unprepared for the shock of the bitter cold. The air was incredible, like he had never known it: it was clear and clean and sparkling, and it felt brittle. His first careless inhalations resulted in cruel tickling in the nostrils, then sharp stabbing pains in his lungs, while the snorts of exhaled breath emerged in visible plumes, so that if he had not been wearing ear muffs as well as the balaclava, he might have heard the resulting tiny ice crystals tinkle as they felt onto the rock-hard snow at his feet.

There was no sign of Speedy or any of the Ramsbottoms: perhaps, snugly bedded down with the animals, they had overslept. The realisation that he would have to make the journey to school alone, without anyone to pummel, stiffened Samson's backbone. He straightened up, put his best foot gingerly forward (walking on the tops of concealed walls was precarious at the best of times) and was soon striding out manfully, even stamping his feet down on the frozen snow in time to *The Road to Mandalay*, *Soldiers of The King*, and anything else he could half-remember. Determined to enjoy the fantastic scenery to the full, he forced his eyes wide open: the cold hurt them and made them stream - but it was worth it. Here and there the snow had been almost completely stripped from the frozen ground, but in other places it had piled up into spectacular drifts, fifty or a hundred feet high in places. The surfaces of these huge ridges had been whipped into a ripple effect and thrown into relief by blackened edges, reminding Samson of a lemon meringue that Mrs. Smalley had once made. It had proved unfit for human consumption, probably through having been made from eggs preserved in water-glass throughout the war, so she had kept it in a cupboard 'in case of unexpected visitors': there it had gradually gathered dust. Eventually a mouse, presumably a very hungry one, had started to devour it, but it paid a heavy price: its life. It had then itself been eaten, presumably by another mouse, so that only a few bits of skin and bone, and most of the tail, were left beside the otherwise empty meringue dish to tell the tale. An alternative explanation, Samson realised, was that the first mouse had not died of food poisoning, but had been ambushed by the second one while tucking into the meringue. He would have given anything to know which explanation was the correct one.

Beyond the slumbering, sighing bulk of Entwistle's, and its frozen lodge and mill race, the rising ground offered some truly surreal sights. In the far distance the mills of Monkey Town smouldered like burnt-out ruins covered in foam. And when Samson continued on his way he was accosted by a forty-foot-tall ghost, perfect in every detail. It loomed up above him, arms outstretched, its all-white clothes hanging in ample folds. Once Samson had stopped shaking, he saw that it had been formed by snow drifting over two bowed-down trees, their main branches outstretched like arms - or wings, even. Nevertheless he took the precaution of turning round many times before reaching the vicinity of St. Peter's, and only truly relaxed when the ghost was out of sight. St. Peter's was not visible as such, nor was the Nine Bells, but their positions were easy to work out with reference to the church spire, which protruded from the drifts quite clearly. The school itself looked like a crudely-constructed giant igloo, and when Samson got closer he saw that the boys' and girls' entrances were completely blocked, and that arrivals were crawling into the building through a tunnel which presumably led to a window -? It did.

From the inside, the school felt very strange. It was very effectively soundproofed by the thick covering of snow, and illuminated by an eerie diffuse light, which had to be augmented with candles. By the time your eyes adapted to the semi-darkness they were reddened and smarting from the smoke from the stove (presumably the chimney was blocked with snow). Keeping-warm exercises lasted until mid-morning, when the last stragglers arrived: the exercises involved marching round and round to the tune of *The Grand Old Duke of York*, hands on the shoulders of the person in front. Then it was time for 'ice cream' - the top of the milk, frozen solid and protruding an inch or so from the neck of the bottle, with the cardboard top as a substitute wafer. It could all have been lots of fun - but not for Samson: day after day, week after week, many children failed to turn up. One of them was

Rita. What a thrill it would have been to go behind her in the crocodile marches, nose in her hair. How could life be so cruel?

There was little opportunity for formal education, other than a bit of mental arithmetic from time to time, or an oral spelling test: the light was too poor. In any case, after the morning break the twenty or so oldest boys had to be sent out to meet the dinner lorry, and after helping push it up the long hill that skirted Preacher's Meadow, to form a human chain to pass the dishes down the short steep slope, leading back down to the school. By the time dinner had been wolfed down, and the utensils returned to the lorry, it was more or less time to pack up and go home.

For most of the children the difficulties in the way of serious learning - spelling, handwriting and sums - did not mean that they were simply marking time: far from it. The lack of opportunities for academic progress was more than made up for by the unprecedented opportunities for improvement in other areas. Creativity was given full rein in the construction of snowmen and igloos, the environs of St. Peter's coming to resemble a mad confectioner's garden, one overpopulated with crudely-fashioned gnomes, then the whole buried under tons of sparkling icing sugar. The making of countless snowballs contributed to the development of motor skills essential for the execution of many adult occupations, and the frequent snowball fights not only taught the participants something about the laws of physics (accuracy could be improved by throwing the snowballs ever harder, and even further by forming them around lumps of clinker), but also social skills such as identifying one's enemies in the confusion of battle, and always protecting one's rear.

But it is perhaps tempting to make too much of the opportunities for learning. Above all, of course, it was simply fun - except for a small minority of killjoys, and for Samson. Nothing could begin to compensate for Rita's continuing absence. Day after day, Samson incessantly patrolled the rising ground in the area through which she would be forced to come to school, but to no avail. By late morning, all hope gone, he would mope and mooch alone, shunning the others. Eventually he could stand the tension no longer, and took to skating on the thick ice covering the Hell Hole, a flooded mine shaft about a quarter of a mile from the schoolhouse. It was not called the 'Hell Hole' for nothing: it had a number of sinister properties, and was bottomless. Over the years it had claimed a considerable number of victims, both human and animal, and none of those who had fallen in - or thrown themselves in, for that matter - had ever emerged to tell the tale: the hole simply swallowed them up ... and yet in warm weather, metal objects such as bicycles and bedsteads somehow floated on the forbidding, oil-smeared surface. For the time being, however, the covering of ice was inches thick - feet even, perhaps - and the only hint of what might lie below the surface was a pair of bicycle handlebars which protruded from the surface like the crumpled horns of a drowned cow.

Samson's motives for risking his life in this treacherous spot were complex: certainly there were times when he wished that the ice would crack open like a gigantic maw, and that he would be swallowed by the icy water, to disappear forever and without trace; at the same time he had the quiet, grim satisfaction of the notoriety which his foolhardy behaviour soon brought him. Unfortunately, by the time Rita returned to school his daredevil exploits had to be abandoned. Having switched from wellingtons to clogs in the pursuit of skating excellence, he suffered a cruel twist of fate. The problem was that the snow trodden underfoot tended to compact under the bottoms of his clogs, perhaps held in place by the clog irons. Within a mile or two it was possible to gain three or four inches in height. However, the compacted layer of snow had a nasty habit of breaking off suddenly and without warning, but only from one clog. Thus it was that Samson came to sprain his right ankle severely. The problem was not so much the pain that he had to endure for weeks thereafter, but the fact that he was compelled to limp along like a real cripple. In the circumstances he chose to keep out of Rita's way: he could just about stand everyone else's taunts, but he would not have been able to cope with hers.

As the appalling weather conditions dragged on throughout February and March even the hardiest souls were worn down, and it was only by having something really special to look forward to that any kind of spirits could be kept up. Fortunately the death toll in Old Guinea rose much above the normally high winter average, with consequent benefits for the church collection box. In normal times the takings found their way quite smoothly to the Nine Bells, and there was no excessive build-up. The only problem was that the then vicar, The Reverend 'Tomcat' Tompkinson, would often need to be carried from the snug to the pulpit. However, in these abnormal times the funds far exceeded even his spending capacity, and he devoted the surplus to the funding of a day at the seaside for the entire top class.

For Samson the timing of the trip was perfect: his ankle was almost back to normal, and stories of his exploits at the Hell Hole had obviously filtered through to Rita, who had begun to give him the glad eye. With careful planning and a bit of luck, he reasoned, it should be possible, in the course of a full day's outing, to separate her trom the herd, get her on her own and make clear to her his undying love.

It had almost been worth the wait.

18. New Horizons

After a seeming eternity the great day arrived. Old Guinea's parishioners were of course never in a position to take a holiday - looking after animals three hundred and sixty-five days a year saw to that, quite apart from the dire shortage of funds - but almost everyone knew someone, or knew someone who knew someone, who had been to Blackpool. Notwithstanding the welter of contradictory rumours and opinions - it rained incessantly, it never rained; it was cold and windy, it was warm and sultry; the streets were paved with gold, the beaches were ankle-deep in shit - one thing was beyond dispute: the tower was the eighth wonder of the world, eclipsing even the Eiffel tower (envisioned by Samson as the eighth wonder of the world, and so not unreasonably understood as the 'Eyeful' tower).

Not wishing to appear over-eager on the great day (already, at this early age, he was showing a predilection for 'playing it cool'), Samson dilly-dallied on the way to school: further delays resulted from his needing to urinate every few minutes, though all he managed to produce each time was the merest dribble. When he reached the Rock of Gibraltar he broke his journey. Deep down he was looking forward to seeing the sea for the first time in his life, but the pleasurable anticipation was tinged with anxiety. On impulse he turned off the track and stepped onto 'T' Rock', and gazed out across the waters of Entwistles' lodge. A gentle breeze had sprung up, and he watched the little waves with interest, enjoying the sound of them lapping over the shore. The sea had to be more or less the same, he decided - bigger, probably, and perhaps with bigger pike in it, but ... detecting an unfamiliar sound, he turned to look in the direction of St. Peter's, and was rewarded by his first sight of the charabanc which would soon be whisking him and his classmates to an earthly paradise - if he didn't miss it.

In spite of the need for alacrity Samson paused a little while more, to drink in the scene down at the school gates. The charabanc had barely drawn to a halt before it was besieged by a heaving mass of jostling children. At that distance they looked like so many ants, and he was reminded of an experience two or three years previously, when he had been walking behind his mother on the way home from a bring-and-buy sale, carrying a jar of home-made raspberry jam. Slipping off the rubber band and cellophane cover, and plunging his fingers deep into the mouth-watering contents, he had let the jar slip from his grasp: it must have landed right next to an anthill, for before he could pick it up and attempt some running repairs, the entire jar was swarming with the beastly creatures.

Quickly forcing a final wee, and pausing further only to give his little member a couple of extra shakes for luck, he broke into a lively canter and arrived at school in time to join the tailenders. Unable to see Rita, he was very relieved to note that her name was checked off on Miss Pollock's list. Part of him would dearly have loved to share a seat with Rita, but at the same time he was relieved that there was no opportunity to do so: apart from all the tongue-wagging that would have resulted, he was totally at a loss as regarded what to say to her. So, he was happy to bide his time, even though it meant sitting next to Speedy.

Every seat on the charabanc was taken up - all thirty children from the top class, plus Miss Pollock as teacher-in-charge (Mr. Thoroughgood being unwell) and of course the man who had made it all possible, Tomcat - an almost unrecognisable Tomcat, resplendent in every detail from his patent leather shoes to a brand new homburg, by way of an equally new pin-stripe suit. Miss Pollock, unfortunately, looked correspondingly dowdy: rangy, skeletally thin and academically bent, she had contrived to make the worst of herself by throwing on a threadbare old coat, several sizes too big, so that she looked rather like a sack of potatoes, but with half the tubers missing.

After a final headcount the charabanc set off, lurching and juddering wildly as the driver avoided, with mixed fortunes, the snow and icy patches, and the numerous boulders and potholes. It was a cold day, with a biting east wind, and once they were on the main road the windows had to be slammed shut. By the time they had reached Bolton the windows were completely steamed up, and it was only possible to see out by constantly wiping away the condensation, or - the preferred option - clearing little oval patches corresponding to the eyes, nose and mouth. From the outside it must have looked as if the charabanc was carrying a cargo of ghosts.

The three-hour journey passed without serious incident. Of course, three or four children were violently sick, and two others cried throughout (one having left her sandwiches at home, the other from missing his mum), but the prevailing mood was buoyant, to say the least. Inevitably there was some fighting, but it was good-natured: other surplus energy was channelled into endless choruses of *For He's a Jolly Good Fellow* - for Tomcat's benefit, of course. Once the initial excitement had died down the journey became very peaceful indeed. The fug was decidely soporific, and many of the children dozed off. Snorky, undeterred, attempted to entertain those around him with a variety of conjuring tricks, and with peeks into his amazing 'collide-o-scope' - a long cardboard tube, at the end of which, when it was turned, brightly-coloured shapes collided with one another to create an infinite variety of fascinating patterns.

Suddenly they were there - more or less, anyway. The faithful charabanc, which thus far had chugged along with only the occasional stop to refill a leaking radiator, shuddered to a halt at the beginning of the Golden Mile. Those who had stayed awake scrambled to open the windows - both for some much-needed fresh air, and to be able to see out. There were gasps of astonishment all round.

Samson was brought out of his reverie not so much by the abruptness of the breakdown, or the magnificence of the sights all around, but by the seashore odours wafting in through the opened window above him, as invigorating in their way as whiffs of the finest smelling salts that money could buy. He had an inkling as to what it must be like to be Rupert Bear, one minute enjoying afternoon tea back home with his mum, the next minute arriving in China, or some equally far-flung and exotic place. Then, as he filled his eager lungs with the intoxicating aromas he was further roused by the raucous cries of seagulls which soared and swooped here, there and everywhere, one moment hanging motionless above the surfline; the next, wheeling away on an invisible breeze. Though Samson had seen seagulls before - during prolonged gales they were routinely blown over from Blackpool - to see them in their element was a revelation.

The hyper-excited children spilled out onto the pavement like maggots tipped from a fisherman's tin can: there, they gazed, they gawped, they gasped, they twisted this way and turned that way as one wondrous sight after another claimed their attention: the terror-inspiring roller coaster, the apparently limitless sands (in the far far distance, they merged almost imperceptibly with a subtle mist) and the myriad brash, bright and noisy entertainments.

'Stick together, everybody! Stick together!' Miss Pollock called out anxiously, and the writhing knot of maggots instantly became a shoal of minnows, darting this way and that for no discernible reason - as if, contained within a tank, they were frightened by their own reflections.

Perhaps alone of the children, Samson needed time to adjust. He wandered round to the front of the charabanc, where the driver had the bonnet raised and was inspecting the radiator. Twin plumes of steam hissed out, putting Samson in mind of a dragon, thereby confirming the magical nature of the experience. Then suddenly he caught sight of Rita - all of her, from top to toe -, and his heart missed several beats. She looked so, so beautiful. Her hair - probably her most eyecatching feature - cascaded more glossily than ever around her proud, reginal shoulders. She was without coat or cardigan, and a burst of bright sunshine helped show off her gingham dress to maximum advantage: the coloured squares were of a stunning mauvy-pink colour, and the fabric itself was either new, or had been meticulously laundered. Her wonderful athletic legs tapered to the shapeliest of ankles, set off by new brilliant white short cotton socks, and on her feet she wore classy patent leather shoes, simple but stylish, rather like the most elegant of slippers, with a slender strap across the arch of the foot. Samson, as so many times before, found Rita's beauty overwhelming at first glimpse, and as if reacting to an excessively bright light shone into his eyes, he recoiled as he caught her eye; then he mingled with the crowd. Little by little he relaxed, contemplating how to spend the sixpence which he had been given for the outing, over and above the regular threepence a week pocket money. He tried to imagine what toffee apples tasted like, and cockles, and hot dogs. He desperately wanted to buy Rita something - anything - but the circumstances didn't seem right, and anyway he had convinced himself that he couldn't afford anything that would do her justice. When, however, he found a brand new penny on the pavement his self-deception was exposed: the coin went straight into a telescope. He was somewhat surprised to find that the telescope did not help him to see further; that instead, it made things look nearer. Nevertheless his pennyworth had a powerful effect on him, stirring an unfamiliar longing, as if he were a recently-hatched turtle, feeling the irresistible pull of the mysterious ocean.

Samson experienced a few moments of panic when he realised that he had got separated from the others, but he was fortunate in being able to pick them out from the gathering crowds as they descended to the beach. Then for the next two or three hours everyone, even Samson, plunged into a seemingly limitless choice of activities: building sand castles, burying Speedy, playing rounders or cricket, or simply mooching around examining the extraordinary variety of flotsam and jetsam, everything from strands of seaweed and dried-up jellyfish to lengths of frayed rope, and splintered planks with intriguing lettering burned onto them. And of course, sand everywhere: inside your clogs, between your toes, in your eyes, in your egg-and-cress sandwiches, in your teeth ... it was almost a relief to be obliged to share them with Speedy, who had come with neither sandwiches nor money. Tired of being pestered for more, Samson handed over the last three rounds and wandered off towards the sea, and when he reached the water's edge he fell into a trance. The horizon puzzled him deeply: what could possibly lie beyond it? Was the world really round (in which case the water would drain away in a spectacular torrent that would shame any ordinary waterfall?) Or was it, after all, flat?

(If not, why did people talk about 'the four corners of The Earth'?) A small boat, chugging towards the horizon, promised to resolve the problem, but unfortunately it dropped anchor about half-way, and Samson was none the wiser.

He must have lost all track of time as he tried to reconcile stories of distant lands and seas with the existence of the horizon, for when he caught the sound of splashing behind him, and either heard or imagined his name being called out, he realised he was ankle-deep in water. It could of course have been anyone at all, but thanks to his ever-reliable sixth sense he knew that it wasn't 'anyone', or even simply 'someone': it was Rita - *the* Rita. He half-turned, just enough to have her at the edge of his field of view, and for the second time that day he was bowled over. Viewed against a vast expanse of empty sands she looked even more beautiful than ever. She had fashioned a necklace from an assortment of seashells, and was fingering it self-consciously, while in her other hand she held her shoes and socks. She had also pulled up her dress and tucked them into her knickers, thereby exposing the thighs of a goddess. As she stood there, hesitating, a light onshore gust caught her magnificent tresses, so that they trailed out behind her, and at the same time the delicate gingham of her dress was pressed firmly against her body, defining the mysterious region between her legs. It was, Samson realised, the same shape as a wasp's rear end, but without the sting. It was a vision that, though only glimpsed, would forever stay etched on his memory.

The breeze subsided. Rita stepped forward, so that she was standing at Samson's shoulder. She patted the water with the sole of one bare foot, perhaps trying to think of something to say. Samson faced the opposite problem: there was too much to say, he didn't know where to start. And still he felt too awkward to look at her directly.

Suddenly the electricity was discharged:

'Tha's weird, tha is,' she said, 'but Ah like thee.'

He mumbled something, even he was not sure what. He hoped that the breeze would freshen, and cool his burning cheeks.

Rita was speaking again:

'.... tha lookin' at? ' he heard. 'There's nowt theer, only watter.'

She would not have talked like that if she had been able to read, Samson told himself. He wanted to launch into an impassioned speech about the South Seas, about crystal-clear lagoons teeming with dazzling fish and giant octopuses, about coral reefs and coconut palms, and about the schooner on which he - no, *they* ... but how would she be able to understand? Instead, he murmured something about her saving a seat for him - on the charabanc, of course. It was only meant as a request, but perhaps it came out more like an order, for the next thing he knew, she was wading back to the sea front. He knew he should have joined her, perhaps offered to carry her shoes, or even given her a compliment about the necklace, but instead he remained rooted to the spot, mesmerised by the far horizon. Perhaps he had missed his opportunity, but the important thing was, that she had declared her feelings for him. There would be other opportunities - sooner rather than later, if she managed to save a seat - and one day, for sure, he would somehow sweep her off her feet and they would travel to the ends of the earth - or to the South Seas, whichever were further away from Old Guinea - and be happy ever after.

19. Educating Rita

By the time Samson came out of his reverie the water was lapping round his knees, and the vast beach was near-deserted. He raced back to the promenade, highstepping like a circus horse. Would they go without him? And if they did -? He need not have worried. Two others had kept everyone waiting: Speedy, and Tomcat. Speedy had just been rescued. Samson would learn later that his fun-loving classmates had buried him up to his neck in sand, then abandoned him. A bit unfairly, Miss Pollock was telling Speedy off, shouting 'Stupid boy!' at him, over and over again, while the culprits sneaked back onto the charabanc. Samson squeezed past Miss Pollock and started to climb aboard. It seemed that his big moment had arrived: he saw that Rita had indeed saved him a seat. She beamed a relieved smile at him, and a barrage of wolf whistles and catcalls left him in no doubt as to what was expected. But it was not to be.

'Samson! And where do you think you're going?' he heard Miss Pollock calling. 'Come here immediately, and explain yourself!'

He turned and dismounted, sheepishly, trying to ignore the barracking.

'If it wasn't for the fact that the Reverend Tompkinson has been unaccountably delayed, you'd be in serious trouble,' Miss Pollock told him. 'Now, wait there.' She clambered aboard and attempted to restore order.

Samson was secretly pleased that he had been told to wait: it gave him time to plan what to do and say, once he and Rita were together. However, his planning was cut short. A police car pulled up - he had never seen one before, but had no difficulty reading the illuminated sign on the shining black Wolseley - and disgorged Tomcat. He was in a terrible state: his new hat crumpled and askew, his collar undone, and what looked suspiciously like traces of vomit down the front of his waistcoat. He stood there, swaying and disorientated, until the police officers helped him to the charabanc. Then he refused to be helped aboard.

'Give me my teachers!' Samson heard him say, his voice

strangely slurred. Everything became clear when the police reluctantly handed Tomcat his bottle of Teacher's Whisky, three-quarters empty. Miss Pollock attempted to prise it from him, but he gripped it tenaciously and she gave up. Then the police, with ill-concealed amusement, helped deposit him in a vacant seat.

The charabanc started up and Miss Pollock called to Samson and Speedy to climb aboard, 'or else'. Samson would normally have led the way, but Speedy looked all in, so he helped push the poor boy up the steps - a bad move, he immediately realised, for Speedy lurched to the seat next to Rita. leaving the one next to Tomcat for Samson. Fortunately for Samson, Tomcat was already asleep, his head lolling dangerously. He was dribbling from the corners of his mouth, and from time to time he mumbled incoherently. Samson was unsure how to respond, but Miss Pollock came back to check, and told him to 'let sleeping dogs lie'. Though unfamiliar with the expression, Samson managed to get the general idea. It seemed that, with the possible exception of Miss Pollock, everyone had had a wonderful day out. Though dog-tired, the children were in excellent spirits, and there was a lot of furtive activity and sniggering from behind Samson. Soon, a song was struck up, to the tune of *Ilkley Moor*:

'Who put the piece of choc-o-lat
On poor Tom-ca-at's to-op 'a-at?
Who put the piece of choc-o-lat .. .

And so on, chorus after chorus. Tomcat stirred, and raised his head in stages, as if it was being operated by concealed strings and pulleys. His heavy eyelids parted, he licked his lips. Then he raised the whisky bottle to his mouth and attempted to take a swig, without having realised that the top was still on.

'Eashy come, eashy go,' he said philosophically, lowering the bottle and closing his eyes.

Samson at first heard the words as 'Here she comes, here she goes,' and looked up, expecting to see Miss Pollock bearing down on them. However, Tomcat's next words, uttered from the corner of his mouth, and clearly for Samson's benefit, enabled him to decipher the earlier statement correctly:

'Do ash I shay, not ash I do.'

Samson nodded. At the time, the words held no significance for him, but years later he would treasure them, as the only time an adult had admitted to their own hypocrisy. There were one or two further utterances, similarly deep. When the charabanc driver narrowly avoided a serious accident after overtaking on a blind bend, Tomcat, without properly waking up, commented that God could see round corners.

After the scare the children quietened down, perhaps subconsciously aware that their noisy behaviour could be distracting the driver, and the charabanc made good progress. However, as they left Horwich behind, the driver pulled off the road and got out, shaking his head and tutting. Clouds of steam, pouring out from under the bonnet, suggested a recurrence of the breakdown in Blackpool.

'We're done for,' the driver announced. 'Oh - unless anyone has any water.'

Nobody had, but urgent requests from some of the girls, to take a toilet break, gave the driver an idea.

'If only we 'ad a bottle, or summat,' he said.

'Will this do?' Samson asked him, easing Tomcat's whisky bottle away and holding it up.

'Aye, just t' ticket!' the driver said, taking the bottle from Samson. Then to Samson:

'Good lad! Thee, come wi' me. Aye, an' a few other lads ... lads only, no lasses.'

Samson and a half dozen others followed the driver off the charabanc.

'Thee first!' he told Samson, after leading the party to the back of the bus, out of sight.

'Eh?' Samson queried. Then he suddenly understood, and after some initial hesitation he urinated into the bottle.

Before long the radiator was refilled and the bus was able to get under way. Samson, the last to reboard, swayed down the aisle, determined to protect the whisky bottle and its contents at all costs: it was still a quarter full, though of course the contents were different from before. Miss Pollock, not realising what had transpired outside, held out an imperious arm.

'I'll take care of that!' she commanded, and Samson handed it over without explanation, before resuming his seat - next to Tomcat, as before.

The rest of the journey passed off without incident, though there was considerable merriment on the part of the boys, and corresponding curiosity from the girls. Finally the valiant charabanc pulled up outside St. Peter's and disgorged its dog-tired occupants.

'Three cheers for The Reverend Tompkinson!' Miss Pollock called out, when finally he negotiated the steps, unaided. 'Hip hip ... !'

Tomcat seemed to have other things on his mind:

'I need my nightcap! ' he shouted. 'Where'sh my nightcap?'

Samson not unreasonably assumed that Tomcat was tired, and wished only to sleep, but Miss Pollock seemed to understand the demand differently.

'Oh-h-h-h! If you must!' she hissed, handing him back his bottle.

Tomcat raised it aloft, a victory salute.

'We live to fight another day!' he shouted, then stumbled off into the darkness.

Samson wanted to go after him, to warn him not to drink the rest of the 'whisky', but by the time he had worked up the courage Tomcat was out of earshot. Samson shook his head resignedly, then collared Speedy ready for the journey home. It had been a strange day, he reflected. Once again he had failed to take advantage of the opportunity to get closer to Rita, yet he felt far from despondent.

'We live to fight another day!' he shouted, as he and Speedy set off. He punched the air, to convince himself: Speedy, though speechless, smiled happily and imitated his action - though without the words.

As the days passed, Samson kept his spirits up by repeating Tomcat's words - not in public of course, but in private and under his breath, like a mantra. He resolved to bide his time, like a hunter: when the opportunity came, he would be ready. This state of mental preparedness would prove important, because the next opportunity to get closer to Rita came sooner than expected. It was nothing less than Miss Pollock's wedding.

It had generally been assumed that, like the vast majority of lady teachers of her time, Miss Pollock would end her teaching days as she had begun them, a bitter and twisted spinster, and judging from the recent deterioration in her dress sense it seemed that she must have resigned herself to her fate. The announcement of her wedding therefore took everyone by surprise. Samson had not even been aware that she was courting. In the circumstances, rumours were at first rife, but it was gradually established beyond reasonable doubt that she had a secret *beau*, a young farmer who was a leading light in the shooting world, being captain of the Rossendale Valley Clay Pigeon Club. Miss Pollock, too, was rumoured to be in the club, and many people seemed to find this amusing, though Samson could see nothing wrong with the notion of a woman wielding a shotgun - in her case, it made perfect sense. In any case, he was more concerned to find out what exactly 'clay pigeons' were - and how he might acquire some, for breeding purposes.

Rumours and speculation aside, the announcement of the wedding triggered off mass hysteria. What the trip to Blackpool had been for the children, the wedding was for the whole community: a much-needed tonic after such a hard winter. Mrs. Smalley summed it up perfectly:

'Just what the doctor ordered,' she said, though her varicose veins had been playing up of late - and so reluctantly, she might have to give it a miss.

Samson, never having been to a wedding, or even seen one from afar, had no idea what all the fuss was about, but could not help being influenced. In any case, one day - for sure - he and Rita would be married, and would live happily ever after, so anything he could learn about the process would stand him in good stead.

If all had gone according to plan, the wedding would have been a very positive experience for everyone, including Samson. He showed great maturity in facing up to his only weakness: his flawed memory. He elected to forgo the pleasures which being part of a crowd can give, and to concentrate instead on observing from afar, and recording with a pencil and paper, every little detail of the entire process. Intuitively, without of course being familiar with the concepts, he recognised the need for objectivity, and surmised that this could best be achieved through non-participant observation. To that end, in the days leading up to the wedding he went to great lengths searching for a suitable vantage point from which he could see everything and everybody, without being seen. Diligence paid off: he found the perfect spot, about twelve feet up in the fork of a bushy sycamore at the edge of the graveyard; from there, he could keep the entire approach to the church under observation, as well as having the altar in view through a hole in one of the church windows, the accidental consequence of a half-brick which had been heaved at a rat sunning itself on the window ledge a couple of weeks previously.

By the day of the wedding Samson's plans were more or less watertight. If Mrs. Smalley had been going he would have feigned stomach ache so as not to have to accompany her, then raced to his post as soon as she had left. However, she had decided not to go, because there had been a heavy overnight snowfall, and the skies promised more of the same: her varicose veins, she claimed, played up 'something terrible' at the merest hint of snow. Samson, undeterred by this unforeseen eventuality, left home earlier than he had planned, and was first on the scene. By the time he was comfortably installed in the sycamore fork, the sky had cleared and the sun finally broke through the mist. It was going to be a beautiful day, and the combination of sun and snow created a fairy-tale setting for which many brides would have given their eye teeth. For the first time in his life Samson wished he had been able to draw, but he knew he lacked the ability, and in any case, how did one draw snow on white paper - and while shivering uncontrollably?

Quite soon, people started to arrive, and to negotiate with some difficulty the slippery slope leading from the lych gate to the church door. The snow, of course, had been brushed to the sides, leaving just ice in the middle. Samson had planned to record how people were dressed, and how they behaved, but he found it more interesting trying to match parents to children, and it set him wondering how Rita would look in ten, twenty or thirty years time ... if her parents came, he could check out her mother ... however, his attention was distracted by the arrival of a solitary black crow, which took up station high up in one of the elms which arched over the slippery slope, announcing its arrival with a loud '*Caw!*' and by dislodging a substantial quantity of snow. There were protests from the assembled guests, shouts of '*Shoo!*' accompanying the clapping of hands, but to no avail: the bird simply turned round and became even more interested in the proceedings.

Samson knew that the presence of such a bird was supposed to signify bad luck, but he was fairly sure that that was an old wives' tale. The important question was, to decide whether it was a rook, a crow or a raven. The bird had, for several weeks, taken to hanging around the school swill bins, and had earned Samson's respect by its coolness under fire: not only did it stand its ground when pebbles were thrown at it, but it almost nonchalantly hopped out of the way if one was particularly well aimed. With that boldness, Samson felt sure, it had to be a raven. The only doubt, a niggling but nevertheless persistent one, was because the bird had never been seen to plummet from a great height, to drop like a stone - the raven's trademark, as it were.

Samson was fascinated by the raven's quaint mannerisms. For example, it was fond of wiping its beak lengthwise on one side and then the other, in quick succession, as if sharpening it; and it periodically stretched out a leg or a wing to its fullest extent for several seconds ... not surprising, if it was even half as stiff as he was getting, stuck in the tree fork and slowly freezing to death in a gentle but persistent ice-cold draught.

Meanwhile the wedding preparations were proceeding apace. By the appointed hour the crowd of guests and the simply curious had grown to well over a hundred; a dozen of the bridegroom's shooting friends had taken up station along the sloping path, forming into six facing pairs, and the bride was being disgorged from a well-decked-out pony-and-trap. How much better she looked, with her ugly face hidden behind a veil! If - God! The tightness of her wedding dress drew attention to Miss Pollock's grossly distended stomach - strange, given her birdlike appetite. But Samson spared her no more than a quizzical glance before resuming his bird-watching. The bird, perhaps actually enjoying the wedding preparations, or maybe with its mind on the leftovers from people's crisps and sandwiches, had started hopping from side to side, its foot movements perfectly co-ordinated, so that it seemed to be bouncing and in perpetual motion. Samson waved discreetly, in the hope of attracting its attention, but just then his own attention was distracted by the sounds of a commotion below. As far as he could judge, the proceedings had had to wait for Tomcat, who was at that moment being helped out of the Nine Bells, very much the worse for wear. He had to be virtually dragged along, his trailing feet making tramlines in the snow. However, when he reached the foot of the steeply sloping path from lych gate to church, he shrugged off his helpers, insisting on negotiating the slippery slope unaided.

By this time the Guard of Honour had stood to, extending their shotguns at forty-five degrees to the vertical to form an arch through which Tomcat, and soon afterwards the bride and whoever it was that was giving her away, would pass. Whereas at the foot of the slope he had been very poorly co-ordinated, with arms and legs jerking out in all directions as if he were a loosely-strung puppet, by the time he came to the arch he had more or less pulled himself together. What happened next therefore came as a surprise, and it al1 happened too quickly for the precise sequence of events to be clear.

As far as Samson could judge, it was the raven's fault. Perhaps over-excited and unable to contain itself, it squirted a volley of huge runny droppings directly onto Tomcat's hat, forcing the brim over his eyes: in the process the bird itself almost overbalanced: more or less simultaneously there was an ultra-loud loud '*CAW!!!*' and a thunderous explosion, then the bird toppled over in slow motion and plummeted to the ground in an enormous shower of snow, immediately in front of Tomcat. Had one of the members of the Guard of Honour deliberately shot the bird, or had the gun gone off accidentally? And did the poor bird's manner of falling to earth confirm the bird as a raven? Unfortunately, before Samson could start to grapple seriously with these and similar pressing questions, the penultimate act of the drama unfolded. Tomcat, jolted in quick succession by the 'bombing' and by the explosion, momentarily became statuesque, and the shower of snow made him look like some kind of half-finished snowman. The delayed shock meant that his limbs jerked into motion anew, but presumably not as intended: he appeared to be walking, then running, and finally dancing crazily on the spot. Then, just as suddenly, he collapsed in an untidy heap, and the heap slowly slid back down the slope to the lych-gate. He was dead, and the wedding had to be aborted.

Samson's immediate response to the calamity was, to keep his eye on the dead bird with a view to recovering it later, and eventually stuffing it. (The thought of stuffing Tomcat also occurred to him, but he was quick to see the impracticalities of the project, and dismissed it from his mind. But the raven ...) Unfortunately one of the guardsmen kicked it into the bushes, then his colleagues peered up into the trees, where the unfortunate bird had been perched, and took provisional aim in case it had had any companions. Samson, by now frozen solid behind a stout branch uncomfortably close to the raven's recent perch, quaked and cursed: in the confusion, he had not been able to make a note of the bird's final resting place.

After Tomcat's death St. Peter's ceased to be a happy place. A new vicar, the Reverend Pilkington, was installed, and the combination of his name, his yellowing white hair and his sharp-faced vicious demeanour soon earned him the nickname 'Polecat'. To make matters worse a visit from the dreaded Schools Inspector had been notified, and this at a time when Miss Pollock was frequently absent with 'morning sickness' - a strange term, Samson thought, because he could not help noticing that she was frequently off work for entire days at a time - surely she could have turned up for the afternoon classes? As for Mr. Thoroughgood, the headmaster, everything was a bit too much for him, and he spent most of his time wittering, and loitering without intent, while Polecat took up the reins and spurred the reluctant pupils on with a mixture of threats and promises. It was a case of 'all hands to the pumps', and so Samson was pressed into service as an auxiliary teacher.

Initially unwilling to co-operate in any way with Polecat, to whom he took an instant dislike, Samson nevertheless soon allowed himself to recognise the sense of fulfilment which can flow from helping those less fortunate than oneself. His first pupil was poor Speedy, and though progress towards literacy was never anything to write home about, there was no doubt that Speedy enjoyed the unfamiliar attention and was motivated to study the pictures in the beaten-up copy of *Black Beauty* which Samson had rescued from a dustbin in Jericho. Samson's real target, of course, was Rita. Once he had established himself as a *bona fide* teaching assistant he felt confident enough to try to help her.

Reading materials were very scarce - these were times of severe post-war austerity, and no paper was provided, even in the lavatories - but Mr. Thoroughgood, obviously impressed by Samson's professionalism and dedication, commandeered Miss Pollock's 'bible', a handbook entitled *School Organization, Hygiene, Discipline and Ethics* by one Joseph H. Cowham, LL.D. and 'designed especially for the guidance of teachers in their professional training, and by educationists generally'. Intuitively recognising the need for educational materials to be relevant to pupils' needs, Samson eschewed the early chapters on abstruse topics such as 'Character' and 'Ethics' in favour of the section commencing on page 100, 'Relation of Bodily Conditions to Mental Vigour', and especially Item 2, 'The Connection of Bodily Vigour with Mental Effort, and The Condition of School Work by which Both May Be Fostered'. It was an inspired choice of text, for in no time at all Rita, by dint of perseverance of the highest order, learned to recognise the words 'the' and 'may' - the former, because of its frequency, and the latter thanks to the fortuitous coincidence that she had a baby sister called 'May'.

It was very much a learning process for Samson too. Not only did he face the challenging task of translating pedagogical principles into practice, but also he was obliged to acquire the art of reading 'upside down' - this term to be understood not in a gymnastic sense, but as a reference to fact that he needed to sit facing Rita across her rickety little desk, a far cry from the handsome 'Model Hygienic Desk' (to be precise, the 'Patent Adjustable Modern Desk') developed by the North of England School Furnishing Company: the virtues of this wonderful invention were extolled on Page 100 of Cowham's illustrious work. Samson's dedication to Rita's education was of course absolute, but an added urgency was injected by the news that the dreaded inspection had been brought forward . This was seen by everyone at St. Peter's as a dirty trick, though there was no evidence to substantiate such a view.

Samson had had a bad dream, in which the Inspector called Rita to the front of the class and asked her to read aloud from an enormous leather-bound tome embossed in gold letters from an undecipherable ancient text. After a cursory glance at the contents Rita panicked, smashing the book over the Inspector's head, then flinging it into the sea of upturned faces. The demented Inspector, picking himself up, leaped off the stage and careered around the classroom, attempting to snatch the precious book from whoever had it at that moment, or to catch it in mid-flight as it was flung from pupil to pupil. As he bounced off the crumbling walls in mounting desperation, the building collapsed in slow motion ...

What actually happened was somewhat different. The tension when the Inspector was ushered into Samson's classroom was palpable: a deathly hush punctuated by nervous coughs and clearings of throats, and by furtive shuffliings and rustlings and scrapings. Mr. Thoroughgood cringed in the sidelines while Polecat, all false smiles and with much wringing of hands, introduced 'His Majesty's Inspector, Mr. Griffiths'. The majority of pupils stared at their desk lids or the floor, or examined their finger nails or flies, but both Speedy and Rita unadvisedly eyed the Inspector - the former with an uncomprehending smile, the latter with an undisguised scowl: Samson, from the corner of his eye, noticed that Rita's right hand was clenched into a fist, and that she was gently punching the palm of her left hand, as if preparing to conduct any hostilities on her own terms.

Polecat cleared his throat and held up a hand to command silence - quite unnecessarily in the circumstances:

'Mr. Griffiths will now begin the inspection,' he announced, adding something to the effect that no-one had anything to fear: they should simply do their best. 'Perhaps ... do we have any volunteers?'

The Inspector, who had been clutching a mysterious black leather bag, now loosened the catch and started to move along the narrow isle which separated the boys from the girls. Samson tensed: immediately to his left was Speedy, by now grinning inanely and just asking for trouble, while to his right just across the isle was Rita. Samson just knew that one of them would be the Inspector's victim, and whether by accident or design - he would never be able to decide which - he cleared his throat at about ten times the normal volume.

'Ah, a volunteer!' the Inspector smiled grimly. 'Excellent!'

Opening his bag wide as he bore down on Samson, he fumbled inside, obviously to locate a suitable reading text, but just then his eyes lit on Samson's borrowed copy of 'School Organization, Hygiene, Discipline and Ethics.' It fell open at Page 100, easily recognisable thanks to its sketch of the Model Hygienic Desk.

'Mmm, interesting ...' He turned it towards him, the better to peruse the text.

All this while Samson stared at the Inspector in panic, still expecting him to target Speedy or Rita. Perhaps that had been the Inspector's original intention - but if so, he had had a change of plan.

'If you would be so kind ...' he said, rounding on Samson and pushing the opened book towards him.

Samson heaved an enormous sigh of relief: Speedy and Rita were safe! He cleared his throat anew, and pulled the book nearer.

'Not that way round!' the Inspector snapped. 'Stupid boy!' He turned the book round through a hundred-and-eighty degrees. '*This* way!'

Samson, shaking almost uncontrollably, nevertheless found

a vein of defiance deep down inside himself.

'No, it's all right, Sir,' he quavered, and he turned the book round to its original, wrong orientation. Then, before the Inspector could react, he began rattling off the familiar words:

'(a) Mental effort is connected with brain exercise. The brain is necessary for all mental operations and, like any other physical organ, is strengthened by judicious effort and becomes wearied with over-exertion. For healthy exercise it needs to be well nourished by means of good food, fresh air, and a vigorous circulation. Exercise of the brain, furthermore, results in an increase in its amount, and an improvement in its quality. The average weight of the brain in an adult European is about 50 ounces, but amongst heathen and uncivilized races -'

Just as Samson was getting to the interesting part the Inspector angrily snatched the book from him, snapped it shut and slammed it back down on Samson's desk.

'Smart Alec!' he seethed, then turned on his heel and marched out, never to be seen again.

For a good half-minute there was a stunned silence. It was broken by Polecat:

'Well, I think we've earned ourselves a day off,' he said.

The announcement was greeted by loud cheers, applause and a general hammering on desk lids - partly in response to the unexpected bonus, of course, but there could be no doubt that much of the exuberance was by way of a 'Thank you' to Samson. He grinned sheepishly, with false modesty. Inside, he was wildly exultant: he was now a hero, and his conquest of the beautiful Rita was now - surely? - a foregone conclusion.

20. Blood Brothers

In a simple, straightforward world the budding relationship between the gallant Samson and the beautiful Rita would have gone from strength to strength after the Inspector incident, with each possessing the other ever more firmly, like sand and cement after the addition of a little water. The reality was different: it was more as though the water had been poured onto a recently-lit firework: the blue touch paper had glowed briefly, sputttered tantalisingly, then fizzled out. So - what exactly had gone wrong? What was the reason? If Mrs. Smalley was to be believed, there was a reason for everything. Samson was not convinced. When he had once asked, 'Why is that?' she had been unable to give a reason, replying weakly, 'Well, there must be' - and finally, her back to the wall after a merciless salvo of 'Why? Why? Why?' she was reduced to insisting:

'Well ... nothing would make sense otherwise.'

The idea of nothing making sense struck a responsive chord in Samson: it made sense. The only trouble was, it was a dead end: if you actually wanted to go on thinking about something it was best to suppose that there was a reason. Anyway ... if there was a reason why things between himself and Rita hadn't quite gone as they should have, it was probably because he hadn't been sure what he was supposed to do, or what to talk to her about. Her action in coming to his assistance by bricking Slattery might have been because the swine had taken to calling her 'stinky knickers' and wrinkling his ugly snout at her. Nor did the chalked hearts prove anything. She could not have written them herself, because ... well ... she held any writing instrument as if it were a dagger, and the dried dog droppings which the Swamps children very resourcefully used as chalk would have crumbled straight away.

It now began to look to Samson as though he had swapped horses in midstream, preferring the certainty of his friendship with Snorky to the uncertainty of his love affair with Rita. Friendship - ha! What a friendship! What a fantastic fellow Snorky had been - and still was, hopefully. The three-card trick, the coin-on-the-glass swindle, the disappearing ten-bob note, the carthorse-turned-racehorse ... the list was endless. It was great honour just to know him, but to be friends, indeed best friends - blood brothers, more or less - was more than any sane person could ever have wished for. It was ... yes, it was too much. From the beginning of their whirlwind friendship they had recognised each other as something special, like twin cuckoos in a nest of hedge sparrows.

It was Snorky who had broken the ice. Samson now recalled how, during the general hubbub following the Inspector's humiliation, Snorky stared at him (Samson) for ages and ages, weighing him up as if he were a prize animal at a show. That was on a Monday. The Slattery business happened the next day, and on the Wednesday Snorky challenged him to a game of marbles. When Samson said he didn't feel like playing, Snorky immediately saw through him and gave him (yes, gave) a dozen ordinary marbles to start him off, plus a priceless pair of matching dobbers. Samson had stood there speechless, fondling the smooth spheres, still warm from Snorky's pocket. He was of course heartbroken when, within two minutes, he lost the lot.

After losing his marbles Samson realised that, although Snorky presented himself to the world as a trickster, he was really a very nice, kind - well, generous - boy who could be relied on in any situation. Whatever you needed - sweets, liquorice, dog biscuits, dandelion and burdock .... anything - you could get, usually without even asking. In the circumstances it was not surprising that Samson was happy to play second fiddle to his newfound friend. Sometimes he felt like a favoured courtier, revelling in his association with a benevolent king: at other times he felt more like a bewildered passenger on a helter-skelter, enjoying the ride, if not the scenery - everything flashed by too fast. However, after the Great Adventure the relationship gradually changed to a more equal footing, a shift which came about partly through their shared passion for collecting birds' eggs. After the dreadful winter, spring came in an unseemly rush. Grass sprang up overnight, greener than Samson had ever seen it. Hedges, trees, bushes and a thousand kinds of weed burst into flower, so that Old Guinea soon took on the appearance of a tropical paradise. The few birds that had somehow managed to survive the big freeze made up for lost time, gorging themselves on overabundant food, mating with reckless abandon and hastily improvising nests. So it was natural that Samson and Snorky should get caught up in this frenetic activity. Every dinner time they gulped down the first helping in seconds, no matter how unpalatable it was, and slipped out; once out of sight, and having checked that they were not being followed, they broke into a trot and headed for the rough ground beyond Jericho. There was to be found an ornithologist's smörgåsbord, all within an area of about a quarter of a square mile: a thicket, a copse, patches of heather and gorse, overgrown hedgerows, and an area of marsh bordering on a reed-infested stream beside which stood the ruins of two tiny old cotton mills. The area, totally unsuited to farming, and in the middle of nowhere, was a natural wildlife sanctuary. Many were the lunch-time hours spent combing this little paradise for the nests of skylarks, peewits, wagtails and kestrels, to name but a few species. Though the boys rarely discovered a nest, and even more rarely a nest with eggs, it was here that they developed the deep mutual respect which, for Samson at least, gave life a new meaning. What Samson admired most about Snorky was his uncanny, unerring instincts concerning the likely whereabouts of particular species, and his confidence in identifying them from the merest glimpse or snatch of song. Snorky, for his part, was obviously greatly impressed by Samson's daring - his downright foolhardiness, sometimes - in climbing disused chimneys in search of kestrels' eggs, or wading boldly into treacherous bogs until the mud came up to his navel, while Snorky meanwhile shouted encouragement from the safety of the nearest stone or hummock, determined at all times to preserve the mirror-finish shine on his coal-black boots.

Sadly, this promising union of knowledge and bravado proven barren at first. The boys found plenty of nests: a beautiful neat-and-tidy miniature nest tucked tidily inside a long-abandoned lidless kettle (probably a robin's nest, or possibly a wren's); the workmanlike home of a blackbird or mistle thrush, the inside expertly smoothed with mud, and the outside camouflaged with bits of wool and moss and lint; and the crude pile of sticks thrown together in an overgrown hawthorn bush by a magpie or carrion crow. But all were empty, though in almost every case it appeared that the birds had only recently flown. Samson began to feel very very guilty, convinced that for some reason he had brought nothing but had luck to the partnership. This conclusion, though unpalatable, was forced on Samson because whenever Snorky went birdsnesting alone, evenings or weekends, he never failed to find nests that were piled high with mint condition eggs just begging to he collected. That this was no exaggeration or downright lie was made clear on two consecutive Mondays when Snorky brought his latest finds to school and secretly showed them to Samson, at the same time regaling his all-ears friend with blow-by-blow accounts of how he had prepared the specimens. However, on the third Monday he must have noticed Samson's chagrin: he patted him reassuringly on the shoulder.

'Tell you what: he said, 'the first proper nest we find, I'll keep just one egg for myself ... you have the rest. Okay? Is that fair?'

'Very,' Samson mumbled, almost inaudibly through being close to tears of gratitude. However, deep down he was sure that they would never, together, find a single egg-bearing nest.

In the circumstances it was hardly surprising that the boys should channel much of their energy into other, more rewarding pursuits. They began to be joined on their forays into the countryside by Speedy, who hopped along behind them as best he could. The first few times, Samson and Snorky, getting wind of Speedy's approach, spontaneously ambushed him. It made for a very pleasant diversion, particularly since when caught, Speedy had a way of shrieking that excited the hunters to wild excesses. From this game more complex games evolved. Samson and Snorky took it in turns to 'be' different animals, moving in their characteristic ways. They learned how to glide silently through thick undergrowth and bracken, or to blunder about as crassly as wounded badgers. One day Snorky smuggled a deer's antlers out of the house and did a brilliant imitation of a proud fallow buck, bold and cautious by turns as it eased its way through a seemingly impenetrable thicket. This initiative spawned a plenitude of big game: an ungainly giraffe, mocked up with the aid of a broomstick and some old cushion covers; a slinking leopard owing much to the 'loan' of Snorky's mother's fur coat; and a trumpeting elephant lent credibility not only by Snorky's outstanding ears, but also by use of a borrowed hunting horn. Speedy, to his credit, eventually got the general idea and wanted to join in, but his talent for doing impressions was limited. The nearest he got to competing on equal terms with the other two esses was when he jinked about like an irate skunk, urged into action by having a broom handle thrust up his behind (by Snorky, of course).

The relationship between Samson and Snorky was, from the beginning, exhilarating - thanks partly to the superfecundity of ideas, partly to an intense rivalry. Fortunately this rivalry, which might at times have brought any other pair of friends to blows, was underscored by a generosity of spirit which would have done credit to two saints. Never was this quality more in evidence than when the boys stumbled upon their first nestful of eggs. Ironically, by this time they had more or less given up birdsnesting as a bad job, and were even becoming bored with stalking - though the number of species which could be inanimalated with an ever-increasing range of props was virtually unlimited, they did not know many, and inventing new ones was not that easy. Fortunately at about this time there was a veritable plague of butterflies, the like of which Old Guinea had never seen before and would never see again. There seemed to be millions of the things, flitting from plant to plant, quivering enticingly when grounded, and occasionally getting caught up in stiff gusts of wind so that they were difficult to catch, in spite of the fact that the boys had home-made nets constructed from broom handles, curtain wire and Mrs. Horrocks' cast-off silk stockings. All of the butterflies were beautiful, of course, but just occasionally an outstanding specimen would pop up, just asking to be netted. Such as specimen was the huge white butterfly which Samson spied on a little patch of wild cabbages up beyond Windy End. Apart from its sheer size it was whiter-than-white and edged with black.

'Flipping heck!' Samson exclaimed. 'What's that?'

'It's .. .. it's a white admiral!' Snorky shouted excitedly. 'Come on, let's get it !'

He leaped towards it and whacked his net down with demonic force. By rights the creature ought to have been pulped beyond recognition, but the cunning thing crawled out from under the net as though nothing had happened, then fluttered off across rough ground with the two boys in hot pursuit. It was Snorky who broke off the erratic chase.

'Look!' he shouted, flinging his net away. 'Look what I've found (*snork!*)'

'What? What?' Samson puffed. Then: 'Oh, ye-e-e-e-es!'

'Beautiful, aren't they,' Snorky whispered reverentially.

'Skylark's?' Samson asked tentatively, still staring in disbelief at the little clutch of sky-blue eggs, so beautifully arranged in a nest that was little more than a lining to a depression in the ground. No amount of time spent studying bird books could have prepared him for this.

'Well, they're not cuckoos', that's for sure,' Snorky pronounced - a little tetchily, it seemed to Samson.

Probably Samson had guessed right, because a few feet away was an extremely agitated bird struggling about with a broken wing and making loud alarm cries - a bit foolishly, Samson felt, because it would have been very easy to catch. Actually, whether it was a skylark's nest was of no importance: starved for so long of success, Samson would have thrilled at the sight of a hen's egg. But would Snorky remember his solemn promise of days earlier?

'I'll have this one, then,' Snorky said, picking out the nearest egg and holding it lovingly in his cupped palm. 'Just this little beauty, okay? You have the rest.'

'Are you sure?' Samson gasped. 'Okay, if you're sure it's alright with you. Thanks! Thanks a million!! *Err* ... where can I put them?'

Snorky searched his pockets with his free hand, pulled out a polka-dot handkerchief, and knotted it with one hand to form a little sling of the kind favoured by storks for transporting babies.

'Here, use this,' he said. Just then, as he held out the handkerchief for Samson to take, he lost his balance slightly, and in the process of recovering he inadvertently stepped on the five remaining eggs. For an age the two boys just stood there silently, heads bowed, looking blankly at each other and at the glistening yellow mess, flecked with blue. Eventually Snorky shrugged, sighed deeply, and went to clean his boots on a tuft of heather. Then the two of them walked back to school like old men returning home from a funeral. In spite of this awful tragedy Samson at no time rebuked Snorky over the accident: Snorky, obviouslyrelieved, soon reverted to his usual cheerful self.

In retrospect Samson was pleased the incident had happened, because it seemed to have brought the two of them even closer together. The frenetic rivalry seemed definitely a thing of the past from now on, and it became the practice for the two of them to spend dinner times going for long walks over the moors, arms round each other's shoulders, sometimes without exchanging a single word. Speedy, at last able to keep up with them, made up a happy threesome. Their favourite route became a wide circuit which eventually led back to the school via Preacher's Meadow. One day the three of them stopped there, leaning on the wall to observe the donkey. There was something about the situation, a feeling that something big was in the air, and Samson thought of issuing a challenge to Snorky before the latter could come up with some devilish stunt himself. However, it was difficult to break the silence.

After what seemed ages Snorky unexpectedly broke wind, then before his friends had time to react he began all of a sudden to talk with great animation about the future, about how their friendship would last for ever and ever.

'Through thick ...... and thin,' he said, looking meaningfully at Speedy on his left and then at Samson on his right.

This tender feeling now off his chest, Snorky motioned his friends to come closer. He himself moved over to Samson's right, then the three of them stood there for an age, arms round each others' shoulders, thinking their own very private thoughts. Eventually, three souls in perfect harmony, the trio wheeled through ninety degrees, with Samson in the middle like a happy hooker in the front line of a scrum, and began to trudge up towards the top of Tit Hill. Snorky broke away from his companions when they reached the old stump, and stood with his back to it. In a more ebullient mood he might well have jumped up onto the stump and shouted 'I'm the king of the castle', then performed some regal conjuring trick such as producing a tadpole from Speedy's free nostril and turning it into a frog - or a toad, even. On this occasion he remained quiet and subdued, a distant look in his eye as he gazed out across Monkey Town. Then suddenly he seemed to get an idea.

'I know (*snork*)!' he said. 'Let's be blood brothers - okay?'

Samson shrugged, not exactly sure what it meant. Speedy gazed at Snorky admiringly, like a dog at its master, having no idea whatsoever.

'Right: Speedy first! Come on!' Snorky said, the sense of urgency underlined by the anxious way he kept glancing at his watch. He helped Speedy up onto the makeshift altar; then, after rolling up Speedy's sleeve, he suddenly produced a huge knife from his own, and scored the back of Speedy's forearm - deeply. For a moment it seemed as though Speedy was not going to react; however, when the blood started welling to the surface he tried to disown the arm by thrusting it away from his body, and started squealing.

'Now you! Quick!' Snorky urged Samson. 'Come on! We haven't much time. Quick! Quickquickquick!'

'Not so deep this time,' Samson begged, bravely rolling up his own sleeve. The knife, however, was extremely sharp.

Now Snorky placed Samson's arm across Speedy's, so that the welling blood mingled symbolically before dripping over the initiates' clogs.

'Brothers!' Snorky announced in priestly tones, addressing his remarks vertically upwards thanks to having an unusually rubbery neck.

Samson had a brief vision of the message being passed from

angel to angel to angel .... until -?

'Brothers!' he said to Speedy. A beautiful expression now stole over the latter's face: he withdrew his crimson tongue from the blanching nose and seemed to be on the point of speaking. But either he had second thoughts, or was unable to formulate the first ones in time, for just then Snorky emitted a long, low-pitched but piercing whistle. At this the donkey, which thus far had been busy browsing in Preacher's Meadow, maintaining a studied indifference to the historic proceedings higher up the hill, raised its outsize head and came rushing to the bluff, braying excitedly. At the same time Snorky ran down the slope towards it, brandishing the knife. For a moment Samson thought that Snorky had taken leave of his senses and was about to include the donkey in the privileged group of blood brothers. In fact, Snorky used the donkey as a stooge: leaping onto the bluff, he raced back and forth along it, brandishing the knife like a sword, making mock attacks on the donkey and shouting 'One for all and all for one', as if, in his confusion, he thought he was playing marbles. Samson, bleeding arm temporarily forgotten, smiled. In particular he was amused by Snorky's cissy style with the 'sword': instead of slashing powerfully from side to side, like a real swordsman would have, he acted more like an old lady prancing about with a knitting needle.

The exhibition of swordsmanship completed at last, Snorky raced back up the hill, leaped onto the stump beside Samson and Speedy, and struggled to raise his own sleeve. Samson offered to help, but just then the school bell rang out. A black expression stole over Snorky's normally angelic face.

'Shit!' he said disgustedly, leaping back to the ground and hurriedly wiping the bloody knife on a tuft of couch grass before thrusting it up his sleeve. It was the first time that Samson had heard Snorky swear in anger.

Where would it all end? Where could it all end? What would happen when, as was inevitable, the precious fountain dried up - when Snorky finally ran out of ideas? He must do, sooner or later - surely?

21. A World Record Attempt

More and more during his last few weeks at St. Peter's Samson found himself pondering the weighty problem as to how his roller-coaster relationship with Snorky would end. In the privacy of his bedroom he tried to find an answer with the aid of a pencil and paper; on lonely walks he took to holding long dialogues with himself, risking the possibility that someone might report him. But, try as he might, the solution was as elusive as a will o' the wisp.

Fortunately Samson's confusion was short-lived. Not long after the 'blood brothers' ceremony, Snorky began to put it about that he was planning a 'farewell spectacular': a comprehensive display of his many talents, to be climaxed by an attempt on his own world frog-skinning record, which stood at just over seventeen minutes for the twelve frogs involved. With typical generosity he offered Speedy the post of assistant: obviously, to be a blood brother meant something very special.

At dinner time on the appointed day a great crowd eagerly climbed the slopes of Tit Hill to enjoy Snorky's so-called 'spectacular', perhaps also to pay tribute to a great performer, or to lament the end of an era. As the zero hour approached, the children ceased fighting for the best places, and settled down to watch Snorky's arrival from The Swamps, sure to be an affair of pomp and ceremony. Only Speedy, out of almost a hundred children, seemed to be unaware of what was going on: perhaps carried away by the honour of being frogmaster, he had climbed on the tree stump and was staring in the opposite direction to everyone else, and making excited *hee-haw* noises.

'He probably thinks it's a panto,' Samson whispered to Rita, enjoying the excuse to stand pressed close against her and feel the warmth of her body through the thin gingham dress.

'Shurrupp and siddown, stupid stinkin' twi,' someone shouted from the back.

Speedy, undeterred, perhaps even encouraged by the unaccustomed attention, began jumping around on top of the stump, making clippety-clop noises with his clogs while continuing to bray excitedly.

'Speedy: the flipping frogs!' Samson warned as the slimy creatures began popping out of Speedy's pockets into the hollowed-out part of the tree trunk - or, if they were lucky enough to avoid his clog irons, out into the crowd. Then, alerted by his ever-reliable sixth sense, Samson turned to look in the direction Speedy was looking. A wonderful sight met his eyes: Snorky was astride the donkey, riding it bareback; in his hands was a long stick, held like a fishing rod; on the end of the line, a delicious-looking bunch of freshly-dug carrots. Samson let out an involuntary shout. The crowd turned and burst into rapturous spontaneous applause, and moved aside to enable the great showman to make his entrance, like the waters parting for Moses. Snorky slid off the donkey's rump onto the tree stump, allowed the donkey to seize the carrots, then gave it a stupendous kick. It burst through the crowd and careered off down the hill, comically kicking its back legs in the air.

Snorky, professionalism personified, waited for the applause to die down a little, then squatted down and began the show with his well-known 'Find The Lady' trick, affecting not to notice the competing display provided by three or four frogs springing about in random directions: one, incredibly, leaped straight back into Speedy's pocket. Next, Snorky produced a mouse from a handkerchief with which only moments before he had blown his nose; then, after waving the handkerchief about to show that it was mouseless, he produced a second mouse ... and a third. Samson was forced to admit that, though the tricks were basically the same as always, they had been developed to new heights.

Time flew. Soon it was time for the grand finale: the world record attempt. Snorky jumped to the ground and cleared a space for himself and Samson. After laying out a whole packet of brand new 'Seven O'Clock' razor blades on the makeshift operating table he took off his watch and handed it to Samson to keep time. Samson examined the watch anxiously - firstly, to see if there was anything fishy about it, and secondly to check the time. It was exactly quarter-past twelve, which meant that Snorky would really have to beat the existing world record by at least two minutes, if they were not be late back to school.

Snorky rolled up his sleeve and nodded tensely to Samson.

'Five ... four ... three ... two ... one ... GO!' Samson shouted, hoarse with excitement.

Snorky's dexterity was amazing. In exactly one minute he laid out the first pelt and flung the rightful owner over his shoulder into the crowd, where it was eagerly fought over.

'ONE!' Samson called.

'One!' Speedy parroted, his face screwed up in a model of concentration.

There was no time to coach Speedy in his role: fortunately Snorky took the initiative, yanking the next frog from Speedy's pocket and in the same fluid movement stunning it against the stump. In a total elapsed time of one minute fifty-five seconds, this second frog was helping to make history.

'TWO!' Samson shouted, hysterical with excitement now he sensed that a new world record was a definite possibility.

'Two,' Speedy repeated, and some of the audience joined in: 'Two! Two! Two!'

Double figures came up in only eleven minutes, with Snorky showing little sign of slowing down: a new world record now looked almost certain. The spectators were jumping up and down, chanting the score - all except Speedy, who was stuck on what sounded like 'Fee!' Nevertheless, in spite of the distractions, Samson continued to keep a careful count ... or would have done. At this point an awful discovery was made: there were no more frogs. Of the original twenty-five or so that Samson and Speedy had collected, only half had stuck around long enough to earn immortality. The mood of the crowd changed very quickly: someone suggested skinning Speedy and counting him as two frogs. Fortunately Snorky, rising to the occasion, quickly defused a potentially ugly situation by distributing packet after packet of penny drops. Then, with everyone munching away contentedly, he jumped back onto the stump, held out a hand for silence (rather like Hitler, Samson thought) and adopted a most solemn air. His prominent ears, with the sticking plaster adrift and the sun directly behind, glowed bright pink.

'Friends!' he began at last, when everyone was silent. 'Friends! Ah mun away soon.'

He paused to give time for the message to sink in, and his ears flapped slightly as though to suggest that he intended to fly away. The crowd murmured reverentially. Samson felt tears welling up. Fighting to control himself, he pressed even closer to Rita. He could feel her heart beating with a slow, regular, infinitely reassuring thud, in contrast to his own, which raced like that of a frightened bird.

'So,' Snorky continued, 'on t' day we break up, Ah've decided to do summat real special ... summat as 'as never bin sin befoor ... summat impossible!' His eyes misting over, he raised his head and gazed towards the steeple of St. Peter's Church.

Samson racked his brain: how could anyone, even the great Snorky, do something impossible? And what was it, anyway? Could he be planning to sprout wings and soar off majestically into the heavens? Would he become the ultimate contortionist and disappear up his own behind in a cloud of steam? Or - Samson gasped - the idiot! The blooming idiot! Without doubt Snorky was planning to throw himself off the church steeple! Why else would he, in recent weeks, have sent him (Samson) to climb onto the church roof and search the steeple for footholds? 'Raven's nest', indeed!

'DON'T DO IT!' Samson found himself shouting out. 'DON'T DO IT. YOU MIGHT BE KILLED!!!'

The crowd tensed, all eyes on him and Snorky.

'Do what?' Snorky asked, all innocence.

'Err ... nothing,' Samson mumbled. 'No, nothing.'

Snorky paused briefly to allow the tension to mount, before going on to explain his real plan with characteristic modesty. He intended to be publicly crucified - not upright in the normal way, but in what he confusingly called 'a patchy style', pegged out on top of the tree stump with six-inch nails through his wrists and ankles; then, within three days, he would free himself 'like the legendary Whodunnit'. Admission, he added almost as an afterthought, was a halfpenny - payable in advance. The proceeds would go to charity.

There was a shocked silence lasting the best part of a

minute. Then questions began to flow, thick but fast. Would they be special nails (in other words, trick ones)? No, they would not: the nails would not be glass ones, nor would the hammer be a rubber one ... everyone was free to bring their own. What would happen if he couldn't free himself? In that case, he candidly admitted, he would have to stay there and rot. Did he plan to free himself before or after dying? Snorky confessed reluctantly that he hadn't thought of that one either: he would cross that bridge when he got to it. What would he do if it started raining? Starting to look hunted, Snorky said he would bring a mac just in case. Then, obviously realising that his plans were not sufficiently watertight as yet, he suddenly shook his head violently from side to side, then held up his hand for silence. Throwing out his pigeon chest, and in every way adopting a brilliant theatrical pose worthy of Lord Nelson, he suddenly screamed out:

'I PROMISE YOU DEATH! DEATH! DEATH-DEATH-DEATH-DEATH-DEATH!! WHAT MORE DO YOU WANT, YOU SILLY BUGGERS!!!'

The power of direct selling, harnessed to an unbeatable product, was immediately evident: money flowed uphill like magic water, until almost every drop that could be squeezed out of the assembled crowd was home and dry in Snorky's capacious pockets. Then the meeting broke up, the children dribbling back to St. Peter's in twos and threes, which here and there coalesced into little rivulets, like water in an estuary finding its way back to the sea after high tide.

22. The Last Biscuit

The coming crucifixion spectacular caught the imagination of St. Peter's children to an extent that surprised Samson, and probably Snorky too. Until that time Samson had always felt that the world revolved around him, but now he was forced to make a Copernican re-evaluation: he could see that everything, directly or indirectly, revolved around Snorky. Snorky was The Sun, the brilliant source of all energy, whereas he, Samson, was more like the dependable old Earth revolving around him; while Speedy, for his part, revolved around Samson like a partially-eclipsed moon. Wherever Snorky went, Samson and Speedy went too: wherever the 'three esses' went, the world was sure to follow. Of course, all the attention was focussed on Snorky: eyes followed him hither and thither; little groups huddled together, whispering about him. One girl, Maria Hoyle, kept stealing up on Snorky crabwise, and trying to touch him; she would then blush like a beetroot and scuttle away. Another admirer, not so little, was the moronic Gladys Dobson, nicknamed 'Goats' Eyes Gladys' from the crazy way she stared at all and sundry with her wickedly-gleaming yellowish-brown eyes, though Samson privately thought of her as 'Goat-Size Gladys' because of her resemblance to a goat standing on its hind legs - she was exceptionally tall, with an enormous distended belly and the spindliest of legs. Gladys needed several well-aimed kicks to persuade her to keep her distance.

It is possible that this unaccustomed adulation, though in some ways unwelcome, went to both Snorky's head and Samson's. (Probably it went over Speedy's). Certainly the two of them adopted a new high profile, strutting around like a couple of bantam cocks, and generally getting above themselves. Samson was soon to regret his newfound cockiness when he inadvertently upset the Wilkes brothers - the great, beefy Hugh and the sickly, scrawny Luke. Their surname had been corrupted to 'Whelks' ever since the trip to Blackpool - Hugh was then renamed 'Huge', or simply 'Muscles/Mussels', whilst Luke became 'Cockles'. Samson should have known better than to pinch Luke's biceps and taunt him with 'How's your cockles, Cockles?' with Huge only a couple of feet away. The next thing Samson knew, he was rolling on the floor in agony, clutching at his stomach and terrified that he was going to die from being unable to breathe: Huge had stepped forward and punched him in the solar plexus. Fortunately for Samson, further violence was forestalled by Snorky, who whipped out a hunting knife and threatened to 'stick' Huge 'like a pig'. The imagery was not lost on Huge, whose father was a pig farmer from somewhere near Jericho.

'Easy when tha's getten a soddin' knife,' Huge sneered.

'Oh yeah?' Snorky said belligerently. However, before anything could develop, Miss Pollock was on the scene, ringing the bell.

'Aye, Ah'lI 'ave thee,' Huge said darkly as he pushed past Snorky; at the same time he managed to give the still-downed Samson a sly kick in the ribs.

The next dinner time, the three esses made a quick getaway from school along the track leading to the Rock o' Gibraltar. They were about halfway there, proceeding at a good dogtrot, when Snorky suddenly pulled up, and put a finger to his lips.

'What's up?' Samson asked.

'*Sssh* ... trouble!' Snorky whispered, motioning to Samson and Speedy to crouch down behind a convenient boulder. 'I smell trouble.'

He himself remained standing in the middle of the track, legs wide apart, and his hands thrust into the opposite sleeves. Before long, Huge's nose slid out from behind a nearby tree, closely followed by the rest of his ugly face. Samson, engaged in some very desperate contingency planning (mainly concerned with deciding which way to run) was astonished when, at the very moment Huge lunged forward, Snorky hurled his hunting knife in Huge's direction: it hit the tree beside Huge so hard that the blade penetrated half way to the hilt, The resulting '*doi-oi-oing;* could be clearly heard above Huge's gasp of astonishment, while Samson was open-mouthed: he had not really seen Snorky throw the knife, there had only been the merest blur of movement.

'Come on, then,' Snorky called out. 'Come on, you great

twerp. T' knife's stuck in t' tree. What are t' waitin' on, eh? Daft gummut!'

Huge, clearly rattled, edged forward. Snorky stood his ground, motionless as a statue. Samson braced himself for the moment when Snorky, obviously with a second knife concealed about his person, 'stuck' Huge as promised. Huge lunged the last couple of yards, and aimed the predictable blow at Snorky's midriff - but it was Huge who fell to the ground. From the way he lay there, he seemed to have broken his wrist.

'Tha'll 'appen teach thee!' Snorky shouted, following up with a vicious kick to the groin.

'God!' Samson exclaimed. His admiration knew no bounds.

'All in a day's work,' Snorky smiled. He strode to the tree, worked his knife loose, made a V-sign at Luke, who was cowering behind a gorse bush, and motioned to his troops to fall in.

'Blooming heck!' Samson exclaimed, when at last they stopped for a break. 'You must have stomach muscles like cast iron!'

'More or less,' Snorky winked. He turned away, delved inside his jacket, and put something on the rock beside him.

'You ... you crafty beggar!' Samson said. The mystery was solved: there on the rock was what Samson for a moment took to be a German World War 2 helmet - until it moved.

'A ... a turtle?' Samson gasped.

'Sort of.'

'What do you mean, "sort of"?'

'It's a tortoise. Same thing, only different. '

'God ... what's its name ... he, or she?'

'It's ... err ... it's called Speedy. Come on, Speedy! Come on!'

At this point the real Speedy pressed forward, tugging at Samson's sleeve. It seemed that he might have recognised a kindred spirit, because he put his hands over the tortoise and bent down to lick it. Snorky snatched the tortoise away and hoisted it aloft, as if it were a sporting trophy.

'Gerrou' o' tha',' he shouted up at the new Speedy. At the same time he performed a triumphant jig. The tortoise moved its legs uselessly, as if trying to swim in a jar.

'Aw!' Speedy cried, jumping up and down in an attempt to reach his namesake.

'*Hahahahaha!*' Snorky laughed, still jigging around. Then suddenly: '*Aarrgh!*'

The cause of his sudden change of tune was clear: either by accident or design, the tortoise had squirted a huge blob of something green and runny over Snorky's head, just behind his elaborate quiff.

Snorky's reaction was extreme: in one fluid movement he lowered the tortoise to the level of his right shoulder, leaned back and to the right, extended his left arm, then - in spite of being very slightly-built - uncoiled with the explosive force of a champion shot-putter. The tortoise now really did fly: it travelled an incredible distance, finally coming to rest deep inside an extensive clump of gorse.

Samson was deeply shocked, lost for words. How could anyone be so thoughtless, so cruel? How could someone who claimed to your best friend sling away a perfectly good tortoise for which you would have given the world? Though in need of consolation himself, Samson recognised that Snorky's need was greater. The poor boy was squatting down, head bowed, trying to shake off the mess.

'Come on,' Samson said with false cheer, 'it's nothing, really - not much different from Brylcreem.'

Unfortunately, the well-meant comparison only served to enrage Snorky further. He pulled away from Samson, turned on his heel, and stalked off without uttering a single word, leaving his two companions to find their own way back to school. Samson was close to tears, unable to face the possibility that he had lost his best friend through a few careless words: to console himself, as soon as Snorky was out of sight he searched the gorse bushes where the tortoise had landed. Unfortunately, all he had to show for his efforts was an abandoned birdsnest and a few dozen scratches.

The next day, Samson learned what it meant to be 'best friends'. Snorky arrived at school looking cool and composed, yet buoyant. His arrival was like a breath of fresh air: the bad smell of the previous day's business was blown away.

As soon as the dinner bell sounded he leaned across to Samson, his face lit up with the friendliest of smiles.

'Coming?' he said, rising to leave.

Samson, heaving a heartfelt sigh, responded with alacrity. For the first time in his life he knew what it must be like to be a dog, given a reassuring pat after being in the doghouse: he could have licked Snorky, and if he had had a tail, he would have wagged it until it flew off. The two friends scampered along for furlong after furlong, until finally they just about collapsed, exhausted. Way back, Speedy followed as best he could. They watched him in some amusement: with his peculiar loping gait, and with his head almost touching the ground at times, he looked for all the world like a badly-trained bloodhound.

'God, I'm hungry!' Samson said, as Speedy flopped down beside him. 'I could eat a horse . .. anything. But we haven't got anything. Oh well ...'

'*I* have!' Snorky responded, licking his lips and looking wolfishly in Speedy's direction. He took out his hunting knife, and began stropping it on the palm of his hand.

'Oh, come on!' Samson remonstrated.

'You're right,' Snorky nodded, returning the knife to his sleeve. 'Don't fancy rotten meat. *Err ... (snork!) ...* how about some biscuits.'

Samson hesitated, the snork alerting him to possible danger, but ... well, a biscuit was a biscuit ..

'Thanks .. err ... two, please ... and a nice cup of tea.'

'No tea.'

'Well, just biscuits, then,' Samson smiled. He was happy to play the game, because obviously Snorky was in a good mood, but the thought did make him salivate copiously.

'All right,' Snorky said, slowly and deliberately. He got to his feet, then wandered over to the nearby wall. The sun began to shine, and a skylark started to sing. Samson, watching Snorky, shook his head. It was difficult to believe that anyone would go to such lengths with a joke - a sort of joke, and not a particularly funny one, at that. He was therefore very surprised when Snorky, who had been bent double over the wall, suddenly produced a bright, shiny tin - a biscuit tin?

Surely not ... and even more surely, not a tin of biscuits?'

'Help yourself,' Snorky said casually, prising off the tin's lid as he approached.

Samson was already drooling. The tin was so so beautiful, decorated all over with delicious-looking golden-brown biscuits shaped like teddy bears. It was all too good to be true: he steeled himself for the inevitable disappointemnt.

'Help yourself,' Snorky said, putting the tin down between them. 'Take two.'

The rich aroma reached Samson's dilated nostrils at the same moment as he caught sight of the biscuits. His mouth opened of its own accord, in amazement, and he felt saliva squirting out from the linings of his cheeks. He more than took Snorky at his word, grabbing three of the bears and biting their heads off together. After his experience with the dog biscuits he was amazed at how these biscuits melted in his mouth. In no time at all the tin was running low.

'Only three left,' Snorky announced. 'Shall we -'

'Four,' Samson corrected, nodding towards Speedy, who was holding his biscuit up to the light, as if he was examining some recently-unearthed treasure.

'Forget that one,' Snorky said. 'Right: one more each, then we'll toss for the last one.'

'Fair enough,' Samson agreed.

'Here you are, then,' Snorky said. Then: 'Good God! (*snork!*) I hadn't noticed before ... some of them are looking to the left, some to the right.' He pointed to the illustration on the tin's lid.

'*Eh*? Oh, yes ... so?'

'I wonder which way the last one is ... I know: guess! If you guess right, you have it. If not ... okay?'

'Okay.'

Snorky reached inside the tin and removed the last biscuit, concealing it by cupping his hand round it. He fixed Samson with a cold, intimidating stare.

'Come on!' he shouted.

'*Err* ...' Samson hesitated, desperately trying to find some way of working out the odds. Unfortunately, he didn't know how many of each kind had originally been in the tin, nor did he know how many of each kind had been eaten.

'Come on!' Snorky taunted. 'Left? Right? Right? Left?' He began marching round and round as he continued chanting. The cunning devil! How could anyone be expected to think, with all that going on?

'It's ... it's looking to the right,' Samson finally blurted out.

'Right? Did you say "right"?' Snorky challenged, his glance switching between Samson and the concealed biscuit.

'Yes, right ... I mean, the bear's right - like this.' Samson turned his own head to the right, to make his meaning clear.

Snorky looked distinctly uncomfortable, Samson thought. If he hadn't known Snorky better he might easily have supposed that his face actually blackened in anger, though of course it could just have been a trick of the light. (At that moment a small but very dark cloud blotted out the watery sun, so effectively that the skylark suddenly stopped singing.) Anyway, Snorky's response to Samson's guess was almost spat out.

'Wrong!' he shouted, and before the word was fully out he had transferred the biscuit to his mouth, which instantly closed around the biscuit-bear's head: the secret was lost for ever. Any doubts about Snorky's mood were dispelled when he threw down the empty tin, stamped on it, then threw the flattened metal away into the bracken.

Samson was more than a little shocked as he watched the crumpled tin's erratic flight, and would probably have had words with Snorky if it had not been for Speedy, who at that moment tugged his sleeve and offered him the soggy remains of the biscuit he had been sucking. In other circumstances Samson might have been duly, or even unduly, grateful for such a selfless and thoughtful action, but unfortunately it went no way at all towards compensating you for the loss of your best friend.

But he ate the biscuit anyway.

23. A Spot of Bother

Now, perched on the Tit Hill tree stump and surveying the panoramic spread of St. Peter's and its environs like a retired general revisiting a crucial battlefield long after the corpses had been cleared away and everything returned to a semblance of normality, Samson began to see the events of those last few weeks in a different light. The possibility had to be faced that Snorky had become temporarily unhinged, like a farm gate with too many children swinging on it. It was clear that his behaviour had swung between two extremes: his usual mercurial, devil-may-care brilliance, and a dark brooding melancholy which sometimes gave way to brief periods of intense rage. Almost certainly he had over-reached himself by announcing the crucifixion (something best left to experts, Samson thought); he had been a victim of his own desperate drive for novelty and sensation. Then probably he had had cold feet, but been too proud to cancel the event.

Samson now began to kick himself. He had failed to see the signs: he had only been concerned about their precious friendship, and hadn't realised what Snorky was going through. Perhaps, if he had glimpsed the gathering storm clouds in time he might just have been able to steer a different course and pilot all three of them to safety. Perhaps ... but he hadn't. They had run into squalls, been blown off course, and finally shipwrecked. Since then he, Samson, had been 'doing a Robinson Crusoe': salvaging what he could from the wreckage, but otherwise reduced to marking time.

When Snorky went into a trance-like state after the biscuit incident, shuffling about about like a sleepwalker who hadn't enough energy to hold his arms out in front of him, Samson had felt numb - as though Snorky had died, almost as though he himself had died. He had hovered about like a bereaved relative keeping watch over a corpse, desperate to detect a flicker of life. He was reminded of the wonderful painting that hung in the Ramsbottoms' kitchen behind the strings of shallots, a poignant work entitled 'The Long Vigil'. Though not sure what 'vigil' meant, and in spite of supposing for some reason that it was pronounced 'viggle', Samson could be in no doubt as to the picture's message: a distraught dog, tears running down its cheeks and its ears drooping pathetically, stood guard over the body of its friend, while in the long shadows thrown by the setting sun (or perhaps by a full moon - the colour was somewhere between crimson and silver) an army of slavering yellow-toothed rats waited for the feast. Apparently the artist had been in the last stages of going blind, and some of the details were not quite right, but the emotional impact of the picture was astonishing: grown men, including war veterans, had been seen to shed silent tears; one or two had even broken down openly and sobbed like women.

Samson realised now that he had let Snorky down somehow. If they had been simply friends, and nothing more, his behaviour would have been excusable. But they were more than friends, or good friends, or even best friends - they were, more or less, blood brothers, pledged to help each other through thick and thin (Snorky's very words). Yes, poor old Snorks had obviously got out of his depth, bitten off more than he could chew, and just when he needed some support his 'blood brother' had only been concerned for him to look cheerful. If Snorky was at fault at all it was through being too proud to ask for help: he had preferred to suffer in silence, humping his heavy burden like an overloaded camel: the crucifixion business had been the last straw. The pattern, Samson realised, had always been the same: when he, Samson, had been in difficulty (for example, when he was at Slattery's mercy) Snorky had rushed to his assistance without hesitation, setting fire to Slattery's shirt tail without any thought for his own safety; yet when Snorky had once asked to borrow Rita for fifteen minutes, to test a 'sawing a girl in two' trick that he guaranteed was completely safe, he had shuffled his feet, *ummed* and *ahed* and made feeble excuses - she wasn't feeling well; she couldn't bear being cooped up ... that sort of thing. Snorky had not pressed the point. He had simply smiled and said quietly, ' It's up to you.' To have offered Speedy as a substitute was poor compensation. There had been other, similar cases. But to have let Snorky down over the crucifixion was unforgivable. Obviously Snorky had been counting on him as an accomplice, to fake the nailing-down or to return and set him free after the crowds had gone. Instead of offering to get involved, he had simply tried to cheer Snorky up - and not so much for Snorky's sake, as because he himself felt deeply uncomfortable whenever Snorky's behaviour was anything less than happy.

It all seemed much clearer now: Samson had expected Snorky's moodiness to be short-lived, but it went on and on, the tension ever mounting, as when a firework has been lit; you say under your breath 'Come on, come on ...' but it doesn't go off; you think it has gone out and you know that, if it hasn't, the bang is imminent and could leave you without fingers or nose or something if you choose that moment to try to find out what is wrong. Well, Snorky had lit his own touch paper and he had smouldered too long. What would the outcome be? What could the outcome be? Would he smoulder a while longer, all smoke hut no fire, like a damp squib? Or would he manage to come up with something special and go off with a fantastic bang, like a dry squib? Perhaps neither ... perhaps he would go fizzing round in ever-decreasing circles, like a well-pinned Catherine wheel ... or jerk into action like a jumping jack, and be gone before you could say 'Where the f -' ... or steal a stick of dynamite from the quarry like Shagger Sharrocks had once done; then grab a broom handle and take off like a witch? Or was his whole scheme like a Roman candle - vivid, colourful, spectacular, but in substance nothing more than a load of balls?

Yes: Snorky, whatever his game, was cutting it fine even by his own standards. The last week drifted by like an owl's world, all silences and shadows and with a pervasive sense of impending violence, right until the last day arrived - the day when all would be revealed ... the day of truth. By a tradition established the year before, there was no afternoon school on the last day of the summer term; the spectacular was set for two o'clock to give time for the teachers to disappear. The morning was given over to prizegiving and exhortation, the main idea being to drag the proceedings out until the special treat arrived. As usual the spelling prize went to Samson, the handwriting prize to Snorky. Samson was eagerly looking forward to his spelling prize, given that in the two previous years he had won first, *Coral Island,* then *Kidnapped* - each, in its way, undoubtedly the greatest book ever written. This year he was sorely disappointed: the prize was a poorly-illustrated and probably second-hand copy of Mother Goose, printed in extra-large characters and with pictures for colouring in. He decided there and then to give it to Speedy, and to use it for coaching him in the rudiments of reading and poultry farming. The prize for arithmetic, as in the previous year, went jointly to Samson and Snorky: each received a handsome cloth-bound ready reckoner. Samson decided to give his copy to Rita, reckoning that it would be quicker to do a sum in his head than find the right page in the book. Right now the only calculation he was interested in was, how many minutes remained until the appointed moment when Snorky would get in position for being nailed down on the Tit Hill tree stump. Unfortunately the calculation could not be attempted, from lack of a watch.

The ceremonies were hastily brought to an end when the dinner lorry arrived. The trestle table were rearranged and the dinner containers, still slightly warm thanks to the time of year, were unloaded. In previous years the children had been wildly excited at the prospect of the special dinner but on this occasion the atmosphere was noticeably subdued, as shown by the fact that when Miss Pollock shouted 'Walk, don't run!' she could be heard. The Headmaster took his place, then Miss Pollock and the infants' teacher Mrs. Lord, and finally the Vicar went to stand behind the Headmaster.

'For what we are about to receive, may the Lord make us truly thankful,' the Vicar intoned. Normally the final 'Amen!' would have been shouted excitedly, understood as a synonym for 'Go!' On this occasion, however, the response was as lukewarm as the food, so that when Speedy dived into the shepherd's pie and started worrying it, his behaviour stood out from that of the other children. Samson stared at him in fond disapproval, to no avail.

About fifty children stayed on for dinner instead of going home early. The number being greater than normal, there was hardly enough food for the first helping. Making his own meal last by chasing the peas round the plate with affected difficulty, Samson wrenched his gaze away from Speedy and quietly surveyed the scene. The atmosphere, though subdued, was expectant, and Samson was reminded of the way that cattle behave when sensing a storm's approach. According to Mr. Smalley cattle felt storms in their bones; Samson was reminded of this by the fact that his own knees were knocking together slightly, and other joints seemed a bit loose: he wondered if, like Snorky, he was becoming unhinged.

Hmph, Snorky! The devil was sitting there expressionless, as cool as a cucumber - half a cucumber, anyway: his free hand was gripping the edge of the table so tightly that the knuckles were white, whereas normally the fingers would have been in perpetual motion, engaged in exercises to promote dexterity. Samson also reckoned that he could make out beads of sweat all over Snorky's dome-like forehead, except for the strange circular red birthmark in the middle of it, somewhat like an eye; it may have been Samson's imagination, but the pale centre of the 'eye' also exuded a bead of sweat, like a tear. Yes, Snorky was tense, alright, as well he might be. There was no going back at this stage, surely? If he funked it he would never be able to hold his head high in Old Guinea ... the same problem if he went through with the crucifixion 'successfully', too ... No, Snorky had made it absolutely clear: he had promised death, publicly. There was no way out for a person of honour, a person so concerned about what others thought that he polished his precious boots ten or twelve times a day, winter or summer.

The meal ground to a halt. A few children shuffled off home but the majority hung around awkwardly, filtering out into the playground in huddles of two and three and four. Samson slipped out alone, unobtrusively, carefully bracing himself for the usual blast of wind, and the sudden brightness which usually made him sneeze. In fact the air was still and breathless, and the sky hung low overhead, heavy and inky-black, like an enormous slab of black stone ready to come crashing down: it felt to Samson as though everyone was going to die, and that St. Peter's was being covered by a funeral shroud even before the Grim Reaper had actually started his grisly work.

The first children to go outside had gathered in little knots in the main marbles area. Most were silent - those that were still speaking did so quietly, conspiratorially. Samson sidled over to the wall that separated the playground from Diggle's garden. The middle section of this wall. for no obvious reason, was twice as high as the ends and provided Samson with an excellent vantage point. He shinned up, then perched there like a vulture - hunched, immobile, head thrust forward and eyelids drooping - slyly keeping an eye out for Snorky whilst pretending to enjoy an after-dinner nap.

A trickle of sweat ran down Samson's nose, tickling him. He resolved to get rid of it by means of a lightning flick of the nose, the moment the drop reached the tip: at all costs he would avoid drawing attention to himself by sniffing or by wiping his nose on his sleeve. The drop, unconcerned, effected its descent irregularly, staying in one place for a while as though waiting for reinforcements to arrive before advancing further, but in the end gravity prevailed until it was hanging there tantalisingly on the very tip. Still no sign of Snorky ... what was the beggar up to? What was his game?

The heavy air stirred slowly, like tepid porage - and again. Each time, a tremor went through the drop, but without dislodging it. The second movement of air did however dislodge something else: the lid of one of the swill bins next to the girls' lavatory - unless ... no: the disturbance had been caused by a huge rat climbing out of the furthest bin ... no, not a rat ... it was Speedy ... Speedy's head, to be precise. Some of the girls noticed the disturbance, and the playground became even quieter. One or two of the bolder souls crept forward to investigate. Samson, shaking with anxiety (but not enough to dislodge the drop), prayed that Speedy would sense the danger he was in, and stay still; otherwise the girls would assume that he was hanging around their lavatory; being so stupid, they would not realise that he was simply after a third helping of dinner.

A little breeze rippled across the playground. Samson glanced up at the church weathercock to see which direction the breeze was coming from, but he was wasting his time: the weathercock had seized up some months earlier and had ever since remained pointing in the general direction of Blackpool, where of course most of the really bad weather came from. However, just as Samson was taking his eye off the bird a stiff gust caught it amidships, so that it suddenly pirouetted through a hundred and eighty degrees before sticking again the opposite way around, as if to turn its back on bad weather for ever more: as it did so it emitted a bloodcurdling rusty shriek like that of a lovelorn peacock. A huge drop of water, a million times bigger than the one on the end of his nose, hit Samson's head, followed immediately by others which landed in an irregular double sequence across the playground dust, giving Samson the impression that an entire tribe of giant cats had just gone by. The next moment, the sky opened and the whole playground seemed to erupt. Normally, of course, there would have been a mad rush for shelter. On this occasion, however, the twenty or thirty girls in the marbles area converged on the swill bins, like fallen leaves sucked into a gigantic fan, even as the great black cloud began to empty itself over them. Samson was slow to catch on, and before he had moved a muscle poor Speedy was buried under a mound of shouting, screaming, scratching, punching and kicking girls. Samson had seen nothing like it since the never-to-be-forgotten incident at Ramsbottoms' farm when a similar number of starving chickens tore a dead rat to shreds. The girls were completely crazed, oblivious of Samson's fists, elbows, knees and clogs when belatedly he mounted a one-man rescue operation. Worse, he was getting buried by late arrivals. With great difficulty he tore himself free, climbed onto the lavatory roof and dived anew into the fray with a vague notion of shielding Speedy. His action, though noble, was ineffectual: within seconds he was overwhelmed, unable to move or even to breathe. To conserve energy and collect his wits, he stopped struggling.

 Thunder crashed overhead. It became louder with each new peal, and jagged flashes of lightning illuminated the heap of writhing bodies. Samson expected that at any moment the whole lot of them would be struck dead. Suddenly there was a tremendous clashing noise, even louder than the thunder, like when the dinner lorry had once run out of control and crashed into the school gates. Bodies dropped away from him, leaving just one - a heavy one, which he soon recognised as belonging to Goat-Size Gladys. Taking advantage of her newfound freedom of action, Gladys rained blows down on Samson's back, everywhere from his neck to his kidneys. He twisted round, hoping somehow to throw her off, and more than winced as a huge bludgeoning fist was aimed at his stomach. Fortunately the blow never properly arrived: instead, Gladys slid off him in slow motion. Though dazed, Samson was able to realise that, as so often, Snorky had come to his rescue: with admirable presence of mind he had seized a couple of dustbin lids and clapped them round Gladys's ears. Gladys struggled to her feet as Samson collected his own scrambled wits, staggered about for a few seconds, and finally collapsed over an open swill bin, her head hanging loose at a strange angle as though her neck was broken. Samson kicked her up the behind, twice: a rangefinding strike with the left foot, followed by the real thing with the right: the ease and depth of penetration suggested that he had scored a bullseye. Then he grabbed hold of Speedy's inert form and half-carried, half-dragged him from the fracas, like an injured leopard struggling with a dead warthog. Snorky covered his friends' withdrawal as the girls reformed for a new attack, and in a brilliant rearguard action used one dustbin lid as an umbrella, another as a shield to protect against a variety of missiles, everything from pebbles and handfuls of mud, to half-bricks and lumps of clinker. When the girls looked like getting the better of him he flung down one lid and took out his hunting knife. The chase was abandoned. Seconds later the downpour stopped, as suddenly as it had begun.

24. After the Deluge

Hostilities over, the battered, bedraggled trio pulled up for a much-needed breather with undisguised relief, flopping down on a heap of stones formed by the collapse of a section of wall alongside the track. Now, for the first time, Samson became aware of the extent of the flooding. The track was like a miniature delta, a confluence of many streams of surface water and farmland slurry, separated by ever-shifting shoals of sand. Signs of destruction were everywhere. Over the opposite wall, on a sloping cornfield belonging to Windy End Farm, Sammy the Scarecrow, a snappy dresser by local standards, looked as if he had been engaged in a titanic struggle to free himself, and in the process had lost his head - this was nowhere to be seen, though his battered trilby had fetched up twenty or thirty yards further down the slope. Beside the boys, where the flash flood had breached the wall and water still rushed down a newly-formed gully, a wheel-less doll's pram, half buried in silt and wedged at an angle between two stones, reminded Samson of the Biblical ark, and the epic struggle between legendary local hero Sam Oglethorpe and the miserly, pennypinching Noah. On impulse, Samson struggled to his feet and inspected the pram's interior, curious as to whether the doll had survived the hectic voyage (the pram must have been tossed around like a coracle): he was somewhat disconcerted to discover, instead of a doll, a dead frog. It was lying on its back, the belly horribly distended, and the skin covered in a disgusting white slime. Samson wondered about the cause of death and, in particular, whether it was possible for a frog to drown, and he was on the point of soliciting Snorky's expert opinion when he noticed that, even though the rain had not resumed, the floodwaters were still rising, so that the three of them would need to get to higher ground by ascending the steep track up to the Rock of Gibraltar. He took a deep breath, nodded meaningfully to Snorky, then somehow found the strength to manoevre Speedy's dead weight, like a sack of turnips, until he could manage a fireman's lift. Then he set off resolutely, wading laboriously but manfully - even, contemptuously - through ankle-deep waters. However, his little legs rapidly turned to jelly as the hill steepened without ever seeming to end, and soon he was floundering around like - well, a flounder. Fortunately Snorky, who thus far had limited his assistance to kicking Speedy's feet free whenever they caught on an obstacle or started ploughing furrows in the mud, now joined Samson and took some of the weight from him for the last few yards of the journey. Samson was just about to murmur a few words of appreciation, but Snorky beat him to it.

'Thanks for your help,' he said, as they collapsed together on top of The Rock.

Samson, though aware that there was something not quite right with the remark, was too exhausted to think about it, and quite content just to lie there on a dryish area, gasping and throbbing, though fortunately his discomfort was largely offset by the warm analgesic glow of heroism.

Now the sun came out. Samson stirred slowly, lizard-like, and changed to a lying-down position to enjoy the warmth of the rock to the full. After a short bask he rose to his hands and knees, shook his head to clear his vision, and looked up to find Snorky grinning at him, with one hand outstretched in a begging attitude; beside him, propped up in a sitting position, was the still-unconscious Speedy.

'Penny for the guy! Penny for the guy!' Snorky chanted, at the same time affecting a funny voice by gripping his nose closed.

'Snorky!' Samson remonstrated. He crawled across to Speedy and poked him a few times: when there was no response he tried shaking him and shouting into his ear. Well, at least Speedy was breathing - he had very bad breath, so there could be no doubt - but otherwise he showed little sign of life. He had certainly sustained a lot of damage. His hair was matted here and there with blood, little trickles of which had tried to run down his forehead and neck; but it was good rich red blood, as thick as cream of tomato soup, and thanks partly perhaps to the recent mud poultice it had congealed rapidly. So there was really nothing to worry about - but?

'Think he'll be alright?' Samson asked Snorky, frowning with worry.

Snorky got to his feet and shook Speedy a few times. Getting no response, he suddenly leaned back and gave Speedy a tremendous slap across the face, as loud as a woodpigeon clapping its wings together - in fact, so hard that Speedy toppled over.

'Shock,' Snorky pronounced, nodding his head to indicate that there could no doubting the diagnosis.

'I'm not surprised,' Samson said, a bit shocked himself. 'So: what are we going to do? No: don't hit him again.'

'There's only two ways,' Snorky said knowledgeably. 'One way would be to give him a cup of nice hot tea with plenty of sugar, and -'

'How the flipping heck can we give him a cup of tea?' Samson interrupted. 'We haven't even -'

'Have to be the other way, then,' Snorky said, and without explanation he got up, clumsily vaulted the wall across the track, and scrambled down the bank to grab a dense bunch of nettles.

'Careful!' Samson warned.

'They're okay if you grab 'em firmly,' Snorky explained. He climbed back up and used the nettles to wipe Speedy's face. For a few seconds it appeared that the treatment was doomed to failure, but then Speedy started writhing about, clawing at his face and making low moaning noises.

'It's working!' Snorky said exultantly. '*Wheeeee! Mmm*, wouldn't mind being a doctor, one day. It must be fun.'

'Enough!' Samson shouted, and in blocking Snorky's attempts to continue the treatment he got his own hand badly stung. 'God ...'

'Yeah, you're probably right,' Snorky agreed. 'Anyway, that seems to have done the trick.' He flung away the nettles, scrambled over the wall again, and this time came back with a handful of dock leaves. 'Wipe him with these,' he told Samson. Amazingly, Speedy's rash soon subsided, Samson's too.

'God,' Samson mumbled.

'Magic, eh?' Snorky said, very self-satisfied. He watched proudly as the patient got shakily to his feet, blinked a few times, looked around, rehoisted his trousers, smacked his lips and finally thrust his tongue up the left nostril where it belonged. Samson heaved a great sigh of relief and lifted his face towards the heavens.

The blood brothers' close shave had brought them closer in every sense, and Samson almost felt grateful to the girls for making it happen. The timing was good too: there was about an hour to kill before the scheduled start of the crucifixion spectacular. It was an ideal opportunity to quiz Snorky about his plans ... an opportunity to be seized boldly, like nettles ... better get straight to the point and pin Snorky down with questions as pointed as six-inch nails. However, just as Samson was opening his mouth in preparation, Snorky started turning out his pockets and checking their various contents - penknives, lengths of cord, a couple of fish hooks, a stick of red sealing wax, and so on - and laying them out on the rock beside him. It was as if he had read Samson's mind. At the same time he started talking rapidly, slightly incoherently - babbling, almost, as conjurors often do as a way of distracting their audience. It was something about his family tree, about how it had so many branches that he didn't know where to start.

'Is it a monkey puzzle, then?' Samson asked. *Hee, hee, hee!* Marvellous! He had been saving that one up for ages, and was extremely pleased that it had come out so pat.

'Something like that.' Snorky said, and an uncomfortable grimace showed that the sarcasm had registered. But he was not to be deterred. 'I think I've told you about my grandad before,' he continued, then when Samson raised a quizzical eye he added, 'You know: Zac Horrocks.'

'Short for "Zaccharias", is it?' Samson queried, managing to keep track of the discussion in spite of being fascinated beyond measure by a bunch of strange little keys and some lengths of bright shiny wire that Snorky had just laid out. He suddenly remembered that Snorky had once called them 'skeleton keys', and perhaps they were called that because dead people could use them to escape from coffins ... or crucifixions???

'No - Isaac,' Snorky corrected. 'Anyway, I found out yesterday that he was one of five brothers.'

'Oh, that's handy!' Samson laughed, thinking that there could be one for each continent. Undoubtedly one would turn out to be a lion-tamer in Africa; another a boomerang-throwing champion from Australia ... 'But listen: are you serious about the ... you know ... I mean, will the nails be real?'

'How can nails not be real?' Snorky challenged, quick as a flash. The question was scathing, hostile, there was no doubt about that, and Samson guessed that Snorky must be angry about something. God! How touchy he had become recently. Samson shrugged, as much as to say 'Forget it', but Snorky continued to stare at him icily.

'Sorry,' Samson said.

Eventually Snorky broke the long, long silence by fishing inside his jacket once more. This time he produced a handful of nails, and these he flung on the rock in front of Samson. Most of the nails were about four inches long and of the type known in the trade as 'wire nails' or 'ovals'. They were beautifully shiny, as though Snorky had spent an age polishing them - though it might simply have been that he had very greasy pockets. There was also a much larger thing, which Samson with some difficulty finally identified as a hat pin. The blunt end sported an elaborate design in what looked like pure silver, depicting the upper half of a man with a funny hat, and one hand thrust inside his jacket.

'Napoleon,' Snorky said.

'Eh?'

'Bonaparte.'

'Oh ...' There were times, and this was definitely one of them, when Samson hadn't the slightest idea what Snorky was talking about. It didn't help that he had misheard the name as 'Bone apart'.

'Well?' Snorky asked. 'Feel it. '

'Feel what?'

'Sharp enough for you? And what about the nails, eh? Suck 'em and see, go on.'

Samson tested the hatpin and two or three nails, trying the points against the tip of his left forefinger. They were all sharp, very sharp indeed, and there was no doubt that they were real.

'What I meant was .. .' he resumed carefully, 'yes ... well, I can see how nails like these will go in. But how the blooming heck will you get them out? Eh?'

Snorky shook his head and smiled in a rather irritating, superior way, as if to say 'Poor boy!' Accessing yet another inside pocket he now brought out the most curious of things, a miniature horseshoe. As well as being very small it was very narrow, and the rounded end was painted bright red, features which suggested to Samson that it must have belonged to a very dainty horse - a fairground one, perhaps?

'What is it?' Samson checked.

'You'll see,' Snorky replied mysteriously. Picking up the horseshoe, he stroked the hatpin with it several times, then held the hatpin near the nails. Several literally jumped into the air - and then, even more amazing, they stuck to it, swinging merrily.

'God!' Samson exclaimed.

'No, just magic,' Samson said cockily. He proceeded to add the nails to each other, end to end, to form a thing like a daisy chain, about a foot long. It was utterly incredible: the nails continued to hang there with no visible means of support - a bit like Speedy's trousers, but more successfully.

'Can I see?' Samson demanded. It was simply not possible: there had to be a catch somewhere.

'See what?'

'The ... *err* .. horseshoe, and the hatpin again.'

'Why?'

'Dunno .. well, just to have a look ... okay, just the hatpin, then.'

'It's real, you've tried it already,' Snorky said. 'But if you don't believe me ...' He separated the hatpin from the horseshoe and nails, but instead of offering it to Samson for inspection he suddenly turned, grabbed Speedy's left ear lobe, stretched it downwards, and plunged the hatpin straight through it - then, before Speedy could intervene, Snorky bent the hatpin double so that the final effect was that of a very distinctive earring.

'Looks good, doesn't it,' he mused, stepping back the better to admire his handiwork.

Samson had to admit (to himself, anyway) that it did look good: it even gave Speedy a touch of class. He smiled fondly at Speedy and patted him on the head, more gently than usual. Speedy looked from him to Snorky and then back again, and began grinning happily and nodding his head vigorously. Samson heaved another sigh of relief, the most heartfelt one ever, then stretched out on his back on the lovely warm stone and closed his eyes.

When at long last Samson opened his eyes, the world was a different place. The sun was beating down strongly, and the last of the clouds were scurrying across the sky, as if eager to escape from the scene of a crime: their shadows, flitting across the battered landscape, looked as though they were being driven to destruction at the edges of the world by an all-powerful sun, like a herd of bison stampeded towards a precipice, that Samson had seen on the poster of a forthcoming film advertised in the cinema foyer on the occasion of the Great Adventure. The great dome of the sky, as it cleared, suggested an enormous open-air theatre in which a little group of diminutive actors played out their insignificant parts on an insignificant stage. Worrying about Speedy's having a hatpin thrust through his ear, suddenly seemed pointless. In any case, if he was happy, why should anyone else worry? Of course, that was not to say that Snorky had done the right thing ...

Any further considerations of situational ethics were pushed into the background by a foul stench, very faint at first but rapidly getting stronger. It was the most awful kind of smell imaginable - like, Samson remembered, one Christmas when he had vomited after gorging himself on Gorgonzola cheese. He rose to one elbow and looked around, wrinkling his nose and blinking. But there was no vomit anywhere - or cheese, for that matter.

'For God's sake!' he shouted at Snorky, who had removed his famous boots and was now peeling off his socks, revealing the most disgusting pair of feet Samson had ever seen. The most striking thing, of course, was the contrast with his boots. Obviously there could be only one explanation for the boots' normally deep shine and the cheesy sogginess of Snorky's feet: he wore them in bed. The other odd thing was the contrast between the lifelessness of the feet, and the incredible dexterity of his hands. It was impossible to imagine how the two types of appendage could grow on the same person. Perhaps, Samson speculated, Snorky had his father's hands and his mother's feet ... or vice versa.

'Half a mo',' Snorky said. 'They're killing me - these boots.' It looked as if the tops of the toes had been skinned.

'What, too big for them?' Samson joked. 'Your feet, I mean.'

'They're new,' Snorky said, scowling.

'The feet? Oh, yes ... the boots. *Mmm*, I can see that,' Samson agreed. 'Now you mention it ...' Even before their exposure to the floodwaters the boots had been only averagely shiny and would obviously have needed weeks and weeks of being polished ten times a day (and worn in bed ten hours every night) before they could have acquired the rich deep Cherry Blossom shine that Snorky loved.

A long silence followed ... a long, long silence during which Snorky continued to mess about with his disgusting feet, apparently attempting to rearrange the toes more comfortably. Meanwhile Speedy happily fondled his new earring, occasionally setting it swinging by shaking his head from side to side. Samson watched his two friends in deep contemplation. He felt he had learned something interesting about each of them. Taking Speedy first, for a change: it was strange that his scalp had bled so little; his ear, so much. Possibly there was not much wrong with his brain as such, just a problem with the plumbing such that his ears got too much blood, leaving his brain a bit short. As far as Snorky was concerned, a definite flaw had been exposed in an otherwise perfect gem ... two flaws, to be precise: his feet. This fascinating realisation led automatically to an exciting idea which, if put into practice, might just result in Snorky having to drop his damn fool crucifixion business. If his feet were playing him up already, what would they be like after a really hard trek over really really rough ground?

'I know!' Samson said brightly. 'How about ... how about a game of hide and seek? Anywhere you like ... you decide. Winner takes all.'

It really was a brilliant idea. If there was one thing in life where they were in different leagues, it was woodcraft, hunting, that kind of thing. A humiliating defeat might just cut Snorky down to size, and his feet would end up so bad that the return journey might be impossible. With a bit of luck he might even sprain an ankle, or break a leg! Then where would he be?

'All what?' Snorky asked cuttingly. 'All the king's horses? All the king's men? All the flipping tea in China?'

Poor Samson! The question, and the sheer hostility of it, took him completely by surprise. Words and images jostled each other and were chopped into useless fragments by the whirring machinery of his brain. He lowered his head and turned this way and that to hide his confusion and the tears that were welling up. He found himself staring at the deep crack across the Rock of Gibraltar, and for the first time in his life he wished the world would open up and swallow him. Snorky's next words were lost on him.

25. Old Man Mountain

Samson's brimming tears split the bright light reflected from Entwistle's lodge into a hundred shimmering iridescent colours, like those reflected from a starling's plumage or from oil too thinly spread on troubled waters. A thousand pinpoint stars were born, doomed instantly to explode or fade away: just four survived, expanding to form four tiny soap bubbles which floated tantalisingly slowly across Samson's field of vision, in the process becoming speech bubbles which entered his right ear. There they popped, each depositing a muffled word.

'Old', the first one seemed to say; the second, 'man'; then 'man' again, and finally 'ten'. 'Old ... man ... man ... ten ... old man ... man ... ten' ...... the words chased each other tiredly through Samson's brain, emerging through the left ear and then circling round to re-enter the right ear. 'Old man man ten ... old man man ten ... old man manten .... old man mountain ... Old Man Mountain! OLD MAN MOUNTAIN!

'Old Man Mountain?' Samson quavered. 'Did you say "Old Man Mountain"?'

Lingering long enough to wipe the most obvious tears away with his sleeve, but without waiting for Snorky to reply, he threw himself at him and embraced him. Old Man Mountain! Ha, ha, ha, ha! Snorky could not have suggested a better place - better for Samson, that is. Because Old Man Mountain was bare and desolate, windswept and strewn with rocks. It provided the best possible test of hunting and stalking skills, with no opportunity for cheating. Best of all, as the terrain was so tough, Snorky's feet would be absolutely destroyed after half an hour spent scampering about like a mountain goat. He would probably have to be taken away on a stretcher!

'Yip,' Snorky replied, calmly but resolutely. He was wrinkling his nose in distaste at the embrace, so Samson released him, then leaped across the crevice, balanced very precariously on the very edge of The Rock, closed his eyes and beat his chest, Tarzan-style. Then he turned to watch Snorky get ready. As always, it was quite a performance.

Snorky carefully rearranged his toes as if he were putting newborn quintuplets to bed, replaced his socks and took out his favourite shoehorn. It was, Samson remembered, the fancy antelope-horn one which had been sent to him by a rich uncle in Tanganyika. What was his name ... his flipping name .... Uncle Bob (the one sometimes referred to as 'Black Bob' on account of being the black sheep of the far-flung Horrocks tribe)? No, probably not .... more than likely it was his Uncle Fritzi, the war hero - the one who had been 'decorated' (the same as 'whitewashed', Samson wondered?) during the Great War after the Battle of Wipers (or 'Vipers' as Snorky pronounced it when imitating his uncle's way of speaking ... a vicious battle, by all accounts). Yes, that would be the one ... the one who had got the V.C. or the V.D. or something ... not the V.E. anyway, that was a kind of rocket ....

Uncle Fritzi's shoehorn helped Snorky make quick work of putting the boots back on, though judging from the frequent winces (hooray!) it was a painful business. Then, all that remained was to give the boots a quick wipe over (aha: Battle of Wipers!) with wet grass (they were too damp to take polish, of course), to tie the laces with the distinctive fancy knots which he claimed to have invented, and which would one day be 'as famous as a Windsor knot', and to stow away the magician's paraphernalia. Finding places to put the various items was magic in itself.

Preparations at last completed, Snorky rose to his feet with difficulty, tottered briefly, like a young girl trying on her mother's high heels for the first time, then turned through ninety degrees so as to face in the general direction of Old Man Mountain.

'Okay,' he announced. 'Okay?'

'Aye aye, Sir!' Samson replied, falling in behind and motioning Speedy to bring up the rear.

The boys, silent and in single file, picked their way through a storm-damaged cornfield towards the ridge at Windy End. Snorky continued to lead the party, as though the whole thing had been his idea. Samson was quite happy just to follow, reckoning that Snorky's eventual crushing defeat would be all the more bitter on that account. Within three or four minutes the party had traversed the ridge without mishap, and started to work their way through a sparse thicket: when they emerged from this they were on the edge of the moors. Here a chill wind whistled, whatever the season, and because of the unpredictable gusts it was one of the worst places in Old Guinea to have a wee - which, however, the boys now did, thereby lightening themselves, as bats do, before engaging in strenuous activity. To the boys' right, dense bracken interspersed with heather-clad outcrops led down to the tired, sluggish Old Man River - a tributary, in spite of its title, of Stranglers Brook. Directly ahead, across two hundred yards of featureless bog, was the forbidding - and forbidden - mountain.

While waiting for Snorky to dry the tops of his precious boots Samson took the opportunity of refreshing his memory of the mountain - in effect, the head of an old man plus a short length of his powerful neck. At the foot of the mountain a thick ridge jutted out like a heavy lower jaw, casting seven o'clock shadows across the bog. Higher up, a long and very straight ledge suggested a determined mouth, especially since it was edged by tiny vertical fissures reminiscent of the puckering which develops around a toothless mouth in extreme old age. Slightly higher still, but a bit too low for the face, a large, gently-curving protuberance, fluted like a scallop shell, could easily have been taken for the right ear, albeit one severely damaged by frost; its mate, if ever there had been one, must have broken away in its entirety, taking a sizeable chunk of skull with it, as if bitten off by a bull terrier.

The features thus far inspected by Samson created an impression of ugliness, of a face ravaged by time. But the upper part was worse, and gave him the creeps - not because it was uglier - which it was - but because of the strong aura of violence and evil, enough to give Samson goose pimples all the way from the crown of his head to the tip of his spine. There was the low, receding forehead, deeply wrinkled by goat tracks; the twisted, sneering nose, with half the bridge eaten away, reminding Samson of an old sailor who had been standing next to him in the lavatory tent at the Whit Monday fête; and the eyes were two sinister black holes, set criminally close together and at slightly different levels. These and several other orifices and pockmarks gave access to the interior of the mountain, but it didn't take much intelligence to realise that the mountain held some terrible secret, a curse or two perhaps, and that anyone daring to enter it would be unlikely to emerge unharmed. However, on the two previous occasions when they had been out of bounds the boys had discovered that, provided they played on the mountain, without trying to pry into its secrets, they were perfectly safe. And certainly it was impossible to imagine a better place to kill time playing 'hide and seek'. There were a million-and-one places to hide, and any sounds made while scrambling about carried in the most peculiar ways, so that your skills were tested to the limit.

'Up on the bridge?' Snorky suggested.

'Aye aye, Captain!' Samson saluted, thereby agreeing the starting point for the game: the bridge of the old man's nose. A good game was guaranteed by starting so high up, and there was on this occasion the added advantage that climbing up to the starting point would take ten or fifteen minutes, thus improving the chance that Snorky would be worn out by the time he lost; given also that he hated losing, more than anything in the world (apart perhaps from getting his boots dirty), he would surely become severely dispirited and want to call it a day and go home to put his feet up, or whatever it was he did with them: any serious injury picked up on the way would, of course, be an added bonus.

'This way!' Snorky commanded. He set off obliquely across the bog, tacking like a dinghy, and led the party safely to the base of the Old Man's neck. Progress became a little faster as they traversed the neck, heading for the left earhole. This was the obvious way to go, since it would have been almost impossible to scale the overhang created by the severe jut of the bottom jaw, and too dangerous to ascend by way of the right earhole because of loose rocks, In the event it took them about ten minutes to reach this first base, and then another five or six to scramble across a wide fall of mini-boulders so as to get onto the upper lip. From this point on the climb was much steeper, and a careless slip could have resulted in a fall of forty or fifty feet, directly onto an irregular line of larger boulders protruding from the bog like knuckledusters. Fortunately there were some excellent handholds and footholds, though just below the nostrils the rocks were slippery where iron-stained water trickled down like old blood.

The boys stopped for a little while to get their breath back. Snorky leaned against the rock face, staring up at the bridge of the Old Man's nose, probably (Samson surmised) plucking up courage for the ascent (he was afraid of heights, but would never admit it). Speedy, meanwhile, peered intently up the nostril, making strange noises, like an old person straining on the lavatory. He tugged at Samson's sleeve, almost causing both of them to overbalance. Samson managed to grab hold of a tuft of heather, then with his free hand he cuffed Speedy in a very committed way. Fortunately, before the situation could get out of hand Snorky set off on the last stage of the climb.

'Come on! Come on, you useless beggars!' he shouted.

Samson, already feeling guilty about the way he had treated Speedy, pushed the latter on ahead, entertaining the vague notion that, if Speedy slipped, he would somehow catch him and save his life. It was a good feeling.

The boys at last reached their goal. They stood there for a couple of minutes to get their breath back and to enjoy the lovely cool breeze. Then it was time for the game to start.

'A hundred?' Samson suggested.

'Make it two,' Snorky responded.

'Okay,' Samson agreed. 'Suits me.'

The idea was that they would count up to two hundred whilst dispersing and getting into position, then the search for Speedy would begin. Speedy, of course, was 'it' and his job was, to disappear as effectively as possible.

'SCRAM!' the two hunters shouted in unison. To help Speedy get the message Snorky gave him a sharp push in the back, then threw a couple of stones at his heels to encourage him to pick his feet up. Fortunately for Speedy there was no chance of sustained target practice, because the hunters were now on the move, skirting the mountain in opposite directions to reach their respective starting positions.

Other than the fact that Speedy was included in the game, there was nothing to motivate him to extreme exertion, so quite understandably he tended to work his way down rather than up the mountain. The hunters would eventually be forced to do the same. However, the game was not a simple matter of finding Speedy: a major part of it was to fool the opponent by such devices as lobbing stones about, uttering Speedy-like noises and so on. Samson decided that, because of the bad condition of his adversary's feet, he could gain an initial advantage by doing something close to the impossible, something that Snorky would not have the wit even to think about, much less to try: making a superhuman effort, he would climb up the extremely dangerous crags at the back of the Old Man's head, scramble over the crown, then get into position above and therefore behind the right eyebrow - the bushier of the two, and hence the better choice.

Samson surpassed himself, reaching the eyebrow by the aforementioned route on the count of a hundred and ninety-six. Collapsing on his heaving belly behind the gorse bushes comprising the eyebrow, faint to the point of dizziness, he waited a few seconds for his vision to unblur, then wriggled forward and surveyed the slopes far below. There was as yet no sign of Speedy or Snorky, and not a single sound which might have suggested where to concentrate his gaze. This was a little odd, because Speedy could normally be relied on the blunder about a bit, and Snorky was wont to do the same in order to create confusion. So ... nothing to worry about for the moment ... in fact, a perfect chance to relax and enjoy the spectacular view.

As far as the eye could see, right up to the blackened horizon where hundreds of smoking mills crowded together along the banks of the lrwell, like chain-smoking mourners lining the route to a civic funeral, the landscape was prettily divided up by irregular dry stone walls into a ragged patchwork quilt of greens and browns, so that the whole looked like a jigsaw puzzle which, after being wrongly assembled, had been thrown onto the fire and had already started smouldering; meanwhile, oblivious, little toy men with toy horses and toy machines crept about like partially-dismembered ants on a cold morning. Samson suddenly felt he knew what it must be like to be an eagle or a falcon, or a buzzard or vulture even, able at the merest whim to soar above all these insignificant little figures. The feeling was obviously one of limitless power and freedom and confidence. God! How wonderful it would be to launch yourself into space from the mountain, float noiselessly over the rolling moors, soar up and up and up with the air meeting the mountainside, glide silently and effortlessly in ever-decreasing circles over the unsuspecting Snorky .... then shit on him!

Suddenly, something moved near the right-hand edge of Samson's field of vision. The movement was sudden and short-lived, and whatever or whoever had made it was now stationary again, invisible amongst the thousands and thousands of boulders and cobbles which littered that side of the mountain in particular. Samson smiled and waited, the experienced hunter biding his time in pleasurable anticipation of the kill. When ... *aha!* Yes, there it was again: a quick blur, then nothing. But what had moved? Was he perhaps 'seeing things'? Could it have been a bush? Perhaps it was a bush that had simply been caught by a little gust of wind, and waved? It .... it was a bush ... well, it was and it wasn't: it was Snorky! The crafty devil - nine out of ten for this - had somehow cut or pulled up a sizable gorse bush and was holding it over his back and shoulders: thus rendered invisible, he was zig-zagging about in short, sharp movements of a couple of feet at most. Now he was crouching behind a boulder, peering round it with extreme caution: obviously it had not occurred to him that his rival would be way up above him, disdainfully watching every move. Poor fool!

Snorky, satisfied at last that he was unobserved, moved from boulder to boulder more quickly. Any moment now he would have to cross a long snaking 'path', less than a foot wide. It started in the corner of the Old Man's right eye, where the tear duct would have been, and the reason that it had the irregular course of a tear drop was that it had been worn away by an occasional rivulet: though having the appearance of a path, it was far too steep to be used as such, by man or beast, and its only possible use would have been as a slide, so that for Samson it was a snake in a snakes-and-ladders game - one constructed on a grand scale, but unfortunately without ladders.

It would be interesting to see how Snorky negotiated the snake: continuing to hold the gorse bush would be dangerous, because the snake was so steep and slippery that you would need six points of contact, like an insect - only achievable by throwing down the bush and getting down on your hands and elbows and knees. *Aha* .. Snorky did in fact discard his bush - albeit temporarily, flinging it across the snake. He then began to pick his way across the snake in a very comical manner, with hands and feet widely splayed, but without letting his knees touch the floor - just like a housefly that Samson had once observed for ages, trying to move across a spiral flycatcher made of brown sticky paper. Perfect! Now, just like the fly when it discovered it was stuck, he was shaking a leg.

Samson shifted his position slightly, like a selfish theatre-goer who had paid a bit over the odds for the best seat and was now determined to get his money's worth regardless of inconvenience to others. In doing so his right hand came into contact with an unusual boulder, the size, shape and smoothness of an enormous brown egg - perhaps one laid by a giant ostrich, Samson surmised - well ... if there was such a thing. It lay about eighteen inches from the edge of the eyebrow, just asking to be pushed over the edge onto the snake: it would meet the snake twenty or thirty feet down the slope, then with a bit of luck it would rumble down towards Snorky and scare the wits out of him! He would be so shaken that his chances of winning the hide-and-seek game would be reduced at a stroke from a thin one to a fat one.

Samson inched to his right. Rising to his knees, he put his full weight behind the egg and tested its weight. Great! It was heavy, but it was rockable. And there was Snorky, still doing his 'trapped fly' impression. It was now or never!

Samson rocked the egg seriously, backwards and forwards, then ... one .. two ... it was easier than he had expected ... three ... and away it went! It landed further down the slope than Samson had calculated, not twenty feet from Snorky. Obviously he was taken completely by surprise: letting out a desperate shout, he somehow scrambled out of harm's way with only inches to spare. But he was still half on the snake, and the avalanche of dust and stones and mini-boulders that soon followed the egg caught hold of him and transported him ignominiously all the way down it. Such was the accompanying cloud of dust that it was some time before Snorky could be located. At last Samson could make him out, coughing and spluttering and manically brushing his clothes down, on the very edge of the Old Man's upper lip: a little extra speed and he would have been swept over the lip and dropped forty or fifty feet onto the knuckledusters. Marvellous! The fright of his life! At that moment Samson would have given anything to see his friend's face. Never one to look a gift horse in the mouth, Samson also realised that the accident had given him a decisive advantage in the game of hide-and-seek

Oh dear! If only Speedy could have ... Speedy ... oh, GOD! Where was he? What if he had been wandering about in the firing line? He could have been scared ... injured   maimed ... killed, even. Worried sick, Samson clambered down from the eyebrow to the snake and, sitting on his haunches, let himself be carried back down the mountain half-way to the upper lip. By managing to stay on his feet throughout he was able to benefit from the braking effect of the clog irons, and he came to a halt level with the bottom of the nose, invisible to Snorky because of the convex contour. It was at this moment that the earlier image of Speedy looking longingly up the Old Man's left nostril, and making strange straining noises came back to him. Of course! That had to be it! Probably Speedy was safe and sound after all, thank God.

Samson rose shakily to his feet, staggered around a little, then stumbled off towards the nostril where, for sure, Speedy was hiding - 'for sure', because the slimy boulders below the nostril revealed signs of a clumsy person (or animal? ... heck!) having recently climbed up. Some of the marks had obviously been made by clogs or boots, and a wide vertical mark must have been where the climber had slipped back a few feet. Anyway, clumsy or not, the climber had obviously succeeded: the marks went to the very edge of the nostril. Thanks to his present position Samson was able to avoid the slippery climb and approach the nostril horizontally without leaving any traces of his movement.

Samson heaved himself into the nostril. Immediately, in spite of being hot and flustered, he shivered - partly perhaps on account of the sudden chill, but partly too through apprehension. The place was dark, damp, dank, with scary hollow dripping noises and whistlings and sighings, as though the Old Man was not quite dead - just sleeping fitfully.

As his eyes slowly adapted to the gloom Samson saw that he was in a kind of cave, one which rapidly narrowed as it curved deeper into the skull, but the far end of which was in complete darkness. Samson inched forward, legs well splayed, ready at all times to drop to all fours just in case a chasm was there waiting to swallow him up. Feeling that his eyes were a hindrance rather than a help, he closed them: this clever move enabled him to use his outstretched arms like cats' whiskers.

Aaaarrrggh! A sudden ripping noise, only inches in front of him, paralysed him. But he relaxed when the noise was repeated, because by then a horrible, disgusting but familiar smell had begun to penetrate his quivering nostrils. Sure enough, when he opened his eyes again he was able to make out, in the dim, dim light, the distinctive figure of dear old Speedy. He was crouched down among some stones - squatting, strictly - and concentrating on 'doing his business', as Miss Pollock liked to put it. Perhaps as an aid to concentration Speedy had his hands over his ears - and something even more interesting, Samson noted: Speedy actually did take his trousers down. Excited by these revelations, Samson thought to check on the most contentious rumour of all: that Speedy had a tail. However, Samson's decent self recognised that it was somehow not quite right to take advantage of the situation to check up on Speedy's private details and he therefore restricted himself to a very brief glance in the general direction of Speedy's rump, very properly refusing to allow his gaze to linger on the something that appeared to be protruding from it - something which might well have been a tail, but to be fair could equally well have been a stiff stool of record-breaking proportions.

Speedy had perhaps detected an intruder's presence: he removed his hands from his ears, and looked up. It was doubtful if he could see Samson, who was by now pressed against the wall behind him, in a very dark recess. It was a wonderful chance to give Speedy the fright of his life. To this end Samson cupped his hands around his mouth, then in the deepest and most tremulous voice that he could manage he shouted:

'*FEEEEEEE ... FIIIIIIII ... FOOOOOOO ... FUMMMM...* I smell the smell of an English *bummmmmmmmmmmmmmm.*'

The effect far exceeded Samson's expectations: Speedy opened his mouth to its fullest extent, like a baboon or a yawning dog, and uttered a most terrible cry, somewhere between a shout of alarm and a scream of terror. It was the kind of cry that, thousands of years earlier, a caveman might have uttered when the starving bears or wolves or a sabre-toothed tiger closed in for the kill, perfectly happy to start eating you while you were still alive and kicking and screaming. Samson abandoned the joke, crept to where Speedy cowered, and patted him reassuringly on the head. Apart from any humanitarian considerations there was an excellent practical reason for quietening Speedy: Samson's finely-tuned hunter's ears had detected sounds coming from just outside the cave, sounds made by someone scrambling up the slimy rocks below the nostril - Snorky, obviously. Far better to give him a scare than to upset a harmless idiot.

'*Ssssssssh ...*' Samson breathed into Speedy's ear. '*Sssssssh ...* it's me, Samson.'

He patted Speedy again, then alternately patted and stroked his wiry head. Speedy leaned closer and trembled self-indulgently. Samson, for his part, concentrated on preventing himself from baulking - such was the foul stench. From the direction of the cave's entrance the sounds of frantic scrambling and of bitten-back expletives suddenly ceased, to be replaced by the sounds of heavy breathing. Snorky's head and shoulders appeared in silhouette, the silhouette's blackness and protruding ears bringing to mind dear old Black Sambo the money box ... Boy Sunday too, come to think of it.

'Speedy! Speedy!' Snorky called hoarsely. trying to shout whilst at the same time trying to whisper. 'Speedy! Where are you, you stupid twerp?' He sounded terrified, which was no doubt why he now crept forward into the gloom in slow motion, crouching so as to make himself the smallest target possible. His hunting knife firmly grasped in his right hand, every few seconds he prodded and slashed the space around before continuing. God! He was out of his mind with fear! With his nerves so on edge, the perfect moment for frightening him was close at hand. Samson cupped one hand over Speedy's mouth while holding his own nose with the other. The moment was ripe.

'*WOOOOOOOOOOO ..... HH*' Samson bawled. In the confined space, and with the benefit of multiple echos, he sounded like a young bullock. '*WOOOOOOOO ... HH!*".
'*AAAAAAAAAAAAARRRRRRRGGGGGH!!!!*' Snorky screamed, and in an unscripted reaction he lunged forward with the knife. Samson heard the knife point strike the rock just behind him, and a fraction of second later a sharp pain seared through his left arm. Then all was cacophony ... confusion ... chaos ...

26. Chicken!

Like a severely injured octopus, with two limbs missing and another badly lacerated, the blood brothers struggled blindly in the inky darkness to untangle themselves. Torsos writhed and heaved: free limbs flailed ineffectually, groped and recoiled. The atmosphere in the cave became ever more heavy and sickly, with foul smells and even fouler language. Screaming disembodied voices flew around like evil spirits, bouncing from wall to wall to create a cacophony worse than in a disturbed roost of bats. A religious fanatic might have given his right arm for inspiration such as this, but Samson experienced no uplifting feeling at first. When finally he was able to extricate himself from the heap he was aware only of being in a cold sweat, and of warm sticky blood oozing around his left armpit. Though the possibility of losing the arm did cross his mind he chose instead to worry about bleeding to death in the darkness. He wondered whether he would gradually shrivel up like an abandoned tomato, or whether the blood would simply drain out in an orderly manner, from the head downwards: already he felt light-headed and sensed there was no time to lose. With commendable presence of mind he squinted his way, half-staggering and half-crawling, towards the tiny patch of light at the mouth of the cave. On reaching the blinding daylight he paused to inspect the damage. It was bad, but not too bad: 'could have been worse' summed it up perfectly. The edge of the knife had slashed through the inside of his upper left arm, to about the depth favoured by a master butcher scoring a joint of prime shoulder pork. Blood was everywhere, but fortunately the precious fluid was oozing rather than spurting, and it already showed signs of wanting to clot. Samson sighed deeply (more because he felt it was the thing to do, than from any genuine feeling of relief), pressed the upper arm tightly to his side and thrust his forearm up his jumper. He was reminded of the proud military man depicted on Speedy's earring, also of a snatch of song, 'Oompah, oompah, stick it up your jumpah!' Able to breathe in more easily than out, he swelled with the exhilaration of hard-won victory and started swinging his clogged feet in time to imagined martial music. Looking out across the bog he conjured up a sea of upturned faces and launched into a royal wave: a searing pain from his cut arm made it one of the shortest waves in history. Well, it was time to move: the others could be heard shuffling towards the entrance, and Samson felt that if he were to make the tricky descent to the bog with them, the obviousness of his crippled condition would detract from the decisiveness of his victory. Using his good arm as a brake he slipped and slithered down the scree, then waited at the edge of the bog for the others to catch up. Then it was he who led the party back cross the bog.

For the first time in the three esses' long-standing friendship Samson felt himself to be the leader, the boss, the king. Partly, of course, this new feeling stemmed from the victory, but it owed something too to the wound. He had often dreamed of doing heroic deeds - single-handedly fighting off battalions of German or Japanese soldiers, or scores of Red Indian braves - but he had always worried about what his reaction might be if he were wounded: he might burst into tears, start screaming hysterically, or simply faint. Now he knew that he would never, never ever, show fear, whatever injuries he sustained. In retrospect the cut on his arm, though it was deep and had bled profusely, was little more than an inconvenience, no worse than being stung by a bumblebee - the potentially alarming sensation of warm blood trickling down the arm was almost pleasant, in the same way that wetting the bed on a perishing cold winter's night could be pleasant - all that was left was a dull, throbbing pain which was already becoming boring. Another day or two or three, and even that would have died away, leaving a lovely scar as a memento of the wounding.

Samson was suddenly reminded of a memorable phrase in a comic passed round St. Peter's: three schoolboys had lied about their age and gone off to teach the Japs a lesson in the far-off jungles of Burma.

'They went out boys, they came back men,' it said.

The three little men successfully negotiated the treacherous bog by a different route from the one taken earlier, and soon arrived at Old Man River. Samson sat down on an old willow root protruding from the bank, and dangled his feet in the limpid water, into which he stared in a philosophic mood until distracted by a loud splash as Speedy inadvertently stepped into the river; moments later, clumsily turning round, Speedy put his foot in it again. Samson wondered how it was possible for anyone, even an idiot, to step into the same river twice. It was the sort of thing that you could think about for a thousand years or more, without ever being able to understand it. He took comfort in a biblical saying which had often been quoted by that fount of wisdom, dear old Tomcat: 'Once, a mistake: twice, a coincidence: three times, a bloody fool', and braced himself for the next splash.

Speedy floundered out of the water, shook himself like a tired old dog, and came to sit beside Samson. He started jiggling his feet, and from time to time he looked up at Samson admiringly. Samson gave him the occasional friendly cuff - with his 'good' arm, of course - to keep him happy. At the same time he contrived to keep a weather eye on poor old Snorky, who had wedged himself in a split willow trunk four or five feet away from his friends. Snorky had a disgusted look on his face, and he was muttering to himself. Seeing Samson look up, he pretended to be staring vacantly into the waters, eyes unfocussed like a poet's. Samson turned back to watch the river again, casually propped his elbows on his knees, in spite of the searing pain when he moved his left arm, and cupped his hands over his eyes: he was then able to observe Snorky through the slits between his fingers. Snorky, now he thought that nobody was looking, quietly took out his knife and started scraping diffidently at his boots: they were in a shocking state, consistent with his having stepped into something very nasty. Samson also noticed that the knife's tip was broken off, and he guessed that that must have happened in the cave, when the blade struck the wall after skewering him.

Now that Snorky was absorbed in his task Samson bent down towards the water and gently immersed his elbow. Even with his pullover and shirt still on he could see the full extent of the wound. It was beyond his wildest dreams: with luck the resulting scar would last him the rest of his life. Watery blood seeped from the cut, and Samson watched, fascinated, as sleek little tadpoles appeared from under some weeds and started nibbling at the ragged edges of the cut. He was reminded how bloodthirsty these harmless-looking creatures were - sometimes, he knew, they turned cannibal, showing admirable perseverance in swallowing a friend or brother or sister whole ... so, they were not really in a position to complain if, after growing up, they found themselves being skinned alive.

Any further exploration of this interesting theme was sharply interrupted by an angry cry from above and behind:
'SHIT!'
Simultaneously something flew past Samson's right ear, mere whiskers away, scattering the assembled diners - Snorky's knife! It struck a stone just below the water's surface, danced through the air, turning over and over, then plopped back into the water as neatly as a trout before finally coming to rest at the bottom of a shallow channel, where it glinted silver.

'Watch it!' Samson remonstrated, turning to scowl at Snorky, but the latter merely looked through him and got on with cleaning his boots with a great handful of wadding. Samson shrugged, and turned back to the river to make a mental note of the knife's position: almost certainly it would be possible, though laborious, to grind the broken tip and make a new point, as sharp as or even sharper than new. How silly of Snorky to throw it away! Oh well ... easy come, easy go. In this way Snorky's potentially dangerous action - which in different circumstances might have sparked off a fight, a riot, a revolution or even a world war - was dismissed. Something about the meandering river - its tranquillity, its timelessness, its soothing sounds, perhaps - reduced the incident to the importance of the tiny ripple created when one of the browsing tadpoles, dangerously bloated, hit the surface - perhaps, Samson speculated, to burp after gorging itself on raw human flesh. He was moved to song:

> Old Man River
> That Old Man River
> He Must Know Something

> He Doesn't Say Anything
> He Just Keeps Roaming
> He Just Keeps Rolling
> Along.
>
> He Doesn't -

Samson broke off, having some difficulty in recalling the words. Partly he was put off by the incorrect grammar employed by the minstrel from whom he had unconsciously picked up the piece; partly he was put off by Speedy, who had just struck up a *fortissimo* sustained '*Aaaaaa ...*', as if he were being examined for a throat infection: it was something Speedy had picked up from school prayers - from the final 'Amen', to be precise.

'Shurrup!' Samson snapped, but on seeing Speedy's pained reaction he immediately showed that he hadn't meant anything, by giving him a nice cuff - then, worried in case the blow was too hard, he ruffled his wiry hair.

'Yeah, shurrup!' Snorky concurred. In his case there was no doubt that he meant it.

Samson, immensely relieved that Snorky was joining in again, shifted to a sitting position and turned to smile at him.

'A good game, eh!' he volunteered. 'Close, blooming close! Very good ... the, err ... that gorse ...' He ended incoherently, discomfited by Snorky's hostile stare, and busied himself flicking off a couple of tadpoles which had locked their jaws so tightly onto the ragged flesh around the cut on his arm that they were dangling in mid-air. Then he turned to contemplate the soothing waters anew. Immediately, the words of the song started to flow again, as if he had known them all his life:

> You and I, We Sweat and Strain
> Body All Aching And Racked with Pain
> Tear that Badge, Lift that Bale
> Get a Little Drunk and You Land in Jai-ail.
> I (*splash!*) Get Weary and
> Sick (*splash!*) of Trying
> I'm Tired (*splash!*) of Living and
> Afraid (*splash!*) of Dying
> But ... *SPLASH!!!* ...

The gentle splashes were made by small stones, thrown into the water by Samson to help punctuate the chorus and emphasise its dirge-like quality. The loud splash, which abruptly terminated the rendition, was made not by Speedy falling in again (though he looked in danger of so doing - attempting, as he was, to throw a stone into the water, without yet having mastered the art of letting go), but by a huge log of wood which sailed over the minstrel's head. It created something like a tidal wave, so that for a few seconds the waters seemed to be flowing backwards; then the log surfaced, its shape, its texture and a couple of suitably-placed knots exactly capturing the essence of a marauding crocodile. At the same time there was a dreadful shriek from above and behind:

'SHURRUP!!! '

Though not musical, Snorky had raised his voice through a couple of octaves and several decibels.

'What the flipping heck!' Samson spluttered, brushing water from his eyes. He broke off abruptly when Snorky wrenched himself out of the tree fork, jumped down, and strode menacingly forward until his face was only inches from Samson's. Samson stared at him apprehensively. There was a long pause as the rivals eyeballed each other, then the tense silence was broken by Snorky:

'If you think you're so blooming clever,' he shouted, 'let's have a real game - see who's really the kiddy (here, he tapped his own chest) and who's fucking chicken!' These last words were screamed rather than shouted, and further emphasised by two stiff prods to Samson's chest.

'If you say so ...' Samson replied weakly. God ... what had come over Snorky?

'The sooner the better, then,' Snorky growled. After maintaining his intimidating, slit-eyed stare for a few seconds more he turned away, performed a few jerky limbering-up exercises, and shouted: 'Come on! '

He set off resolutely, with Samson and Speedy following close behind. Like the remnants of an unsuccessful peasant uprising they lurched along: Snorky limping gamely at the front; Samson, almost at his elbow, nursing his bleeding arm;

and Speedy bringing up the rear, dropping back from time to time when his trousers started to carry out their constant threat of falling down. Notwithstanding these technical difficulties the three of them soon reached the vicinity of St. Peter's, and after shinning over the umpteenth dry stone wall they arrived in a field overlooking the quarry, a little out of breath but otherwise in working order.

The quarry seemed deeper than on Samson's previous visit. It looked as though a great deal of stone had been gouged out from the southern face, causing the crumbling church to teeter precariously on the very edge - an effect emphasised by extensive undermining. Almost every building in Old Guinea, from once-imposing edifices such as Foxgloves Hall and St. Peter's Church, to the meanest hovel or pigsty, likewise the miles and miles of tumbledown dry stone walls - all these were constructed from sandstone hacked from the quarry. During building booms the quarry was busy from dawn till dusk, with blasting twice a day. A makeshift railway was used to raise rock from the face, down in the bottom of the quarry, to a platform of old railway sleepers at the summit, where the waggons were unloaded. The waggons were hauled up the long, twisting incline by a noisy stationary engine working through a complex system of cables and pulleys, and unloaded by manual operation of levers which opened their bottoms. After being unloaded the waggons were allowed to freewheel back down to the workface. At first their progress was very slow, because the axles were never oiled and the track poorly maintained. Occasionally waggons would be derailed by stones on the track, and once, a quarry worker had been killed by a waggon which jumped the track and plummeted some thirty or forty feet onto him: it still lay there over patches of rust, upside down and with one set of wheels at a crazy angle. Samson wondered if the patches of rust had originally been pools of blood.

The most dangerous area was, of course, the lower slopes. Once the waggons got moving they came to a steep section of the track, down which they plunged with a shrieking rusty roar; they then raced round a long, curved, almost level section (in effect, a ledge of up to fifteen yards wide, before descending, more steeply again, to the workface.

The level section was where the fun was to be had, and fortunately (being technically out of bounds to St. Peter's children) it was out of sight both from above and below, thanks to substantial overhangs. The game was, to wait behind the dynamite hut, about ten yards from the track, like novice steeplechasers under starter's orders - and there, with bated breath and bumping heart, to listen for the roar of the waggons as they began their descent of the steep upper section. Then, of course, the first one to run across the track in front of the roaring waggons was 'chicken', and the last one 'the kiddy'. Both Samson and Snorky excelled at the game: both were experts at cutting it fine. Speedy, of course, was never invited to play: instead, someone would shout 'Corner!', whereupon he would shuffle off and stand at the back of the hut until collected.

A chain of three loaded waggons was now clanking up the last few feet of the upper section, just prior to unloading. Within a minute or two they would have been emptied and cast loose. It was time to get ready.

'Okay?' Snorky checked, getting to his feet and performing a few jerky limbering-up exercises.

'Right when you are,' Samson replied resolutely.

'Right: the showdown,' Snorky said grimly, his tense voice reduced to a whisper.

'The showdown,' Samson agreed. Then, remembering Speedy, he turned to him and shouted: 'Corner! Corner!'

Normally Speedy would have obeyed the command mechanically, but on this occasion he failed to budge, even when Samson repeated the command twice. There was nothing for it, therefore, but to resort to a bit of quick magic that never failed: Snorky's 'magic circle'. This involved using a clog toecap to inscribe a crude circle in the dust around where Speedy stood: he would stay there all day, if necessary - or if, as on the trip to Blackpool, he was forgotten. (Once, he had been accidentally left inside a circle all night: he was only found the following lunchtime, as cold as a hibernating skunk.) On this occasion he failed to follow precedent: he stepped out of the circle.

From far above came the noise of the waggons being emptied, and a vast cloud of dust rose up, plunging the level section into semi-darkness. Time was running out. Something had to be done, and soon: a bit of inspiration was called for.

'Stay there, you thick twit!' Snorky shouted.

'Yes, stay where you are - please.' Samson's voice was tinged with desperation.

In response, Speedy smiled angelically, and slowly and deliberately withdrew his tongue from his left nostril. Then his lips parted as though he was going to belch: instead, incredibly, words came out:

'Me pay, Sansan. Me pay,' the unfamiliar voice wheedled.

'You haven't got any flipping money, you stupid gormless idiot!' Snorky shouted.

'No ... I think he means "play",' Samson said. 'What do you think? '

Snorky blinked and shrugged, but said nothing.

'Okay ... come on, then!' Samson shouted to Speedy, then all three of them sidled over to the starting line. Urgently, Samson tried to explain the rudiments of the game to Speedy, who - after returning his tongue to the nostril where it belonged - began nodding enthusiastically.

Samson himself, in addition to having lightning reflexes and a wonderful sense of timing, had developed a foolproof system based on careful observation. Reduced to its essentials, the system was, to start counting when the waggons' roar changed quality, and to start running on the count of three-and-a-half. This, unfortunately, was slightly beyond Speedy's counting range, so some other system would have to be adopted - and soon.

'Any moment now!' Snorky called out, setting himself.

'I know: we'll give him a start,' Samson shouted back, and Snorky appeared to nod agreement, though he might just have been counting down. Samson motioned Speedy to a point about three yards from the track: from there, even a tortoise would have ended up 'chicken'.

Samson gouged a line in the dust, making it extra bold by repeated use of his clog toecap: his head was lowered, and his breathing was hard, more from tension than exertion.

The overall effect was not dissimilar to that of an angry bull. Speedy watched him, perhaps wondering if the line was a new kind of circle.

'Listen!' Samson commanded, racking his brain for a suitable instruction ... a simple instruction ... an instruction so simple that even an idiot would be able to understand it. Fortunately, inspiration was immediately forthcoming:

'Listen!' he commanded again, and unconsciously switched to the vernacular. 'Reet? When tha 'ears t' truck, run like fuck!' The rhyme was the important thing, of course, not the swearword.

'Tuck ... fuck,' Speedy repeated, intense concentration contorting his features.

'Again!' Samson demanded, using his hands as might an Italian choirmaster, to elicit a *fortissimo.* 'Again! Truck ... fuck!'

'Tuck ... fuck,' Speedy obliged, this time more fluently thanks to having withdrawn his tongue from his left nostril, for the second time in as many minutes - a world record, Samson wondered? 'Tuck ... fuck .... tuck ... fuck ...... tuck ... fuck .. fucktuck ...'

Speedy's incantation echoed back and forth across the quarry and set itself up inside Samson's head. Samson felt faint, perhaps from loss of blood. His heartbeat seemed to double in speed, then to double again.

The noise from above changed character. Samson settled beside Snorky in his special crouch, which favoured a particularly explosive start and hence permitted a very late one. At the same time he began his silent count, half-closing his eyes in an effort to overcome the interference from Speedy's continuing chant. It didn't work, but at least it reduced Speedy to a blur, so he didn't have to think about him.

'One!' Samson shouted, inaudibly. *Damn!* At this moment, the blur shifted: Speedy had turned round and was looking back at him.

'RUN!' Samson shouted - this time publicly, exaggerating his mouth movements to compensate for the fact that the words were probably inaudible above the roar of the approaching waggons. Speedy grinned, as though he was getting the hang of the game and beginning to enjoy himself.

'TWO!!' Samson shouted hoarsely. 'RUN!! RUN!!'

Momentarily, Speedy turned towards the track: then, clearly confused, he turned back as if awaiting new instructions - though his mouth movements, like those of a drowning fish at the surface of a polluted pond, suggested that he was still continuing the original chant.

'THREE!!!' Samson screamed. 'RU-U-U-U-U-N!!!!'

He and Snorky shot forward at virtually the same moment. Speedy, crazy boy, started to run back towards them: finding himself going the wrong way, he turned to follow them across the track.

It was too late. There was no special sound distinguishable from the terrifying roar of the waggons, only inches away: no shout, no scream. But when Samson and Snorky skidded to a halt and turned, as one, to look back, they saw Speedy's body lying face down beside the track, absolutely still except for the erratic swinging of his 'Napoleon' earring. There was a huge bloody gash across his left temple, but blood only seeped from it, rather than gushed or spurted.

White with shock, Samson and Snorky looked at each other, back at the body, then at each other again. Snorky grabbed hold of Samson's lapels and pulled him close.

'Listen!' he wheezed, his burning eyes seemingly on stalks. 'I know nothing ... you know nothing ... we know nothing - okay?'

'Nothing?' Samson quavered.

'No, nothing.'

'What - nothing at all?'

'No: nothing ... nothing at all ... absolutely nothing.'

Slowly, Snorky released his grip. Then the two of them spontaneously did what Speedy should have done: they ran like fuck.

27. Goat Island

'RUN! RUN!! RUN!!!' A volley of tremendous shouts caused Samson to spin round. As he turned he started running, and as he started running he saw a wall of stone flying towards him. Huge lumps of stone, some the size of hams or even sides of bacon, hurtled at him in slow motion, and even as the first lumps - mercifully, these were no larger than chunks of stewing steak or smallish pork chops - hit him, he was floored by the accompanying rush of air from the blast. He rolled over and over and would have lain where he came to rest, deafened and winded, if the words reverberating in his head had not held a special significance for him. He struggled to his feet, as awkwardly as a downed warhorse, and though blinded by clouds of dust and acrid fumes which overtook him in an instant, he careered rabbit-wise across the floor of the quarry, scrambled up a steep bank, staggered across twenty or thirty yards of rough ground and dived over a low stone wall. Like a tired steeplechaser carrying too much weight he tumbled head over heels, landing on his back on something soft and yielding, supporting and enveloping.

After an age Samson opened his eyes, and as he struggled to co-ordinate their movements, and to get them focussed, he saw that Mrs. Smalley was standing over him accusingly. Her purplish-black eyes, multi-faceted like a blubottle's, gazed fixedly into the darkest recesses of his soul.

'I know nothing,' he gasped. 'Nothing ... nothing at all ... absolutely nothing.'

He put out his hand to block her gaze. She, not to be put off, pricked him with something really really sharp.

'*Ouch!*'

She pricked him again, this time in several places at once.

'*Ouch! OUCH!* Nothing ... nothing at all ... absolutely nothing.'

As much as anything, what upset him was the awful appearance of her face - all blotches of red and green and brown and purple, and with one eyebrow missing. It was not until the surviving eyebrow started walking away, with a curious rippling movement, that Samson recognised it as a bristling fat caterpillar: the eyes, ripe blackberries; the instruments of torture, thorns.

The picture assembled itself in slow motion, the pieces coming together as when the film of an explosion is played backwards. He remembered the spell created by Speedy's earring as it swung erratically like the last movements of the pendulum of a clock that was about to stop ticking. A trickle of memories had developed into a flood that threatened to engulf him, so that he had clung to the tree stump on Tit Hill as desperately as Sam Oglethwaite had clung to the top of Blackpool Tower. He remembered everything - except that he had no recollection whatsoever of making the journey from Tit Hill to the quarry. The distance was about two hundred yards by the most direct route, though for all he knew he might have gone via Timbuktu and taken a whole year.

A year or an hour ... five minutes, or whatever ... it was time to be going. Samson made an effort to sit up, and immediately wished he hadn't. He kicked out angrily, then realised with horror that any effort he made to extricate himself from the bramble bush would result in his being trapped more securely. He deeply regretted laughing himself stupid once when Speedy had got similarly stuck in some brambles, and he and Snorky had only just managed to pull him out - backwards, his clothes ripped to shreds and his skin torn and bleeding. Oblivious to the pain Speedy must have been in, he had been obsessed with the desire to catch a glimpse of Speedy's feet. Speedy's wellingtons had come off, and one of his socks. Samson was fascinated by the discovery that Speedy's feet (at least, his right foot) was neither webbed (as Snorky had once insisted) nor (as Snorky had claimed on another occasion, unaware that he was contradicting himself) - cloven. Nor were they half-way between ... no, their outstanding feature was the peculiarity of the toes, which were long and straight and had great bulbous swellings at the ends, like xylophone hammers.

The muted sound of returning waggons crashing into the buffers down in the quarry jolted Samson back into the there-and-then. He renewed the attempt to free himself, but this was easier thought than done. With each jerk he sank deeper, and was held more tightly. With enormous difficulty he lifted his head and shouted 'Help! Help!' - weakly, and with the first and last consonants inaudible, so that he must have sounded like a distressed kitten. He immediately wished he had kept quiet: there was a loud answering 'Moo!' in response. Squinting along his nose, he espied a number of cows converging on his bush, a mean-looking crumple-horned Friesian at their head. He renewed his struggles, more frantically: as before, with each successive jerk he sank even deeper and was held even more tightly.

Blinking cows! He yelled angrily, at the herd in general and at the leader in particular. The latter, by vigorously rubbing its neck against a fence post around which the bush had grown, shook him ever deeper. The cow looked up briefly, perhaps to check on progress, then carried on rubbing itself. What was to be done? Lie there quietly, possibly for days or even weeks, until somebody came across him? Or make one last, do-or-die attempt to get free, accepting the risk of ending up as bramble jelly? Opting for the latter course of action, Samson jerked his body straight, reckoning that this way he would be less likely to sink than if he simply thrashed about in a panic. His head now thrown back, he suddenly spied a strand of barbed wire running along the top of the wall behind him. He was just able to reach out, grab the wire with both hands, and haul himself out of the bush inch by painful inch.

So, the bush was bested - but at a price: scores of scratches, clothes badly torn, and one clog captured. The clog just stood there in the exact centre of the bush, like an abandoned bird's-nest. The animals, though wary, immediately followed the limping one-clogged figure, mooing derisively. With a show of bravado Samson stopped and turned to face them, and wildly waved his arms: the cows backed off a little, but it was clear that their interest was stimulated by the strange antics. Finally, in desperation, Samson lunged at them, and as he reached the enemy front line he kicked a huge cowpat in their direction. Unfortunately he had failed to keep his eye on the ball, as it were: the clog, not helped by having a loose iron, ploughed deep into the cowpat and stuck irretrievably. Samson elected to leave it where it was, and thanks to this snap decision he was able to make a quick getaway while the cows contemplated their next move.

The immediate danger over, Samson started chuckling. What amused him was the thought of the two abandoned clogs - the left one deep inside a blackberry bush, the right one buried in a cowpat about ten feet away. What would anyone finding them think? That they had been lost by a giant with a ten-foot stride but only Size 2 feet? Or by two much smaller giants, engaged in some bizarre contest - perhaps savouring the thrill of shin-puncing? Interesting ... Samson shrugged, turned to check where the cows were (they had resumed their grazing, thank God) and slackened his pace. There was nothing to worry about now. The field ahead looked quite safe to cross, with not even a scarecrow to contend with ... deserted ... almost ... all except for a solitary sheep which suddenly popped its head over the wall and took a good look at him. It looked very nervous, ready to run away at any moment, and only standing its ground out of curiosity. Samson smiled to himself, because the sheep's behaviour proved something that he had suspected for a long time: that all animals (like most people) were cowardly when alone, and only acted big when in a group.

God! Samson suddenly noticed what a strange sheep it was, with its greyish-white face, black nose and black ears. Was it a Black Berkshire? Was it a sheep at all? Or was it perhaps a goat? It was difficult to tell, because only the head was visible. Samson cursed himself for knowing less about farm animals than about wild ones. *Hmph!* If it had been a lion or a tiger ... He suddenly remembered something that Snorky had once told him, about how it was possible for lions to marry tigers, the resulting children being called ... what was it - 'liars'? No . . 'ligers', that was it ... or of course 'tions', depending which one was the father. So: might not this peculiar specimen be a geep - or a shoat, even? And if so, how on earth was anyone expected to be able to know the difference between them, given the difficulty of telling a sheep from a goat in the first place? Of course, if the whole animal had been visible ... but it wasn't. In fact, as Samson got closer, the thing's head popped down out of sight. He pressed forward eagerly: frustratingly, by the time he reached the wall, the thing had gone ... vanished.

It was quite extraordinary ... it must have scampered off at a tremendous rate of knots, covering seventy or eighty yards of rough ground in the time it took him to hobble less than twenty. Half-convinced he was 'seeing things', Samson vaulted over the wall, and struck out across the next field with scarcely a backwards glance. He must put the strange beast out of his mind (it was out of its, for sure). However, the tingling of hairs rising on the back of his neck made him suddenly stop and look around. To his expected amazement the self-same stupid creature was now staring at him from over the wall he had vaulted! He made a two-fingered sign. The animal responded immediately, bleating (for want of a better word) in what seemed like a deliberate mocking tone; at the same time it sawed its stupid head from side to side, as if intent on cutting its own throat. Samson regretted not having a knife with him, to help put the animal out of its misery. He felt tempted to run back towards the animal and lob a stone at it - and, if lucky enough to score a hit and down it, to then pound it with the stone ... utterly jellify it. But he continued on his way: he had had his fill of adventure, for one day.

Samson pressed on. Although it was not possible to use the lanes, because of the sharp cinders underfoot, he made excellent progress - so much so that Foxgloves Hall soon came into view, about a mile further on. Oh God ... what to say when his mother asked him where his clogs were? 'I know nothing ...'? Hardly ... it was alright to know nothing about a missing button; at a pinch, it might just be possible to know nothing about the odd tear or two in his trousers; but it would be absolutely impossible to know nothing about a complete pair of missing clogs. No matter how absent-minded you were, or how accident-prone, to lose your clogs and not know you had lost them was inconceivable. Of course, there was always the old excuse about them having been stolen by Catholics, but by now that one was beginning to wear a bit thin: already they had enough items (a scarf, a raincoat belt, a balaclava, two pairs of socks and a handkerchief, if he remembered correctly) to equip an army, or at least to open a second-hand clothes shop. No, it was as weak as water. And there was another worrying thing: was it actually possible to know nothing? If you knew that you knew nothing, then - surely? - you knew something. Tricky ... a pity Snorky wasn't around, to give a second opinion ... unfortunately the blighter not only wasn't on hand, he wasn't in contact at all, hadn't been around for ages. He might just as well have been a million miles away, in London or America or Australia or somewhere ... anywhere ... so: what was to be done?

Samson did not know what to do: fortunately, his feet did. They had already changed course, as though shying away from Foxgloves Hall. He felt like saying to them, 'Hey, feet! This isn't the blooming way!' or some such thing. After all, his clogs always seemed to know the way home - his wellingtons too, for that matter. Actually, he had to admit, his feet had a point. By the look of things they were taking him to Dead Man Clough - their owner, by staying there till nightfall, would then have a plausible excuse for having lost the clogs. Yes, he could have tripped, especially in the dark ... very easily ... how many times had he asked his mother for the loose iron on his right clog to be repaired? So, it was really her fault. Right: he had tripped, felt as if he had sprained both ankles, then taken his clogs off to inspect the damage and been unable to find them in the inky darkness. Excellent! Exultant, Samson turned to face Foxgloves Hall. He was about to make a rude sign in that direction, but realised that from that distance it wouldn't be seen (and if it were, he'd be in serious trouble). Fortunately a better idea came to him:

'*B-E-E-E-E-E-H!*' he bleated derisively, investing much feeling. '*B-E-E-E-E-E-H!*' And again: '*B-E-E-E-E-E-E-E-E-H!*'

'*B-e-e-e-e-e-e-h!*'

Christ Almighty! An answering bleat, seeming to mimic his own as perfectly as an echo, made his hair stand on end. The whatsit! The stupid blooming animal, frightening him like that! Well, not exactly frightening, but ... where the heck was it, anyway? Aha: as far as Samson could tell, without actually turning to look in the direction the answering call seemed to have come from, the animal was concealed behind the hedge to his left, about thirty yards away. What on earth did it think it was playing at, wandering about from field to field, spying on people? Just who or what did it think it was? Good God ... no self-respecting sheep or goat in its right mind would waste its time doing things like that, when there were lots of lovely buttercups and thistles and things just asking to be munched and cudded. Of course, if on the other hand it was a geep or shoat, it might be in two minds ... or half a mind, for that matter ... it could certainly be confused. Well, anyway - confused or not, the beggar needed to be taught a lesson ... but what? Then straight away, before Samson could say or even think 'Jack Robinson', a brilliant idea came to him ... an idea for teaching it a lesson that it would never forget (more precisely. one that it would not live to remember): he would lead it to a place where, if it chose to follow, it would surely lose its footing and plunge to a certain death. If, however, the stupid cretinous animal chose not to follow, than he (Samson) would be guaranteed absolute peace and tranquillity. This special place was more than just special - it was specially special ... unique. It was the only place in Old Guinea, Samson reckoned, where you could be absolutely sure of being absolutely alone. It was the place that, though he had never been there, he had been thinking about for a couple of years, off and on. He had even christened it. Purely for reasons of geography, and without in any way prejudging the true identity of his four-legged adversary in this battle of wits which would soon reach its climax, he had called it simply 'Goat Island'.

Soon Samson was skirting the western side of T' Neck o' T' Woods, and entering Dead Man Clough. Never in his life had he moved so noisily - cracking twigs, splashing in puddles, crashing through bracken, all the while humming and cursing. This out-of-character behaviour served two purposes. First, it enabled him to block out the jumpy feelings he had on account of being shadowed by a deranged animal - just as, when once he had had a bath, he had burst into song to allay the fear of drowning. Second, it enabled him, by stopping suddenly and then listening intently, to verify that the whateveritwas - or, was not - was - or, was not - following him. Sure enough, it was picking its way through a patch of sycamore saplings about fifty yards behind him. For a good two seconds after he had stopped, it continued on its way, then it too stopped and made no further sound.

Haha! Just as I thought, Samson thought.

Samson set off again. This time he proceeded very very quietly, taking full advantage of being in stockinged feet. There was no way that a clumsy four-legged beast with hooves could keep up with him without making a tremendous din and giving the game away, so that as he worked his way downstream he was able to put a greater and greater distance between himself and his shadow. By the time he reached T' Cut he was well and truly on his own. This was just as well: the lack of proper footwear now meant that negotiating the narrow, slippery and treacherous path along the edge of the ravine was extremely difficult. The animal might now be catching up.

Soon Samson was opposite the Belle Vue houses, literally reduced to a crawl by virtue of the frequent absence of any path at all, because of landslides. It was here that he had once come across a dead sheep (on second thoughts, perhaps a goat) impaled on a jagged spur of rock a few feet down the face of the ravine, and it was perhaps this image which had given him the idea of luring the thingummy to its death - though from where he now clung, it seemed far more likely that it would have the advantage, and might turn the tables: it could race up behind him and tup him to his death. One possible course of action would be to grab its horns at the moment of impact and hang on like grim death, so that it could kill him only at the cost of its own miserable life. Another possibility, one requiring very fine timing, would be to leap up into the air as it charged, so that it sailed to its death alone ... as against that, a less-than-perfect jump could have very painful consequences indeed. Fortunately, it seemed, the stupid thing had missed its chance: it was still not in sight when he reached the point where the ravine changed course and The Whacker came into view. Safe at last ... phew!

Perhaps the beast had a bit of sense, after all: it knew when to quit. Another fifty yards, and the wall of the ravine split, forming a spur about a hundred yards long. Slightly bent about half way along, the spur resembled a stuck-out thumb attached to an otherwise-clenched fist. Descending into the fissure between thumb and fist was an eerie experience. The muffled rumblings and thunderings of Strangler's Brook, far far below, suddenly became conspicuous by their absence, and were replaced by sounds of water seeping from the rock face and dripping from ledge to ledge. Almost every step set off a mini-avalanche of loose shale which occasionally dislodged larger lumps of rock, which in turn bounced off into the depths. Neither light nor air seemed to penetrate this space, so that Samson suddenly felt very cold, and his breathing became very shallow. He paused to get his bearings. Up above, T' Whacker's huge head seemed to be balanced as precariously as a top about to stop spinning: it appeared to be swaying slightly, though of course that was not possible. Down below, the rock face was sheer, and because of a slight overhang the ravine seemed bottomless. Experiencing a touch of vertigo, Samson sensibly squatted down: then, relying on his hands and heels, he let himself slide down an oblique groove. This took him to the end of the thumb nail, where his ultimate goal was suddenly revealed, a hundred feet or so further down.

Samson gasped: Strangler's Brook, which higher up the valley was quite lazy, with assorted debris bumping tiredly along, was here forced through a gap of five to six feet wide, so that it became a raging torrent. Even as he gasped, a whole tree branch visibly accelerated on reaching this section, crashed from one wall to the other, jammed across two rocks and was immediately snapped like a matchstick, and the pieces unceremoniously swept away towards the spectacular waterfall which, based on something Snorky had once talked about, he had christened 'Nigeria Falls'. At the head of the falls, the aptly-named 'Goat Island' was a small lump of black rock, protruding defiantly from the middle of the torrent, not three feet from the lip of the fall.

After a long pause and several false starts Samson steeled himself to make the final descent. Real climbing was called for here, with a premium on handholds because of the increasing soreness of his feet. With each new mini-drama

Samson's shaking intensified, Skill and patience were no longer enough, and faith was difficult to come by at such short notice. However, the journey was in the nature of a pilgrimage, and when Samson reached the foot of the cliffs he had enough courage to leap about eighteen inches across the foaming torrent, to land on Goat Island.

Splat! Samson had intended to make a four-point landing, as might a cat, but this was not to be. The smooth, convex lump of rock was permanently wet, and covered in green slime, so that he was lucky not to slide straight off it. Fortunately his hands and feet splayed out like a tortoise's, so that he ended up performing a belly flop. Winded, worse even than when Huge Whelks had punched him in the stomach, Samson indulged in a long bout of controlled convulsions, whilst his mind went into a spin. The world itself was spinning, like a wobbly top. Hundreds of confused thoughts and feelings were being stirred, like folded bits of paper being shaken around in a hat that was still being worn. Nothing made sense. There had been a time, not so very long ago, when the whole world was a gigantic playground, when even porage tasted exciting. Then all this had turned to ... shit. This turned to shit, this turned to shit. Tomcat gone ... Snotty ... Speedy, dear old Speedy ... Rita going somewhere else, Snorky disappeared off the face of the earth ... this to shit, THIS to SHIT, the same but rearranged, like GOD'S WILL written wrong on one of the St. Peter's gravestones: GODSWILL. Pigswill. Shit, piss, piss, shit ... how long till Rita again? Thirty days hath September April June and November all the rest have thirty-one ... thirty for September, thirty-one for October, sixty-one, ninety-one, a hundred and twenty-two ... February: twenty-eight? One thousand nine hundred and forty-eight, divide by four ... four eight ... seven ... four hundred and eighty-seven a hundred-and-fifty-three plus four hundred and seventy-eight ... seven hundred and ... seven hundred and ... start again, work back from Whit ... Whit, shit, shit, Whit ... forget it . No way to see into the future, to Hell with the Grammar School ... anything for an eye in the back of the head to see the past what the hell had happened why why whywhywhywhywhy? Please God give a sign a crack on the back of the head a kick up the backside a message in the sky a dogshit drawing on the wall anything anything ...

'*Cuckoo! Cuckoo!*'

Eh? Samson raised his heavy head clear of the rock, the better to concentrate his ears on this familiar but unexpected sound. Too late in the year for the first cuckoo ... perhaps the last one, then ...

'*Cu-ckoo! Cu-ckoo!*'

There it was again - as unmistakable, in spite of the roaring of the waters, as a church bell in a fog. But coming from where? At risk of dislocating his neck Samson scanned each wall of the ravine for signs of the bird or birds, but it was hopeless. Nothing could be made out against the dark rock.

'*POW!*' Samson shouted, imitating the sound of a gun going off. '*POW! POW! POWPOWPOW1!!*' The idea was, to scare the bird or birds into taking off. Instead, the shouts seemed to encourage them:

'*CUCKOO! CUCKOO! CUCKOO! CUCKOO!*' came the calls, regular as clockwork - as from a Swiss-made cuckoo clock. It was as though the birds were trying to tell him something, and getting frustrated because he wasn't catching on.

Suddenly Samson got the message. Bobbing downstream towards him was a small bottle, a medicine bottle by the look of it, with a piece of paper sticking out of the neck. God! He willed the bottle towards him.

Come on, come on, come on ... it bobbed teasingly, tantalisingly, like a fishing float being toyed with by a foolhardy fish. Then it got stuck, held up by a branch wedged across the stream. Samson broke a length of dead wood from the branch and tried to coax the bottle closer. It ducked away and briefly submerged, as though controlled by an invisible thread, like the ten-shilling note in the Great Adventure. *Ha!* There it was again, about to joint the surging stream which skirted Goat Island on Samson's right. Wriggling like a wet seal, he turned clockwise and plunged his hand into the water, hoping to grab the bottle as it sped past. However, the force of the water was so strong, and the rock on which he lay was so slippery, that he was spun round like a propeller and came close to being forced off the rock and into the raging torrent. He stopped rotating just in time to see the bottle, complete with message, shoot the fall. Miraculously, at the bottom of the fall it bobbed up again, apparently undamaged. For a few seconds it lingered at the foot of the fall, going round and round in the eddies of a minor whirlpool - then it rejoined the stream, its secret intact.

With a deep sigh Samson picked up his stick and threw it over the waterfall after the bottle. Perhaps, like himself and Rita, the stick and bottle would meet again somewhere, some day. It was a lovely thought, and it certainly merited the beautiful rainbow which appeared at that very moment over the fall, magically suspended and seeming to dance in the spray like a giant dragonfly. Overcome with emotion, he was moved to song:

>   There Was a Boy
>   La da da da dee da da da
>   A Boy Who Wandered Very Far
>   Near and Far
>   O'er Land and Sea.
>   So Ve-ry Shy, dee da da dy
>   Dee da dee da da dee.
>   And then One Day
>   One Magic Day dee da da day
>   Da dee dee da dee da dee da
>   La la la
>   Wa wee wa wee.
>   The Greatest Thing
>   Ding dong dong ding
>   Is to Ding and be Donged
>   In Return.

The rainbow disappeared as abruptly as it had begun, as though switched off. Samson felt a deep chill strike through him. A message from Rita? No no no no no ... ridiculous ... stupid ... crazy ... absurd, yes, that was the word. He had only recently come across it, and without being quite sure what it meant, he felt that it sounded just right.

'Ha ha ha ha ha!' He fell into a self-mocking laugh, imitating the sound of a cross-cut saw, enjoying the way the alternating sounds mingled with echoes, just audible above the roaring of the waters. 'Ha ha ha ha ha!' And again, 'Ha ha ha ha ha.' Absurd, absurd!

'*Ha ..... ha ..... ha ..... ha!*'

Eh? What? What was that? Christ: an answering call, from somewhere up above. Had the world gone mad? An answering call? Couldn't have been ... but it couldn't have been an echo, after such a long delay, and the gaps were longer than in his own forced laugh. Heck! This was no sheep or goat, or geep or shoat ... nor, for that matter, was it a cuckoo or an echo, or a cucko or an echoo ... it was another human being - either that, or an escaped hyena. His imagination, playing tricks? Trembling with apprehension, Samson felt compelled to solve the mystery. With great difficulty he turned over so as to lie on his back, propped on his elbows, the better to scan the walls of the ravine. He squinted against the brightness.

'*HA HA ... HA HA HA!*' he laughed, hysteria more than compensating for shortage of breath. He waited, not daring to breathe.

'*Ha ..... ha .... . ha .... . ha .... . har ...*' Funny ... the answering call was even slower now, as though produced by a puppet whose clockwork mechanism had started to run down.

Suddenly something extraordinary became apparent - something so amazingly extraordinary, so extraordinarily extraordinary, that Samson would remember it vividly for the rest of his life: the laughter was coming, for sure for sure for sure, from T' Whacker: at the same time, and in time to the laughter, the huge stone head was nodding:

'*Ha ..... ha ..... ha .... . ha ..... HAAAAAAAA!!!!!*'

Samson, craning his neck, and in statuesque silence observing the Whacker's nodding, was slow to react to what happened at this point: the Whacker's head broke away from the body and plunged into the ravine, straight towards Goat Island.

Desperately scrabbling at the rock beneath him, but gaining no purchase, Samson waited for the inevitable impact, which would squash him like a fly. Then, miraculously, one of his hands gained a grip and he managed with a superhuman effort to throw himself over the waterfall. Yet, in spite of reacting so slowly to the threat of extinction, Samson's otherwise agile brain had managed to run through all the possible authors of this murderous deed - sheep, goat, geep, shoat, cuckoo, echo, echoo, cucko - and discounted every single one of them in favour of the true perpetrator, who fleetingly revealed himself in silhouette, then identified himself beyond all possible doubt by means of the catapult V-sign that had become his trademark: the blooming blackamoor!

Then the world started spinning ...

―――― *Also by* **Janus Oggsford** ――――

The **BOOLEAN BEAST**
Vol. #1 of the (monu-)mental
13-volume *Moose Mysteries*
[The OX Press, 2012: ISBN 978-0-9573932-0-2]

Originally conceived as a spoof on Colin Dexter's 'Chief Inspector Morse' novels, Janus Oggsford's Moose Mysteries *soon developed along completely different lines.*

Deep underground in the bowels of Oxford's world-famous Boolean Library a vicious serial killer is on the loose. Described by the sole eye-witness as 'half-man, half-beast, like a black panther on its hind legs', the killer strangles, rapes, disembowels and partially dismembers his terrified victims. Meanwhile ace detective Manfred Moose resigns on a matter of principle, and looks forward to progressing his research into the 'Shakespeare Authorship Question'.

In the ensuing public hysteria Moose is reinstated in unusual circumstances, and appointed to lead the pilot unit of a new off-the-record Criminal Justice Directorate, set up to bring serious criminals to justice 'by any and every means'. He is teamed up with tough New York cop Lewis Luther Armstrong, a 'Mr. 5 x 5' Afro-American. But before the new unit can get into gear the killer doubles up on his savage attack, then doubles up again. Moose and the team find themselves in a desperate race against time.

That's the serious stuff ... but *The* **Boolean Beast** is also a humorous *tour de force*, a *smörgåsbord* of comic situations, biting irony, exuberant wordplay and whacky dialogues. The narrative sparkles, and the characters are three-dimensional.

At 704 pages, and close on a quarter of a million words, *The* **Boolean Beast** is a banquet of a read. In spite of its length, the narrative never flags.

Subsequent volumes in the 13-volume saga will be published at roughly 9-month intervals. Volume #2, *The* **Last Word**, is scheduled for publication in September 2013.

View extensive extracts **free** at: **www.theOxPress.co.uk**

— *and* —

The Illustrated *OGGSFORD* DICTIONARY
[Scorpio Humour, 2001: ISBN 978-1-904209-00-9]

Published in 2001, **The Illustrated *OGGSFORD* DICTIONARY** established Oggsford's reputation as a master wordsmith. Initially modelled on Ambrose Bierce's *The Devil's Dictionary* of a century earlier, the work is enlivened by over 400 whacky graphics - cartoon illustrations by Harper, montages by Anton Maverick, and a miscellany of other graphics.

The dictionary is built around over 1000 apocryphal definitions - witty 'joke' definitions such as:

ALCHEMY the science of the impossible

BOOKER PRIZE literary award for writing parking tickets

CAVALRY CHARGER speedy steed which darts impulsively into the fray - and is thereby distinguishable from a brewer's carthorse, which farts compulsively into the dray

DEFINITION, CIRCULAR *see* CIRCULAR DEFINITION

... and so on. Over 90% of the entries are Oggsford originals, rather than having been culled from other authors' works.

There is extensive cross-referencing, enabling the reader to open the book at any page, then be effortlessly transported, as on a magic carpet, to other pages.

The *A*-MAZE™

This is a free Internet game built around an extended set of apocryphal definitions (over 1200) and whacky graphics. Derived from **The Illustrated *OGGSFORD* DICTIONARY**, it exploits the cross-referencing potential of the dictionary - but whereas the book's cross-referencing is logical, the game's cross-referencing is largely cryptic - a crossword addict's delight!

Access the game free at: **www.thea-maze.org**

——— *and 'Coming Soon'* ... *Captain Cock-Up™* ———

Captain Cock-Up™ is another humorous 13-volume saga by Janus Oggsford. The opening volume, *Independence Day*, is scheduled for publication by The OX Press on - you've guessed it! - 4 July 2013.

The saga chronicles the fall and fall of Britain's 'oldest private bank', the 200-year-old Bloggs Bank, from the day that seventh-generation Sir Dennis Percival Bloggs-Gusset takes over as Chairman and MD. Fat, feckless and fifty, Sir Dennis is cajoled by socialite mistress Nicola Bolingbroke-Hoare into launching an ambitious 'GOD' project designed to propel the sleepy old bank into the world's top ten by 2010. Meanwhile ...

... for 35 years prodigiously self-educated Bert Gutteridge has held down the lowly job of 'Desk Sergeant' at Bloggs' Head Office. Then, thanks to the passing of his immediate superior, he looks forward to being promoted to the latter's prestigious 'Desk Captain' role.

Gutteridge races back to his sordid Shoreditch hovel in the hope of finding a letter confirming his promotion. And there it is! He celebrates by trying out his new home-made snuff, prepared by drying the fruiting bodies of the hallucinogenic mushroom *Amanita muscaria*. Feeling no effect, he doubles and redoubles the dose, and kills time by going through a vast pile of unopened mail - which includes a redundancy notice, posted on the same day as his promotion letter.

At a stroke, Gutteridge's ecstatic feelings turn into rage. Then the hallucinogen kicks in. He feels dizzy and nauseous, and regurgitates his dinner; his skin becomes hot and prickly, and sprouts feathers; his eyes become huge orbs; his toes, talons; and his arms, wings. In no time, he has been transmogrified into an invisible owl, the eponymous Captain Cock-Up™, able to fly at will through walls and ceilings, to settle undetected on victims' shoulders, and there to implant suggestions designed to bring the mighty bank to its knees by a process of attrition. The only signs of a visitation are a sprinkling of dandruff-like feather dust on the victim's left shoulder, and a nearby crudely-stencilled message in a medium resembling gooey grey birdshit ...

Check on Captain Cock-Up™ at **www.captaincock-up.org**

... and finally ... introducing the newest addition to our stable of thoroughbred authors ...

Justine Booker-Price

and her
brilliant
debut novel

Full English Breakfast
A Sexual Comedy

Graduate linguist Georgia Brown is in limbo. Approaching 30, still without a proper job, and not yet recovered from an inexplicable relationship breakdown, Georgia reacts to intense parental pressure by applying for a post she has no hope of landing: as 'Production Executive' with London-based film company Videococo. Though totally lacking in relevant qualifications and experience, she lands the job and takes up residence in Leamington Spa's 4-star Royal Terrace Hotel, where Videococo plan to produce a new Reality TV series.

But all is not as it seems. The tourist industry is in crisis, and the hotel's owner-manager, John Julius Lord, is heading for a breakdown. Nevertheless the hotel survives, and begins to prosper, largely thanks to gratuitous help from frequent guest Melanie Beste-Goodenough, owner of a magazine publishing empire, and a bevy of her beautiful 'nieces'. Within 3 months Lord is acquiring other hotels and being hailed as saviour of the British tourist industry.

The bubble bursts when, coincidentally, filming commences, an ecumenical conference is hosted, and a ghost from Georgia's troubled past comes back to haunt her. A sexual scandal envelopes the hotel and its Establishment clientele, Lord is indicted on a murder charge, and Georgia's life is once again in ruins.

Full English Breakfast is due to be published in mid-June 2013. Check out details at **www.theoxpress.org**